KT-211-350

CARDIFF
CAERDYDD

ORCHARD BOOKS
First published in Great Britain in 2016 by The Watts Publishing Group

First published in the United States in 2016 by
Little, Brown and Company, a division of Hachette Books Groups, Inc.

1 3 5 7 9 10 8 6 4 2

All characters and events in this publication, other than those clearly in the public domain, are fictitious and any resemblance to real persons, living or dead, is purely coincidental.

A CIP catalogue record for this book is available from the British Library.

ISBN: 978 1 40833 584 0

Printed and bound in Great Britain by Clays Ltd, St Ives plc

The paper and board used in this book are from well-managed forests and other responsible sources.

Orchard Books
An imprint of Hachette Children's Group
Part of The Watts Publishing Group Limited
Carmelite House
50 Victoria Embankment
London EC4Y 0DZ
An Hachette UK Company.

www.hachette.co.uk
www.hachettechildrens.co.uk

VIRGINIA BOECKER

For Holland
and
For August

Harrow-On-The-Hill

Cambria

Gallions Reach

River Wye

The Mudchute

Whetstone
Rochester
High Street
Hatch End
Hexham
Anglia
62 miles to
Upminster

ONE

I sit on the edge of the bed waiting, the day I've feared for months finally here. I look around the room, only there's not much to distract me. Everything is white: white walls, white curtains, white stone fireplace, even the furniture – bed, wardrobe, and a small dressing table set below a looking glass. On cloudy days, this lack of colour is soothing. But on the rare sunny winter day, such as today, the brightness is overwhelming.

There's a gentle rapping on the door.

'Come in,' I call.

The door squeaks open on its hinges and there's John, standing in the doorway. He leans against the frame and watches me a moment, his brows creased in a frown.

'Are you ready?' he finally asks.

'Would it matter if I'm not?'

John crosses the room to sit beside me, somewhat gingerly. He's dressed well today, in stiff blue trousers and matching blue coat, and a white shirt that somehow isn't wrinkled. Hair that manages to be curly but not unruly. He looks like he could be going to a masque or a ball, someplace festive. Not where we're really going.

'You're going to be fine,' he says. 'We're going to be fine. And if they make you leave, well' – he smiles then, but it doesn't quite reach his eyes – 'Iberia is beautiful, even this time of year. Think of the fun we'll have.'

I shake my head, feeling a rush of guilt at his being forced to make light of what's about to happen: the council hearing. To face my crimes, to answer to the charge of treason against Harrow.

When I was first summoned to attend, it was the week after Blackwell's masque, after John and Peter brought me to their home. After we'd learned of Blackwell's plan to steal the throne, to turn the hundreds of witches and wizards I helped capture into his army; after I gave John my stigma – the inky-black, elegantly scrawled XIII on my abdomen, the mark that healed me and gave me strength – and nearly died myself.

I wasn't conscious then, nor was I conscious when I received the second summons, nor the third. I received a total of six before I even opened my eyes, six more before I could take a step unassisted. They were coming at a rate of one or two a week before Nicholas put an end to it, assuring the council I would meet with them when I was ready.

It took two months.

And for two months, I've lived in the shadow of this hearing, wondering what will become of me. It's unlikely the council will allow me to remain living here, not without a price attached. Becoming their assassin is Peter's guess; their spy, John's. But mine is exile: given an hour to collect my things, then an escort to the boundaries of Harrow, ordered never to return.

'If they make me leave, you're not coming with me,' I say. 'Fifer, your father, your patients...you can't leave them.'

John stands up. 'We talked about this.'

Actually, John did all the talking; I did all the protesting.

'I don't want to leave them, but I refuse to leave you,' he continues. 'And anyway, it won't come to that. Nicholas won't allow it.' He takes my hand, gives it a gentle tug. 'Come on. Let's get this over with.'

I get to my feet, reluctant. I'm dressed well, too, today, in a gown Fifer gave me. Shimmery, pale blue silk skirt, the bodice a darker blue brocade, trimmed with silver thread and white seed pearls. It's the prettiest gown I've ever owned. It's the only gown I've ever owned. Fifer even plaited my hair, pulling it into an elaborate rope that falls over my shoulder. I wanted to wear it down, like I usually do. But she insisted.

'With your hair like this, you look about fourteen,' she said. 'The younger you look, the more innocent you look. It'll make the council think twice about exiling a child.'

John reaches forward and gently grasps my plait, running his fingers down the length of it. I close my eyes against the sensation, against the feel of him standing so near. When I open them, he's watching me carefully, and

I know I'm looking back the same way.

The sound of someone clearing his throat in the hallway breaks the spell. John steps away just as Peter appears at the door, concern etched into every line on his weathered face. Like John, he doesn't quite look himself today. Dark curly hair, carefully combed. Dark beard, closely cropped. He's clean, ironed, and starched, and if it weren't for the sword at his side – broad, curved handle, a pirate's blade – I might not recognise him.

He gives us a quick once-over.

'Good, good. You both look good. Proper but not prim. Well groomed but not overly so.' Peter leans in closer, taking in whatever he sees on our faces. 'Mind, you might want to try and look a bit more sombre. Save the celebration for after, hmm?'

I step back, away from John, but he only laughs and rolls his eyes.

'We should start out,' Peter continues. 'Best to be there early. We don't know what kind of crowd we might run into.'

At the word *crowd*, my stomach seizes into a knot. It's something else I've feared since I was summoned to this hearing. Facing the people of Harrow, hearing their stories. Learning how I, or someone I know, have killed someone close to them; how I, or someone I know, have ruined their lives.

Downstairs, John helps me into my coat. Long, made of blue wool and lined in rabbit fur – another gift from Fifer – and the three of us slip from the cottage into the bitter late-February air, the wind biting our faces and numbing our cheeks.

John and Peter's home, nicknamed Mill Cottage for the enormous waterwheel built into the attached barn, lies outside the village of Whetstone in northern Harrow, tucked at the end of a narrow dirt road that runs alongside a slow-moving river. It's peaceful here, and quiet today as usual. Nothing but the sound of the water mill splashing softly in the banks and a pair of mallards swimming along the edge, squawking at us for food.

Mill Cottage is a funny, charming little place, once three separate smaller homes that, over time, Peter combined into one larger one. It still maintains a rather haphazard look: The front house is long and low, brown stone with a weathered blue door and large, blue-paned windows. The middle house is red brick and the tallest of the three, the façade lined with small windows and a brick-columned smokestack. And the back house, where my bedroom is, dark grey brick with a thatched roof, surrounded by John's lush physic gardens. He says they'll be full of birds come spring, building nests and hatching chicks; nearly unliveable for all the noise.

Not for the first time, I wonder: *Will I still be here come spring? Will Mill Cottage? Will Harrow?*

It's just over an hour's walk from Whetstone to Hatch End, where the hearing will be. Peter says it's tradition for every council meeting to be held at the residence of the head councilman – no longer Nicholas, not after his illness kept him from performing his duties, but a man named

Gareth Fish. I met him once, at Nicholas's home after I'd first arrived: tall and cadaverous in black, taking dictation. Peter said he's a fair man, if a bit ardent; John and Fifer said nothing, their silence telling me all I needed to know.

Our path runs across sloping, grassy terrain, marked occasionally by weather-logged signposts with arrows that point to the nearby hamlets that make up Harrow's settlement: THEYDON BOIS, 3.2 MILES. MUDCHUTE, 17 MILES. HATCH END, 3.7 MILES. The sign reading UPMINSTER, 62 MILES has been crossed out and now reads in untidy scrawl beneath it: *Hell lies this way*.

Winter has settled in everywhere I look. The grasses in the meadows and distant rolling hills brown and dotted with unmelted snow; the trees barren and lifeless. Farmhouses dot the landscape, smoke from fireplaces seeping from chimneys, sheep and cows and horses huddled in quiet, shivering masses under the brightness of the heatless sun. The scene is peaceful but with an underlying current of tension: a village lying in wait.

'Nicholas will be there already, along with Fifer.' Peter's voice breaks the frigid silence. 'We debated whether Schuyler should come, but decided it was too much of a risk. We don't want to draw any comparisons between his somewhat…capricious past and yours.'

Schuyler. A revenant, lifeless and immortal but with almost unimaginable strength and power. He saved Nicholas's life by helping me break the curse tablet that Blackwell used to try to kill Nicholas; he saved all our lives by pulling us out of Blackwell's palace and onto

Peter's ship, bound for safety. But for all that, he's still a thief and a liar, a goad and a miscreant, and despite Peter's delicacy what he really means to say is that Schuyler's past was violent, unpredictable, and untrustworthy. Just like mine.

'As for George,' Peter says, 'he wrote a lovely letter, which will be entered into evidence on your side.'

In the days that followed Blackwell's usurpation of the throne and Malcolm's subsequent imprisonment, and before Blackwell closed Anglia's borders, George – a spy once in the guise of the king's fool – took a ship bound for Gaul. He was to meet with their king in a bid for troops and supplies, knowing that sooner or later, probably sooner, Blackwell would attack Harrow. There are too many people here who have the power to oppose him. And as long as Harrow exists, it will be a threat to him: an unsteady king on an unsteady throne.

'Then there's Nicholas,' Peter continues. 'While it's true he's a bit diminished, politically speaking, after everything that's happened' – he waves his hand vaguely, but it's clear he means me – 'he's still influential among the older Reformists. Of course, there are some in the council who argue that Nicholas is complicit in Blackwell's takeover. That if he hadn't been intent on helping you, on making sure your life was spared' – a glance at John, who scowls – 'we could have somehow stopped him.'

The idea, it's so absurd I almost laugh.

'Blackwell has been planning this for years,' I say. 'Decades, even. Since he started that plague that killed the king and queen. My parents. Half the country.'

Peter holds his hands up, a conciliatory gesture. But I go on.

'Even if you'd known, you couldn't have stopped it. I would have said that even before I knew he was a wizard.' I think of the man I knew – the man I thought I knew. The man who was once Inquisitor, devoting his life to rooting out and destroying magic. Who spent his life plotting in secret and lying in attendance; who used me, Caleb and the rest of his witch hunters to capture witches and wizards so he could build an army, overthrow the king – his own nephew – and take over the country. 'You don't know Blackwell the way I do. You don't know what he's capable of.'

I've stopped walking, and now instead of shivering I'm sweating beneath all this rabbit fur. John gives my hand a slight squeeze, and only then do I realise I was shouting.

'I do know,' Peter says. 'And the council needs to know, too. What Blackwell's done, everything he's done. With any luck, it will tell us something about what he plans to do next.'

We've been over this strategy countless times. Nicholas wants to put me on the stand and have me tell them what I told him, things I've never told anyone else before. About my training, about how I became a witch hunter, about Caleb.

Caleb.

My stomach twists into a tight, painful knot the way it does every time I think of him. And I think about him often – too often. The way I raised my sword to try to kill Blackwell, the way Caleb threw himself in front of him.

The way I killed Caleb instead.

He needed me out of the way, I know that now. He saw me as an obstacle, as something keeping him from the ambition he so desperately needed to reach. But knowing that is still not enough to quell the guilt that eats at me, that has eaten at me every single day in the two months since his death.

'...and that's it,' Peter finishes. 'That's all you have to say. I realise we've been over it a hundred times. But it's important to be prepared.' I nod again, even though I didn't hear a word he said. I never do. Every time he starts to talk about it, my thoughts drift to Caleb and I don't hear anything else.

We travel the rest of the way in relative silence. I'm too nervous to talk, Peter too tense, John too worried. John walks alongside me, brows furrowed, running a hand through his hair until his once-neat curls are nearly standing on end. It makes him seem boyish, younger than his nineteen years.

The path before me begins to narrow, passing through a squeeze of trees lining the road. The trunks are high and twisted, their leafless branches curling and intertwining like fingers, forming a dense canopy to throw shade on the damp dirt beneath our feet and obscuring the view ahead.

'Mind your step.' Peter points to the felled trunk blocking our path in the centre of the road. 'These trees, they're quite lovely in summer. But after the first of the winter rains, it seems as if half of them come down, quite a pain in the – *God's blood.*'

I hear John's sharp intake of breath, and I look up and see them. Hundreds, maybe even a thousand people, lining the road to Gareth's. For a moment, we stand there, the three of us rooted to the ground, staring at the faces of the men and women before us, who wear expressions ranging from curiosity to disgust to hatred.

We push past them, shivering beneath wool cloaks and hats and scarves and gloves. I don't recognise any of them but I recognise the look they give me, the way their eyes sweep over my too-fine gown and too-fine coat, and all at once the effort Fifer put into making me look respectable, into making me look innocent, all of it seems at best a farce, at worst an insult. I don't belong here, and they all know it.

'Head up,' Peter whispers. 'You look hangdog. Worse, you look guilty.'

'I feel guilty,' I say. 'I do feel guilt.'

'Feeling guilt and looking guilty are two very different things,' Peter says. 'Now look, there's Gareth ahead. He'll lead us inside.'

The endless sea of people ends at the low stone wall surrounding Gareth's home. Sand-coloured brick two stories high, surrounded by an expanse of manicured gardens, trimmed low for winter. It's bordered by a hill on one side, thick with dark, winter-hardy trees, and on the other, a cathedral. Separate from the home but built from the same sand-coloured brick, it's fenced by a tall iron gate and fronted by a crumbled cemetery, full of irregularly planted slabs and crosses, mossy and weatherworn.

Gareth, dressed in black council robes, the red-and-orange badge of the Reformists emblazoned on the front, strides toward us. He's as I remember him: spindly and grey, pale blue eyes flashing behind wire-rimmed spectacles. He offers his hand to Peter and then to John, who shakes it without enthusiasm.

'I trust you found your way here without incident?' Gareth says.

'We're here, aren't we?' John mutters.

Peter throws him a sharp look; John ignores it.

'No incident,' Peter replies. 'Though that's down to luck more than intent, I reckon. I seem to recall your wanting to keep this a private affair? Looks like half the northern hamlets showed up.'

Gareth offers a thin smile, a glint of an apology. 'News travels fast in Harrow, you know that. Especially news of this magnitude.' He looks to the crowd, now pressed in so close they're nearly surrounding us. They've fallen silent, those in the back craning their heads, trying to hear him speak. 'For many, this was the first they'd heard of Nicholas's illness. It's natural for them to be concerned for his well-being. He is a popular figure, of course.' Gareth's smile wavers just a bit. 'I'm sure many here are grateful to Elizabeth for sparing his life.'

'She didn't spare it, she saved it.' John's voice is sharp, irritated. Peter lays a hand on his shoulder but John ignores that, too. 'And if people are so grateful to her, then why are we having this hearing at all?'

'I'm afraid it doesn't work that way.' Gareth spreads his

hands, as if he himself is helpless to the machinations of the council, as if he himself is not the head of it. 'The council calls the hearings, not the populace. Although I am sure the vote will bring their gratitude into consideration.'

Of all the looks levelled in my direction, not one could pass for gratitude.

'In any event, the council is convened inside, waiting for your arrival. Shall we?' Gareth gestures not at his home but at the neighbouring cathedral. 'With the crowd such as it is, we had to move the hearing there. I assume there are no objections?'

'Would it matter if there were?' John snaps.

'None at all,' Peter says cheerfully. 'Shall we?'

Gareth leads us down the short path to the cathedral's gate, the crowd pressing close behind. He opens it and waves us inside, striding quickly toward the front door, black cloak billowing behind him like a storm cloud. Peter steps through but I hesitate, feeling a sudden shiver of foreboding at my surroundings. The gates: like those at Ravenscourt, tall and forbidding. The crowd: like the one that protested in front of them, angry and demanding. The spire atop the cathedral: a judge pointing an accusatory finger. The tumble of tombstones: a jury waiting to pass sentence.

'It will all be over soon,' John whispers in my ear, his hand steady on my back.

I turn to him and that's when I see it: a split second of movement, a man in a blur of black, and that familiar sound, the creaking of wood, the sound yew makes when strung with hemp; a bow with an arrow nocked and ready to fly.

The scream tears out of my mouth just as the arrow tears through the neck of the man standing right beside John.

TWO

The man's mouth opens wide, in shock as much as horror. Blood fountains from the wound in his neck, saturating his shirt even before he drops to the ground with a heavy thump, like an overstuffed sack of turnips.

The crowd around us erupts in screams. Another arrow, two, zing through the air. Another man goes down, then a woman.

Peter yanks his sword from the scabbard with one hand, points toward the cathedral with the other. 'Go! Get inside. Both of you. *Now.*' He charges past us, back out the gate, and disappears into the crowd.

John grabs my arm, vicelike, and pushes me down the path ahead of the people who push and scream behind us. He shoves open the cathedral door and Fifer stands on the threshold, pale and pretty in an emerald velvet gown, her hair pulled back tightly from her face.

'What's happening?' Her normally gravelly voice is

thin with fear. 'I heard screams—'

'We're under attack.' John thrusts me through the door. Throngs of people crowd behind him, push around him, come between us. He's released me and is now disappearing from sight, back out the door again. 'Stay inside,' I hear him call. 'Don't come out, no matter what.'

'John!'

'Don't come out!' he repeats. I hear his voice but I don't see him. I call his name again, but he's gone.

I skirt along the back wall of the cathedral and down the side aisle toward the transept, Fifer on my heels. People crowd the nave, fill the pews, all of them screaming and pushing.

'Where's Nicholas?' I shout.

'With the rest of the council,' she shouts back. 'They convene in the crypt before hearings; they hadn't come up because you weren't here yet.'

I stop before a tall arched window overlooking the graveyard. A dozen or so men, John and Peter among them, stand huddled beyond the gates. Peter presses a sword in John's hand and before I can make sense of what's happening, before I can reconcile the sight of John holding a weapon, they scatter.

I slip off my rabbit coat, let it slide to the ground. Lift up the outer skirt of my gown, tear off the kirtle underneath.

Fifer's mouth drops open in horror. 'What are you doing?'

'What does it look like?' I kick the fabric aside. 'I'm going to help.'

'I see that,' Fifer snaps. 'I meant, what are you doing to that gown?'

I shoot her a look.

'You can't go out there.' She changes tack. 'You could get hurt.' She casts a furtive glance around, but the people crushed around us aren't paying attention; even if they were, they couldn't hear us above the fray. 'You could die.'

'Which is why I need weapons,' I say. 'Some of the men here must be armed. A sword, or knives, preferably, but I'll take anything.'

Fifer hesitates, scowling. Finally she picks up the hem of her heavy velvet skirt and pushes into the crowd. I turn back to the window. Arrows fly indiscriminately; men – I can't see who – dart behind trees, hedges, headstones. There's shouting inside, shouting outside; I can't make sense of anything. Moments later, Fifer reappears behind me, carrying a handful of silver-handled knives. She passes them to me one by one, handle first.

'I don't know if they're what you want,' she says, 'but I had to steal them, so I don't want a word of complaint.'

A grin slides across my face at the feel of their cool, comforting weight. I pick up my discarded kirtle, slice off a strip with one of the knives, tie it around my waist into a makeshift belt. Shove the rest of my weapons inside, then step to the small door beside the window and unbolt the latch.

'Lock it after I leave,' I tell her. 'Don't open it again, not for anyone.'

'Don't do anything stupid,' she replies before shutting

the door and sliding the heavy bolt back into place.

Before me, the cemetery and the surrounding gates. Beyond that, trees, and then an expanse of brown rolling hills. To my right, men fighting and shouting, Peter among them. I don't see John but I do see two others, not archers in black but townsmen in simple winter robes, lying face-up in the grass, arrows lodged in their chests. Dead.

I edge my way toward the front of the cathedral. I don't make more than a few feet before an arrow sings by me, lodging itself in a crack in the stone. It's followed by another, then another. They arrange themselves in a neat little row, not six inches in front of my face. The aim is not a mistake, it's a warning. I crash to the ground. Crawl on my stomach across the dirt and grass, take refuge behind a crumbled slab pocked with lichen and moss. Arrange my thoughts, as neatly as the arrows messaged before me.

First, find the shooter. The arrows came in high, landed low; somewhere in the trees, then. Second, kill the shooter. I slide a knife from my belt and dart from behind the headstone to another, my eyes on the shadowed branches above me, inviting him to show himself.

Where are you? I think.

A reply comes in the form of yet another arrow, this one skimming the space between my third and fourth fingers, wrapped around the corner of the stone. I jerk my hand away, the smallest yelp escaping my lips as a stream of blood runs down my fingers, a crimson streak against pale skin. Out of habit, I wait for it, but it doesn't come. Not the flash of heat in my abdomen, not the sharp, prickling sensation.

Because out of habit, I forget I no longer have my stigma.

I duck behind the slab again and assess. I'm bleeding, I'm cornered. I'm armed but not as much as I'd like, and I can't spot my attacker. I have no advantage. But I didn't survive two years of witch-hunter training without knowing how to make the most of a disadvantage. Unbidden, Blackwell's voice rings through my head: *In order to regain lost advantage, you must always do the unexpected.*

So I do the one thing I shouldn't do when surrounded by a hidden enemy: I stand up. I hear it then, the tiniest sound – a ruffle of leaves, a barely suppressed grunt of surprise. It's enough. I spot him perched in a low branch of an oak tree, camouflaged by the boughs of a nearby evergreen. I slide one of the heavy silver knives from my belt. Pull back my arm, take aim, throw.

And I miss.

Damnation.

A short, derisive laugh; the soft thud of feet hitting ground. Whoever was in the tree is out of it now, and he's coming for me. Footsteps. The rustle of fingers on fletching, the drawing back of an arrow. So I do the only other thing I can do when surrounded by a hidden enemy:

I turn. And I run.

The arrow whistles over my head, just barely and by mistake – my foot gets tangled in the hem of my gown and I tumble to the ground. Roll to my back, scrabble for another knife, but it's too late: The archer is standing over me. Dark hair, stocky build, early twenties. I don't know him, but he seems to know me. He regards me with a half-suppressed smirk, a shake of his head.

'From everything I've heard about you, I'd hoped for a better fight than this.'

'Who are you?' I ask.

The archer doesn't bother to reply. He pulls another arrow from his quiver, slowly nocks it in place, never taking his eyes from mine.

'I like a good sport,' he says. 'Blackwell assured me you'd be one. He'll be disappointed to hear he was wrong.' He cocks his head to the side, considering. 'Perhaps not that disappointed.'

I shuffle back and away from him, from the arrow now aimed directly at my face. I don't get far, backing into another headstone, the rough surface digging into my spine.

The archer swings his bow back and forth, slowly, as if taking inventory of my features. 'You have pretty eyes,' he says. 'Seems a shame to shoot you there, but it's the best place, you know. It'll only hurt for a moment.'

I notice it then: the badge stitched on the front of his black wool cloak. It's a grotesque thing: a red rose strangled by its own thorny green stem and pierced through the top with a green-hilted sword. I've never seen it before now, but I know exactly what it is: Blackwell's new emblem.

'He won't win,' I whisper. They're my last words; I should make them count. 'Blackwell. He thinks he'll win. But he won't.'

A shrug. 'He already has.'

I don't reply; I only wait. For the arrow to pierce my skull, my brain; wait for death. I close my eyes, as if it will hurt less that way.

Then, in the space between one moment and the next, it happens. A footfall, the tread of boots on the soft grass, the snap of a twig. My eyes fly open as the archer whirls around but not in time, not before the blade lands hard across his neck and down his back, nearly slicing him in two.

His dark eyes go blank. A spray of blood spurts from his mouth onto my face, my arms, my dress. The archer sways once, twice, then topples to the forest floor like a felled tree. Behind him is John, his blue jacket and trousers no longer stiff but wrinkled and torn, his white shirt no longer white but red with blood.

He drops to his knees beside me. 'Are you all right?' He cups my face in his hands, turns it gently from side to side. 'He didn't get you, did he?'

My eyes dart from the downed archer, his blood spattered all over the tombstones and pooling crimson beneath him, to the sword in John's hand, also dripping blood.

'Elizabeth.' John tilts my head toward his with a finger on my chin.

'He got my hand,' I finally reply. 'But I'm fine.'

John swipes his thumb over the still-bleeding cut. 'It's not deep, but I should take a closer look at it later anyway.' He pulls me to my feet. 'I saw him watching you. He was in the tree, firing at us, then he stopped as soon as you stepped from the cathedral. Why did you do that? I told you to stay inside. You could have been killed.'

A look passes between us, and in it is the unspoken

realisation of how different things are now. I am not the person I was when we met, not the person I was three months ago. A witch hunter then, invincible; bearer of a stigma and the subject of a prophecy: the most wanted person in Anglia.

I don't know who I am now.

'You shouldn't be out here,' he goes on. 'It's too dangerous. You're not well enough, and you're not...' He stops himself, but I seize on his words anyway.

'I'm not what?' I pull away from him. 'Not strong? Not useful? That I'm not able to fight anymore so I should just stay away since I'm not wanted anyway?' The words pour out of me before I can think better of them.

'That's not what I meant and you know it.'

'I'm sorry,' I reply quickly, because I do know it. 'I shouldn't have said that, and –' I fall silent as it hits me then, what John has done. He used a weapon, and he killed someone. The boy who has done nothing but save lives has now gone and taken one. 'You killed him.' I glance at the archer at our feet.

'Yes,' John agrees. 'But I'm not sorry for it. I would do it again if I had to, if it meant protecting you, or anyone else.'

I blink at the sudden vehemence in his voice.

'I don't want you to do that,' I say. 'That's not what you do.'

'I think we're all going to do things we don't want to before this is all over,' he says. 'Let's go. We got them all, at least I think we did. But we'll want to do a head count inside, make sure everyone's accounted for.'

We thread through the cemetery to the front of the cathedral where a huddle of men gather – Peter, Gareth, a handful of others I don't recognise. They stand beside a line of bodies, a trail of blood leading up to and soaking the ground beside them.

'How many?' I ask. 'I saw one man down when I came out, one of ours. Did they get anyone else? Did we get any more of theirs?'

'Five.' John shoots me a grim look. 'Four men, one woman, all of them ours. Of theirs, we only got the one. The others – we counted four more – disappeared as soon as we gave chase.'

Harrow is a ten-mile-long stretch of land surrounded by a magical protective barrier, allowing in only those who reside here or, like me, are accompanied by those who reside here. But with Blackwell's claim to the throne, and the revelation that he, too, possesses magical ability, Harrow has become exposed and vulnerable. With hundreds of witches and wizards missing since the Inquisition began four years ago, there's no telling who are dead and who may have turned traitor, either by choice or by force. But someone has, and now they're letting Blackwell's men inside Harrow.

The first breach happened a month ago. A single man – he was thought to be a spy or scout – was caught in the village of More-on-the-Marsh, about halfway between John's house in Whetstone and Gareth's in Hatch End. He was discovered quite by accident: He fell out of the tree he'd been sleeping in, frightening a pair of wizards fishing in a nearby pond at dawn, and ran away before they could catch him.

The second breach was more sinister. Three men were caught creeping through the Mudchute, a desolate area full of patchwork fields that stretch south from the populated settlements in northern Harrow, to the border. They weren't after anything, they weren't armed, and they didn't run away when they were caught. They simply disappeared into thin air.

Despite the fear running through Harrow that Blackwell's men are being allowed through, there's a contrary undercurrent of hope. Because for many, the idea that someone they love, someone they thought was dead but is instead traitorous and alive, is a seductive one. But since John watched his own mother and sister burn to death on the stake in front of him, it's not one he can indulge in.

Over a year on, he still struggles with it. Although I may not be responsible for their capture, I am complicit. And I know he struggles with that, too.

'Where did you learn how to use a sword?' I ask.

'I've known how to use a sword since before I could walk,' John replies, a wan smile on his face. 'A benefit of having a pirate for a father, I suppose.'

'You use it well,' I say cautiously.

He nods, noncommittal. 'I've never had much use for it, but I'm glad for it now. Especially after today.'

I want to tell him to be careful. I want to tell him how it goes. That first you kill for a reason, then you kill for an excuse. Then you kill for neither, and bit by bit the lives you take begin to steal from your own. I saw it happen to Caleb just as I felt it happen to me. I can't watch it happen to John.

But before I can say this, before I can get out a word, Nicholas rounds into sight. I feel a rush of relief to see him alive, unharmed, but that relief quickly turns to dread the moment he joins the other men, all of them pointing at me, at the cathedral, Gareth nodding, adamant.

Peter breaks away as we approach, Nicholas following close behind. Peter grasps John in a tight embrace before turning to me and doing the same. Nicholas regards me closely, his clear, dark-eyed gaze moving from the blood on my clothes to the blood on my hand. We both say nothing as the others descend upon us, still in rapid conversation.

'What's going on?' John says.

'I wanted to gather the women and children into small groups, escort them back to their homes,' Peter replies. 'Set up a revolving perimeter, armed men to patrol the barrier around Harrow day and night to ensure no further breaches.'

'To which I agreed,' Nicholas says. 'I also agreed that the hearing can wait. With what's happened today, we have more important matters to attend to.'

I breathe a sigh of relief at this stay of execution, that I can have a few more days, a week, perhaps, to prepare. Until Gareth says, 'On the contrary. I think now is the perfect time to hold the hearing.'

THREE

John steps in front of me, as if to shield me from the idea. 'No. We don't have to hold the hearing today. It can be postponed.'

'Unfortunately, that isn't how it works,' Gareth says. 'The council has been convened, the font to tally the votes has been readied. Neither can be adjourned until a resolution is met.' He looks to Nicholas. 'These were the rules you yourself instated, when you set up the council.'

'The rules were put in place to prevent treachery within the jury, as you well know,' Nicholas replies. 'It's to prevent threats from within the council, not without.'

'Precisely,' Gareth says. 'Which is why they do not apply. The people in Harrow came today for answers. That is what they will get.'

'They came for answers, but instead they got an assault,' Peter says. 'They're frightened. Let them go home.'

'If you're asking me to reconvene the council in order to

give our enemies yet another chance to attack us en masse, I must decline,' Gareth says. 'It's no coincidence the attack happened today, that it happened here. Blackwell's men knew where we would be. Where *she* would be.' He glances at me, whatever ease he felt toward me earlier now gone. 'They're looking for her, there is no doubt about that. And we need to decide what to do about that. Today.

'However, I will not stop you from leaving if you feel you need to,' Gareth continues, looking to Nicholas. 'Bylaws state that the head of the council can enter in a vote for an absentee member. I would be more than happy to do that for you.'

Nicholas doesn't reply, but the anger in his dark eyes speaks for him.

The first time I saw Gareth, I thought he was a clerk. That night, Peter told me he was actually a member of the council, and now he's the head of it. Something about that reminds me of Blackwell, gaining advantage at the expense of someone else's disadvantage. And that's when I decide. While it might be to my benefit to put the hearing off until another time, I don't want Harrow to suffer.

'Gareth is right.' I turn to Nicholas. 'We should have the hearing today. There's no sense in putting it off any longer.'

Perhaps Nicholas expected I would say this, perhaps he hoped I would; either way, his only response is a crisp nod.

'Excellent.' Gareth claps his hands, then gestures back toward the cathedral. 'Shall we?'

'Can she change clothes, at the very least?' John says. 'She's covered in blood. There's no need for anyone to see her like this.' He doesn't say it but he doesn't have to – all the effort Fifer went through to dress me and make me look like a young girl, an innocent girl, it's undone, and now I'll stand in front of the council looking like the very thing they're trying to hide.

A killer.

'I'm afraid that's not possible.' It's Nicholas who replies this time. 'If the council has been called to session and the subject of that session is physically within the grounds, they may not leave until it has been adjourned.'

Gareth nods. 'Those are indeed the rules.'

John throws me a quick glance, then peels off his jacket and drapes it around my shoulders. My once-beautiful blue silk-and-brocade gown is now ripped and stained with dirt and grass and blood, my once-carefully plaited hair tumbles in disarray over my shoulders. John's coat covers some of it. But more than what it covers is what it uncovers: my reliance on him, his allegiance to me, our connection to each other that hurts him as much as it helps me.

The doors creak heavily on their hinges as Gareth pushes them open. Inside, in the relative calm, I see things I didn't before. A font of water in an elaborate stone vessel standing in the narthex, the water swirling around of its own accord. Rows of shining oak pews, blood-red kneeling cushions hanging from tiny hooks along the back. The red, blue, and white Anglian flag draping from the timbered ceilings alongside the Reformist flag in black, red, and orange. The entire space smells sharply of incense – frankincense, benzoin, myrrh. Soothing scents, though not today.

As before, the pews are filled with people, so many that they spill into the aisles, along the back and the sides. And they're all looking at me.

Maybe it's the dim, kaleidoscopic light, maybe it's the chill inside the cathedral, maybe it's fear, but the edges of my vision go dark and I'm seized with an urge to run. Out these doors, through that tree-felled tunnel, across the sloping meadows and past the borders of Harrow. But where would I go? It's been a constant question ever since those herbs spilled from my pocket, branded me a witch and landed me in jail, turned me into a traitor and changed my life forever.

A hand grasps my shoulder, spins me around. Nicholas steps in close, his tall, dark figure towering above me.

'You'll be tempted, but do not lie.' His voice is low. 'They will ask you questions you will not want to answer but if you do not tell the truth, they will know it. Tell them what you know, how you know it, just the way you told me. The rest,' he adds, 'will take care of itself.'

The rest will take care of itself. Everything else will follow. These words, these catechisms, they continue to demand an audience of me. First Nicholas asked me to allow someone else's prophecy to be my guide, now he asks me to let someone else's judgment be my fate. His faith is meant to be encouraging, I know. But this same faith is asking me to put my life in someone else's hands, and so far, experience has shown me that's the worst place for it to be.

Gareth steps forward and takes my arm. John releases me and reluctantly, I walk up the aisle with Gareth.

Everyone else remains seated as I pass. I can feel their eyes on me, hear their whispers. I feel like a bride, in the most ill-conceived, ill-fated marriage ever imagined.

We reach the pulpit, scrolled and elaborate and painted gold, the stand carved into the shape of a raven: a messenger of truth but also a symbol of misfortune and deception. Lined up before it is a row of chairs, all of them plain but for the one in the centre. It's large and uncomfortable-looking, all sharp angles and battered wood, the back spiked to a point. All four of the fat wooden legs are carved into the shape of a lion.

A door behind the altar opens. Out walk a line of men, all dressed identically to Gareth and Nicholas. Plain, floor-length robes, hooded and velvety black, adorned with the Reformist herald: a small sun surrounded by a square, then a triangle, then another circle, a snake devouring its own tail: an Ouroboros. The councilmen. My judge and jury.

Gareth leads me to the chair in the centre, gestures for me to sit. Immediately, a set of chains spring from the arms and legs, bracketing themselves around my wrists and ankles. The carved wooden lions roar to life, snapping their jaws, growling, flexing splintery-sharp wooden claws. I jerk away but go nowhere as John, seated in the front row beside Fifer and Peter, clambers to his feet in protest. Peter grabs his shoulder and pulls him down.

Gareth steps to his place behind the pulpit – the seventeenth councillor but the only one who counts – and clears his throat.

'Before we begin, I think it's only appropriate to observe

a moment of silence, in honour of those killed in the attacks today.'

He reads the names of Harrow's four dead men and one dead woman, then turns and addresses the crowd.

'As you all know, we have convened here today to determine whether Elizabeth Grey should be allowed the privilege of remaining within the protective borders of Harrow, or whether she should be banished, never to return.'

There's a low murmuring from the pews.

Gareth continues. 'Today's attacks mark the third breach of security, the third time Blackwell – the new ruling king of Anglia – has managed to infiltrate Harrow. But it is the first time he has sent his men to retrieve what I believe he sees as his property. While it is our policy – that is to say, a Reformist policy – to offer protection to those who seek it, we must determine whether this protection can and should be offered at the expense of our own safety.'

'The attacks on Harrow are no fault of Elizabeth's,' Nicholas says. 'Whether she is here or not, Blackwell's men would come.'

'We have lived in Harrow in safety for many years without incident,' Gareth replies. 'I find it impossible to believe that her arrival and these attacks are mere coincidence.'

'I imagine we all found it impossible to believe that the former Inquisitor would turn out to be a wizard,' Nicholas responds. 'Yet so it is.'

'The girl is dangerous,' begins one councilman. He's the

oldest of the men, even older than Nicholas, his pale skin and wispy white hair stark against his black robe. 'I cannot discount that. But she saved Nicholas's life, and I cannot discount that, either. Were it not for her, he would be dead.'

A pair of men sitting side by side nod in unison. 'Indeed, she did save a life,' one of them says. 'Of course, one could argue that saving one life is not quite recompense for the lives she has taken.' He fixes me with a pair of mismatched eyes: one deep brown, the other canary yellow. 'And how many lives would that be, Miss Grey?'

I pause a moment, considering a lie. As if on cue, I catch the minute shake of Nicholas's head. I feel the weight of a thousand pairs of eyes on me, and I start to sweat beneath John's heavy blue coat. And I look away as I answer the question that not even he has dared to ask me.

'Forty-one,' I murmur.

'What's that?' The man's single yellow eye gleams with malice. 'I don't think the people in the back can hear.'

'Forty-one,' I say again, a little louder.

The man gives a grim nod. 'As I say. Forty-one lives gone, one life spared—'

'Saved.' Nicholas corrects the man, the same way John corrected Gareth. 'She did not spare my life, she saved it. And she has saved others.' Nicholas looks to Fifer but not to John. No one on the council knows what I did to save him. 'Given the opportunity, she may save far more.'

'You're not suggesting we allow a witch hunter—'

'Former witch hunter,' Nicholas interrupts quietly.

'To fight with us? For us?' The two councilmen look at

each other, puffed as a pair of crows. 'How are we to believe this isn't all part of a trap? A plan she concocted with Blackwell to get inside Harrow and do away with us all?'

Silence falls as the whole of the cathedral considers his words. Considers the idea that I might be playing my part in a trap, one set by Blackwell and that results in my killing everyone inside Harrow. It's impossible.

Except that it's not.

'It isn't.' I grip the hard, square armrests, hating the tremulous sound of my voice but afraid to raise it any higher. 'I would never help Blackwell. Not anymore.'

The councilmen look down the line to one another, exchanging glances that range from surprise to disbelief. Mainly disbelief.

'I don't want to hurt anyone. I never did, not really,' I say. 'When I became a witch hunter, I was just a child. I didn't realise what it meant – what it would mean. But I didn't know what else to do.' It's a pitiful excuse, the worst. But it's the truth.

'But whether I stay or go, whether I am here or not, Blackwell is coming after you,' I continue. 'He wants Harrow. Under his thumb or gone, but he will not stop until he gets what he wants. That is something you have to know about him – he always gets what he wants.'

The councillors look down the row at one another again.

'If you do allow me to stay, I can help you,' I say. 'I can help keep him away. I can help try to do away with him.' I purposely avoid the word *kill*. 'I worked with him for three years, lived under his roof for two. I know him.'

'Not well enough, I'd say,' the yellow-eyed councillor retorts. 'Otherwise you'd have known he was a wizard. Despite everything you say you know about him, somehow the most important thing managed to escape you completely. It was right in front of you.'

'I thought he was using one of you!' My voice rises to a pitch; the lions at my feet bare their teeth at me in warning. 'I thought he was using a wizard to perform magic for him. He told me he hated magic. I didn't know it was a lie!'

'How could you not know?' This from the old white-haired man. He doesn't sound angry, just bewildered. 'Nicholas assured us you were an educated, intelligent girl.'

'But that's just it,' I say, and my voice is quiet again. 'I'm just a girl. Or, I was, when I went to live with him. I was thirteen years old. I was looking for him to be a teacher, a mentor.' I almost don't say the next word, but then I do. 'A father, after I lost my own. Not a wizard.'

That's when I tell them everything: the truth the way Nicholas wanted me to tell it. How I was the king's mistress. How I was arrested for carrying herbs that prevented me from conceiving his child, then sentenced to death, only to be saved by Nicholas. How I discovered Blackwell was a wizard before setting out to find the tablet Blackwell cursed in order to kill Nicholas, that the only reason I could find it, resting in that dark, dank, mouldy, and deathly tomb, was that Blackwell wanted to kill me first.

'He betrayed me, too,' I finish. 'I believed the things Blackwell told me. I didn't have any reason not to. I didn't go around looking for lies, like I do now. But I know now, and I can help you stop him.' I look at John then, his hazel eyes going wide as he guesses what I'm about to say next: 'I will fight for y—'

John is on his feet before I finish the sentence.

'She can't fight,' he says. 'She's still recovering. She's still not strong enough. And she doesn't—' John cuts himself off as he catches himself, about to announce to the whole of Harrow that I no longer have my stigma.

It was Nicholas's idea to keep this a secret from the council. His fear was that if they knew I didn't have it, the threat today wouldn't be exile; it would be execution.

'She nearly died,' John finishes, and it's a long moment before he sits again, resistance giving way to resignation.

'I'm afraid I have to agree.' A councilman, quiet up until now, speaks from his chair to my right. 'She's a child. And as Mr Raleigh points out, an unwell child at that.' His eyes, a deep cornflower blue, sweep over me, observant but not unkind. 'I fail to see what she can do for us that we cannot do for ourselves.'

I bristle a little at this: at being called a child, at being underestimated.

'She was one of Blackwell's best witch hunters,' Gareth points out. I feel a rush of gratitude at his defence, until I realise it is most likely an offense. 'And there is the inarguable truth that she did manage to infiltrate Blackwell's fortress, fight her way from that tomb, and destroy the curse tablet.'

The line of councilmen erupts with comments.

'She showed a tremendous amount of courage—'

'—went back into that tomb after nearly being buried alive the first time—'

'She managed to get into his palace once before, perhaps she can do it again—'

'Aside from fighting,' Nicholas interrupts, 'there are many other ways in which Elizabeth can help. She can help train an army. She can provide us with information. About Blackwell's strategy, his home, his defences. His witch hunters. Of course, you understand this is why he is intent on hunting her down. He knows that in the wrong hands, this information could be a weapon.'

'You speak of training an army,' another councilman says to Nicholas. 'What army? All we've got assembled are guards, a handful of pirates, and some noblemen.' He glances into the pews. 'We don't have strength, and we don't have numbers. Not unless we want to start *requiring* men to fight. Men who have no experience fighting.'

'We will get troops,' Nicholas says. 'But negotiating for them is not a straightforward matter. Gaul has offered men but understandably, they're wary. They've got their own borders to protect, and while they certainly do not side with Blackwell, they also do not want to risk his animosity. What happened with King Malcolm is not something the Gallic king wishes to repeat.'

The night of the masque, after Peter came for us and we disappeared from Greenwich Tower, Malcolm and Queen Margaret were arrested and thrown into the depths of Fleet, the most notorious prison in Anglia. Their arrest frightened everyone in Harrow. To orchestrate the incarceration, and possible murder, of a monarch is something not even the staunchest Reformist would consider.

'And in the meantime?' The blue-eyed man addresses Nicholas. 'You can't expect Blackwell to wait until we manage to recruit troops. He won't wait for them to arrive before he attacks. That's weeks from now at the earliest. What do we do until then?'

'Prepare,' Nicholas says. 'Assemble our guards, recruit more men. Men who are willing and able to train, men who are not able but who are willing. Open our borders to outsiders willing to fight for us.'

He turns to the pews. Makes eye contact with those sitting toward the front.

'It's not enough to wait; it's not enough to deny. Nor is it necessary to place blame, point fingers, punish.' Nicholas looks to the councilmen then, at each of them in turn. 'We've hidden long enough. The fight has not just been brought to our doorstep, it's through the threshold and it stands inside and it carries a sword. Sending Elizabeth into exile will not close that door, nor will turning her over to the enemy. We must show Blackwell that he cannot simply take what he wants, that Harrow will not fall as long as we are here to defend it. And Elizabeth can help us do that.'

The men and women in the pews, moved by Nicholas's words, murmur and nod to one another. Gareth looks from Nicholas to me, to the councilmen.

'Let us prepare to vote.'

FOUR

The councilmen rise from their chairs and start down the aisle toward the entrance, stopping beside the water-filled font I passed on my way in. The man at the front holds up a hand, index finger pointed to the sky. Holding back his velvety, bell-shaped sleeve with the other hand, he plunges his finger into the bowl.

From where I'm seated, I can see the water, a slow, tepid swirl before, begin to pick up speed, a few droplets splashing into the air. After a moment, a small puff of steam erupts and he removes his hand from the bowl. Then, one by one, each councilman repeats the process.

As the last man steps from the font, the water stops swirling, turning placid and still as a mirror, silvery and beckoning. It's not a font of holy water, as I first thought when I saw it. It's a scrying bowl.

I've found a few inside the homes of wizards I've arrested, but I've never seen one in use before. They're used to read the thoughts of many people instead of only one, the way a scrying mirror does. Water is a conductor, and an element of truth: impossible to lie to, no doubt to prevent votes from being fixed or made under duress. This must be part of the council rules that Nicholas instated; the magic bears his hallmark: simple, honest, resolute.

Each councilman steps forward and peers inside. Some give a quick glance; some take a longer look. But they each, after seeing whatever it is they see, nod before proceeding back up the aisle and settling into their chairs again, their velvet cloaks a sigh against the wood.

Gareth steps behind the pulpit. Before I can swipe my damp palms against the wooden armrests, he speaks.

'It's a tie.'

Fifer looks to me, then John, a grim smile of solidarity passing her lips. Peter's face shows alarm; he knows it's likely I will be sent away, and his only son with me. Because eight against eight, a tie, must be broken, and only Gareth, as head of the council, can do it.

'To stay or to go.' Gareth's voice holds the tone of a man who revels in every eye being on him – which they are – and having the fate of someone in his hands – which it is. 'It's clear some of you see Elizabeth Grey as a danger. Someone untrustworthy, someone violent, someone disloyal.'

Fifer opens her mouth to object, but closes it quickly. She can't object, because it's true. If I were loyal, I'd still be with Blackwell. The way Caleb was, until the very end.

'By that same token, because we are up against someone

untrustworthy, violent, and disloyal, I see that many of you consider that an advantage.'

Nicholas watches Gareth as he speaks. His dark eyes harden, obsidian, and I know that look well. It's the look he gave me when his seer, Veda, told him I was a witch hunter. That I was not the wronged innocent girl he believed me to be. I feared him then, and despite everything he's done for me, I fear him still.

'Despite my initial misgivings, I, too, see this as an advantage,' Gareth continues. 'But the condition by which you will be permitted to remain in Harrow is not only that you fight. It is not enough for you to train our army, not enough to catalogue what you know. I want you to use your training to turn against the man who trained you.' A pause before his words, hard as steel, clash through the silent cathedral. 'I want you to kill him.'

Here I sit: chained to a chair in a blood-soaked gown with a blood-soaked past, being asked once more to trade on violence for the sake of peace. I look to John. He holds my stare, the weight of it telling me what he wants me to do. He wants me to decline, to refuse, to be exiled so that we can leave Anglia together, for somewhere he believes we will be safe.

But I was never one to do what others wanted me to.

'Yes,' I say. 'I will fight for you. I will' – I stop on the word before pronouncing it with more force than I feel – 'I will kill him.'

Gareth nods at me, satisfied; he gets the response he wants. But John startles me with one I don't when he climbs to his feet and says, 'Then I will fight for you, too.'

The pews erupt with voices but one, more musical than the rest, cuts through them all.

'You can't. He can't.'

I – along with everyone else – turn to see Chime, that pretty dark-haired girl from the Winter's Night party who laid claim to John before I came along, on her feet. She glares at the councilman to my left, the one with the same cornflower-blue eyes as hers. At once, I know who he is; Fifer told me all about him. Chime's father, Lord Fitzroy Cranbourne Calthorpe-Gough.

'I really must object.' He glances at his daughter, then back at Gareth, his handsome face etched in a scowl. 'I don't see how allowing a healer to fight will help us.'

'I don't see how it can hurt,' Gareth says. 'You yourself said we had no army, no men. Now we have one more.' He flashes a brittle, indulgent smile at John, who doesn't smile back.

'This is war,' Lord Cranbourne Calthorpe-Gough continues. 'There will be injuries. John Raleigh is a healer. He saves lives. He does not take them.'

'Yet he took one today with very little hesitation,' Gareth responds. 'And from what I saw, he did it very well. He's already in this fight.'

There's nothing to say to this, because Gareth is right. For better or worse, John was in this fight the moment we met. But Chime's father is right, too: Taking lives isn't what John does.

'It simply makes no sense,' Lord Cranbourne

Calthorpe-Gough says. 'We need a healer to attend—'

Gareth waves it off. 'We have other healers.'

'Surely there are other—'

'Enough.' John's voice, deep and sure, rings through the cathedral. 'I appreciate your objections, but they're unnecessary. I already said I'll fight, and that's final.' He shifts his attention to Gareth. 'Are we done here?'

I wait for Gareth to reprimand John's disrespect, maybe to deny his pledge. Instead he only smiles.

'The council is adjourned.'

The chains around my wrists and ankles snap open, falling to the floor with a loud clank. The lions cease their restless prowling, wrap themselves around the wooden legs of the chair, and become inanimate once more. The crowd is silent as they file from their pews, row by row into the aisle and out the front door.

Gareth gathers his book from the pulpit and exits through the side door along with the rest of the councilmen, the same way they came in. John rises from his seat and pushes his way toward me, but he's stopped every few feet by men and women who approach him, shaking his hand and offering their thanks.

Harrow has suffered since the rebellions in Upminster – Anglia's capital and the seat of Blackwell's new power – began two years ago. Witches and wizards from all over the country sought refuge here, safe from the Inquisition and from witch hunters, from prison and torture, flame and death. But more people meant less to go around, and there have been rations for food, land, supplies, and weapons.

John is well liked here, of course he would be. He helps people when they're ill, often for very little money, more often for free. Now he's going into battle on my behalf, many of those here no doubt assuming he won't return.

It's Fifer who reaches me first, emerging from the crowd in front of my chair.

She pulls me to my feet and, together, we make our way to the door that opens into the cemetery, to avoid the stares of the men and women still idling in the hall. We step into a patch of shade beneath a tree, not far from where Blackwell's archer had me cornered against a headstone, not far from where his blood still stagnates sticky in the bright sun. Then she turns to me, her hands crushed against the hips of her green velvet gown.

'Have you gone completely mad?' she demands. 'Fighting? Killing Blackwell? Why would you agree to that?'

'I had no other choice.'

'Yes, you did,' she says. 'You could have, oh, I don't know, not agreed.'

'If I still had my stigma, it's the first thing I would have done,' I say. 'Not fighting would have created more problems. The council would have asked questions, and one way or another, the truth would have come out.'

Fifer casts about, to make sure no one is nearby, listening. There isn't, but she lowers her voice anyway.

'You could die.'

'I won't die,' I say. Empty words: It's not a promise I can

make and she knows it. 'But I also won't sit back and do nothing.' I search the people spilling from the cathedral, looking for one in particular. 'I don't know what John was thinking, telling the council he would fight, too.'

'I do,' Fifer says. 'He was thinking of you.'

'It doesn't matter. He still can't do it.'

'I know you think that,' she says. 'But if I'm being honest, they could do worse. He has your stigma, so he can't be hurt. And he's pretty good in a fight. Peter trained him well.'

'I saw.'

'At least you didn't make an utter fool of yourself like Chime, the whey-faced thing,' she continues. 'What right does she have speaking up for John? But there she was, on her feet before the whole of Harrow, bellowing like a fishwife guarding her bucket.'

'She was hardly bellowing,' I say. 'She was just defending him. She did what I should have done.'

'He's not her bucket to defend,' Fifer says with finality. 'And speaking of.' She jerks her head toward John, at last making his way out of the cathedral.

The blood has dried on the front of his white shirt, stiff and dark. He has his sleeves pushed up past his elbows, hands and forearms stained red. His hair is unruly and sweaty, his face harried and unsettled. When he reaches us, he wraps an arm around me and pulls me to him.

'I'm in dire need of a bath,' he whispers before kissing me.

I smile against his lips; Fifer makes a retching noise.

John pulls back then. 'You shouldn't have agreed to fight,' he says to me.

'That's what I said,' Fifer says.

'No choice,' I say again. 'Council's orders.'

'I know. But I still don't want you—'

'I don't want you fighting, either,' I interrupt. 'I know you can, but that doesn't mean you should. You're a healer. I already said this, but fighting isn't what you do.'

'And I told you before, things are different now,' he replies, an edge slipping into his voice. 'I will do what I have to.'

'But it doesn't make any sense.'

'Things stopped making sense a long time ago. I don't see why they should start now.'

'John—' It's all I manage before a familiar voice interrupts.

'John, may I speak with you?' Chime stands off the dirt path, under a tree by the gates. She's dressed in a cerulean-blue silk-and-velvet gown, the same colour as her eyes. Real, live butterflies adorn the shoulders, their wings blue and edged with black, fluttering softly. Her jet-black hair is pulled off her face into a loose knot and adorned with blue-jewelled butterfly-shaped pins.

The whole effect is beautiful, ethereal, just as she is. I can easily see what John saw in her, even though he says when they were together he was too drunk to see much of anything. Fifer says she's trouble and while that may be so, I can't imagine she's more trouble than me.

'Of course.' John arranges his irritated expression

into something resembling calm.

'In private, please?' Chime glances at Fifer, then me. 'If you don't mind.' Her voice is high and soft, warm and melodic, the sound of a summer's day.

'Not at all,' I say. John gives me a small smile before the two of them turn and walk down the path together.

'We'll be waiting,' Fifer coos. I shoot her a look; she jabs me with her elbow. 'Why'd you let them go off together?' she hisses when they're out of earshot.

'She just wants to talk,' I say. 'There's no harm in that.'

Fifer purses her lips but doesn't reply.

John and Chime stop under the tree at the end of the path. She appears to be doing most of the talking; John watches her intently, and every now and again he nods. Seeing them together, I feel a sharp pang of jealousy, but there's something else, too: inevitability.

Chime touches her hand to John's, says something in parting. She glances at me, those deep blue eyes sweeping over me, her face carefully neutral. She ignores Fifer entirely. Then she turns and walks away to join her father. Lord Cranbourne Calthorpe-Gough nods at me, then John, before taking Chime's arm and leading her away.

John walks back to us, his face expressionless.

'What did she want?' Fifer demands.

'Nothing,' he says. 'Well, not nothing. She wanted to talk to me about her grandmother. She's very ill.' John turns to me. 'She's my patient; I've been treating her for years. It's actually how I know her. Chime, I mean.'

Fifer purses her lips again.

'Anyway, she was asking me if I could come by and spend some time with her grandmother before things got under way.'

Fifer makes a noise partway between a scoff and a snort. 'Can't it wait until it's all over?'

'Fifer,' I say, my voice reproachful.

'It really can't,' John says. 'And it's better if I do it now anyway, just in case.'

'In case what?'

'In case something happens to me.'

'Nothing is going to happen to you,' Fifer says.

John smiles a little, but it doesn't reach his eyes. 'I don't think anyone can promise that.'

FIVE

That evening, Peter avoids looking at me during supper, too busy beaming at John as if his son had managed to fulfil all the fatherly dreams he'd held for him, all in one afternoon. In turn, John avoids his gaze, too intent on trying to catch mine, the echo of our earlier disagreement still hanging between us. I want to fight; John doesn't want me to. Peter wants John to fight; I don't want John to. John is angry with me, for reasons I understand, and I'm angry with him, too, for reasons I don't.

I avoid looking at both of them entirely, staring down at my trencher of beef stew and bread, which goes largely untouched.

'You'll wait for your summons, but I expect it'll be here within the week.' Peter waves his glass of brandy around, his third – a celebration – and continues. 'You're to report in when you do. Straight to Rochester Hall.'

Rochester Hall. Lord Cranbourne Calthorpe-Gough's

home, Chime's home. Where camp is to be set up, where training is to take place, where the troops from Gaul, when they arrive, are to be stationed. Where John and I, as new recruits in the fight to protect Harrow, are to live for the foreseeable future.

'Is Rochester Hall well suited for a camp?' I pick up my bread, tear off a piece. 'Does it have adequate grounds? Spaces for people to live? To train?'

I think of Blackwell's home at Greenwich Tower. Hidden behind forty-foot walls, guarded day and night, protected on one side by the Severn River, on all sides by a moat. And I think of all the magic inside: As much as inside Harrow, I realise now. Magic used to train us, to frighten us, to harden us into soldiers, all done by the hardest and most frightening man I know.

John and Peter exchange amused glances, and I feel my irritation grow.

'Quite so,' Peter says. 'Fitzroy's grandfather, the Fourth Earl of Abbey, he was a prophetic man. Not a seer, mind, just observant. He foresaw trouble with magic, foresaw that it would no longer be tolerated. He founded Harrow, you see. Most of the land we're living on belongs to the Cranbourne Calthorpe-Goughs.'

I'm surprised, though perhaps I shouldn't be, that Chime is heir to all of Harrow.

'Some of it he sold to Nicholas, some to Gareth, and I own some, of course,' Peter continues. 'But the majority of the men who live in Harrow are tenants. Fitzroy, he's a hard man, but he's a good man. He won't conscript them to fight if they do not wish it.'

'Unlike Gareth,' John mutters.

Peter nods. 'Even so, conscription isn't necessary. We've got plenty of volunteers. Messages have been pouring in all afternoon, since the trial.' He gestures to his desk at the stack of letters half a foot high. 'Men to hold the line, to stop the attacks until the troops arrive.' Peter touches his snifter to John's goblet, a toast. 'And a girl, too, of course,' he says to me, as if I'm an afterthought.

Finally, it settles into me, with clarity, what I'm angry about: I'm an afterthought in my own fight.

'Of course,' is all I can manage.

To an outsider, this exchange is innocent. Pleasant, even. But with the intuition John has, part of that healer's magic he possesses, I know he senses the tension simmering beneath the surface. He's on his feet, a beat before me.

'It's late,' John says to Peter, but his eyes are on me. 'It's been a long day, and I'm tired. I'm sure Elizabeth is, too.'

'I'm fine,' I say. 'I want to clean up first.' Since I arrived at Mill Cottage, and since I've been able to, I've helped Peter and John with the cleaning and cooking. They don't do it, not well, anyway, and though they don't ask and most of the time they try and stop me, I do it anyway.

'Leave it,' John says. I throw him a sharp look and he adds, 'At least until tomorrow. All right? You need to get your rest.'

I snatch the dishes off the table and stomp into the kitchen with them, ignoring John's advisement completely. I don't need to rest. What I need to do is to get strong again, to start training. I need to learn how to fight – and to fight well – without my stigma. I can't do any of that if I'm resting.

Peter and John give me a wide berth, doing and saying nothing as I grab up linens, rattle around cutlery. Finally, I finish. The dining room is clean now, and awkward in its silence. Nothing but the crackle of the fire in the hearth, the ticking of the clock on the mantel, the rustle of branches on the trees against the mullioned windows. I can almost feel the weight of the pair of matching dark eyes on me, watching me.

I don't know what to say to either of them. I'm embarrassed by my outburst, but not enough to apologise for it. Angry, but too much to ask for forgiveness. After a moment I settle on 'Good night', pushing past them both, out of the dining room and into the foyer, then upstairs to my room. Soon enough I hear the creaking of footsteps on the wood staircase, the careful shutting of John's door across the hall from mine. The sound of it is somehow lonely.

I'm not tired, but I change into my nightdress anyway. Something else Fifer gave me: pale green linen with a square neckline and wide sleeves, both trimmed with dark green ribbons. Almost too pretty to sleep in. I move to the dressing table in the corner of the room, sit in front of the mirror. Pull a brush from the drawer and begin to run it through my hair.

Once again, I don't recognise myself. Six weeks ago, I was deadly. Today, I am cautionary. My reflection confirms it: Pale. Fragile. Weak. The loss of my stigma took more than just my strength and my ability to heal – it took away my identity. I don't know where to find it, or even where to begin looking.

I cram the brush back into the drawer, slam it shut. As I do, a piece of parchment slips from the bottom, flutters to the floor.

After I woke up but before the weather cleared enough for us to spend our days outside, John and I spent all night writing notes and passing them to each other beneath our closed doors. Peter was adamant we not see each other after dark; he still is. But to John's way of thinking, it didn't mean we couldn't speak to each other.

It was simple. He fashioned a loop of twine, one end slipped under my door frame. He had the other end. He'd write me a note, fold it around the twine, then give his end a little tug. I'd reel it around, read it, and write back, then give my own end a little tug. Back the note went. Sometimes we'd have several pieces going at once, so neither of us was waiting on the other.

I pick up the note, unfold it. The page is filled with a series of botanicals, carefully etched and labelled in Latin. *Angelica sylvestris*, a fine-petaled plant with a spray of white blossoms. *Salvia officinalis*, a grey-leafed shrub full of deep purple flowers. *Berberis vulgaris*, another plant marked by spiked leaves and fat red berries. The delicate beauty of each rendering is a stark contrast to John's crooked, nearly illegible scrawl.

He drew them for me, in part, after I teased him about

his penmanship. The other reason, he said, was that these were some of the plants he used to heal me. They were beautiful to him, he said, because they brought me back to him.

I drop my head into my hands, the parchment fluttering to the floor. I don't have a lot of experience with what it means to be with someone the way I am with John. None, in fact. I don't know how to navigate waters in which half the time I feel as if I'm drowning. But I do know there are better ways of treating someone who loves you than by flinging beef stew at them, falling into stony silence, then storming out of the room.

A cool breeze snaps in through the open window, rattling it against the frame. I get up to close it, glancing at the dimly lit gardens below. Most of John's carefully cultivated plants are dormant now, pruned back for winter. But the trellis that snakes up the stone wall is choked with winter honeysuckle, wild and flowering, the scent heady even in February.

The trellis.

In less than a minute I'm out the window and over the edge, down the wall and on the ground. A quick glance through the blue-paned window of the front house shows Peter at his desk, busy with his letters. I duck beneath it and pass to the other side, my bare feet crunching in the narrow gravel pathways until I'm standing in the garden beneath John's window. There's a trellis here, too, full of the same winter honeysuckle.

I start to climb.

Within seconds I'm at the top, peering into his window. John is sitting at his desk, propped up on one elbow, his head resting in his hand, reading. He's tired, I can tell; his eyes are at half-mast and even as I watch him, they slide shut and his head bobs forward.

I tap on the window.

His head snaps up, eyes wide. He glances toward the door.

I tap again.

John whips his head around, catches sight of me outside his window. I smile at the way his jaw drops open, shocked. He's on his feet in an instant, crossing to the window, pulling it open, and tugging me inside. I clamber over the sill, clutching my nightgown around my legs so it won't tangle.

His eyes travel from my hair, loose and hanging around my shoulders, down to my bare, mud-stained feet then back to my face, but not before lingering slightly on the low, square neckline of my nightgown that shows more than it should.

I really should have changed.

'Elizabeth,' he starts.

'Before you say anything, I need to talk to you.' I step away from him, out of reach of his arms, of the way his shirt is unbuttoned too low, his hair that looks like it's had my hands in it. The way he looks at me, a half smile bordering on a smirk, and the way he smells, lavender and spice and something unmistakably him. My insides do a long, slow twist.

He takes a step closer.

I hold my hand up. 'You stay right there. I can't have you distracting me.'

John sighs, running a hand through his already-dishevelled curls. Then he points at the chair at his desk, the one he was sitting and almost sleeping in moments ago.

'Please, sit.'

I do.

'I'm sorry,' I say. 'For how I acted today. Earlier. Downstairs. You know.' I shake my head at the ineptness of my apology.

'It's all right.'

'No, it's not,' I say. 'I was terrible. You didn't do anything. And I never even thanked you for what you did do. Standing up for me at the trial. Agreeing to fight with me. I know it couldn't have been easy.'

'You're wrong.' John sits on the edge of his mattress facing me, resting his bare feet along the dark wooden bed frame. 'It was very easy.'

'I know that's what you think now,' I say. 'But nothing about this is going to be easy.'

'I only meant that the decision was.'

'You say that only because you have the stigma,' I say.

'It has nothing to do with that.' John considers. 'No, you're right. It has everything to do with it.'

'I don't regret giving it to you,' I say quickly, before the seed of the idea can take root. 'I never regret that.'

'But you do regret not having it,' he says.

'Yes,' I say. And there it falls: the truth. 'I would

be lying if I said I didn't. It would make what I have to do…doable. Because right now it isn't. Right now it seems impossible.'

John falls silent, in the way that tells me he's thinking something he doesn't want to say. So I wait for it. For him to tell me I can't kill Blackwell. To tell me, as he's done so many times before, that it's too dangerous, that I'm not strong enough.

'I know you think I'm going to try to stop you from doing what you want with this,' he says finally. 'But I'm not.'

'You're not?' I enjoy a second of relief before it falls into distress. 'Oh. Is that because…you don't want, you know, you, and me, and…'

'No!' He gets to his feet, takes my hand, and pulls me off my chair and onto the bed to sit beside him. 'Of course not. That isn't it at all. Do I wish I could lock you away until this is all over? Yes. But you would hate me for it, and anyway, that's not who you are. And I never want you to be anything different.'

I blink. 'No?'

'No.'

'And…that's it?' I say. 'No arguments, no fighting?'

John huffs a quiet laugh. 'Would you prefer I pull a sword on you? Duel it to the death?' I smile, and he goes on. 'I've got your stigma, but I'll be damned if I'm not going to protect you with it. As much as I can, however I can. I won't stop you. But I don't want you to try to stop me, either.'

I hesitate, but only for a moment. The conditions of the

truce he's offering aren't ideal, but they're unlikely to get any better.

'I guess we're in this together, then.'

He grins. 'That's what I've been trying to tell you.'

I laugh at that. I can't help it.

John shifts a little, moving closer to me. The light in the room is dim, the tired candle on his desk having already extinguished itself. The last one sits on the table beside the bed, the flame bobbing softly in the night breeze. He slides his hand into my hair, cupping my neck, his thumb skimming across my cheek. I lean into him and I don't know who kisses who first but it hardly matters.

We half push, half pull each other down onto the bed. We're tangled together on the sheets, kissing and fumbling and tugging at each other's clothes. I don't remember deciding to take off his shirt but there it is, off. His hand moves to my bare leg, sliding up to my hip and taking my nightgown with it. I let out a little gasp; he kisses me harder.

The feel of his hands on my skin, of mine on his. His lips on my neck, his hair tangled between my fingers, his breath in my ear. I can't think. Maybe it's the control we spent staying apart while living so close in this house, maybe it's the control spent keeping ourselves together today, but it's falling apart now. My heart is racing, my breath is coming fast, we're doing what we've done before but it's never felt like this: all urgency and carelessness and need, and I want it all to carry me as far as it will take me.

A flurry of wind blows through the window then; the candle on the bedside goes out with a hiss. The room plunges into darkness. The sharp, opaque scent of sulphur from the extinguished flame; the mattress creaking under our weight; the feel of his bare skin pressed against my own. At once, I'm not in John's room, kissing him, feeling his body on top of mine. Instead, I'm in Ravenscourt Palace, in Malcolm's room. I'm coerced, I'm unwilling, and I'm frightened.

The heat I felt just moments before gives way to a sudden snap of cold. I push him off and away from me. Scurry to the head of the bed, pulling my nightgown down to cover my bare legs. My breath is still coming fast.

I can't see through the darkness in the room, not really, but I can make out John's silhouette as he sits up. His breath is still coming fast, too.

'Hold on a minute.' John gets up, fumbles around for his shirt, pulls it on. Makes his way to the table. I hear the scratch of a match, watch as he relights the candle in front of him. He glances at me, then crosses the room and lights three more, set into brackets at intervals along the wall. Light floods the room.

'I'm sorry,' I say, before he can say anything. 'I don't know what happened. I don't know why I did that.'

'You don't have to know,' he replies. 'And you don't have to apologise.'

'I guess it was the dark,' I continue. 'It reminded me of being somewhere else, with someone else—'

'Elizabeth.' John moves to the bed again and sits at the very end of the mattress, as far away from me as he's able. 'You don't have to explain it to me.'

He slides his hand forward across the mattress until his fingertips touch mine, tentative.

I'm reminded of the way he did that on the morning after we first went to Veda's, after I reacted the way I did in the tunnel beneath her cottage, remembering my final test, filled with so much fear I couldn't stand, couldn't walk, couldn't do anything but curl into a ball. Reminded of how he carried me in his arms back to Nicholas's, stayed with me all night. How, even then, he cared for me in a way no one else had before.

I'm also reminded of how none of this is easy for him. Nothing about me, or him and me, is simple. I know it would be easier if I had never come into his life at all. If he had stayed with Chime, if he'd preferred her over me. The guilt eats at me, but I can't tell him this. Because if I do, it will be just one more burden he will take on for me, when he's already taken on so many.

'I should go.' I swing my legs over the edge of the mattress.

'Wait.' He catches my arm. 'Please, stay. I'll sleep on the floor,' he adds quickly. 'You don't have to if you don't want to. But I don't want you to go.'

I start to say no, that it's best for me to leave. But just like every other day, when I stay when I know I should go, I don't.

'All right,' I say. 'But you're not sleeping on the floor.' I turn back to the bed, sliding under the clean, lavender-scented linen sheets.

John pauses, then slides in beside me, pulling the

bedcovers over both of us. He's careful not to touch me, too careful. But after a moment I roll over to face him, wrap an arm around his waist. He pulls me closer, my head resting on his chest, his face buried in my hair.

And we sleep.

SIX

Cough.

The sound cuts through my slumber, pulling me awake. I open one eye, then the other, taking in the dark panelled walls, the deep blue bedcovers, John's arm slung around my waist. We're still in the same position we fell asleep in, curled up in each other.

Cough.

Peter.

'God's nails,' John murmurs into my hair.

'How long do you think he's been out there?' I whisper.

Cough. A pause, then a horrible choking sound of Peter clearing his throat. *Cough.*

'Judging by that noise he's making, I'd say awhile.'

I press a hand to my mouth to smother a laugh.

'Shh, you'll make it worse,' John says, only he's laughing, too. 'I guess I'd better talk to him.' He pulls away from me and climbs out of bed. His warmth goes with him, leaving me cold.

'Wait.' I sit up. 'You can't go out there looking like that.'

'Why?' John looks down at himself. At his wrinkled trousers, his rumpled shirt that looks exactly what it is: slept in. What he can't see is his tousled hair, or the smirk on his face that makes him look as if he's been up to no good – or quite a bit of good, depending on the one looking.

'Because you look as if you've been doing exactly what your father thinks we've been doing.'

'Ah.' John grins. 'Here's the thing: If I go out there with neat hair and proper clothes, he'll think I've got something to hide. Because if I were really guilty of something, there's no chance I'd go out there looking like this.'

'Oh.' I think about this a moment, then scowl. 'Done this before with other girls, have we?'

'I've never done this with other girls. Only you.' He dips his head, brushes his lips against mine. 'You'll always be the only girl.'

My lips curve into a smile as I kiss him back.

Cough.

'Into the breach.' John crosses to the door, flinging it open with a flourish. 'Sounds like you've got the croup,' he announces, stepping into the hall. 'That's quite a feat, you know. Croup is almost exclusively a child's illness, and exceedingly rare in old men.'

John closes the door then, but I hear Peter's response anyway.

'I'll give you the croup, young man.'

I press my hand against my mouth again to stifle my giggles.

John and Peter continue talking, their voices muffled through the wood so I can't hear what they're saying. I can't exactly leave and go back to my room, not with them standing in the hallway. I could climb back out the window, but there's no point in that now. May as well wait until John returns, to hear our punishment.

I climb out of bed, examine the tangled sheets and coverlet before pulling them over the mattress, smoothing them tight. Then I remember what John said about looking guilty and pull them back down again.

The window is still slightly open, the cold morning breeze slipping inside. I pace the room, and in the light of day I can see just how transparent this linen nightgown is, how you can see nearly everything underneath. So I sit down at John's worktable and tuck myself in as far as the chair will allow.

It's a mess. Books, parchment, ink, and quills scatter the surface. Scales, mortars and pestles, strainers and stirring sticks made from wood and glass and metal. Half the drawers in the table are open, spilling forth with herbs and powders, roots and leaves. I'm overcome with an urge to clean it all up, but I leave it all be. I've seen enough of the way John works to know there's some sort of method in his madness.

A familiar scent hits me then, drifting in with the breeze. It's deceptively soft and sweet, like scented talcum, but with a bite that lingers in your nose afterward – a warning. I peer into drawer and there it is: *Aconitum*. Also called wolfsbane, or devil's bane, it's extremely poisonous. It can cause paralysis; it can stop someone's breathing; it can stop a person's heart.

While devil's bane is recognisable by scent in its raw form, it can be mixed with other herbs to become neutralised, making it odourless, tasteless, untraceable: the perfect poison. There's no use for it except to kill.

I look through a few more drawers. Dig through more sachets, more jars, more bottles. Find more poisons. Belladonna. Mandrake. Foxglove. Why does John have them? More than that, how did he get them? Even in Harrow, where magic is allowed, these herbs are banned. Fifer said that Harrow's prison, Hexham, was once filled with wizards who tried to settle one grudge or another using poison: a salting of devil's bane in someone's soup or a dusting of deadmen's bells on a letter.

I set the poisons on the table, thinking to ask John about them. Then I reconsider. If he hasn't told me about them, there's a reason for it. So with the skill born of years spent ransacking wizards' homes – finding things they didn't want me to, rearranging them back the way I found them before leaving and filing a formal report with the office of the Inquisitor, and eventually, inevitably, returning to arrest them – I tuck them back into the drawers.

When John returns moments later, I'm sitting in his bed on top of the blue coverlet, smoothed tight over the mattress again. I've plaited my hair down my back, securing it with a piece of twine I found on his table. My hands are folded in my lap. John stops on the threshold, takes one look at me, and starts to laugh.

'I've never seen anyone look guiltier than the way you look right now.'

I don't reply, not right away.

'What did your father say?' I finally manage.

John shuts the door and leans against it. He's grinning.

'He says I'm to remember my manners, and your modesty. I'm also to consider my future instead of my present, weigh my intentions against my impulses, eschew vagary and vulgarity, caution against capriciousness, reject foibles, and embrace virtuosity.'

'Those are a lot of words.'

'There were a lot more besides that.'

'He talks a lot, doesn't he?'

'You have no idea.' He tilts his head, his grin fading into a look of sympathy. 'You look so glum. Don't be. If this were at all a problem, I would tell you. It's not. It's just his way of showing he cares. It's odd, I know. But believe me, if he didn't act this way there would be a problem.'

'If it's not a problem, then why are you still standing there instead of over here?'

John's grin is back. 'Because he's on the other side of the door, waiting for me to escort you back to your room.'

'Oh.'

I get up, cross to the door. Stop in front of him. He looks down at me, his eyes full of warmth and amusement and something else, too: love. When he leans down to kiss me, I push down my guilt, as far as it will go. Wrap my arms around his neck and kiss him back.

'Vagary,' he whispers.

'Vulgarity,' I whisper back.

The following day, Harrow is hit with another attack. Five more archers, just like last time. Only this time they get farther, all the way to Gallion's Reach, the very centre of Harrow. Where the high street is, where the shops and taverns are, where a hundred or so people were when they came roaring through in a swirl of inky-black cloaks and arrows and violence. They fired at random, killing two unarmed men, a horse when they missed, one of Peter's pirate brethren when they didn't.

The archers escaped as quickly as they invaded, before what little guard we have could rally a chase. Our men spent the morning picking through the surrounding villages but came up empty, the attackers no doubt returning to Upminster to fill Blackwell's ears with yet more information on Harrow: the layout, the security and lack thereof, where people congregate, where people do not.

Nicholas and the other council members spend the week increasing and adding to the spells around Harrow. Before, only those without sovereignty were disallowed. Now there are three veils of magic: sovereignty, sanction, and intent. Three chances to pass, three chances to fail.

But as Blackwell's men are armed with magic, magic is not enough. So within that same week, the Watch was formed – a group of two hundred armed men patrolling the thirty-odd miles of Harrow's borders, day and night, determined to prevent another breach. Peter and John were among the first to volunteer. Not wanting to disrupt the fragile peace that's settled between us, I encouraged it. And when they packed their bags and stowed their swords and left Mill Cottage, I hid my reservations beneath a smile and a bid of good luck for Peter, a kiss and a whisper of care for John.

While Peter and John and every other able-bodied person inside Harrow either guards the border or assists in setting up camp inside Rochester, Schuyler and Fifer decide to use the time to try to make me battle-ready.

They come for me one morning at dawn, the pair of them striding into my room with a bang of a door and the knock of a boot on my bedpost.

'On your feet, bijoux.'

I sit up, squinting at Schuyler's tall, pale frame at the end of my bed. Fifer stands beside him, a fiery contrast.

'What time is it?' A glance at the window shows no light behind the curtain.

'Time to take a little pounding.' Fifer tosses a handful of clothes in my direction. A pair of trousers, a tunic, a pair of boots, and a steel-buckled belt nearly hit me in the head.

'Watch it,' I grumble.

'Blackwell didn't coddle you during training, so neither will we.' She yanks the covers off me, the cold predawn air an assault.

'At least give me a minute to wake up,' I say. 'Or eat? You can't expect me to work on an empty stomach.'

Schuyler tosses me something, and I snatch it out of the

air just before it hits my face. It's bread. 'According to my sources' – he taps his forehead, reminding me of the power he has to hear my thoughts – 'this is what you ate, the only thing you ate, every morning before training. Any more and you'd vomit it up, any less and you couldn't finish. So get it down and let's get going.'

'We'll wait for you in the hall,' Fifer adds, then shuts the door.

I climb out of bed, a sick sense of dread roiling in my stomach. It's the same feeling I had every morning of every day spent at Blackwell's. Wondering what I would face, how much I would be hurt, if I might die. I stare at the piece of bread in my hand. It even looks the same. Not white manchet bread made from fine flour but coarse, grey wheaten bread. I take a bite; it tastes like gravel.

I pick up the clothes Fifer tossed my way, starting a little when I see what they are. Black trousers, white shirt, tan coat, black boots. The belt I thought was for my trousers is for weapons instead. Witch-hunting clothes.

Damned Schuyler.

I pull them on. Tie my hair back the way I used to, twisted into a knot at the nape of my neck. Walk to the dressing table, look at myself in the mirror mounted above it. Freckles standing in relief against pale skin, pale blue eyes made paler by uncertainty. I'm wary and I'm afraid but I cling to it, comforted somewhat by the familiarity.

As promised, Fifer and Schuyler wait for me in the hallway. Without a word they lead me downstairs, past the dining room and through the kitchen, out the back door.

The sun is just now creeping over the horizon, the sky grey and cold, the air misty with dew. I hurry after them, past John's physic gardens and the low stone fence that surrounds them, into the rolling meadows, the frozen grass crackling under our feet.

'Where are we going?'

Fifer points ahead, where the meadow begins sloping upward into a hill. 'We need privacy,' she says. 'We thought about doing this at Nicholas's, but Gareth is always popping in and out like some damned spying spectre. But he never comes out this way, and neither does anyone else, really.'

'Privacy?' I repeat. 'What are you doing that you need privacy for?'

Fifer turns to face me, now walking backward. 'Scared?' She smirks.

'You wish.' But I am, and she knows it.

We reach the top of the hill, and there, in the flat ground below, I see what they've got planned for me. It's a tiltyard. No sand, stands, or crowds, but a tiltyard nonetheless. Long and narrow, measured and marked by small flags and lined with weapons. Rows of targets, racks of polearms, crossbows, and swords, and a large wooden chest that I can only presume holds even more. Despite my fear, I feel a little thrill rush through me.

The pair of them walk to the edge of the tiltyard and I follow. Schuyler kicks open the lid on the chest and pulls out a mace, a battle-axe, and a handful of knives. One by one he tosses them to the ground; they land on the grass with a wet thud. Finally he pulls out a set of mail – a hood and a long-sleeved tunic, the small iron rings tinged red with rust.

I pull a face. 'Mail? Only pageboys wear mail. I never wore it, not even when I was a recruit. Not even when I knew nothing. Not even the time I got sick and could barely—'

In a blur, Schuyler whips a knife off the ground and flings it at me. It spins end over end, heading straight for my heart. I dive to the ground as it whistles overhead, lifting my head just as the blade buries itself in a birch sapling ten feet behind me. The trunk is barely three inches wide.

'Have you lost your mind?' I wipe mud from my face in a furious swipe. 'You could have killed me.'

'Better wear the mail, then.'

I haul myself to my feet. My trousers are already stained and wet, my hands and face dirty, and we haven't even begun. Fifer holds up the offending mail; I pull off my coat and slip it on over my shirt.

'Headpiece, too.' Schuyler flips his wrists, miming the motion of putting on a hood.

I pull the hood over my head, cursing the way the metal rubs against my ears, the way it blocks my hearing, the way it tugs on my hair, cursing Schuyler with every profanity I can think of.

'Stop complaining.' Fifer pulls out a necklace, one I recognise – brass chain, ampoules filled with salt, quicksilver, and ash – and slips it around my neck. 'So he can't hear you during the fight.' She grins. 'Don't say I never did anything for you.'

Schuyler watches me, his face impassive. Then he snatches a sword off the ground, tosses it to me. Walks to the rack, snatches up a swallow: a long, double-sided sword. Spins it around and around, the blade a flashing blur.

We step into the centre of the field. Schuyler circles me, slow; I match his movement step for step. He strikes. Once, twice. I parry the first two; the second he lands a hit, knocking the sword out of my hand and sending it skittering along the grass.

'Point.' Fifer raises a hand.

'You're scoring?' I retrieve my sword.

She nods. 'If you win, you choose your next test.'

'And if Schuyler wins?'

'He does.'

'Again, bijoux.' Schuyler steps toward me.

I lunge forward and attack, but he's ready. He blocks, then blocks again. Frustrated, I drop to the ground and swipe my leg under his. He's not expecting this; he stumbles and I throw up my other leg, kick him in the groin.

Schuyler falls to one knee, groaning a catalogue of curses. I toss my sword aside and jump him; he's not expecting this, either. We hit the ground, rolling over and over. He hooks an arm around my throat, throws me to my back, pins me there. I jam a thumb into his eye, an old trick. He yelps like a child, rushes at me with a roar. Slams on top of me, reaching for my wrists, trying to pin me. But before he can, I yank a dagger from my belt, thrust it against his throat. The blade pierces his skin, a drop of curiously black blood bubbling to the surface.

'Point,' Fifer calls. I glance at her. She's grinning.

Schuyler gets to his feet, a shadow of pain etched across his face. He swipes at the blood on his neck, glances at it, then at me. His blue eyes glitter with antagonism.

'Again.'

SEVEN

As it did the first time around, training exhausts me.

Most days I fall asleep before the sun sets, only to wake with the kick of a boot against my door at dawn, Schuyler and Fifer bidding me to rise, to get dressed, to follow them to whatever new test they've devised for me. Day after day the tests get harder, more painful, draw more blood. But day by day I get stronger, more confident, less afraid.

In the week since I began training and John left with the Watch, he's written to me twice, both letters delivered in the bony clutches of his falcon, Horace. He tells me about the patrol along the border: uneventful. He tells me how he is: tired. Horace perches on my windowsill, patiently preening his feathers as I write back, telling John about my training with Fifer and Schuyler. I don't mention how hard it is, I don't mention how I ache. In reply, he doesn't tell me to stop; he only tells me he misses me.

On the evening John is due to return home, I'm

determined to stay awake long enough to see him. I lost today's scrimmage with Schuyler and he sentenced me to a ten-mile run, fully armed, through the hills of Whetstone. My muscles scream for rest, but I manage to stay awake.

I lie in my white bed, the quartered moon shining through squared panes, sending pale shafts of light along the floor and up the darkened walls. The cottage is quiet tonight: There's no patter of rain on the roof, no winged rustle of an odd barn owl or the soft tapping of branches against the window. I've got an ear half cocked, listening for the door to finally open, for the familiar thud of footsteps on creaky stairs. The only thing that breaks the silence is the clock on the mantel downstairs, softly chiming out the hours.

Twelve. One. Two.

I don't remember hearing the clock chime three, so I suppose I drifted off. But then I hear the smallest whisper of noise, hovering just above me. I feel a smile work its way across my face.

'You're back.' My voice is sleepy, half dreaming. 'I tried to stay awake for you, but...' I trail off, wait for his hand in my hair, for the familiar weight of him as he sinks into the mattress beside me.

'Playing cottage with a new paramour, are we? How sweet.' The voice is oily, dripping with sarcasm, and it's not John's.

My eyes fly open.

Looming above me, a figure in all black. Black hooded cloak, black heavy boots, and a black, stupid smile. And it's a figure I recognise: Fulke Aughton. A witch hunter.

I lurch to sit up, but Fulke slams his hand around my throat, forcing me back down.

Fulke was the lowest-ranked of all Blackwell's recruits. The slowest, the clumsiest, the most fearful. Caleb and the others called him Fluke Naughton – they reckoned he made it through training by a combination of sheer accident and luck. To see him here, in my bedroom, my first feeling isn't fear, nor is it dread. It's outrage.

I jam my thumb into his eyeball. Fulke bites back a grunt of pain, then snatches my hand, twisting my thumb so far I hear a pop as the bone dislocates from the joint. I let out a gasp, but I refuse to scream. Not for him.

I reach up, grasp the back of Fulke's head with both my hands, and slam my forehead into his. Fulke, the idiot, bites his tongue, hard, and lets out a strangled cry. He backs away from the bed and I leap on top of the mattress and launch myself at him. He's caught off guard and the two of us stagger backward into the white brick fireplace. We hit the hearth and I jump off him, grab his head again, and slam it into the brick. Fulke lets out another cry and drops to his knees. I snatch a poker from the fireplace, hold the sharp end to the vein on the side of his neck. He's trapped between the wall and me, and neither of us is yielding.

There aren't a lot of ways to kill a witch hunter. But a broken neck or a knife to the jugular or a sword to the eye or ear, something that penetrates to the brain, that's something not even a stigma would be able to heal.

'What are you doing here?' I keep my eyes on his. As

long as he's looking at me, he won't try anything. It's another reason Fulke isn't a good witch hunter. He's not smart enough to plan a move without first shifting his eyes to the target, alerting them to his next move.

'I don't have to tell you anything.'

'I hold the weapon, I make the rules,' I say. 'If you want to see the sun rise, tell me why you're here.'

'No.'

I thrust the poker into his neck and with a tiny popping noise, the point breaks the skin. I can just see his blood in the pale moonlight, a running rivulet down his neck.

'Stop!' His voice is a high-pitched whine.

'Why are you here?' I repeat.

'Why do you think?' Fulke's brown eyes are steady on mine. 'We're here to bring you back to Blackwell.'

A pause, then it sinks in. '*We?*'

Fulke's eyes flick to the window. I whirl around just as it slams open and there, sitting on the ledge, is another witch hunter in all black: Griffin Talbot. Short blond hair, dark blue eyes, handsome and charismatic, a friend of Caleb's and a favourite of Blackwell's. Unlike Fulke, Griffin isn't slow. Nor is he stupid, or clumsy, or fearful. He's everything a witch hunter should be: Smart. Strong. Fast.

Deadly.

'Fluke, you idiot.' Griffin slides off the ledge, his heavy boots a menacing thud against the floor. He saunters toward us, his gaze traveling from Fulke, still on his knees with his back against the fireplace and my poker in his neck, to me crouched beside him in a thin white linen nightdress, low-cut and trimmed with pale pink ribbons, my hair spilling down my back.

Griffin smirks.

'You're looking well these days, Elizabeth,' he says. 'I was never one for your particular brand of charm, but perhaps I was wrong.' His eyes roam the length of my body; I'll gouge them out given half a chance. 'Being a traitor becomes you.'

I fire off a string of obscenities.

'Enchanting, as always.' Griffin switches his attention to Fulke. 'You had one job,' he says. 'Watch a sleeping girl while I checked the house. Jesus, Fluke. She had you against the wall in under a minute, and she's not even dressed. Nor was she armed. Unless she sleeps with a fire poker under her pillow.'

Fulke pouts. 'You know who she is.'

Griffin shrugs and turns back to me. 'I didn't know you had it in you, Grey. Your healer gets killed and you go and cozy up with his father?'

Fulke lets out a sycophantic laugh. 'That's right. Who do you think you are? Myrrha?'

'No, that's not Myrrha,' Griffin says. 'Myrrha was in love with her own father. Not her lover's father.'

'Jocasta, then?'

'No, she's the one who married her son.'

I tune out their bickering as my stomach drops. John? Killed? But that's not possible. He's got my stigma, they couldn't have killed him. He can't be dead, he can't be...

That's when it occurs to me, with a sigh of relief they

don't hear: The night of the masque, Blackwell stabbed John – but Blackwell left before Fifer transferred my stigma to him. They think John is dead, and they think I'm still what I was.

I think fast. Two witch hunters in my room, one I could easily kill, another who could easily kill me. John and Peter are still gone, but that could change any minute. John could hold his own in a fight, at least for a while. Peter, too. But Griffin is good – too good. He's an excellent strategist; his only weakness is he gets too aggressive in the heat of battle and makes stupid mistakes. But this won't be a battle, it'll be a massacre. Unless…

Schuyler. I think his name in my head; I shout it. *They're here. Witch hunters. Two of them, inside my room, they're here…*

'…no, Nyx and Erebus were siblings. Jesus, Fluke. Remind me to tell Blackwell to send you back to remedial—'

'Shut it, Griffin.'

'Blackwell must be hard pressed for help if he's sending Fulke to do his dirty work.' I break into their ridiculous conversation. Maybe if I get Griffin talking, I can buy time for Schuyler to reach me.

'Not hard pressed at all,' Griffin says. 'It's an honour to serve the king. The rightful king.'

'Blackwell is not the rightful king.'

'He's the one sitting on the throne. That seems rightful enough to me.'

'What are you doing these days, now that Blackwell's a wizard and witchcraft isn't against the law?' I ask. 'Do you call yourself witch hunters still?'

'We're knights now,' Griffin replies. 'Knights of the Anglian Royal Empire.'

'Fulke is a knight?' I glance at the motto stitched beneath the herald on their cloaks. In Gallic it reads *Honte à celui qui ne peut pas atteindre.* Shame be to him who achieves less.

I scoff then. I can't help it. 'They got the shame part right, anyway.'

Griffin doesn't reply.

'How many of you are there?' I continue. 'Is it just witch hunters? Or is Blackwell recruiting new members?'

'Nice try, Grey,' Griffin says. 'I'm not telling you a damned thing.'

'What are you going to do, then?' I say. 'Try to kill me? Because I'll tell you right now, that won't end well for you.'

'Always picking a fight, aren't you?' Griffin tuts. 'No, we aren't here to kill you. But then, we don't kill. We never did. Just you. You're the one who kills.'

I'm the one who kills.

'I saw Caleb's body,' he continues. 'When Blackwell brought it back. You know, I always thought you had a thing for him. Caleb, that is. The way you followed him around, made sheep's eyes at him. We all saw it. Then we saw his body. The way you flayed him open, eviscerated him, really. You must have hated him. Deep down, you must have. Maybe because he didn't care for you back. Not in that way, anyway.'

Griffin's trying to rattle me, and it's working. I can feel

Fulke beside me, loosening his posture, about to make a move. I can feel myself disconnecting from this moment and moving into another, into the past where I see Caleb coming, where I stay my hand, where I don't kill him...

'Grab her, Fluke.'

Before Fulke can make a move, I shove the fire poker into his neck until the point thrusts out the other side.

Blood hurls itself across my face with a sickening splash. Fulke slumps to the boards, thrashing and jerking, pawing at the poker with his hands, trying to stem the flow of his own blood spurting from his neck.

I'm on my feet but Griffin is on me in a second, his dagger raised, steel flashing like lightning in the moonlight. I dodge it once, duck from it twice; he won't miss a third. I back across the room, stumble into the wardrobe. Griffin lunges for me; I throw open the wardrobe door, hear a crunch as his face meets wood, then his muttered curse. I scramble over the bed, snatching my bedsheet as I go, balling the white linen in my fist. Rush to the window, smash my fist through it. The broken glass falls in satisfyingly large shards and I snatch them up, holding them in front of me as if they were knives.

Griffin wipes the smallest smear of blood from beneath his nose. It must have broken on the wardrobe door, but it's healed now. He's watching me as he prowls around the bed, his eyes glittery with anger and the thrill of the hunt. I know that feeling, or I did: part nerves, part fear, part excitement.

I don't feel it now.

He starts for me again and I pull back, narrowly miss

stepping on a shard of the broken window glass. I stumble from it; the delay is enough. Griffin tosses his dagger to the floor, snatches my wrists, and hauls me across the bed. I slash at him; he twists my arm, hard, to get me to release the glass. I don't. We scuffle around on the mattress, him on top of me, me thrashing beneath him. I knee him in the groin and he grunts in pain, rolling off me and onto the floor, dragging me with him. Somehow in the tumble the glass gets loose again, raking across my forearm, the cut smooth and sharp.

I slap my hand over my skin but it's too late: Blood leaps from my veins and seeps between my fingers, running fast down my arm to join the rest of the blood – both mine and Fulke's – on my nightdress.

Griffin pushes me off him and scrambles to his feet. He stands there a moment, silent, pointing at my arm. 'You… your arm. It's not healing,' he says finally. His eyes are wide. 'Why isn't it healing?'

Before I can think of what or how to reply, he grabs me by the throat, lifts me off the floor, and slams me into the wall.

'Where is it?' Another slam, then another. 'What happened to it?'

My head is spinning, and not just from Griffin throttling me like a rag doll. He knows I don't have my stigma; this is nothing but trouble for me. So why is he acting as if he's the one hard put by it? If he's here to bring me back to Blackwell, he's got me right where he wants me.

A creak of a window frame. Another rumble of boots on

the floor. A tsk of impatience, amusement, irritation, or all three, and there's Schuyler standing in front of the window, arms crossed, eyebrows raised. He takes in the bloody scene before him and shakes his head.

'Isn't this a treat, then? A witch hunter inside Harrow.' Schuyler's eyes, alight with anticipation, lock on to Griffin. 'Managed to evade the Watch, did you?'

Griffin releases me and I slump to the floor, gasping for air. 'Your watch leaves much to be desired.'

Schuyler glances at Fulke, drained of blood and pale as moonlight, sprawled out beside the fireplace, the poker still crammed in his neck.

'I wouldn't go that far.' Schuyler shrugs. 'As they say, it's the end that counts, not the beginning. And so far, your side isn't making a very good end.'

Griffin yanks the fire poker from Fulke's neck with a sickening squelch and steps toward Schuyler. He swings it slowly in front of him, droplets of blood falling onto the floor, dark as ink.

'Pyrrhic victory,' Griffin says. 'Whatever small wins your side manages to achieve, they'll never outweigh your losses.' He looks Schuyler up and down, cold and appraising. 'But let's be honest. When I kill you, I'm not sure they'll consider that a loss.'

And here it is: Griffin's aggression, his overconfidence, his inability to see what's really happening. He doesn't see what I do – the malice lurking beneath the surface of Schuyler's calm demeanour, the shine of violence that in a revenant is never truly tarnished.

Griffin hurls the fire poker at Schuyler as if it were a javelin. Schuyler bats it away just as Griffin yanks a sword from his scabbard, so fast it's a silver blur. He lunges toward Schuyler, blade flying. He swings the sword toward Schuyler's neck while simultaneously reaching into the bag knotted by his side, full of salt, sending a spray of it directly into Schuyler's face. It's a move Blackwell taught us: The salt is meant to blind and confuse a revenant, allowing the blade to land somewhere, anywhere. It's not meant to kill, just to stun long enough to allow for escape. Much like what I did to Schuyler the first time I met him, inside the Green Knight's tomb.

Only escape isn't Griffin's plan.

Schuyler ducks the shower of salt, evades most of it. By this time Griffin's got a dagger, a weapon in each hand now. He jabs at Schuyler, but Schuyler knocks the dagger away with ease; it flies from Griffin's hand and skitters across the floor. Then Schuyler grabs the sword with the other, wraps his fingers around the blade. I wince as it cuts into his hand, that curious black blood flooding to the surface, watch as he bends – *bends* – the shaft of the sword. Griffin lets go and it, too, clatters to the floor.

Schuyler holds out his palm, then squeezes it into a fist, as if wringing himself of his own blood. He steps toward Griffin, weapon-less. But not powerless.

Griffin pulls out another dagger.

To watch them is to watch a game of cat and mouse. A cat swiping at the mouse, over and over, toying with it, making it think it's on equal footing just for the sport of it when you know – even if the mouse doesn't – that it never even stood a chance.

It happens so quickly then.

The dagger, knocked from Griffin's hand. A futile reach for another fireplace tool, missed. A thrown punch, also missed, a tossed piece of furniture, the dawning recognition on Griffin's face that he's out of options.

Hands on either side of the head, a quick and savage snap, and Griffin is gone. Slumped to the floor, his eyes and mouth both open, the defeat on his face a surprise, even in death. For a moment, the room falls back into the silence of before. No patter of rain, no rustling barn owl, no brushing branches. Not even the chime of the clock downstairs to break the sound of my ragged breathing.

Schuyler crosses the room, his boots crunching on the glass, and looks me over, his nostrils flared slightly at the heavy, iron scent of blood in the air.

'You all right?'

'I think so.' I hold up my arm. 'I'm cut, but I don't think it's serious.'

Schuyler snatches the blood-spattered bed linen from the floor, tears off a piece, and hands it to me. 'Don't get up. You'll cut yourself again if you can't see where you're standing.' He starts for the door. 'I'll be back.'

Schuyler returns a moment later with a handful of candles and a bundle of matches. In seconds, the room comes alive with light and the sight of carnage. He looks around, shakes his head. 'This is a damned fine mess you made.'

I almost laugh.

'Witch hunters, eh?' Schuyler nudges Griffin's body with his toe, then glances at Fulke. 'You know, I rather thought Blackwell's men were after Harrow in general, but this time it seems as though they're actually after *you.*' A pause. 'D'you have any idea why?'

''Course not,' I say, irritable. The cut on my arm stings like hell. 'If I did I'd do something about it. If for no other reason than to keep idiots from breaking into my bedroom and making this happen.'

Schuyler looks around. 'What do you want to do, then? If you want to get rid of them before the guard arrives, you'd better do it quick, because – *ah.*'

Seconds later the door to the bedroom slams open and Peter and John stand on the threshold, broadswords in hand. The emblem of the Watch, a simple orange triangle, is embroidered on the front of their short grey cloaks: a symbol for stability. Almost in unison, their eyes go round as they take in the scene. Griffin, lying on the floor, eyes wide open to the ceiling, his head set in an unnatural angle. Fulke, who has emptied every bit of his blood onto the floor, like a sponge that's been wrung dry.

'What happened here?' Peter rushes to the window, looking out as if he's expecting men to come pouring in at any moment. 'They left the front door open, then we saw footsteps leading up the stairs. Mud,' he adds. 'What the hell happened?'

Schuyler gives them a rapid rundown.

John crouches beside me. It's only been a week since I

saw him, but somehow he looks different. His hair seems tamer than usual, curls pushed back instead of falling into his eyes. He's unshaven by more than a few days, he's got deep circles under his eyes, and the furrow in his brow now seems etched there, as if it belongs. He drops his sword and picks up my arm, gently peeling off the strip of linen. He hisses a swear at the sight of it.

'It's not as bad as it looks,' I say. 'It's just a scratch.'

'It's more than a scratch.' He flings aside the bloody fabric. 'I don't think you'll need stitches, but I'll need to attend to it anyway. Can you stand?'

John helps me to my feet. Schuyler rummages around in the wardrobe and pulls out my black leather boots and passes them to John. He looks confused for a moment, until Schuyler points at the shards of glass scattered along the floor.

'What else did they say?' Peter turns from the window to face me. 'Did they say why they were after you?'

'No.' I tug the boots from John's hand and slip them on. 'It's as Schuyler said. They broke in, said they were here to take me to Blackwell. We fought, I got cut. But then he said something, I don't know…'

'What did who say?' Peter is beside me then. He plucks a clean handkerchief from somewhere beneath the folds of his cloak and presses it against my arm, which has begun to bleed again. I look to John, but his attention has drifted back to the bodies on the floor.

'Griffin.' I point to the feet sprawled on the floor at the end of the bed; it's all I can see of him from here. 'When he saw I was injured and didn't heal, he knew I didn't have my stigma. He wanted to know what happened to it.'

'Not to worry, love.' Peter pats my hand. 'He won't be able to tell anyone about it now, will he?'

'That's not it,' I say. 'It's that I expected him to be glad, when he found out. To taunt me for being weak. Or to get in a few punches on me, knowing I couldn't retaliate. I expected him to do anything but what he did.'

'Which was?'

'Act afraid,' I say. 'You don't know, because you don't know Griffin, but he's not afraid of anything. Anything except Blackwell. But he acted as if he were the one in trouble, not me.'

'Elizabeth, what are you saying?'

Schuyler and I exchange a rapid glance, a look of surprise settling into his face as he hears my thoughts before I say them out loud.

'I'm saying I think they were after my stigma.'

EIGHT

Peter slides his sword into his scabbard. 'I want you to get cleaned up,' he says to me. 'And then I'm going to take you to see Nicholas.'

'Now?' John says. 'Why?'

Peter makes a gruff noise. 'Because Elizabeth was attacked in her bed by a pair of witch hunters and nearly killed,' he replies. 'Because she thinks Blackwell sent them after her stigma, which she doesn't have, which you do. I expect that's reason enough?'

'We've got more pressing concerns at the moment, don't you think?' John says. 'Elizabeth's arm. And these two.' He looks back at the bodies on the floor. 'We can't just leave them here. What if there are more of them on the way? Shouldn't we be out there, looking for them?'

'The area was clear when I arrived,' Schuyler says.

'Obviously it wasn't that clear,' John snaps.

Schuyler raises an eyebrow but doesn't reply.

'I'll take care of matters here,' Peter says. 'John, you take Elizabeth to Nicholas's once you've got her cleaned up. Schuyler, if you don't mind going ahead to let him know what's happened, and that we're on our way? You can check for more men on your way out.'

Schuyler nods, then turns back toward the window, going up and over the sill in a flash. But John doesn't move, nor does he respond.

'John.' Peter turns to him and, finally, John wrenches his gaze from the massacre on the floor. 'Did you hear what I said, son?'

'Don't you need help moving them?'

A brief scowl crosses Peter's face, then he steps forward and grasps John by the shoulder. Gives it a little shake. 'I'd like you to help Elizabeth,' he says, his voice gentle. 'Fetch some hot water. Prepare some medicine, and some bandages for her arm. She'll meet you across the hall in your room.'

John looks to me, his eyes at once going wide at the sight of Peter's handkerchief, damp and crimson with blood, still pressed against my forearm.

'Of course. Yes. I'll do that right now.' He moves toward the door, then back to me, an uncertain dance. Finally he leaves, his footsteps creaking on the staircase as he makes his way downstairs.

Peter offers me a wan smile. 'He's upset, of course. This evening might have gone differently, and you might be lying on the floor instead of them. It's a lot for him to take in. I daresay he's in shock.'

I don't know if that's it at all, but I nod anyway.

'And you? Are you all right?' Peter pulls me into a fatherly embrace.

'I'm fine,' I reply, my voice muffled against his shoulder. 'A little shaken, but otherwise fine. And I'm sorry about all this.'

He releases me. 'Don't apologise. I should apologise for leaving you alone. But please. Let John take care of you now; I'll manage the rest.'

As Peter sets about wrapping up the bodies, I take a stack of clothing from the wardrobe and step across the hallway. I haven't been in John's room since I spent the night there, shortly before he left for the Watch. But something seems different. Last I saw, it was untidy to say the least: wrinkled clothing in a heap on the floor, the table under his window a riot of herbs, powders, and sachets. His desk scattered with books and parchment, pens and ink.

Now it's clean. Books stacked neatly on the desk, the table surface clear, everything tucked neatly into the drawers and shelves below. The room even smells different – what was once a heady mix of spices, herbs, and him – is gone. Now the air is crisp, clear, sterile.

I pull out a chair at the desk and sit, waiting for John to return. A moment later he does, bumping in through the door, lugging a pail of water. Wordlessly, he walks to the basin on the stand beside his bed and starts to empty water into it. But he's not paying attention, not really, and the water spills over the rim and splashes onto the floor.

He doesn't seem to notice his boots getting wet, nor does he seem to notice me watching him. And when the bucket is empty, he doesn't seem to notice that, either; he's still holding it aloft, faint dripping the only sound in the room.

'John.' The word comes out a whisper.

He jerks his head around to look at me and, at once, his expression both lifts and crumples, as if he's just now seeing me for the first time.

'Are you all right?' I say.

'You shouldn't be asking me that. I should be asking you that.' He drops the bucket with a clatter. 'This shouldn't have happened at all. If I'd been here, it wouldn't have. I could have fought them off. Kept them from hurting you.'

John pushes away from the basin and makes his way to the table under the window. He rummages around in his drawers, pulls out a small amber bottle. I can just make out his untidy scrawl on the label. *Oil of jasmine.* He crosses back to the basin and taps a few drops of the scented oil into the water.

'Jasmine is good for a lot of things, such as soothing a cough or stopping snoring,' he says. 'Which you don't need, of course. It also helps with a woman's labour pains, which you don't need, either. Really, you don't need it at all, only I like the scent of it. It makes me think of you.'

I blink at his rapid change of topic, at his nervous stream of chatter. Both are unlike him in every way.

'Thank you.' I manage something between a frown and a smile. 'I like the smell of it, too.' Finally I rise from the chair and move to stand beside him at the basin.

There are no bathing sheets or cloths to wash or dry myself with, but I dunk my arm in the water anyway, hissing a little as the jasmine oil burns into my cut. I recall the first time John tended to a cut on my hand, after I learned Caleb was the new Inquisitor and squeezed my wineglass so hard it shattered. I remember the scent of mint, the pleasant way my skin tingled when he set my hand in the bowl of water. The way he held my hand in the water, his long fingers wrapped around my smaller ones with his careful touch.

It wasn't like this at all.

John stares unseeing into the basin, the water now swirled through with blood and stained pink. Perhaps Peter is right; perhaps John is in shock. He's been on watch for a week, he's tired and thought he was coming home to rest, but instead he came home to bloodshed – and the possibility that Blackwell's men may be after the stigma – and him.

'If they really are after the stigma, I won't let them find it,' I say. 'I won't let them find you. I will protect you.'

This jerks him out of silence. 'I don't need you to protect me. I need you to show me what to do if they do find me. How to use it.' His gaze is sharp. 'You were asleep. You had no weapons. You weren't even dressed and you still managed to hold them off. You even managed to kill one of them. How did you do it?'

This is so unlike anything John would ever say, or even think, that I'm nearly struck dumb.

'I did what I was trained to do,' I finally manage. 'Knowing how to do that, it doesn't only come from the stigma. It came from three years of training, from facing danger every single day. From facing death every single day.'

'I haven't been facing death every day?'

'You have,' I say. 'But this is different. You know it is.'

John makes a dismissive noise.

'My stigma wasn't handed to me,' I say. 'I earned it. It may not belong to me any longer, but it is still a part of me that will never go away. I earned it.' I repeat it because it needs to be repeated.

'I never said you didn't.'

'You didn't need to,' I say. 'You've made it clear – you and your father both – that you think my value rests on it. You think I cannot do what the council wants me to do, what they kept me here to do.' The anger I've felt since the trial flares up once more. 'I suggest you go back into that bedroom and take a look at what I'm capable of doing.'

I regret the words as soon as they're out of my mouth. John recoils, his face going dark.

'I know full well what you're capable of.' He backs away from me. 'Not a day goes by that I don't know that.'

'John—'

'I'll wait out in the hallway for you to finish.' He slams the door behind him, so hard it rattles the frame.

My hands begin to tremble, ruffling the surface of the water. It's not until now that I realise it's cold. Not because it's gone cold, but because it was cold to begin with.

I pull them out of the basin, shake them dry. Walk to John's table, search the drawers until I find a simple paring knife. I remove my nightgown and set about slicing it into strips to wrap around my arm. It's no longer bleeding, but it's still angry, red, and weeping. Unhealed. And my thumb.

Swollen and blue and bent, gone nearly numb with pain. I take a breath, press down on the bone and bite back a groan as it snaps back into joint. I use the last of the linen strips to bind it tight, then I slowly dress, pulling on simple brown trousers, a pale blue tunic, and a long dark blue cloak. Run my damp fingers through my hair, pulling it into a knot.

When I step into the hall I don't expect to see him, but he's there, leaning against the wall, arms folded, eyes on the floor. But he doesn't look up when my footsteps creak against the floorboard, nor when I pull his bedroom door shut with a click.

'John.'

He pushes off the wall and makes his way downstairs. I'm tempted to call after him, to apologise, to tell him I didn't mean what I said.

Only I did mean it.

I trudge down the stairs after him. I can just make out the imprint of a pair of muddy boots on the threshold where Fulke made his entrance. They lie beneath scattered droplets of blood: his exit.

I step through the front door into the cold, moonlit night. Across the river from Mill Cottage, in the meadow that stretches for miles behind it, Peter stands beside Griffin's and Fulke's bodies, spade in hand. John stands motionless, watching. He's changed into his old black coat, the grey cloak of the Watch left behind. The collar is flipped up so I can't see his face, but I'm warned by his posture – still, stiff, intractable – to keep my distance.

I pause to watch Peter at work. Take in the sound of iron

hitting dirt, the sight of sheets stained with blood and the limp, lifeless limbs splayed beneath them. It hits me then, all the trouble I've caused since coming into John's life. Not just for him, but for everyone around him, everyone he knows and loves. They took me in and stood by me when they could have tossed me aside. It would have been easy enough; it was for Blackwell and Caleb.

I turn to tell him this, to once again apologise for once more failing to understand what he's done for me. But without a word and without waiting for me, he starts down the path that leads from Mill Cottage into town, toward Nicholas's house.

Reluctantly, I follow.

NINE

It's three miles to Nicholas's house in Theydon Bois, a walk we take entirely in silence – John leading, me following. He does not ask me how I am, he does not try to comfort me. I don't know what to say to this John who says nothing to me, who stares ahead in stony silence, wielding a sword before him as if he's about to be attacked.

So I say nothing at all.

We walk along an open, uncomplicated road over gently rolling meadows, the fractured moon helping to guide a path John already seems to know well. Eventually it ends at an arched wooden bridge, the water beneath dark and still. On the other side is a house I presume belongs to Nicholas.

It's different from his home in Crouch Hill, where Nicholas first brought me after rescuing me from Fleet. That house was large, grand, built to impress. This house is smaller, cosier; a country home. Rough-hewn stone walls, slatted wood roof, the front lined with a dozen square shuttered windows.

John leads me down the narrow path to the front door. Dozens of rosebushes in every colour, enchanted into bloom even in winter, line the walk. Red ivy and pink honeysuckle crawl their way up the walls, lavender bushes bursting beneath them. I turn to say something to him about it; the delicate wildness of it all is something I know he would appreciate. But he walks inside without even a glance at them, or at me, pushing past Schuyler as he appears in the doorway.

Schuyler walks out to meet me. He's dressed in the same black clothing he wore earlier but his hands, face, and hair are clean of blood. I find myself wondering if Fifer helped him, if she brought him warm water and bath sheets, or if she stood by while he washed up with cold, stinging water and strips of dirty, bloodied fabric.

'I've seen better nights, haven't you?' he says.

'I've seen better months,' I mutter in reply.

Fifer hurtles out the door then, throwing herself at me in an embrace that nearly knocks me over. 'Schuyler told us everything. You're not hurt too badly, are you?' She pulls back to inspect me. 'I can't believe it. Witch hunters inside Harrow! Rather, what do they call themselves now?'

'Knights of the Anglian Royal Empire,' Schuyler and I reply in unison.

Fifer pulls a face. 'Nicholas is inside, waiting for you. And John.' She pauses, considering. 'Why didn't he wait for you out here?' She peers at me closely, green eyes narrowing.

'Everything all right with him? And you?'

'He's fine,' I lie. 'It was a long week on watch. I think he's just tired and a little shaken up. I'm fine, too.'

Fifer tugs me inside the house, through a short entrance hall into the drawing room. It's cheerful and inviting: Upholstered chairs and settees are scattered over rugs, woven with flowers and vines in vivid shades of yellow, orange and green. Tapestries of woodland scenes cover the white plaster walls, and the ceilings are open to the rafters in the country style. An stone fireplace takes up nearly an entire wall, crackling flames throwing light and warmth into the room.

Nicholas crosses the room to greet me. He clasps me by the shoulders, his eyes creased with concern.

'Schuyler told us what happened. I'm relieved to see that you're safe, and on the mend.' He says this last part almost as if it's a question.

He settles me in a plush seat beside Fifer, then looks to John, sitting beside the fireplace and staring into the flames as if he can read them.

'John?'

He turns his head.

'I wondered if you'd be so kind as to make Elizabeth a tonic?' Nicholas smiles, but it doesn't quite reach his eyes. 'She's a bit pale and appears to have a chill.'

The room falls quiet, and I feel as if everyone in it is watching me, watching us; trying to piece together what's happening while it's still falling apart.

'You can help yourself to my stores,' Nicholas prompts.

'They're right where you remember them.'

John rises from his chair and finally – finally – looks at me. 'Of course I'll make you something. I won't be long.'

Fifer jabs her elbow into my side. We both watch as he walks from the room, his hands jammed in the pockets of his coat, the one he still hasn't removed despite the warmth in the room, almost as if he hopes he won't be asked to stay long.

Nicholas turns back to me.

'The Knights of the Anglian Royal Empire.' This is how he begins. No questions. 'They were after you. They knew where you were. They knew you'd be alone.'

'They didn't know I was alone,' I say. 'Not for certain. Fulke – he's the one I killed, the one who came in first – was sent to watch over me while the other one, Griffin, searched the house. And they were only looking for Peter. They thought John was dead.'

Fifer starts to speak, but Nicholas holds up a hand to stop her. 'Go on.'

'Fulke said they were ordered to bring me back to Blackwell,' I continue. 'I didn't ask why; I didn't think I needed to. I know too much, both about him and about you. I thought that was why he wanted me back, just as you said at my trial. But now I'm not so sure.'

I pause, thinking again about Griffin. About the look on his face when he saw me cut, when he saw me bleed.

'Griffin, he acted the way he always does,' I say. 'He didn't seem worried that he was here, in Harrow, surrounded by enemies. He didn't seem worried that he could be caught. He didn't seem worried about anything, not until he cut me. Until he knew I didn't have my stigma.' I recall the way Griffin threw me against the wall, over and over, demanding to know what happened to it. 'Why? It should be nothing to him if I don't have my stigma.'

Nicholas steps to the window overlooking the front of the house, moonlight falling through the panes and illuminating his expression. There's a world of difference in the way he appears now compared to when I first met him, alone in my cell at Fleet. Thin and haggard and grey then; now bright and full of life. Even so, there is a gravity in his face that hasn't changed.

Finally, he speaks. 'Elizabeth, I want you to tell me about Blackwell.'

I open my mouth to say – I don't know what – but shut it as John steps into the room, carrying a copper goblet. He's flushed and dishevelled, his coat finally gone, the sleeves of his blue cambric shirt pushed up past his elbows. His eyes are bright and he's grinning. He looks and acts so much like the John I know that I'm able to manage a brief smile in return.

'I'm sorry it took me so long.' He hands me the quietly smoking cup. A scent drifts from the top and there's something about it that makes my stomach curdle. 'It's wormwood, dill, and horehound boiled in wine,' he tells me. 'It's nice, and I think you'll like it. At the very least, it should warm you up.'

Wormwood. I know enough from his notes that while wormwood is used in soothing tonics, it's also the primary ingredient in absinthe – which is also the primary ingredient in the ale I drank too much of the night I dropped witches' herbs in front of the king's guard, got arrested, and nearly lost my life.

Another jab from Fifer.

I nod my reluctant thanks but John doesn't acknowledge it, already moving back to his chair beside the fire. After a long moment, I turn back to Nicholas.

'What about Blackwell?' I set the cup down on the table beside me. 'What do you want to know about him?'

Nicholas switches his attention from John back to me. 'I want to know about your relationship with him.'

'Relationship?' The word, in conjunction with Blackwell's name, confuses me. 'I don't think I understand.'

'When you trained with him, did he single you out in any way? Did he train you differently, or treat you differently? Did he provide you with anything – weapons, advice, warnings, even, about what was to come – and not the other witch hunters?'

'No.' Then I reconsider. 'Not really. But I do remember something he said to me once, after I completed a test. It was toward the end of training and by then, I knew what he was like. And what he said was so unlike him, it was hard to forget it.'

Nicholas is watching me closely. 'What did he say?'

I hesitate. I don't like talking about training. I didn't then, and I don't now. Not only because reliving it forces me to remember things best left forgotten, but because it forces everyone in this room to remember who I really am.

I don't want them to remember they should hate me.

I hope for a smile from John, or a look of reassurance, something to let me know it's all right. But he's drifted away again, head bowed, hands clasped tightly together. Closed off.

So I go on without him.

It was the maze test, the second-to-last test before our final. Those who were left – there were eighteen of us then – were given four days to get through it. We had no supplies. No food, no water, no weapons, no provisions except our wits, our knowledge, our courage, and our resourcefulness: better news for some than for others.

We were led to the test at midnight; they always began at midnight. The night was thick with fog; it was like walking inside a cloud. Then we saw them: massive hedge walls, stretching too far and too high to see where they ended. The fog clung to them like wisps of snow, twisting and curling around the branches, making them look alive, as if they were breathing. As if they were waiting to devour us.

Three days. That's how long it took me to get through the maze. I'd been attacked, twice, by things inside; things I couldn't name. Creatures that looked like wolves but snaked around corners like serpents. Things that flew like hawks but looked like bears, wearing their teeth and claws and shape. My clothes were in shreds, as was the skin on my right arm. I lost a boot along with a big chunk of my hair when something, I still don't know what, grabbed hold of me and almost didn't let go.

When I finally made it out, it was morning. Dawn, or just before it. There was dew in the grass, pink in the sky; there were birds and sun and freedom and success. I crawled out on all fours, bloody and sweaty, hungry and thirsty, and so, so tired. I got as far as I could manage – ten feet, twenty maybe – before flopping to the ground. I wanted to cry; I wanted to sleep. Instead, inexplicably, I started to laugh.

Maybe it was joy, maybe it was madness. But to know I was sent in with the expectation that I wouldn't come out – the feeling went beyond relief.

That's when I heard it. The tiniest noise, footsteps in the grass, the heel of a boot on a twig. I rolled to my back and there he was. Blackwell. He stood over me, a shadow between me and the sun. Turning light to dark in the way only he could.

'My lord.' I scrambled to my feet and dipped into a clumsy curtsy.

'Elizabeth.'

I waited. His eyes, cold as wet coal, looked me up and down. Took in my tattered clothes, my missing boot, the hank of hair missing from my scalp. I swiped a lock of what was left behind my ear, to try to hide it. My hand came away red.

'You did well,' he said finally.

'Thank you, my lord.' My voice was a hoarse whisper, leagues away from the wild, shrieking laughter of just moments ago.

He stepped toward me; I willed myself not to back away.

He took another step, then another, until I was staring directly at his doublet: fine cloth of gold and trimmed in emerald velvet, sleeves slashed to show the white of the fine linen beneath.

'Look at me,' he said.

I did.

Tall. Dark hair, shaven nearly to his scalp. Short, closely cropped beard. Well over six feet. Attractive, if one could get past those hard, cruel eyes.

'You were a mistake,' he said.

I didn't know what to say to that, if I should say anything to that. Finally, I settled on 'Yes, my lord.'

'Yet with all that, here you are. Again. Still. Here.' He began to circle me, the way a wolf does its prey. It took every ounce of control I had to stand in place. 'Why do you think that is? Why are you here, Elizabeth?'

I had a thousand replies, none of which I could voice. *Because of you? In spite of you? No thanks to you?* Instead I said, 'To learn, my lord.'

'To learn,' he repeated. 'And what, pray, are you learning?'

He was behind me now; I couldn't see him but I could feel him, and every hair on the back of my neck stood on end, shrieking their warning. His words were mild but I could hear the pique behind them. I didn't know how I'd displeased him but then, I never did.

'How to serve you.'

He stepped around me so that he was facing me again. But I didn't relax. And I didn't look at him, either. I kept my eyes on his golden tunic, the still-rising sun glittering off the fabric.

'How fortunate am I to have such a servant in you.'

He was taunting me, I knew that. Once again I didn't know how to respond, so once again, I repeated myself. 'Yes, my lord.' It had become a mantra.

Blackwell looked toward the maze. I didn't know what other recruits were inside, or who had already returned. It occurred to me to wonder: Was he waiting for me? Was that why he was here? Or was he waiting for someone else?

'Do you think, Elizabeth, that you will make it through training?'

This, I knew the answer to. I didn't have to hunt around for what to reply and I didn't hesitate when I did.

'Yes, my lord.'

Blackwell nodded. 'Yes. I see that you believe that. And I can see you wish me to believe it, too.' He smiled, or at least gave the nearest approximation to a smile I'd ever seen from him. It transformed him. It turned him from someone you would fear into someone you could almost trust.

Almost.

'And do you know? From what I saw today, I very nearly do believe it.'

My heart swelled, and I felt a flush of pleasure race through my limbs all the way into my cheeks, burning bright with what was, from him, the highest of praise.

'I think, in time, you'll either be my greatest mistake or my greatest victory.'

* * *

'Then what?'

Nicholas's voice snaps me back to the present. For a moment I'd been there, at Blackwell's, at the mouth of the maze. I could almost feel the dew on my hands, the smarting in my scalp, the burn of sunlight in my eyes.

I look up to find everyone watching me.

'Nothing,' I say. 'He walked away, and that was it. I didn't see much more of him, and I didn't talk to him. Not until the night of the final test.'

'The test in the tomb,' Nicholas clarifies. 'After which you received your stigma.'

'Yes.' I rub my eyes. The weight of the evening is bearing down on me, and all I want is for it to be over.

But Nicholas presses on. 'Elizabeth, do you know how stigmas are created?'

There's a shift then, a tension that springs from his words and coils around the room. I feel it in the way Fifer stiffens beside me, see it in the way Schuyler moves to stand behind her. The way John jerks his attention from the flames, past me to settle on Nicholas.

The front door opens and Peter emerges from the entry hall into the room. 'My apologies for being late.' He shrugs off his cloak, holds it out. It's plucked from the air by an invisible hand – Hastings, Nicholas's ghost servant – and disappears from the room. 'The ground is harder to dig into, what with the cold. Nearly broke my spade on that second grave –' He stops himself. 'How are things here?'

'Enigmatic,' Nicholas says mildly. 'Though we're working

to change that.' Peter pulls up a chair beside John, who doesn't acknowledge his father's presence.

'I don't know how stigmas are created,' I answer Nicholas's question. 'No one had them before us, so there was no one to tell us how it was done. A lot of our guesses were ridiculous and most didn't make sense, but we all agreed that it had to be some kind of spell.'

Nicholas nods. 'Magic – all magic – works the same way. It is the direction of a witch or wizard's power into an external object, be it a person or thing. A love spell placed on a slip of parchment. A healing enchantment planted within a potion. A protective charm embedded into a ring. A curse placed onto a tablet. A stigma given to a witch hunter.'

The hair on the back of my neck prickles in warning.

'Magic, the order that is magic, is to seek unity and balance within all things,' Nicholas continues. 'The power that is inherent in your stigma: that of strength, of healing, of preventing death or in some instances the death of others' – a glance at John – 'disrupts that balance. It is to give power to do what no human, magic or non-, should be able to do. To attempt a spell of this consequence would deplete their magic. All their magic.'

'Magic can be depleted?'

Nicholas nods. 'When a witch or wizard casts their magic into an object, say, a letter intended to entice, a potion meant to heal, it decreases. How quickly it is restored, and the degree to which it is restored, depends on the spell, as well as the witches or wizards themselves.

For an old wizard, or a wizard compromised in some way, their magic may never fully return. The same is true of a curse. My own magic was depleted somewhat by the curse Blackwell set upon me. And while I am not fully restored, I am quite close.' He looks to Fifer, who manages a small smile.

'If the spell to create a stigma requires so much power that it could deplete a person's magic entirely, how could it be done?' I say. 'There were sixteen of us. Sixteen stigmas, which means sixteen spells, sixteen witches or wizards giving up their power to give us ours – ' I stop as I realise. 'They didn't give up their power, did they? Their power was taken from them. Stolen.'

In the silence that follows, I come to understand the remainder of Blackwell's plan. The first, I already knew: to take the witches and wizards we captured for him and turn them into an army in order to overthrow the kingdom. And now, I know the second: to steal the magic of those who resisted in order to empower his men so they could never be defeated.

'But it still doesn't explain why Blackwell wants my stigma,' I say. 'There's nothing special about it. Its power isn't any greater than anyone else's. Griffin's, Fulke's, Caleb's—'

'No?' Nicholas breaks in. 'Are you sure about that?'

I hesitate. Think of the things I can do; used to do. I think of my strength, my speed, the way I could hunt better and fight fiercer than anyone. How I rose to the top of the ranks, how I was Blackwell's best witch hunter, second only to Caleb. But that was because I wanted it, because I fought for it. It was because of me.

Wasn't it?

'You said yourself there was no precedent,' he continues. 'No one to tell you how stigmas were created. Did it occur to you that someone had to be first? Someone had to be a test subject in Blackwell's experiment?'

In time, you'll either be my greatest mistake or my greatest victory.

'A wizard's power is not cumulative,' Nicholas says. 'Magic is not cumulative. Blackwell could not take power from one man after another, or one woman after another, in order to increase his own. Again, the laws of magic, and that of balance, do not allow for it. You only take on the power, the magic, that is greatest of the two. He would not risk diluting his own power, as it were, with that of a lesser witch or wizard. So, no. He is not trying to increase his power.' A pause. 'I believe he is trying to restore it.'

There it hangs: the truth on a knife's edge. The dawning realisation of what Nicholas knows, what he's been trying to get me to piece together on my own.

I leap to my feet. Peter jumps to his, too; he turns to John as Fifer snatches my hand, saying something to me in a soothing tone but I can't make out her words through the rush of blood in my ears and the words Nicholas says next:

'I believe your stigma came from Blackwell. And for reasons I cannot begin to fathom, he needs his power back.'

TEN

The following week is nothing short of agony as we pick apart what it means, what it could mean, for Blackwell to be after the stigma.

Arguments between Peter and John are an almost hourly occurrence. Instead of being frightened by possessing Blackwell's power, by possibly becoming a target of that power, John is determined to use it. He wants to do what Gareth kept me in Harrow to do: He wants to kill Blackwell. Peter, once heartened by his son's desire to throw himself into this fight, has since turned tack, pleading with John to leave Anglia, for him to take me on his ship – the one Peter gave him when he left pirating – and sail away from Anglia, as far as it will take us.

But John won't quit; he can't. The stigma won't let him. The balance of magic is tipping, and not in John's favour. I have a cause for the change in his behaviour now. The distance, the violence; every day he heals less, every day he fights more. Blackwell's magic has taken hold of him, and every day that passes it grows stronger.

For now, his secret – and mine – is still safe. But for how long? Each day I train with Schuyler and Fifer, and each day I get stronger, more agile, more battle ready. But John trains alongside me now, and whatever improvement I make he outpaces tenfold. The disparity between us cannot be ignored, and it can no longer be hidden.

It's a problem without a solution, at least, not one I've been able to land on. And I'm running out of time. This morning a pair of fat, creamy envelopes arrived at Mill Cottage, sealed with wax and stamped with a double quatrefoil, Lord Cranbourne Calthorpe-Gough's badge: our summons. John's duty to the Watch has officially come to an end, and he and I are to report to the camp at Rochester within twenty-four hours.

Rochester Hall is located in the northernmost part of Harrow, in a town named for itself: Rochester. It's a two-hour walk from John and Peter's home, down a pretty country lane bordered by hedgerows and bramble-covered wood fences, the landscape dotted with trees, red-roofed farmhouses nestled in low-lying valleys, and fields littered with clusters of sheep in their dirty, tangled winter wool coats.

We've been on the road for an hour, Peter leading the way, John and I falling behind, each of us laden with a hastily packed bag filled with clothes and weapons. I've not seen much of Harrow, just a map John drew for me once. But I understand the landscape enough to recall that

Rochester is surrounded by hills on the north, Anglian territory to the east, and the country of Cambria to the west. It's an odd place to set up camp. If Blackwell and his men somehow managed to breach the barrier en masse, we would be landlocked, and there would be no escape.

'I've been thinking about the spy,' I say. It's the first thing I've said all day so far. 'The one letting Blackwell's men inside Harrow. I think we can all agree it's someone still living here. It has to be. They know too much. Enough to tell them exactly where to go, how to get there, and in some cases, when to be there.'

I think back to the first breach: the archer found halfway between Nicholas's home and Gareth's. The second breach at the Mudchute, the third at my trial, the fourth in my bed, the fifth on the high street a day later. And now this: the camp.

'What if it's him? Lord…Three Surnames?' I can't continue calling him Lord Cranbourne Calthorpe-Gough, it's ridiculous. 'And what if that's why he's setting up camp there? It's so remote. What if he's leading everyone into Rochester with the plan of locking us inside with no means of escape, and handing Blackwell the key?' I flinch at the thought of it. How easy it would be, were it true. How fast. One traitor, one battle, no survivors.

Peter opens his mouth, but it's John who speaks first.

'He's not the spy.' John turns to me. 'Look, I know how he seems. I know he seems privileged and arrogant and, well, an ass.' He smiles a little. 'But I've spent a lot of time at Rochester. With Fitzroy – sorry, I call him that, his surname is just too long – and with his family. I've known him a long time and he'd never turn traitor. He would never put his family in danger, no matter what the gain.'

I want to tell him that sometimes people don't do things for gain, they do them to prevent loss. That sometimes people fall into something, get in over their heads, and the hope is never to get back up, only to do whatever is necessary to keep from falling further.

'John is right,' Peter says. 'There's nothing Fitzroy wouldn't do for his family, for his daughter. He's as loyal to Harrow as Nicholas. I'd trust him with my life, and I do.' Peter's tone is placating, eager to keep the uneasy peace between him and John. 'As for why the camp is there, it's simple. There's no other place big enough – or safe enough – to house an army. Southern Harrow is naught but open fields and forests, hamlets and cottages. Rochester Hall is the largest and safest home in all of Harrow, a castle in its own right.'

'And there's a benefit to it being remote,' John adds. 'If anything were to happen, there are plenty of means of escape. There are tunnels that run beneath it, straight across the border into Cambria, and an inlet that runs in about a mile from there, with access to the sea. But most of all, Rochester has as many protective spells on it as Nicholas's house in Crouch Hill. Though a lot of them are – *stop*.'

John holds out an arm, and Peter and I halt in our tracks. John breaks away from us, looking along the ground until he spots a fist-sized rock. He tosses it down the centre of the road, as if he were playing a game of lawn bowls.

From nowhere comes a roaring sound, then a sudden drop in air pressure like that before a storm. A thundering gust of wind hurls its way toward us, picking up debris from the road as it goes, whirling into a grey, dusty cyclone.

I take an involuntary step backward, but John moves toward it, his hand outstretched. 'Field of Bulls. The Mount Inn. Snows Hill Arms.'

Like that, the wind dissipates, exploding into a cloud of dirt, leaves, and twigs. John starts off down the road again, motioning for us to follow.

'What was that? That you said?' I'm coughing and wiping grit from my eyes. 'They sounded like taverns.'

'They are.' John swipes a hand through his hair, shaking debris from his curls. 'To get past the cyclone, you have to list three pubs in Harrow. Three pubs you've been to.' He shrugs. 'Fitzroy said that if someone wanted to see him but they couldn't name three places they've had drinks, then he didn't want to see them.'

Peter explodes into laughter and I smile, the first real smile in days.

As we continue down the lane, the countryside yielding nothing more than what I've seen all day – hills, valleys, trees, sheep – I begin to have my doubts about the supposed grandness of Rochester Hall. If it is as large as Peter says, I should have seen it by now. It should be visible for miles, the same way Greenwich Tower lurked in the horizon, a stalwart blight on the vista of Upminster.

John raises his hand again. He snaps his fingers twice, fast, then lets out a short whistle. I begin to grow irritated at the theatrics of this place, for all its show but very little substance. Until it happens: The air before me shimmers, goes blurry, and at once the hills, valleys, trees, and sheep – there not just seconds ago – disappear, an illusion in tapestry. And in their place: Rochester Hall.

I feel my eyes go round.

Peter called it a castle in its own right, but in truth I expected a home like Gareth's or even Humbert's, with its many gardens and waterways, protected by a moat and a portcullis. I wasn't expecting a fortress.

It's massive. Made entirely of deep red brick and ringed by hundred-foot-high curtain walls, its many spires and towers are cut with arrow slits and connected by parapets. It's surrounded by a large, algae-choked lake, and the only access to the entrance – a heavily fortified gatehouse on the other side – is via a footbridge, easily a half mile long. Beyond the lake the grounds stretch on and on, farther than I can see, all the way into the densely wooded hills.

Peter smiles at my grudgingly impressed silence.

John leads us across the bridge, our footsteps the only sound under the blue, eerily silent sky. 'Where is everyone?' I say. 'It's so quiet. And how are we to get in? That doesn't exactly look welcoming.' I wave my hand at the iron gate looming before us, closed and forbidding.

'At Rochester, you can't believe everything you see,' John tells me. 'And you can't believe everything you hear, either.'

My earlier irritation is back.

John steps up to the gate, places his palm flat against the iron. I expect it to creak upward on its hinges, or to disappear, or perhaps some ghostly ministration to arrive and usher us inside. What I don't expect is this: for the arrow slit that was not a second earlier eight feet above my head to now be in front of me. And for it to be no longer small, nor an arrow slit, but a door-sized opening.

Peter whistles his approval as John steps through, gesturing for us to follow. Inside, a tunnel winding into darkness.

John navigates it with ease, leading us left, right, up and down corridors as if he's done it a hundred times, which he no doubt has, until we're outside again. It takes a moment for my eyes to adjust once more to the bright sunlight but when they do, I see a camp so large it seems almost a village in and of itself.

The park stretches out for miles, every inch of it occupied by people, tents, supplies, wagons, dogs, horses. Smoke fills the air from a thousand small campfires; tents and marquees of every shape and size rise from the ground, some striped and multi-pitched, others white and single-poled. Crates are stacked everywhere, spilling over with cookware, flatware, lanterns, linens.

Past the park and down a long, sloping incline lie the training fields. Two jousting pits lie side by side, filled with sand and lined on one side with wooden stands, covered by a canopy. Beside them, the archery butts, rows of meticulously racked bows and arrows, colourful targets painted on canvas and wrapped around bales of hay. Next to that, an open meadow bare of anything save for several dozen fat wooden chests filled with weapons – knives and chains, sickles and maces, daggers and axes.

I also see, though perhaps I'm not meant to, the carcasses of several dozen catapults, lurking at the edge of the woods, to be loaded and sprung, then moved to strategic points around the camp in the event of a siege.

Once again, Peter whistles his approval. 'Fitzroy's outdone himself.'

'There must be a thousand people here,' I say.

'He says just under, yes,' Peter replies. 'We've petitioned Gaul for two thousand troops, and they'll fit.'

'What about the rest of Harrow?' We pass a trio of wagons, a dozen men still hauling out supplies. 'How many are there? Do we have room for them, too?'

'Three thousand, give or take,' John replies. 'Not all of them will move here, though, not even under threat of war. But there's space for them if they do.'

Six thousand people. It seems impossible that Rochester could shelter them all. Once again, my thoughts go back to the spy, the enemy, the traitor in our midst. What would happen if Blackwell were to gain access. I know what John said, what Peter said, that it isn't Chime's father. Maybe they're right. But I also know what Blackwell always said: *Warfare is based on deception.* To win, you must present yourself to the enemy in a way that makes them believe what they want to believe. I should have listened then, when he all but laid out his secret in front of us.

What am I not hearing now?

As if on cue, he appears then: Lord Three Surnames himself. Up close, he's taller and more attractive than he was at the trial. Finely dressed in brown leather breeches, a steel-grey-and-green harlequin jacket over a steel-grey doublet, and a brown leather scabbard fastened about his waist, only it's empty. He's commander in chief of this army, but he looks like a man playing at war, not planning for it.

He slaps John on the back, gives his hand a hearty shake. Does the same to Peter. Then he turns to me, blue eyes brightening as he takes me in. I watch them closely, as if I could spot deception swirling along their surface.

'Miss Grey.' He extends his hand to me; I take it.

'Lord Cranbourne Calthorpe-Gough.'

'Please, call me Fitzroy,' he says. 'It's lovely to see you again, outside the confines of the council. And it's a pleasure to have you join our forces. You're one to be reckoned with, as I understand.'

I open my mouth to respond, but Peter speaks for me. 'She's quite skilled with a knife,' he offers. His grin is broad but I can see the strain behind it. 'Her swordplay is nonpareil, and I'm eager to get her to the archery butts. She's far too modest to claim it, but I daresay she's a better shot than you, Fitzroy.'

It's uncomfortable, this: Peter extolling virtues learned in order to capture and kill the people of Harrow, now repurposed to save them. Virtues that nearly no longer exist. But Peter has his part to play in all of this, just as I do.

There's a roar then, the sound of men cheering and laughing, coming from the jousting pits. I can just make out a dozen or so men, watching two others circle each other in the sand, their sword blades flashing in the early-afternoon sunlight.

'Sparring,' Peter says with some satisfaction.

'Every day,' Fitzroy replies. 'They'll make their way through their own ranks, then they'll start looking for opponents.' He gives my shoulder a clap. 'They're throwing away a small fortune down there. But I'd be willing to place my own on Elizabeth.'

He smiles. John scowls. Peter swallows.

I smile back.

Fitzroy lifts a hand and from nowhere, a young boy in white livery scurries up.

'Take their bags to their tents, if you please. Elizabeth Grey and John Raleigh. They're both inner ring five, I believe.' The boy nods, takes our bags, then dashes away.

'Those fighting are in the white tents,' Fitzroy says as we make our way to the jousting pit. 'The circles increase by rank. I'm in the centre, along with the field marshal, the captain, the lieutenant. You'll meet them later. The company makes up the outer rings.' He glances at me. 'Does Blackwell employ a similar ranking among his men?'

I allow a smirk. 'I'd say he favoured a more 'first among equals' type ranking.'

Fitzroy throws me a smile; it lights up his face. He really is breathtakingly handsome. 'I wager he did.'

'Elizabeth!' A familiar voice cuts through the noise around us. 'John!'

I turn to see Fifer waving at us through the crowd, Schuyler behind her.

'What are you doing here?' John says as she pulls up before us.

Fifer jerks her thumb at Schuyler. He's got four bags slung over his shoulder, wearing an expression that's equal parts amused and annoyed.

'It's his fault,' Fifer says. 'He told Nicholas he didn't think it was safe for me to live at home. Not with all the attacks, and not after what happened to you, Elizabeth. So Nicholas sent me here.' She looks around, grimacing as she does. 'It's the last place I want to be, living in a tent. With all these men. It's unseemly and barbaric.'

'I'm going to be living in a tent,' I say.

'As I said.' Fifer grins. 'Barbaric.'

We gather at the edge of the jousting pit, watching the bout until it ends: a thrust forward, a jab to the chest that would have been fatal in a real fight but instead ended with a nick to the skin, a bloom of red against a white linen shirt.

The losing man swears; the winning one laughs. The rest of them join in, tossing around coins and insults. The victor, tall and broad and pock-faced, looks around the pit. Finally his eyes land on John and light up.

'Come on, son. Let's see if your swordplay is as pretty as your face,' he calls out. He snatches the cutlass from the losing man's hand and tosses it to John.

John catches it easily, a smirk breaking out on his face again – the same smirk I've come to know and dread. 'It's certainly not as ugly as yours,' he calls back.

The men all laugh and jeer; even Peter joins in. A dozen or so others, attracted by the noise, wander over to watch.

Fifer and I exchange a rapid glance.

'John,' Fifer whispers. 'I don't know if this is a good idea. You can't win, you really shouldn't even try, not with all these people watching…'

He glances at her, an unmistakable look of contempt crossing his face. 'Not you, too.' Fifer's eyes go wide. I don't know if he's ever looked at or spoken to her that way before.

John shrugs off his coat, tossing it into the grass. Spins the cutlass once, twice in his hand, and steps into the sand. The man who challenged him, a pirate by his clothing and his attitude, walks forward, flips him an obscene gesture. In return, John kicks up a spray of sand, dousing him with it. The crowd laughs and catcalls.

'Here we go,' Fifer mutters.

John and the pirate circle each other, swords held high.

The sun is bright today: too bright. I turn to shield my eyes from the light and as I do, I see a riot of colour opposite the pit from me. A cluster of bright girls in even brighter gowns, cerulean blue and emerald green and cardinal red, Chime among them. Her dress, in canary yellow, is the brightest of all. She sees me watching her, but her eyes skim right past me and land on John, and there they stay.

I look back to the match. The gambling has begun in earnest now, men throwing around coins and barbs, catcalls and challenges. John ignores it all, focussed entirely on the man before him, who advances blow after blow, all of which John deflects. I know what he's doing; it's what I was taught to do: Allow your opponent to expend all his energy on showing off while conserving yours.

The crowd around us continues to grow. Soldiers in red-and-blue colour-blocked surcoats, pageboys in white livery, servants in brown muslin, and one man in black: Gareth. He stands down the line from me, arms folded, eyes fixed on the fight.

John takes a blow from his opponent's sword, parries it once, twice, then ripostes. He makes as if he's about to lunge but stomps his foot instead, a feint. The pirate strikes and John steps aside; there's a shiver of metal on metal before John thrusts his blade forward.

Gareth looks from John to me and back to John again, as if he's beginning to understand something. And he's not the only one. Chime has stepped away from her group of friends to stand beside her father. She tugs his sleeve; they exchange a word, two, before turning back to John, matching eyes narrowed in suspicion.

'He's too good,' Fifer mutters. 'He needs to stop. They're going to figure it out.'

Without a word, I edge away from the pit. Wander to the one beside it, some twenty feet away. There's no one here but two small boys, wrestling in the sand. They take one look at me, scramble to their feet, and scamper away.

I glance again at John, who is circling the man before him, ready to attack.

News travels fast in Harrow, you know that. It's what Gareth said at my trial, to account for the hundreds who showed up to watch it. If he figures out there's more to account for John's skill than his father's tutelage, how long before he tells the council? Before the council tells everyone

ELEVEN

Schuyler's head jerks in my direction from across the tiltyard; he was as focussed on watching John as everyone else. Even from here I can see his startled expression, but it quickly gives way to understanding. We need a distraction. Something to take the attention off John and onto something else and it may as well be me.

What are you waiting for? I think. Then, for good measure I add, *Scared?*

I barely have time to blink before he's slamming into me with the force of a battering ram.

I'm knocked to the ground, my breath knocked from my lungs. I'm momentarily stunned at the pain of it but I shake it off, just as I've done every other time he's caused me pain these past two weeks. Get to my feet. There's a murmur from the crowd nearest us; someone saw, someone is paying attention. It's not enough. I need everyone to be watching.

Again.

Schuyler digs his feet in the sand like a restless lion and crooks his finger at me, a mocking gesture. I lunge for him. Catch him around the waist, rear back, then knee him in the place all boys are vulnerable – even hundred-year-old revenants. Schuyler groans and staggers backward. He lobs a fist at me as he goes, a half-hearted swing I duck easily. He's going easy on me; he can't go easy on me. Already our fight has lost interest from the crowd, they're back to watching and cheering for John.

I reach for my weapons belt, for the line of knives I keep there. Schuyler's already recovered, coming for me again. Before I can think better of it, I slide one out, take aim, and plunge it into his chest.

He sucks in a nonexistent breath, a darkness stealing across his face. That smirk he wore before now turns menacing, and I see it: that feral, wild look revenants get when they're in the heat of battle, when they sense blood. The instinct they get when they return from the dead, the one that wants to put others in their place.

Schuyler yanks out the knife, tosses it aside. Then he's on me, smacking me across the face, hard, the force of the blow turning the world black around the edges. I pull my leg back and slam it into his left kneecap. I hear it crack and Schuyler groans and crumples to the ground, his handsome face twisting in pain, lunging for me as he falls. I leap away but I'm not fast enough; he catches my foot in his hand and yanks and I land with a thud in the sand.

He gets to his feet, kicks me in the ribs. I twist and dodge his second attempt; I'm not so lucky with the third. His heavy, black-booted foot lands squarely in my gut; the force of it knocks the breath from my lungs and sends me flying. I tumble across the sand before finally stopping on my back, arms and legs splayed, eyes unwillingly closed. I feel the rumble of feet along the ground. Schuyler, he's coming for me again. I need to move; I have to move.

But when I crack my eye open I see that it's not Schuyler. It's John.

He slams into Schuyler with the same force Schuyler used on me, knocking him into the sand. John pulls back and punches Schuyler in the face once, twice, then jams his thumb into the spot in Schuyler's chest where I stabbed him with my knife.

Schuyler grabs John by the front of his shirt and pushes him off, or tries to. John yanks from his grasp, then rears back and knees him in the stomach.

Damnation, John. Everything I was trying to achieve he's about to undo, and possibly make it worse.

'John! Schuyler!' I throw myself on top of both of them. 'Stop!' We tumble together in a tangled heap of arms and legs and obscenities.

'Elizabeth, get off!' John grabs my arm and shoves me off him. I lunge for him again, this time wrapping my arms around his neck, pulling him on top of me, forcing him to look at me. His face is inches from mine, he's breathing heavily against me, his dark curls plastered to his face with sweat. He's staring at me, so intense, and for a moment I forget what I was going to say.

He's hauled off me then, none too gently. Before I can

register what's happening, I'm wrenched to my feet, too.

'Move.' It's Peter and Nicholas. 'Now.'

Peter, still grasping my arm, gives me a little shove. Nicholas is holding John, and together they push us across the grass like scolded schoolchildren, Schuyler and Fifer trailing behind us. I glance behind me and, to my horror, a crowd of people stand behind us, watching. Not a dozen, or two, or even three. No, this crowd numbers into the hundreds. I wanted a distraction; instead I caused an attraction.

We trudge across the field, away from the tents, away from the noise and the smoke and the bustle and the crowds. Through a nest of trees to a stretch of wide, flat grassy ground that leads through a long, yew-tree-lined alley and straight into the large inner courtyard of Rochester Hall.

Were I less angry, less worried, I might be able to appreciate the beauty of it. The carefully planted gardens, the fountains, the marble statues, the walls crawling with ivy and bejewelled with stained glass windows that sparkle in the sunlight. As it is, all I can do is look at John. He's long since shrugged off Nicholas's grasp, his face like thunder as he storms ahead of us, looking at and speaking to no one.

'The solar, I think, John, in the west wing?' Nicholas says. 'We'll have privacy there.'

John doesn't respond, but leads us through one of a dozen archways into an exterior hallway, to a closed but still guarded wooden door at the end. The guard sees John coming and immediately steps aside to let him in. A few turns down a corridor lands us in a cosy room overlooking the courtyard we just came in through.

Nicholas hails one of the maids bustling nearby and motions her over. He looks at John expectantly.

'What?' John throws his arms up. 'For God's sake, what do you want from me?'

'Herbs,' Nicholas replies, his voice soft, his eye contact direct. 'For Elizabeth? For her injuries. What do you need?'

John throws me a half-appraising glance, then turns to the maid.

'Arnica for the bruising. Calendula or chamomile for swelling. Water. One bowl hot, the other cold. Clean cloths.' A pause. 'Bring some passionflower, too, if you've got it. That should help calm her down.'

'I don't need calming!' I shout.

The others look at me.

'Then what in God's name did you do that for? Fighting Schuyler – have you gone mad?' John swings an impatient hand. 'Look at you! Your face. *God's nails*. How the hell do you expect to hide that? Never mind that. He could have killed you.'

'I wouldn't have killed her,' Schuyler says at the same time I say, 'He wouldn't have killed me.'

'I had it under control,' I continue. 'We were just… practising.' I resist an urge to press a hand to my rapidly swelling eye.

'Why, Elizabeth?' Peter's calm voice is a stark contrast to John's rage. 'You're not ready. Not for a match like that. Swordplay you could have managed, and I had Fitzroy ready to wager on your archery. Something noncombative. You didn't have to do this.'

'It was Gareth.' I glance at the solar door to make sure it's shut. 'He was watching you fight, John. Chime was, too, and Fitzroy. They could see how good you were.'

'So what?' John snaps. 'So I was good. Why does that matter? It doesn't have anything to do with you.'

Beside me, Fifer lets out a small squeak of protest. 'It has everything to do with her.'

'Goddammit.' John paces the room, threading his hands through his hair. His shirt is untucked and ripped down the front, his trousers are coated in sand and blood – not his own, but mine. 'If you two don't shut your mouths about that stigma—'

'John.' Peter's voice is firm. 'That's quite enough.'

'Then I don't want to hear another word about it,' John retorts. 'The stigma is mine. You gave it to me.' He flashes me a look, not one of gratitude or affection, but one of anger and entitlement. 'If you want it back, it's the same as wishing I had died. Is that what you're saying?'

The way he's manipulating me in this conversation, boxing me in to get the response he wants, it feels familiar. It's the way Caleb used to speak to me.

'No,' I reply, and I wish to God we were having this conversation in private. 'I'm not saying that, of course I'm not—'

'Then stop trying to protect me!' he shouts. 'You act as if I need you to swoop in and save me at every turn. I don't. I don't need you.'

I feel as if I've been punched in the gut. My mouth goes dry and my face fills with the heat of embarrassment and humiliation, of having others witness it. I try one more time, one last time.

'You don't know what having it means,' I say. 'I know the strength you feel, I know you feel invincible. But you're not.' I pause, measuring each explosive word as if it were gunpowder. 'I never regret giving you the stigma, I told you that. I also told you it has to be earned. What I didn't tell you was what earning it does to you.' I'm aware of my voice echoing through the room, of everyone's eyes on me. 'It takes away your compassion. Your humanity. It will take everything that makes you a healer. Everything that makes you who you are.'

John shrugs. 'And I told you, things are different now. As for my compassion, I have none. Not for Blackwell. Killing him has nothing to do with humanity, it has to do with revenge. I'll be damned if you or anyone else is going to stop me from getting it.' He turns and pushes through the door into the hallway, Peter on his heels.

'He doesn't mean that.' Fifer looks at me, her face waxen with horror. 'He's just angry. He needs time to calm down. I'll go talk to him; maybe he'll listen to me.' Even I can hear the uncertainty in her voice. She gives me a weak smile before following John and Peter out the door. Schuyler goes with her, and I'm left alone with Nicholas.

'What is happening to him?' I sink into a soft, golden chair and drop my head into my hands. 'I don't understand what is happening to him.'

'Blackwell's magic is taking over,' Nicholas replies. 'John's magic, the magic he was born with, gifted with, it cannot exist in the same plane as Blackwell's. The stigma is simply too powerful, and the balance that magic requires cannot be maintained.' He eases into a chair beside me, as if that will ease the words that come next. 'It is destroying John's magic.'

'Then transfer the stigma back.' I jerk my head up. I don't know why I didn't think of this before, but I'm desperate now. 'Your magic did it once before; it can do it again. Give it back to me.'

'I cannot do that,' Nicholas says. 'For one, John would not allow it. For me to force it from him would be the same as Blackwell forcing magic from all those other wizards without their consent. Even if I could,' he adds above my objections, 'it would not work the way we'd want it to. Blackwell's magic is too entangled with John's now. There is no way to separate the two.'

'What if I kill Blackwell? If he's dead, if the source of the stigma's magic is gone, will it disappear from John?'

Nicholas shakes his head. 'The stigma's magic is not attached to the source, the way my curse was attached to the Thirteenth Tablet. Were the stigma to operate the same way, it would be dependent on that source. Which is to say, if the witch or wizard who gave up their power were to die, a witch hunter would lose his or her power. You know, as I do, that Blackwell would never allow his machinations to fall upon the chance of others.'

I drop my head back into my hands. The only sound in

the room is the pendulum on a clock somewhere, ticking off seconds.

'I still have to kill him.' I say the words not in anger or desperation, but in manufactured calm. 'And I have to do it before John makes good on his threat to do it himself and gets himself killed.'

'You're not ready to face him.'

'The hell I'm not!' I lose the hold on my composure, tether it down again. 'I think it is he who is not ready to face us. Why the knights, why the archers, why this spy? If he needs the stigma so desperately, why isn't he coming after it himself?'

'Have you ever known Blackwell to do something when he could send others in his stead?'

'No,' I admit.

'Blackwell not being here himself is not indicative of a lack of readiness,' Nicholas says. 'Our sources confirm that he's marshalling troops in Eastleigh and Spellthorne, Portsmouth and Somerset, and, of course, his own county of Blackwell.'

'That's the whole of the southern counties,' I whisper.

'Yes,' Nicholas replies. 'He is moving exceedingly fast, even in winter; especially in winter. He is more than ready to face us.'

'Then all the more reason for me to stop him before he gets here,' I say. 'You have to help me do it, I don't care how. Spell me, curse me, give me an army, or just give me your blessing. But give me something. Give me' – I stop as it occurs to me; I can't believe it hasn't occurred to me –

'the Azoth. I wounded Blackwell with it once; this time I can finish the job. I can sneak into Ravenscourt, I can kill him in his sleep—'

'You will not,' Nicholas says, stern as the father I barely remember. 'The Azoth is magic beyond you, beyond me; it is beyond even the stigma. Were you to use it, it would curse you. It would take you over, take every ounce of your power, until there was nothing left.'

'I thought you said I didn't have any power,' I mutter.

Nicholas throws me a sharp look. 'I said this before at your trial, and I meant it: There is much for you to do to help us, but it does not entail you throwing yourself into death in order to achieve it. I understand you are accustomed to this being expected of you, but we do not expect it of you. I do not expect it of you.'

'But John—'

'You cannot help him if he doesn't want to be helped,' Nicholas says. Then he is gone, his red cloak billowing behind him as he sweeps from the room.

'The hell I can't,' I whisper. My eyes begin that familiar, uncomfortable burning that always seems to follow that familiar, uncomfortable feeling of pain.

The maid comes back into the solar with a silver tray full of the things John requested and sets it down beside me. Three tiny sachets of herbs; two bowls of water, one hot, one cold. I don't know what to do with any of it so I do nothing with it. I'm about to tell her to take it away when a soft, musical voice speaks.

'He left without healing you.'

I look up to find Chime standing in the doorway, watching me. Up close, her yellow dress is even more beautiful, the skirt iridescent and shimmering, the bodice thickly sewn with seed pearls. But her face is shadowed by worry and beneath that, fear.

I swipe a hand across my eyes. 'Yes.'

'That's not something he would do.'

'No.'

'And you're not healing on your own.'

'No,' I repeat, my voice cracking on the word.

With a swish of silk and a patter of slippers on stone, Chime steps inside and shuts the door, moving to sit in the chair beside mine. With a sweep of her hand, she dismisses the servant and gestures at the tray between us.

'Start with the calendula, for swelling. That's the orange flowers. You'll need to steep them first, but not in the hot water. It'll burn the leaves. Use the cold instead.'

'What do you know about healing?' I'm suspicious, remembering Fifer saying Chime's speciality was love spells.

'Not a lot,' she admits. 'But I've watched John work often enough that I know more or less what he would do. And anyway, I don't think I can make you any worse than you already are.' It was meant as a joke, I know, but neither of us smiles.

It occurs to me, in a sickening, resigned sort of way, that Chime is the only one who cares for John the same way I do. She sees the difference in him now. She doesn't even know about the stigma but she knows enough to know he's not himself.

There's nothing Fitzroy wouldn't do for his daughter.

Chime is not my friend, nor will she ever be. But maybe she can be something more than that. Something that, in the end, will be more valuable. Maybe she can be my ally.

We sit together in the solar, empty and silent now but for the flutter of Chime's hands in water and the whisper of herbs as she steeps sachets and I dunk and wring out cloths, holding them to my eye, my cheek, my nose.

And I tell her everything.

TWELVE

Tonight, as it has done each night in the week since I arrived, the iron bell in the mess tent clangs three times, calling us to supper.

It's a different experience, living and training at Rochester, than it was in Greenwich Tower. There, we had our own living quarters. Warm beds, roaring fireplaces, fragrant rushes on the floor, linens smelling of lavender and changed daily. We ate formally: five-, even six-course meals on plates of silver with flatware made of pewter, wine in crystal goblets. We displayed our table manners, part of our education and a requirement foisted upon us at mealtimes, one we all abided unless we wanted the disgrace of being made to dine in the kitchen with the lesser servants.

Here at Rochester we sit at crowded tables, eat meals off trenchers of wood, often with no flatware at all. No goblets, either; we drink from shared wineskins. Dinner is not quail, or roast lamb, or even chicken: It's porridge and beans, cabbage and turnips, bread and cheese. Once a week, on Sunday, we're served meat, whatever is caught and killed from the surrounding park. It's not what I'm accustomed to, but I don't fault it. Feeding a thousand people is no small feat, even with the fleet of volunteers and servants Fitzroy has on hand. Not just that – these supplies have to last for who knows how long, and be enough for several thousand more.

I'm pushing my barley and onion stew around with a hard piece of millet bread when John appears, surrounded by a group of boys in uniform. They squeeze in around and across from me, all of them dirty and sweaty from yet another sparring match. I know them by sight but not by name: tall, well-built, attractive boys around John's age, laughing and confident. Some of the girls farther down the table watch them as they settle into place and begin reaching for their trenchers, cramming down bread and stew as if it were a delicacy.

John slides in beside me and gestures at the boys around him. 'Elizabeth, this is Seb, Tobey, and Ellis.' The boys look at me appraisingly. One of them winks. 'And this is Bram.' He points at the boy across from me. Dark hair, dark eyes, a twisted nose that looks as if it's been broken a few times. 'His father's one of Fitzroy's lieutenants.'

'I remember you.' Bram looks at me across the table. 'From Winter's Night. Remember? I congratulated you on your and John's wedding.'

I don't say anything to this, but the other boys laugh and catcall John. Accuse him of being henpecked, of being smitten, wife-ridden.

'I'm not getting married,' John says. 'Never was. It was just a joke.' The tone in his voice, the dismissal in it, makes my throat close up and my cheeks burn. I look down at my plate, whatever little appetite I had now long gone.

The way John has treated me this past week, since the incident in the solar, it's wearing on me. He's always surrounded by these boys, always fighting. He doesn't seek me out anymore, not the way he used to. If anything, he's avoiding me. I saw him just last night with his new group of friends, Chime among them. He saw me, too, I know he did. But he didn't invite me over, and I didn't go. I just walked on by.

'Right,' Bram says. 'But joke or no, I enjoyed talking to you anyway. I remember your dress, the white one with the flowers. It was quite lovely.'

I look up at him then, and the smile he gives me drops into the pit of my stomach and makes me feel even worse. He pities me, and to be pitied is the worst kind of humiliation. But I stay quiet. It's a trick I learned from training: If I make myself as invisible as possible, danger may just pass me by.

John and his friends continue eating, devouring everything in front of them. Seb, a tall boy with ginger hair and an unpleasant smirk, pulls a flask from beneath his jacket and uncorks it, the harsh scent of whiskey wafting over the table. He passes it around and when it comes to John, he takes an enormous swallow. I open my mouth to remind him he doesn't drink, at least not while he's healing.

Then I remember he's not healing at all and shut it.

'You're not eating,' John says finally, nudging my shoulder with his. It's coming up on four in the afternoon, but the sun is already making its way into the horizon, spilling red across the grounds. The short and bitterly cold days of winter have taken hold, despite the warmth of a thousand fires – some real and rooted in kindling, some magical and free-floating – that heat the camp.

'I guess I'm not hungry.' I wait, with useless hope, for him to tell me I should eat. That I need to in order to keep my strength up, or to prevent illness, or to stay healthy.

Instead he says, 'You don't mind if I have the rest, then?' He slides my plate in front of him before waiting for my response. 'Fighting makes me so hungry. Seems like there's never enough.' A pause. 'Maybe you should train more. You might eat more, if you did.'

With a clatter, the boys rise to their feet, pulling on cloaks, strapping on weapons, snatching last-minute bites of bread off the table. John finishes the last of my food and turns to me.

'We're going to the tiltyards, see if we can't get in on the last matches of the day. Those pirates, they've got more money than sense. There's a fortune to be made off them, and you barely have to try.' He shakes his head. 'Idiots.'

The other boys laugh. I wonder what Peter would say if he heard John speaking about his friends that way.

'I don't suppose you want to come, do you?'

His words, they're so similar to ones Caleb used to

dismiss me, the way he'd invite me to things out of habit instead of desire. It hits me hard as a slap.

I shake my head.

'Suit yourself.' John unfolds himself from the bench and that's when I see them: A brace of men making their way through the narrow aisles between the tables. Not the Watch, but members of the guard all the same. Black cloaks, silver pikes, the red-and-orange Reformist badge, stubborn on their lapels. There may not be Persecutors, not any longer; Blackwell took that away. But there are still lawbreakers to persecute.

The crowds around us, they pull back to let them through, following them with bemused looks. The men stop in front of me, but I know they're not after me.

'John Raleigh,' one of them says.

'Yes?' John looks down at the guard; he towers over him by at least three inches. 'What d'you want?'

'By the order of the council, we are sent to arrest you for possession of materials herewith banned within the parish of Harrow-On-The-Hill.'

John opens his mouth, then snaps it shut, a muscle twitching in his jaw.

'What materials?' The boy called Tobey steps to John's side. His hand strays to his hip where his sword is hilted, an aggressive gesture.

'Leave it, son,' the guard says to him. 'You'll only make it worse.'

Another guard pulls out a slip of parchment from his cloak, unfolds it, and begins to read. The gesture is so familiar, so like what I did for all those witches and wizards I arrested not so long ago, that I begin to tremble.

'Aconitum, a known paralyzing agent,' the man starts. 'Belladonna, which causes convulsions. Mandrake, which arrests breathing. Foxglove, also called deadman's bells, which causes tremors, seizures, delirium, and death.'

Tobey turns to the red-haired boy, Seb. 'Go fetch John's father. Peter Raleigh. He's at the tiltyards with the rest of the pirates. Now.'

Seb pushes from the table and disappears into the crowd. Beside me, John pales; I can actually see the blood draining from his face. And slowly, slowly, he turns to me.

'You,' he says, the disbelief evident even in his hushed voice. 'You found them, didn't you? In my room. And you told them.' He swipes a hand across the table then, sending trenchers and wineskins scattering. The crowd around us, they've fallen so silent I can almost hear my own heartbeat, pounding wildly in my chest.

I wish I could deny it, but I can't: Every word he says is true. I told Chime, and I struck a deal with her father, and now John is to be arrested and charged and thrown in prison. And there he will stay. He will not go to war, he will not fight, he will not try to kill Blackwell, he will not be forced to give up his stigma and be killed himself. He will be safe. And he will hate me.

That was the other, unspoken part of the deal.

John and I continue to stare at each other – him in anger and betrayal, me in grief and agony – as the guard continues speaking.

'According to the laws of Harrow, possession of any one of these materials carries a mandatory punishment of a year in prison.'

There's a rustle and a collective murmuring as Peter appears, pushing between the tables in the tent. 'Now see here!' He steps between John and the guards. 'You cannot arrest my son. He's a healer. The things he had, he used them to cure, not to harm. To put him away for a year—'

'Four years,' the guard corrects. 'He was in possession of four poisons. Per the rules of the council, that's a term of four years.'

He takes John's arm; John yanks it away. Turns back to me, fury turning his hazel eyes nearly black. It's not the same look he gave me when I lay on the table before him all those months ago, injured and bleeding, when he found out I was a witch hunter, when he made the decision whether he was going to save me or let me die. No, it's not the same.

The look he gives me now is worse.

'You cannot do this.' Peter lunges for the guard and with a flick of his wrist disarms him in an instant. He points the sword into the guard's chest. 'You will not take my son.'

'Unless you'd like to find yourself in a cell in Hexham beside him, you'll lower your weapon,' the guard says.

'It's your weapon, you idiot,' Peter mutters.

'We're to escort Mr Raleigh to Hexham prison, where he will officially receive his sentence and be given the opportunity to enter in a defence, if he wishes.'

'He'll enter a defence,' Peter snarls. 'And I daresay you'll be needing to enter one before this is all over.'

'Father.' John turns to him. 'Let's go. The sooner we get there, the sooner I can be back. This is all a mistake.' One final glance at me. 'Nothing but a mistake.'

The guards reach for John again; this time he lets them. They clamp his wrists in iron bindings and escort him through the mess tent and across the field, Peter at his heels. John's friends, the girls at the end of the table, everyone in the tent, they all turn to watch them go. And when John passes out of sight they all look back to me, some with anger, some with confusion, some with bright, greedy eyes as if the scandal unfolding before them were their dessert, sorely missing.

I grab my trencher, and John's. Step through the aisles and the people who don't give way for me, forcing me to push through them so they can push back, vaguely threatening.

At the entrance I glance over my shoulder, just once, and see her. Chime. She's surrounded by her friends, now aflutter with whispers and gasps and poorly concealed smiles. But Chime's face is unhappy, and it, unlike Bram's, is not pitying. She holds my gaze and for a moment, we are united in shared misery.

I step from the mess tent and make my way to the adjoining kitchen tent, where a group of women huddle around vats of water, washing up. I drop the trenchers in the pile at their feet and make my way across the field. I don't know where I'm going, not really, but I find myself pushing through the rapidly darkening sky and into the yew alley, making my way up to Rochester Hall, retracing the steps I took a week ago, following John into the solar.

I don't go there; I'm not allowed into the west wing of the house – no one is, save for council members and Fitzroy's friends, family, and, of course, John. But Fitzroy opened the east wing and a few of its many rooms up to the camp: the library, the music room, the chapel, the dance hall. The library and chapel get much use; the music room and dance hall do not.

The guard posted at one of the doors that lead inside moves to let me pass. Like the rest of Rochester, the east wing is lovely, if not a bit gaudy. Walls covered in rich yellow brocade. Black-and-white-tiled floor covered in an expansive, deep-blue-and-red carpet. Gold chandeliers, dripping with crystal, hang from arched ceilings. There are even suits of armour mounted on ledges set high upon the walls.

I pass room after room but enter none of them. Not the library with its spiralling towers of books; not the frescoed and gilded dance hall, so like the great hall at Greenwich Tower where the masque was held; not the music room, empty save for a girl and boy who stand entwined in a darkened corner. They all remind me of John.

The last room I try is the chapel; I know it by the yellow cross etched into the stained glass door. I push it open. Marble floors, oak pews; a constellation of stars painted on the ceiling against a midnight-blue backdrop. A thousand candles, set in brackets along the walls, spring to life, magically alerted to my presence.

I crawl into an empty pew – they're all empty – and draw

my knees to my chest, wrap my arms around myself, rest my head. I don't cry; it seems too insignificant, too selfish for what I've done. And I had to do it. But it doesn't mean I'm not sorry for it, and it doesn't make it any easier to bear.

There's a rustle then, the whisper of a door on its hinges, the soft sound of two sets of footsteps on the threshold but only one breath. I tilt my head to see Fifer standing there, Schuyler behind her.

She slides in beside me, saying nothing. She doesn't have to. Because after a moment, she moves closer, reaches for my hand, then drops her head on my shoulder, sighing deeply.

Schuyler sits on my other side. He cups the back of my head, just briefly, before leaning forward, head bowed, his forearms resting on the seat back in front of him.

We sit together, a silent trio of misery, until the last of the candles burns out and there's nothing left but darkness.

THIRTEEN

'We've come to see John Raleigh.'

Fifer and I stand before the entrance of Hexham. She tells me it was once a stable before being converted into a prison: long and low and built from stone, inset with squared windows and rounded doors. The only sign there are criminals inside is the high wall that surrounds it. Even so, it's not like Fleet: not meant for torture, or a place for holding until a death sentence is carried out. I winced when I saw a platform in the yard, but Fifer assured me it wasn't for executions but a holdover from auctions, selling off animals to merchants. There's no one dangerous here. Most of the prisoners are debtors, the occasional petty thief or miscreant, a drunk or two.

And a healer who did nothing except make the terrible mistake of getting involved with a witch hunter.

The guard, armed and dressed in black, that red-and-orange Reformist badge emblazoned on his chest, glances between us.

'I can only permit one visitor at a time.'

'You go,' Fifer tells me. 'I'll wait for you here.'

My stomach squirms with dread. The guard checks me for weapons; I have none. Then he unearths a key and unlocks the gate, the creaking hinges echoing across the courtyard. He leads me inside, into the wide, empty corridor, light spilling in through unbarred windows. But for all that it is unlike Fleet, it still smells the same: mould and moisture, anger and abandonment.

We wind up a flight of stairs then down another hall. There's no sound of death here, no bodies bruised and battered and dying in the corner. But it is cold, several of the windows open wide to the frigid winter air. And, as most prisoners in Hexham serve short sentences for their relatively minor crimes, Fifer says it's entirely empty.

Not entirely.

The guard leads me past cell after cell until we reach one at the end, the barred door closed and firmly locked. Inside, on a cot pushed against the wall, is John.

He's sitting with his back to the wall, his boot heels on the edge of the mattress, arms draped over his knees, head down. He's dressed in grey trousers and a long grey cloak, the hood pulled over his head to keep away the chill.

He heard us coming, he must have; it's deathly quiet and there's no one around but for us. Still, he doesn't even look up. Not even when the guard clears his throat: Once, twice. Finally, the guard speaks.

'You have a visitor.'

John looks up then. But not at me, at the guard. He still says nothing.

The guard clears his throat again. 'You have twenty minutes.'

John mutters something under his breath I don't hear. The guard walks away, back down the hall and the stairs, the same way we came, leaving us alone.

'How are you?' I say, awkward.

A scoff. That's his only reply.

'I wanted to see you,' I continue. 'Talk to you. And to bring you these.' I open the bag slung across my shoulder, pull out a pair of books: *Physika Kai Mystika* and *Monas Hieroglyphica*. Both alchemy texts I borrowed from the vast library at Rochester Hall.

'I don't want to see you, and I don't want to talk to you. You had me arrested,' John says. 'Don't bother telling me you didn't. You went through my stores in my bedroom and you saw them, and you turned me in. It was you.'

'Yes,' I confess. 'I did have you arrested. But I did it to help you. I know you don't see that now. I only want to help you.'

He fires off one obscenity, then another.

'The books, I think they will help you, too,' I go on. 'To remember your magic, the magic you were born with. Gifted with.' I use Nicholas's words not to manipulate him, but to remind him. 'You're not yourself right now. I know you don't see that, either, but we do. Your father. Fifer. Schuyler. Even Chime.' He frowns a little at the mention of her name. 'This isn't the John I know.'

'You don't know who I am,' he says. 'You don't know me at all.'

'That's not true.' I lean forward, touch my forehead to the bars. 'I do know you. At least, I did.'

I think of the stack of notes he wrote me. Every last one I have with me, tucked carefully into my bag. Notes I've read and reread a hundred times, for the comfort I needed when he was no longer there to give it to me, and to prove to myself that what we had wasn't just something I imagined.

'Blackwell's magic. The stigma. It's part of you now.' I tell him what Nicholas told me. 'It will take you over, if you let it. It is taking over.' I squeeze the bars to steady myself. 'But I want you to fight it. I want you to use the time in here to try to remember who you are.'

John charges across the cell then, so fast I don't have time to react. He reaches through the bars and snatches my wrists, gripping them hard.

'Do you know what you've done?' He gives me a little shake. 'Do you have any idea?'

'Yes!' I try to pull away but his grasp is too strong. 'I know exactly what I've done. I've kept you from harm. I've kept you from harming others. I've kept people from learning your secret, and from discovering mine. I've saved your life, again, only you're too far gone to see it.'

'It's not your right to do that,' he shouts back. 'Don't you get it? You aren't my mother. You aren't my sister. And you sure as hell aren't my friend.' His eyes narrow into cruel, hard slits. 'You don't get to say what happens to me.'

I close my eyes, just for a moment. Try to remember his breath on my cheek, his lips on mine, the warmth and the love he once felt for me. But even those memories are slipping away now, insubstantial as a ghost.

'You aren't who I thought you were,' he continues. 'The girl I thought I knew, she would have been pleased for me. She would have helped me to fight. Not shut me away in a cage as if I were an animal she was trying to tame.'

That's not what I did, I want to say. Only I don't, because it is exactly what I did.

'I did it because I care about you,' I say instead. It's more than that, so much more. But the words that should be said in private, in whispers and in love, don't belong here.

'Funny things happen to the people you claim to care about,' he says, the words cruel and sharp and cutting deep. 'You cared about Caleb, yet you killed him. I suppose I got off easy, didn't I?'

I jerk away from him, flinching as if he'd struck me. He doesn't try to hold me back.

'How dare you throw Caleb in my face,' I say, my shock turning quickly to anger. 'You know what happened that night. You were there. You know I didn't mean to kill him.'

John shrugs, utterly careless. 'You had me thrown in jail for no reason. You've lost the right to be indignant. And now, I want you out. The sooner you leave the sooner I can put this behind me. Whatever the hell it was.' He lunges for the door again, and again, I flinch. But he only bangs the heel of his hand against the bars.

'Guard!'

The man arrives quickly, too quickly. No doubt he's been lingering at the top of the stairs, listening to every word we've said.

'Get her out of here. And make sure she never comes back.' He turns his back on me.

'John,' I start. But then I stop. I won't plead for him. I won't make him take back the words he said to me. I won't make him turn back and tell me he didn't mean them. *I love you*, I say. Only it comes out as 'Goodbye.'

Fifer waits for me at the entrance. She's pacing back and forth, gnawing a fingernail. At the clank of the key in the door she stops midstride and rushes over.

'How did it go?' She tosses the guard a nasty look before taking my arm and pulling me across Hexham's empty courtyard, toward the gate.

'He told me to leave,' I say. 'He said he never wanted to see me again.' My voice cracks as his words, the reality and the finality of them, sink in.

'Elizabeth—'

'Don't,' I say. 'Don't tell me he's not himself. He is. This is who he is now.'

'That is what I was going to say,' Fifer replies. 'But better this way and alive than any other way and dead.'

We step through the prison's open gate and onto the narrow dirt road that leads north to Gallion's Reach, past Whetstone, and, beyond that, Rochester. It's desolate here, nothing but frozen fields decorated by clumps of barren trees, fences, and the occasional lone farmhouse, their chimneys sending up fat, erratic plumes of smoke as if they were distress signals.

A mile or so on I catch sight of a group of a half-dozen men standing a few hundred feet off the road. They're members of the Watch; I recognise their grey cloaks, that aggressive orange triangle on the lapel. I can't see who they are, though, not from this distance. But I can see they're having trouble with what looks like prisoners they've captured.

Two men in grey hold up a third man in black. By the way his head hangs limp and his feet drag along the ground, he looks to be unconscious, possibly dead. Two more men in grey are wrestling with yet another man in black. He's not unconscious, but he's well on his way – he stumbles, falls to his knees, gets up, stumbles again. Their grunts and expletives cut through the still, frigid air.

Fifer and I exchange a rapid glance.

'More of Blackwell's men,' Fifer says. 'And look. Is that Peter?' She points to a dark, curly-haired man in grey, dragging the still-conscious captive across the field.

'Yes.' I step off the path into the grass, making my way toward them.

'Wait.' Fifer snatches at my sleeve. 'I don't think we should go over there. It could be dangerous.'

I shake her off and don't reply. I'm too busy watching the man Peter is holding. He's got manacles clamped around his wrists and ankles, and he's been beaten, badly. His movements are jerky, erratic, and as he falls to his knees once again, he groans and coughs out a mouthful of blood.

He's one of Blackwell's men, that much is clear. I know by his familiar the black cloak and the emblem on the front – that damned red rose, strangled by its stem and pierced with a green-hilted blade. But there's something else that's familiar, too. The way he moves, the sound of his voice, the way his dark hair falls across his forehead. Something stirs in my chest then: dread and a dawning recognition.

Peter shoves the man to the ground; he hits the dirt with a groan. Peter then reaches for his sword, the sing of the blade against the scabbard echoing across the barren field. As if in response, a flock of birds takes flight nearby, screaming their retreat into the dull grey sky.

I break away from Fifer. Move across the frozen grass, picking up speed as I go. Peter grabs a fistful of the man's hair and yanks him to his knees, the other men of the Watch urging their approval. Peter grips his sword in two hands, swinging it high above his head. The man before him tries to hold himself steady. But even from here I can see him trembling, his body swaying like a stalk of wheat in the wind.

It's Malcolm. The king – former king – of Anglia.

'Peter.' His name comes out a choked whisper. I try again, louder, my footsteps pounding to the beat of my heart as I run across the field. 'Peter, stop!'

But Peter doesn't hear me. He's too entrenched in the violence of what he's about to do, too caught up in bloodlust, too caught up in the justice he's about to mete out. I scream his name again.

'Elizabeth, stay back.' Peter lifts one hand from his sword, holds it out in warning. The other men see me sprinting across the field, Fifer on my heels. Some of them draw their own weapons, unsure of me, of what I'm going to do.

'Don't!' I shriek. But my plea is ignored as Peter turns from me, places both hands on his sword again, and turns back to Malcolm.

Malcolm shuts his eyes.

Peter raises the blade.

And he swings.

FOURTEEN

I leap in front of Peter, pushing Malcolm out of the way. Malcolm's not expecting it; he lets out a grunt and we both hit the frozen ground with a muffled thud. I feel the blade swish the air above my head, the hair on my neck prickling at the near miss.

Somewhere behind me, Fifer shrieks.

Malcolm utters something then; I can't make it out. But the sound of his breathless voice brings back a thousand memories and they all come flooding in along with a thousand other sensations: the feel of him beside me, lean and strong. The smell of him, a curious mixture of soap and fir trees, now mingled with the sharp metallic tang of blood. The sight of his dark, rumpled hair, his hands, his neck, and his unshaven face fills me with repulsion, just as it's always done. But just as I've always done, I push the feeling away, and I stay by his side. I'm afraid of what will happen if I don't.

'By God and his mother!' Peter bellows. 'What the devil are you doing?'

'You can't kill him.' I disentangle myself from Malcolm and climb to my feet. 'He's not who you think he is.' I look around at them, at the men advancing on me. At Peter looming before me, his cutlass poised like an axe, ready to strike.

Malcolm turns his head toward me: slowly, as if he's afraid to call attention to the fact that it's still attached to his body. Finally, he sees me. At once his eyes go wide, pale grey and bloodshot and wild.

'Elizabeth. Oh my God, Bess.' I cringe at his nickname for me, too intimate to be said aloud in front of a crowd, too intimate to be said at all. 'It really is you. I heard your voice, but I thought I was imagining it.' He staggers first to one knee, then the other, looking up at me. 'What are you doing here?'

'My lord,' I say, the old habit of deference slipping into place, smooth as bed silk. 'This isn't the time—'

'I heard you'd escaped,' he continues. 'But Uncle didn't tell me what happened to you. I asked – demanded – but he wouldn't tell me.' Malcolm shakes his head. 'I didn't know you were in prison until after you were already gone. Still, no one would tell me anything. I should be told everything!'

Malcolm is babbling now, a combination of shock, fear, of being beaten half to death before nearly being executed. He talks as if he doesn't realise we're not alone, as if he's forgotten there are men around him, listening to every word he says.

'My lord.' I keep my voice low so no one can hear. 'Please, stop—'

'I don't know if anything he said was true,' he continues. 'About your being a witch. It doesn't matter if it was. I would have stopped it, if I'd known. You know that, don't you? That I wouldn't let anyone hurt you?'

Malcolm takes my hand then, curling his fingers around mine before bringing them to his lips. This time I don't grit my teeth and bear it, this time I flinch from it and this is what finally gets his attention. He drops my hand and sees – finally – the men around us, their weapons pulled and poised. It jerks him into the present: shock and understanding first colouring his face, then paling it.

'What is the meaning of this?' Peter steps before me, his eyes dark and angry. 'Elizabeth, who is this man?'

I start at the realisation: Peter doesn't recognise him; the Watch doesn't, either. They don't realise that the man they captured, the man they nearly executed, the man on his knees before them, is the king – the deposed king – of Anglia.

'He's—' I start. Then I stop, thinking quickly. Is it better if they don't know it's Malcolm? Worse? Would they dare to kill the king? Or would it only make them kill him faster? Malcolm doesn't seem to know, either; he hasn't moved, not an inch. I can hear his ragged breathing, mingled with my own.

It happens so fast then. The man beside Peter lunges forward, snatching my arm and yanking me from Malcolm's side. Peter raises his sword once more, and we're back to where we started.

'He's the king!' I shout. 'You can't kill him. He's not one of Blackwell's men. He's the king.'

A terrible silence falls then, as weighty as an axe to a block.

'You're lying.' The man holding my arm gives it a savage shake. 'This man is not the king. He's a witch hunter. He's one of your friends, and you're trying to save him.'

'I'm not lying.' I turn to Malcolm. 'Tell them your name. Tell them who you are.'

Malcolm looks at me, uncertain. He doesn't know if this will save him or condemn him.

'If you want to live, tell them.'

Malcolm lurches to his feet, unsteady, what little colour he has left draining from his face. He's in no condition to stand, or even sit, but that doesn't matter. Malcolm would never state his elevation from his knees.

'My name is Malcolm Douglas Alexander Hall.' He glances at the men, his earlier hesitation gone. 'Son of William Hyde Alexander Hall, House of Stuart, and Catherine Johanna Louise Hesse-Coburg, House of Saxony. Titles: Duke of Farthing in Gael. Duke of Cheam in Southeast Anglia. Supreme Head and Lord of Airann.' A pause, then: 'First in line to the kingdom of Anglia and Cambria. Interrupted.'

Interrupted from his own throne, by his own uncle. Thomas Charles Albert Louis Hall, also House of Stuart in Anglia, officially titled Duke of Norwich, but who styled himself Lord Blackwell after his principal holding in South-west Anglia.

Interrupted from certain death, by me.

'Oh my God,' Fifer whispers. 'Elizabeth, what have you done?' Voices erupt around me, from all the men in the Watch but one: Peter. His mouth has gone slack, as has his weapon, as he stares at the man responsible for the death of his wife, his daughter. He could have had justice, he could have avenged them. He almost did. And I stopped it.

'He is the king of Anglia,' I tell him. 'To kill him is regicide. That's against the law. It's a treasonable offense, punishable by death.'

At once, I know this was the wrong thing to say.

'The law!' Peter's voice, never spoken to me in anything other than honeyed tones, even after I had his own son arrested, rises to a pitch. 'Punishable by death!' He rounds on me, dark eyes lit by anger but something else, too: grief. 'His laws are nothing but death. He killed my wife, my daughter. He killed them.'

'He's done that, yes,' comes a voice, thin with pain. 'And he's a blackguard, no doubt, and it's a puck to spare him. Even so, the worth of his trouble is still more than the trouble he's worth.'

The men whip their heads around and I do, too. The man in the field. The one we'd forgotten about, the one I thought was dead. Only he's not dead, and he's not a man.

It's a woman.

By all rights, she looks like a man: tall, broad-shouldered, well muscled, even; a shock of pale red hair cut above her ears. Early twenties, if I had to guess. But the tell is her voice: sweet and high and girlish. She's on her knees now, and I can see the hilt of a knife protruding from over her shoulder.

The men of the Watch look around at one another, puzzled.

'Who are you?' Peter steps toward her. He lowers his sword, raises it, then lowers it again, as if he's unsure whether to pull a weapon on a female.

'Keagan Hearn.' The woman extends a shackled hand to him. Peter doesn't take it; she lets it fall. 'From Airann, 'course, the lovely river city of Dyflin.'

'That's all very well and good, Keagan from Airann,' Peter says. 'But what are you doing here in Anglia? And with him?' Peter jerks the point of his sword at Malcolm.

'I reckon that's clear enough, no? Sprung him from prison, there in Upminster. Fleet. Wretched place.' Keagan sits back on her heels, grimacing. 'Taking him back to Airann. Was, until we ran into you lot. No chance you could let us on our way – no.' Peter's sword is against Keagan's throat now, his decision made. 'I suppose not.'

'Why would you rescue him?' Another man of the Watch steps forward. 'Are you a sympathiser? Traitor? Persecutor?'

'No, sir,' Keagan replies. 'None of those things. But then, none of those exist any longer, do they? They, like everything else, exist under a different rule now.'

'Don't play games, lass,' Peter says. 'You're in enough trouble already.' He glances at Malcolm, still swaying on his feet. 'Why were you taking him to Airann? What are you planning to do? Gather troops? Invade Anglia? Take the throne?'

'You can't take what already belongs to you,' Malcolm says. 'The throne is mine. It was taken from me, and I have every intention of getting it back.'

'*Ach.*' Keagan turns to him. 'What have I told you about that? Don't lead with that. Never with that.'

'I only speak the truth,' Malcolm says, a haughtiness to his tone. 'A king and his words are divine. You would do well to heed them both.'

'That attitude is precisely why you are here' – she points to the ground – 'instead of there.' She jerks her thumb behind her, vaguely toward Upminster.

'Your lack of respect offends me,' Malcolm says.

'And your lack of humility offends *me*,' Keagan snaps. 'My God, man. If you expect to live through this, you'd best learn to read a room.'

Malcolm opens his mouth, then shuts it. I feel my eyes go wide. I've never heard anyone speak to Malcolm that way. Not his councillors, not his advisors, not even his own uncle, who hated him and wanted him dead. But Keagan clearly cares for none of this: the deference nor the consequence.

'Looks as if we've got company.' She jerks her head toward the road and straightens her posture, the slightest wince the only giveaway to the knife still lodged in her shoulder blade.

Striding across the field are Nicholas, Gareth, and Fitzroy, their robes flapping in attendance. On their heels is

Schuyler. I glance at Fifer, who nods: It was she who summoned Schuyler, told him what happened, told him to come and to bring Nicholas.

Malcolm seems to recognise Nicholas immediately. He'll know him from when Nicholas was in his father's council, from once charging him as the most wanted man in Anglia. He draws himself to his full height – not considerable, as Malcolm is only a few inches taller than I am.

The three men pull up short, take in the scene before them.

'Ye mus' be the cavalry.' Keagan's brogue is thick and sarcastic.

'Schuyler's been so good as to inform us of what's happened here,' Fitzroy says. 'But we've not heard why. Or how. And who you are.' He steps in front of Keagan.

'Some lass from Airann,' one of the Watch says. 'And a traitor.'

'*Ach*,' Keagan mutters again. 'I told you, I'm no traitor. I'm a militant. A member of the Order of the Rose.'

The men exchange rapid glances; even I'm surprised. The Order of the Rose is a resistance group comprised of students at the university in Airann, founded four years ago – just after Blackwell became Inquisitor – in response to his anti-magic laws. But it makes no sense that this girl, Keagan, is here in Harrow; even less that she's with Malcolm. The Order, at least as I know it, is an intellectual organisation. They distribute pamphlets, write scathing treatises for underground journals. They don't kidnap kings.

'The Order,' Fitzroy says. 'Of course. A fine group. I've

been following your movements since you began. I always did enjoy your tracts.' He rocks back on his heels. '*A Tale of a Tub* was my favourite. When the brother relied on inner illumination for guidance, then walked around with his eyes closed after swallowing candle snuffs? Amusing.'

Keagan grins.

'Your protestations of late have certainly moved beyond satire, though, haven't they?' Fitzroy continues. 'Rudimentary explosives. Burning effigies. Defacing buildings. And, most recently, bridges.'

Keagan lets out a girlish peal of laughter. 'Defaced is right. Did that one myself. Crawled up onto Upminster Bridge, stuck pamphlets on the spikes through those severed heads. Reckon they don't mind, though. What with being dead and all.'

'Heads?' Gareth says. 'Whose?'

Keagan shrugs. 'Some of Blackwell's, some of yours, some just in the way.'

Gareth doesn't reply.

'And now you've taken a king captive.'

Keagan nods, all earlier levity gone. 'That's just the start.'

'A student group,' Peter repeats in a mutter. '*God's blood.*'

'No need to invoke,' Keagan says calmly. 'Now, much as I'd like to chin-wag all day long, I've got a bit of a pressing matter.' She lifts her chained hands, points her thumbs over her shoulder. 'This dagger you clapped in me, she stings diabolical.'

Fitzroy starts toward her.

'Wait a moment.' Gareth holds out a hand. 'You don't

know who she is. She said she's part of this Order, but we don't know that. She could be one of Blackwell's. She could be lying.'

'I told you—' Keagan starts.

'She's not lying,' Fitzroy finishes for her. 'Her actions prove that. Were she one of Blackwell's, she wouldn't have broken his nephew out of jail, she would have killed him. Hold very still.' He places one hand on Keagan's shoulder, the other around the hilt of the dagger. 'On three,' he says. 'One, two –' Before he can get to three, Fitzroy rips the knife from her back.

Keagan lets out a soft groan, pitching forward onto the ground. Fitzroy fishes a handkerchief from inside his doublet and presses it against the wound to stop the bleeding.

'You said taking the king – Malcolm' – Nicholas glances at him; Malcolm has wisely kept his mouth shut since Nicholas's arrival – 'was just the start.' He steps to Keagan's side, touches a finger to her back. A soft white glow emanates from his hand and at once, the cut is healed. Keagan shuts her eyes, briefly, in relief. 'The start of what, exactly?'

'The plan to knock Blackwell off the throne, 'course,' Keagan says. 'What else?'

I could laugh – I very nearly do – at the idea of a student group believing they can overthrow Blackwell. But Nicholas doesn't look amused at all.

'I see,' he says. 'And you've taken Malcolm because you believe he should remain as king?'

'Him? No. I mean, he had his chance, didn't he?' Keagan

glances at Malcolm, a look of utter disdain on her freckled, ruddy face. Malcolm stares back at her, jaw and fists clenched; I've never seen him look this angry and I almost – almost – feel sorry for him.

'Didn't do much with it,' Keagan continues. 'If he had, we wouldn't be here, would we? No.' She answers her own question. 'But he does have his uses. If Malcolm is dead, Blackwell's no usurper: He's the rightful heir to the throne of Anglia, and no country in this world would support overthrowing him. The only chance we have is to keep Malcolm alive. Dead? We're no longer resisting. We're contending. You'll find, I think, we won't last long if that's the case.'

I hadn't considered this. And judging by the way the men of the Watch look around at one another, shifting uneasily in their grey cloaks, they hadn't, either.

Nicholas nods, his dark eyes intent. 'So you were planning on holding him as a political prisoner. Have you facilities for that? Guards? Troops?'

'In a manner of speaking,' Keagan replies.

'To take custody of a deposed king puts you, your university, your city, and your country at terrible risk,' Nicholas says. His voice is firm, but it is not unkind. 'You risk attacks from Blackwell, once he discovers you have Malcolm. You risk attacks from those in Airann who oppose his being there, and from those in Anglia who want revenge. You risk retaliation from opposing countries. Retaliation from supporting countries. Interest from neutral countries hoping to profit from the chaos, sending in spies and bounty hunters.'

For the first time, Keagan's bright eyes flicker with uncertainty.

'He can't stay here,' Gareth says. 'We cannot risk this falling on us. We are enough of a target as it is. First her' – he glances at me – 'now this.'

'We cannot kill him,' Fitzroy says.

'No,' Nicholas agrees. 'We cannot. But we can detain him for the time being, until we determine the best course of action.'

'You're not suggesting we keep him here,' Peter says. 'You're not suggesting you put this man in the same prison where my son is.' It's too much, then, for him. Too much that his son is in jail because of me, too much that Malcolm still breathes air because of me. Peter sheathes his sword, spins on his heel, and walks across the field toward the road.

'Fitzroy, could you and Gareth escort our two guests to Hexham?' Nicholas says. 'And Schuyler, could you please accompany them? Schuyler is a revenant,' Nicholas adds. 'With all that it means. So I very much advise against an escape attempt.'

Malcolm swallows. Keagan's eyes go wide again.

Nicholas turns to the remaining five men in the Watch. 'I'd like you to go with them to Hexham, and to stay as additional guards there this evening. And I would request that you not speak of this to anyone else.' He looks at Fifer and me. 'You're dismissed.'

The men of the Watch step forward, grasp Keagan and Malcolm by their shackled arms, and lead them away. Keagan goes without protest. But Malcolm twists in their grip, as much as he can, looking over his shoulder at me. In his face is a plea: for me to speak to him, to speak for him. For me to stay with him.

But he is not the king anymore and I am no longer his mistress, so I do neither. Instead, I turn on my heel and, for the first time, I walk away.

FIFTEEN

'Dismissed!'

I'm halfway across the field before Fifer catches up to me.

'Nicholas hasn't dismissed me since I was twelve,' she goes on. 'Since the time I was angry at him and cursed him and made his eyebrows fall out. He looked ridiculous, he was furious with me but it was so funny –' She stops. 'Either way, I'm going to hear about this later, we both are, and it won't be pleasant.' A pause. 'It's always trouble with you, isn't it?'

I don't reply.

'What do you make of all that?' Fifer switches tack. 'That girl, Keagan. Bold as brass, going into Upminster like that, breaking into Fleet. I wonder how she did it.'

Still, I don't reply.

'And the Order of the Rose. I've heard of them, of course, we all have. There've been a fair few from Harrow who are supposedly members, but no one really knows. Their membership, their magic, it's all shrouded in secrecy. I suppose it has to be, doesn't it? Otherwise it's just more names for the Inquisition.'

I step from the field onto the road and keep walking. I don't make it more than a few dozen yards before I feel a hand on my sleeve.

'Elizabeth.' Fifer's breath comes short. 'Rochester is this way.'

I spin on my heel, begin walking in the other direction.

'Elizabeth!' Fifer steps in front of me then, takes me by the shoulders. Leans into me, her eyes searching mine. 'What is it? It's him, isn't it? Malcolm?'

I open my mouth, close it. Fifer heaves a sigh.

'I thought as much.' She takes my arm and tugs me back down the road. 'That must have come as a surprise.'

I'd laugh at the understatement, were I in a laughing mood.

'I never thought I'd see him again,' I say. 'I never wanted to. But I did, and then I went and saved him. I don't know why I did that.'

'I don't know, either,' Fifer says. 'But it's a good thing you did, isn't it? I hadn't thought about what it would mean if he were dead, not until Keagan said it. I don't know if any of us had thought about that.'

I wasn't thinking about that when I pushed him out of the way of Peter's sword, but I don't tell Fifer that.

'Blackwell must have,' I say instead. 'Otherwise he wouldn't have put him in Fleet. He meant for him to die eventually. No one gets out of Fleet.' *Unless it's to the stakes.*

'You did,' Fifer says shortly. 'And now Malcolm has, too. The Order must have some strong magic, not to mention strong connections inside Upminster, to manage that.'

'I suppose.'

'I'll admit, though, he's not what I imagined he would be,' she says. 'The way he looked at you. The way he spoke to you. I guess I expected something different.'

'Which is?' My tone takes on a bite but Fifer continues undeterred.

'I imagined him being rather cruel. Summoning you, dismissing you. I imagined he treated you as, well' – she pulls a face – 'a servant. But the way he looked at you today, the way he took your hand. He tried to kiss you, for God's sake. He called you Bess.'

'He was in shock.' I stop to relace my boot. It doesn't need relacing, but it hides my face and the uncertainty I know must be showing. 'He thought he was going to die. People do and say strange things when they think they're going to die.'

I rise to find Fifer watching me, eyebrows raised. 'Seemed to me a little more than that.'

'There's nothing more than that. Nothing at all.' I throw that last bit over my shoulder, already making my way down the road again. She catches up to me in an instant.

'What do we do now, then?'

'Same thing as before,' I reply. 'Same as always. Kill Blackwell. Looks like I have to do it even faster now. With Malcolm here, how long do you think it'll be before those guards shoot their mouths off to everyone they know? Before the spy inside Harrow finds out and Blackwell sends in yet more of his men?'

'Nicholas told the guards to keep it a secret,' Fifer says.

I look at her.

'Nicholas said you're not ready.' She tries again. 'He wants you to focus on training. On getting stronger. He told you to let the council sort out what to do about Blackwell. Schuyler told me,' she adds hurriedly. 'He heard what Nicholas said to you in the solar.'

'Nicholas doesn't have to know everything, does he?' I pull my coat tight against the gust tunnelling toward us, hardening my already frozen cheeks. 'You don't mean to tell me you've never done anything without his permission. Never disobeyed him. Never done the direct opposite of what he—'

'I get the point,' Fifer snaps. 'But you don't see mine. You're not ready.'

I stop. Turn to her. Whatever she sees on my face is enough to make her reconsider.

'Fine.' She holds her hands up. 'Be a fool. Kill Blackwell. Get yourself killed in the process. By all means, allow me to help.'

'That's more like it.' I gleam at her. 'I want the Azoth. And I want you to help me get it.'

'I don't know where it is.' She says this fast – too fast. I smile; she glowers. 'You'll never get it,' she continues. 'It's hidden inside Nicholas's house; not even I'm allowed near it. It's protected by spells, and then there's Hastings. Even if you do get in, he'll never allow you to take it.'

'You seem to forget who I am.'

'Who you were,' Fifer corrects. 'And I never forget that.'

Since we became friends, it's the closest Fifer and I have come to an argument. The road before us, the fields around us, the wind whipping against us, none of it is as cold as the look that passes between us.

'I'm going to take the Azoth, and I'm going to kill Blackwell with it,' I say. 'And while I'm at it, I want Schuyler to come with me.'

This time it's Fifer who walks away from me, the wind carrying the stream of expletives over her shoulder. 'You won't stop until everyone hates you, will you?'

'I won't stop until he's dead,' I reply, but she's too far away to hear me.

In the three days since John's arrest – and since Malcolm's capture – I've kept to myself, in a virtual state of hideout. It wasn't long before the news spread of my betrayal, how I tipped the guards to John's illegal herbs, how I was jealous of his attention to Chime, how I allegedly got my revenge.

It was enough of a scandal to bury the real scandal: that the deposed king of Anglia, once Harrow's greatest enemy, now resides in prison not ten miles from camp.

I no longer sleep in my tent, not after I returned the first night and found it unpoled, trampled, and slashed. I don't join the others at mealtimes, not after the second night I cleared an entire table as if I had the plague, the air full of mutterings: *traitor*, *liar*, and worse. Instead, I've spent all my time training, resting in the chapel, planning, and waiting: for the opportunity to steal inside Nicholas's home, take the Azoth, get Schuyler, go to Upminster, kill Blackwell.

Waiting for tonight.

I choke down another meal of oat, pea, and barley stew with a slice of brick-hard bread, hand off my trencher at the mess tent, weave through the sea of soldiers in the field. It's mostly empty now, as everyone is either at supper, the sparring pitch, the library, or, in Nicholas's case, at Gareth's in a private meeting, held to determine what's to be done with Malcolm.

My bag, already packed with what few things I own, is at my side. I carry it with me everywhere now, as I have nowhere safe to leave it. It doesn't arouse suspicion – I look no different this night than I have the past two.

The sun dips over the horizon as I slip over the bridge across the lake, pausing to give Rochester one last look before starting out for Nicholas's. Somewhere inside the grounds is Fifer, still simmering with anger at me, made worse by Schuyler's enthusiasm for my plan.

'Blackwell already tried to steal the Azoth once,' Fifer shouted at me last night, before turning the full force of her fury on Schuyler. 'If he gets his hands on it again – which he may, if you die' – she glared at me – 'he'll be invincible. That will be on you.'

'If Elizabeth's going to try to kill him, the Azoth is the best option.' Schuyler tried to reason with her. 'It's her only option.'

'And you wanting to help her has nothing to do with you wanting to get your hands on it.'

'Not in the slightest.'

Fifer crossed her arms, unrelenting. 'Then swear it.'

That was how we reached a compromise. Schuyler would accompany me to Upminster and to Ravenscourt, acting as my scout, my guard, and my protection. But he would not help me steal the Azoth, nor would he touch it once I had it, by pain of death or Fifer's wrath, whichever came first.

Three hours later I reach Nicholas's house, following to the letter Fifer's reluctantly given instructions. A fresh bundle of sage and pine tucked into my pocket, pulled out and set alight when I reach the front door. As it begins to sputter and spark, sending up plumes of thick, fragrant smoke, I wave it before me in two long, sweeping diagonal lines. The smoke hangs in the dark evening sky: an X.

I count to sixty, then enter the house.

It's empty inside – and not just because Nicholas is gone. There are no ghostly hands to pluck my bag from my shoulder, or to take my coat and ferry it from the room. Hastings is gone, and would stay gone, until the last of the herbs turned to ash. Sage and pine, burned together, interferes with a ghost's energy, dissipating it into almost nothing. I didn't ask Fifer if it was cruel, but I didn't have to. Forcing someone from his or her home always is, no matter what the reason.

I recall the rest of Fifer's instructions. 'Walk to the third beam, beside the painting of peaches in a silver bowl,' she'd fairly spat at me. 'Kick the bottom – what I'd like to do to you – to release the hinge. Then push. It'll lead you to the wizard pit, and to the Azoth.'

Wizard pits. Small, secret chambers built into homes throughout Anglia to protect men and women from the Inquisition, from the witch hunters, from me. Some I'd seen accessed through gaps in staircases, some through false chimneys, others through the privy. Most were skill-less, easy to find. This one is masterful.

I pluck a candle from my bag, light it with another one of my matches, and slip through the narrow gap beneath the beam, finding myself in a small room, maybe six feet square. There's nothing here – no furniture, no adornments. It's completely bare, save for a wooden panel built into the brick wall, narrow and shut and locked.

Tucked into the seam is a note from Nicholas.

Elizabeth, it says. *If you're reading this, I ask you to reconsider what you're about to do. There are some matters that are too great, even for you.*

This stills me.

The care he's taken of me since I entered his life, it's more than I expected of the man who was once my enemy, a man I once would have killed. He has not become like a father to me, not like Peter; he would never be that. But he is a protector and a saviour, both of which I am in exceedingly short supply of as late. Even so, his warning falls short.

It is not enough to stop me.

I fold the note back up, tuck it in my bag alongside all of John's, and fish out a cluster of silver thistles. Fifer assured me there would be magic on this panel, a spell or curse to keep me out if Nicholas's words failed, and thistle would help to reduce the harmful effects. It'll still be painful – she assured me of that, too – but I can endure a little pain to get what I need.

I drive my thumb deep into a barb at the tip of the stem, drawing a drop of blood to ignite the thistle's magic, and reach for the door. The moment my hand touches the latch there's a spark, a white-hot flash of blue flame, and a sizzling noise as whatever curse it's imbued with leaps into my skin, up my arm, and into my head, ringing and shaking and vibrating and deafening. I feel as if I've got my head stuck inside a cathedral bell. I grit my teeth against the sensation – I've felt worse – and twist the dials on the lock: 25, 12, 15, 42. December 25, 1542. Fifer's birthday.

The door swings open. With some trouble I wrest my hand from the latch, the ringing in my head subsiding enough to allow me to see it, in the shallow depths of the dark cabinet, lying there, alone: a steely corpse in a wooden coffin.

The Azoth.

I reach in, wrap my hand around the hilt. At once I feel it, surging through my skin as if greeting an old friend: the heat and energy of the Azoth's latent curse, dripped into me the last time I used it – when I tried to kill Blackwell and killed Caleb instead. It hums, erratic at first, a flickering beat in my blood before finding its rhythm, one that matches my own heartbeat. A rapid thump that, as the seconds pass, grows slower, steadier, and surer.

A grin steals across my face.

I slide the Azoth into the scabbard beneath my cloak, snatch up my candle, then retrace my steps through the house until I'm outside once more. I step over the bundle of still-smoking herbs on the threshold, and pull a single mint leaf from my pocket, dropping it in the centre. Mint increases energy, and it will help make Hastings's return easier. It wasn't part of Fifer's plan, but I do it anyway: a weak apology.

I'm meant to meet Schuyler in the early hours before dawn, at the desolate crossroads between Theydon Bois and Gallion's Reach, before making our way south through the Mudchute, east out of Harrow, and on to Upminster. But it's not yet midnight, and it's a short distance to our meeting place, maybe forty-five minutes. I've got hours before I need to be there. So I start off on the second part of the plan, thought of and devised by me but wholly unbeknownst to Fifer.

I will go to Hexham to find Malcolm and that student, Keagan. They both just came from Upminster, and they were both just inside Fleet, managing to make it out without detection. They may know things about the city, about Blackwell, about his guard, and about his protection. It could mean the difference between me returning victorious or never returning at all.

SIXTEEN

At Hexham, a complement of guards mills about the door, six that I can see: four in grey cloaks, two in black. I take note of their posture, the way they walk, shift their weapons. Listen to snippets of conversation that echo, into the still night sky. The men are tired but not exhausted, bored but not frustrated – at least not enough to become restless. Restlessness can lead to gambling, sparring, or fighting, that burst of energy making them jumpy and nervy, alert to things that aren't there.

Or that are.

I move north along the wall, cutting left at the junction, until I'm facing the back of the prison. I run my hand along the wall: rough, knobby, and dry, not at all like Fleet. The walls there were always damp and slick with black mould. I sling my bag across my back, secure the Azoth at my side. Plunge my hands into the dirt along the ground, gathering grit for traction. Then I dig my toes into the grooves in the stone and begin to climb.

The walls are high, thirty feet at least, but it's not a hard climb and I reach the top a few moments later, perching along the narrow ledge. I look around, listen. No guards heard me, none of the Watch saw me. There's a certain irony in that, and my earlier grin is back.

Below me is a clearing between the wall and the prison, maybe six feet wide, running the length of the building. There are no doors on this side, only a dozen or so windows, large and unbarred. There's a possibility one of them is unlocked; the day I visited John I recall a few of them were open, filling the hall with frigid air.

I scurry down the wall. Pause, dash across the clearing to the first window. Locked. The second window is also locked, as is the third. And the fourth. My heart speeds up, my breath comes fast. If the guards were to come around the corner, they'd see me, and I'd have to explain what I'm doing here in the dead of night. They could detain me, they could learn where I'm going, they could take away the Azoth.

I run to the last window, the sixth one, slip my fingers under the ledge, and pull. It opens. I nearly laugh with relief, hauling myself in and over the ledge. Inside, an empty cell. Locked, but that poses no problem. I tug a pin from the knot in my hair – tucked there for just this reason – and slide it into the keyhole. A click, a twist, and a pull, and the barred door swings open. I shake my head. The magic on Hexham exists to keep those marked as prisoners inside, and visitors, guards – and, in this case, intruders

– out. Even so, it really is a most unsecure prison. If I survive killing Blackwell, I'll have to bring this up with Nicholas.

I search the corridor for Keagan and Malcolm. They're not on the first floor; every last cell is empty. I find the stairs, take them quietly, and make my way down another wide, moonlit hall. I pass cell after empty cell, confusion rising with every step.

Were they not taken here? Did Peter convince them to place them elsewhere so as not to be near John, somewhere like Gareth's? Did Nicholas have them removed – knowing, the way he knew I would go after the Azoth, that I would come here looking for information?

Or, worse: Was tonight's council meeting a ruse for yet another trial, an excuse to put Malcolm in that hard-backed chair, chains on his wrists and snapping lions at his feet, subject of an interrogation and a scryed, watery verdict? Malcolm is nothing to me. But he is the king of Anglia, the rightful king. Not a common criminal, not a traitor.

Not like me.

I keep searching. But as I approach the end of the still-empty hall, my footsteps slow. Because every cell that ticks by brings me closer to the one at the end. John's. Finally I stop, unsure whether to continue or to leave.

'I know you're there.' That girlish, Airann-accented voice calls from the end of the hall. 'No sense hiding it. Come on, then, show yourself.'

I hesitate a moment longer, then step in front of the cell the voice is coming from, two from the end. Keagan stands there, leaning into the wall beside the cell door. 'Well, well. If it isn't the little sparrow. Bess, is it?'

I glance in the direction of John's cell, then back at Keagan. She's watching me closely, a grin pressing dimples into her cheeks.

'Elizabeth,' I say. 'If you don't mind.'

'Why should I mind? It's your name.' Keagan shrugs. 'I was just going off what Your Former Highness calls you.'

'Bess!' Malcolm's face appears then, pressed between the bars of the cell between Keagan's and John's. His dark hair is mussed, the way he looks when he wakes. I turn my head from it, and from him. 'What are you doing here? How did you get in?' He looks around me into the corridor. 'Where are the guards?'

'The guards are occupied,' I say. 'I let myself in.'

'Did you now?' Keagan says. 'Why would you do that? It's late, and this is a prison. You should be home, asleep.'

'You've just come from Upminster,' I say, going straight to the point. 'I need to know what's happening there. How the city is being guarded, and by whom. What Blackwell's doing. How you got in and out of Fleet without detection.'

The grin Keagan has worn since I arrived slides from her face. It ages her like a spell, the amused girl at once becoming a suspicious woman. 'And why would you want to know that?'

'Tell me the information I want to know, and I'll tell you what I plan to do with it.'

Her bright eyes rake over me. They take in my tight black trousers, tall black boots, my hair pulled tightly back, the bag slung across my shoulder. Then they land on the bulge beneath the folds of my cloak, where the Azoth is hitched to my waist.

'What are you up to, little sparrow?'

'Fine, I'll bite,' I say. 'Why do you keep calling me that?'

'You're a little thing, aren't you? Too little to pay mind to, some might say. Some might even take you for granted. But I say different.' She cocks her head. 'I think the things people think you can't do are what gives you your advantage.' A pause. 'Why do you want to know what's happening in Upminster?'

'That's my concern. Not yours.'

'Another thing about sparrows,' Keagan continues conversationally, 'is that in some cultures, they're seen as harbingers of death.'

I glare at her; she grins back.

'Have you come to break us out?' Malcolm's face is still pressed against the bars, his eyes still on my face. He doesn't see what Keagan sees, what's right in front of him. But then, he never did. 'You are, aren't you? I knew you would come for me, I knew it.'

'*Shhh.*' Keagan waves her hand in Malcolm's direction. 'You're going in, aren't you?' she says to me. 'To Ravenscourt. You're going to find him.' Her eyes once more land on the sword beneath my cloak. 'You're going to try to kill him.'

'What? No.' Malcolm reaches for me and without thinking, I step away. Keagan's eyes follow the movement, her teeth catching her bottom lip; an incongruous gesture.

'You can't do that. It's too dangerous. You don't know what Upminster's like now.'

'Which is precisely why I've come. To find out.' I step closer to Keagan; she steps closer to me. 'Blackwell's after us now, you know that. He's after –' I stop. I nearly say me, I nearly say *John*. I nearly say *the stigma*. 'Them. And he won't stop until he gets them, unless someone stops him first.'

'Interesting.' Keagan wraps her hands around the bars. Her fingers are long and slim, but her nails are short and ragged; they look bitten off. 'First you said us, then you said *them*. Which is it, sparrow?'

'I don't have time to play games,' I snap. 'You can tell me what I want to know, which helps you, which helps your Order. Or you can keep this information to yourself, which helps no one. You've got sixty seconds to decide, or else I'm leaving.'

She hesitates only five.

'I'll tell you what you want to know,' Keagan says. 'But first, you tell me what I want to know. Anything I want to know.'

There's something sly about Keagan. She wants to trade in information, the way all watchers, players, spies, and operatives do. But something tells me the information she's looking for isn't political.

'Fine. Ask me what you want. One thing,' I stipulate.

'What are you doing here?' Keagan says. 'And I don't mean here, in this prison. I mean here, in Harrow. With them. *Us*.' Her smile is once again gone, the woman once again returning. 'What is a witch hunter – former witch hunter – doing sleeping with the enemy?'

I scowl at her words, forked as a serpent's tongue and no accident.

'I was arrested,' I say shortly. 'Nicholas rescued me.'

'I know that,' Keagan says, impatient. 'Everyone knows that. Your little story is becoming quite the legend in our world. But as with all legends, there are untruths. I want to know what they are.'

'Why?' I say. 'What does any of this have to do with what I'm here for?'

'Because I need to know if I can trust you,' Keagan replies. 'I can't trust you with what I know unless I can trust you.'

I turn around then; I almost leave.

'Your debt was repaid,' Keagan says to my back. 'A life for a life, so they say. But you're not liked here, you can't be. Yet you stay on, and now this.' A pause. 'I know you'll say Blackwell is after you, but I also know that's only part of it. I want to know the rest of it.'

'I stayed because I thought I belonged.' I don't look to him, but I think of him anyway, at the cell at the end of the hall, poisoned by the stigma I gave him and hating me for it.

'And now?'

I don't know. The answer belongs to me, but it also belongs to him: John if he can find a way to forgive me, Blackwell if he'll allow me to live; Schuyler if he'll help me to return, Nicholas if he'll permit me to stay if I do.

‘I told you what you wanted to know,’ I say instead. ‘Now you tell me. A deal’s a deal.’

‘This wasn’t about a deal. It was about trust. It’s always about trust, sparrow. Don’t ever forget that.’ She smiles then. ‘And I trust you. You’re tough, and I like you. Lose that sweet, fresh-faced-daisy look, you could be a real warrior.’

I step to the bars, grip them hard. The Azoth, sensing my anger, fires its solidarity hot and fast against my side.

‘You think you know something about me; you know nothing,’ I say. ‘And I don’t give a damn either way. You tell me what I want to know or I swear to you, imprisonment will be the least of your problems.’

I reach beneath my cloak, place one hand on the hilt of the Azoth, pushing the fabric aside just enough for her to see the emeralds glinting in the dim light. If she’s heard my story, she’ll have heard of the Azoth’s, too: No legend is complete without a legendary sword.

Keagan’s eyes widen. She goes quiet and she stays quiet, a goddamned prodigy.

‘Troops,’ she says finally. ‘Blackwell’s got them, of course, mobilising in the south. Your old contingent. Witch hunters. Knighted now, but hunters nonetheless.’

‘I knew that,’ I say. ‘Continue.’

‘They keep guard at Ravenscourt around the clock. West, at the gate. North, where it meets the Shambles. South by the Severn River has no physical protection, but it does have magical. The gargoyles embedded in the walls? They’re enchanted now. If they see an intruder, they screech.’

I think rapidly, turning over the layout of Ravenscourt in my head. The south garden by the Severn River was going to be my route in. Unless…

'How far do they see?' I say. 'All the way to the Severn? Beyond?'

'We've not gotten close enough to find out,' Keagan replies. 'Fleet is full of people who got too close.'

'Is Blackwell there full-time?' I ask. 'At Ravenscourt, I mean? Has he left Greenwich altogether?'

She nods. 'We've been tracking his movements. He's not been back to Greenwich since the night of the masque. No one has seen him. He's not made any public appearances; well, except the one. Where he was crowned at Leicester Abbey.'

So he's done it: made it official. Malcolm swipes a hand across his dark jaw, not in resignation but in anger.

'I can help you.' Keagan's voice is low, persuasive. 'I could help you get in and out of the city. I've done it before. I could help you kill him.'

I step back from her cell. Rearrange the folds of my cloak over the Azoth.

'You can't help me. I wouldn't want your help, even if you could. You got yourself caught.' I allow myself a small, recriminating smile. 'Perhaps you can tell me more about being a real warrior another time.'

'Sparrow, crafty as a magpie.' Keagan's smile is nearly feral. 'Stand back.'

'What?'

'Stand back, Bess.' At the sound of Malcolm's voice,

at the command in it, I do.

Keagan raises her hands, palms flat, toward the cell door. Mutters something, an incantation by the sound of it, only I can't make out the words. Intrigued despite myself, I watch the skin on her hands turn orange, then red, then white. The air around her palms shimmers with light, with heat; I can feel it, even from where I'm standing.

Then: fire.

A rope of it shoots first from one palm, then the other. They meet in the middle, twisting and turning together before hurtling toward the door. The bars turn the same colour as her hands – orange, red, white – and with a small sizzle, like fat in a frying pan, they simply disappear, collapsing into a molten pile of smoking metal.

'Come on, little sparrow.' Keagan steps over the rubble into the hall. 'Time to fly.'

SEVENTEEN

I step in front of her, blocking her path. 'You're not coming with me.'

'Considering I've already broken out, I really don't have much choice,' she replies. 'If I hang around here, I'll just get tossed back in and I'd rather not go through that again.' Keagan snatches her borrowed black cloak from the bench and pushes past me into the hall.

I scowl. This situation is rapidly spiralling out of control.

'You'll never get out of here,' I say. 'Hexham's guarded by more than just men. There's a spell on it. Only those who aren't prisoners are free to come and go. You can't leave.'

'One problem at a time, sparrow.'

'If they find you, they'll catch you.'

'Which *they* is this, now?'

'All of them!' I lower my voice to something resembling reason. 'If you're caught again, I can almost guarantee prison will be the least of your worries. I may have pushed him out of the way of a sword' – I jerk my head toward Malcolm's cell – 'but I'm not doing the same for you.'

'They won't kill me,' Keagan says. 'And they're not going to catch us, because there's no chance they'll think we're going right back to the place we just escaped from.'

'There's no *we*,' I say. 'There is no *us*.'

Keagan moves to Malcolm's cell. A single hand held out this time, aimed at the lock. Before I can utter a word of protest there's a sizzling sound, a clank, and the door swings wide open. But before Malcolm can exit, I slam it shut.

'Bess!'

I ignore him. 'What are you doing?' I say to Keagan. 'He can't come with us. You're supposed to make sure he lives. Remember? That's what you said. If he dies, Blackwell is rightful king.'

'Aye, I said that,' she replies. 'But if you're going into Upminster to kill one king, you need another to take his place. Killing a monarch has repercussions, you know. If Malcolm's not there, one of Blackwell's men will take over as regent, and we'll be in this all over again. It's not what I planned when I started this, but sometimes plans have a way of making themselves.'

'Is that what you want? What the Order wants?' I cannot voice the traitorous words that come next; I cannot ask her if she wants Malcolm back on the throne, not while he's standing right in front of me.

But I don't need to.

'It doesn't matter what they want,' Malcolm says. 'They don't have a choice.'

'He's right.' Keagan pries my hand off the cell door. 'Current King Thomas or former King Malcolm, that's all the choice we've got. Scylla and Charybdis, to be sure. But things would be different this time.' She swings the door open, sweeps her arm in an ushering gesture. 'Malcolm takes the throne again, he won't forget who saved him, and who got him there. Isn't that right, Your Majesty?'

Malcolm's expression is cut glass. 'It's one of many things I won't forget.' He spins on his dusty boot heel and strides down the prison hall as if it were an aisle to the throne. Keagan raises a pale eyebrow, then starts after him.

I don't follow, not right away. Because I can feel John's eyes on me, as certain as if it were his hand on my shoulder. I turn around and see him standing by the door to his cell, half lit by shadows. For a moment we stare at each other; I still can't reconcile the change in him. His eyes dark and cold, shadowed as if someone's smeared dirt beneath them; the furrow between his brows no longer a guest but a resident.

I don't give him a chance to turn from me first. I don't give him the chance to throw one last barb at me, as if the sting from the others weren't painful enough. So even before Malcolm can whisper another 'Bess!' from the end of the hall, I walk away.

Keagan, Malcolm, and I huddle together at the bottom of the stairs. From where we stand we can make out the door that leads into the courtyard, locked and guarded by the same man I saw earlier. He's leaning against the bars, watching the others play some kind of game. There's the sound of something heavy hitting the dirt, one after the other, then laughter and cheering.

'Are they playing bowls?' Malcolm whispers.

Keagan kicks the wall once, twice. The guard idling by the door turns at the noise, frowns, pulls out a sword. Unlocks the door and steps inside, blade out.

'What are you doing?' I hiss. 'He may not know any magic. Not everyone in Harrow does, you know. He may not be able to let us out.'

'*Shhh.*'

The guard draws near. He's three feet away, two, when Keagan leaps out from behind the wall, pulls him into a headlock, then drags him into the stairwell. His eyes go wide with recognition.

'Lift the spell,' Keagan orders. 'Let us out.'

'I can't,' the guard whimpers. 'I don't know any magic.'

'Untrue,' she says. 'You cast a spell on that guard to make him miss his target, because you have a wager with the other guard across the yard.'

'How…how do you know that?'

Keagan's neat white teeth are bared in a grin. 'When a man watches bowls as if it were blood sport, it's always down to finances. Now. Let us out and I'll let you keep your secret. And your winnings.'

The guard curses under his breath. In the next he utters some kind of spell, an incantation. A wasplike buzz stirs the hall, then goes silent.

'You've got ten minutes,' he says.

Keagan grabs the back of his cloak and shoves him down

the corridor. She finds an empty cell, pushes him inside, and fuses the lock with a blast of heat from her hand.

'Show us the way, sparrow.'

I lead them to the cell and the open window I came in through. We climb up and over it and, once outside, make our way across the short clearing to the outer prison wall.

'I scaled it,' I tell Keagan. 'To get in. I don't think we can do the same to get out. You might be able to, but I don't think he will.' I nod to Malcolm.

'You'd be surprised at what I can do,' he says.

'I'm sure I would not, my lord.' Keagan pulls a face at my servility. But formality is the only weapon I have against him, the only weapon I ever had.

He approaches the wall with the same arrogant posture with which he approaches everything. Spits in one hand, rubs it together with the other, and places both along the stone, feeling for a hold. Keagan throws me a glance; I shrug. Maybe he can do it.

Malcolm begins to climb. To my great surprise, he does it easily, makes it three feet above the ground, five, ten. I move to the wall, too, hoisting my bag over my shoulder before swiping my palm cautiously along the sand, lathering my hands with grit. Beside me Keagan does the same, then starts up the wall beside him. But I don't go, not yet.

About twenty feet up, Malcolm's foot hits scree. He shifts his weight to compensate, but the stone doesn't hold and breaks from the wall in a soundless fall, hitting the ground below with a thump. Malcolm hangs by his hands, his feet dangling in midair, reaching and stretching for another hold. He doesn't find one.

In a breathless moment he falls, silent; I think of the things he's going to break when he lands: a foot, a leg, his knee, or even his back. But he lands on his feet, dropping and rolling to absorb the impact, the way I know to do but had no idea he did.

Malcolm rises and brushes the dirt from his trousers. He doesn't look hurt; he doesn't even look embarrassed.

'You could have broken something,' I say. 'How did you learn to climb like that?'

Malcolm shrugs. 'I spent nearly every night of my thirteenth year inside taverns in the Shambles,' he tells me. 'I assure you they were not sanctioned visits.'

'An enthralling tale.' Keagan drops to the ground beside him, nimble as a cat. 'But now you've cost us time. And if you had broken something, you'd have cost us even more. And I assure you, I'm carrying you nowhere.' She bites her lip in thought. 'I'll just have to create a distraction.'

We tread along the prison wall until we reach the edge. The guards' laughter and the thudding of rocks echo across the empty, shadowed courtyard. Keagan points to a small guard building posted along the front.

'I'm going to set it on fire,' she says. 'A small one at first, so it doesn't look intentional. Just know, though, it won't be long before they figure out it is.'

'And then what?' I say.

'Look for my signal,' she replies. 'You'll know it when you see it. And when you do, run. Straight for the front gate, as fast as you can.'

'Don't hurt anyone,' I tell her.

'I won't.' Keagan runs across the courtyard, disappearing into the shadows. I can just make out her crouched figure, edging toward the guardhouse. I keep my eye on her but I'm acutely aware of Malcolm edging up behind me, his shoulder pressed against mine.

'Bess.' His voice, whispered in the dark, sends a rope of tension up my spine.

'My lord?' I don't turn around.

'Are you really going to kill him? Uncle?' A pause. 'I can't ask you to do that for me.'

'I'm not doing it for you.' The words come out before I find the sense to stop them. 'It has nothing to do with you.'

Silence. A shoulder that goes stiff beside mine.

'Majesty.' I spin around, dip into a hasty but always clumsy curtsy. 'My apologies. I did not mean to speak out of turn. But these are…' I fumble around the foolish niceties, unpractised of late. 'Trying times.'

Malcolm blinks at me, twice and fast, as if he's clearing something from his eyes. 'No apologies necessary.' Then he nudges my arm and points behind me. 'Look.'

A single tiny bird made of flame flits through the sky, zigzagging its way to the prison gate before alighting upon the square iron lock. The metal begins to glow a faint red: It's melting. With a wink, the bird disappears and though I can't see, I know the gate is now unlocked.

'Was that our signal?' Malcolm whispers. 'She doesn't mean run now, does she?'

I hesitate. The guards are still playing bowls; they're not

thirty feet from the gate. If we run now they will see us, but we may not get another chance.

'My lord,' I say. 'Run.'

We make it five steps, maybe ten, when it happens: A rumble, a crack, and the front door of the guardhouse is blown wide open, flames pouring from within.

'Ho!' a guard shouts. They all drop their stones and rush toward the building. But they don't know what to do, not really; they stop halfway there, heat and confusion making them wince. They don't see us so we keep running.

Twenty feet from them. Ten. A glance at Malcolm confirms he's slowing down. I reach for his sleeve, yanking it hard just as a wall of fire erupts beside us, tall and wide and crackling hot. The entrance is free and clear in front of us. There's a pounding of footsteps as Keagan appears and the three of us sprint through the gate. She pulls it shut and with another handful of red-hot flames, she melts the lock, trapping the guards inside. I can see the fire rising higher and higher into the sky.

'We can't leave them there,' I say. 'They'll burn, the prison will burn. John—' I turn around; I start to go back. Keagan swipes her hand through the air and at once the crackling red sky turns black once more. I can't see it but I can smell it: the lingering scent of smoke, the acrid stench that reminds me of Tyburn, and of death.

'I said I wouldn't hurt anyone.' She snatches the back of my cloak and pushes me into the field, away from Hexham. 'And I'm of my word.'

'But the smoke—'

'Will clear. It's not enough to incapacitate. But I can't have you running back in there. We've got fifteen minutes, I wager, before they figure out what's happened. We need to be long gone before then.'

I lead them over dark, sloping meadows and through brackets of trees to reach the crossroads where I'm to meet Schuyler. We have to stop a few times for Malcolm to catch his breath. He said the fall didn't hurt but the way he favours one leg tells me different.

Judging by the position of the moon, already beginning to dip west, it's maybe two in the morning. I'm not due to meet Schuyler until five. But when we come upon the intersection of two small roads and the low, broken stone wall nearby, I'm not at all surprised to see him lounging there, a pale silhouette against the night sky. He sees us approaching and hops off the wall, his boots crunching against the frozen grass.

'Well, you've really done it now, bijoux,' Schuyler says by way of greeting. 'Breaking this lot out of jail, practically burning the place down. I don't recall this being part of our plan.'

'Believe me, it wasn't.'

His eyes land on Keagan, bright and menacing. 'You're trouble,' he says. 'I don't like trouble.'

Keagan laughs, not afraid of him in the slightest. 'You're a revenant, are you not? By my measure, I should think you live for it.'

Schuyler turns from her laughter to face Malcolm. But Malcolm does not flinch, does not step away.

'And what of you?' Schuyler says. 'Do you plan on causing me trouble, too?'

'I don't answer to you,' Malcolm says levelly. 'In the future, I'll thank you to address me as sire. Or lord. Or Majesty.'

'I'll be in hell first.'

'You're a revenant, are you not?' Malcolm repeats Keagan's words and the sarcasm in them. 'By my measure, I should think not even hell will have you.'

'Enough.' I step between them. 'If this is to work, and God knows that's question enough, it'll be without your childish bickering.'

Malcolm blinks, that bewildered look again. He's never understood me, that's true, but he understands me even less now, outside the palace and outside his rule; outside the part he's written for me that I no longer play.

Schuyler reaches down, picks up several canvas bags I didn't see before. He tosses one to Keagan, who catches it with ease, and the other to Malcolm, who doesn't. The bag hits the ground, spilling its contents all over the grass: clothes, a waterskin, a bundle of linen filled with food, and a cache of weapons.

'Fifer's idea,' Schuyler says, before I can ask. 'I told her what happened. She's still angry with you, so don't get it in your head that she's not. But she said you couldn't very well take these two into Upminster looking like that. So she packed some provisions.' He pulls out another carefully wrapped package from his bag and hands it to me.

'Your lady did this?' Keagan's already rifling through her

bag, grinning as she pulls out bread, cheese, and an array of fruit. She crams an apple into her mouth, groaning as she chews. 'She is kind, delightful, an angel.'

'She is absolutely none of those things,' Schuyler says shortly. 'Now hurry up and eat. We need to get as far as we can tonight, in case the Watch decides to come after us.'

Fifer may still be angry with me, but it doesn't escape my notice that she packed my favourite foods: strawberries and cold quail and soft bread and hard cheese. It didn't come from the camp at Rochester, that's for certain. I'm filled with unexpected warmth at the lengths she must have gone through to get it.

Malcolm, Keagan, and I eat quickly – revenants don't need to eat – then repack our bags before making our way through the Mudchute and its wide-open fields, broken only by the occasional farm or cluster of livestock. We walk until the sun begins to rise, the grey sky turning orange and yellow around the edges, until our eyes and backs droop with exhaustion and cold.

We come upon a small, recessed valley near a small brook, under a copse of trees. It's enough to shelter us from the wind and the rain that's beginning to leak from the leaden skies. Schuyler pulls a tarp from his bag and strings it across two trees. Keagan conjures a blast of heat to dry the damp grass, then a low, smokeless fire that heats the space to the warmth of a summer's day.

We stretch out along the ground, tucking our bags beneath our heads. The warm air, the crackle of the fire, and the patter of rain on the tarp soothe and relax me. My lids droop, and I'm nearly asleep when he whispers my name.

'Bess.'

My eyes fly open. Malcolm's voice, soft and close to me, even in daylight, makes me stiffen. Across the clearing, Schuyler watches me carefully.

'Are you awake?'

I could say nothing; I could say *Go to hell.* He's no longer the king and I'm no longer his mistress: I am no longer beholden to him and I owe him nothing. But the habit of obeisance is too ingrained now; the pattern too set. I don't know any other way of interacting with him.

'I'm awake.' I pull to a sit beside him. His arms are wrapped around his knees, and he's shivering despite his woollen cloak and the warmth of the air. 'Is there something the matter?'

'No,' he replies. 'Not entirely. There's just something I want to ask you. Something I need to know.'

The uncertainty in his tone makes me cautious. 'Of course.'

'Why didn't you tell me about the herbs? The ones you were arrested with,' he clarifies, as if he needs to. 'I could have helped you, if you'd told me. I could have done something.'

As if he hadn't already done enough.

'What could you have done?' I say instead. 'You were the king, a persecuting king. I was a witch hunter. I made my living enforcing your laws. I wasn't going to lay them at your doorstep.'

'You were more than a witch hunter to me.' His eyes and

his words are pleading. 'You are more than that. And I thought – hoped – I was more than the king to you. You could have told me,' he insists. 'I would have done everything I could to save you.'

There's a world of malevolent naïveté in his words. He couldn't save his throne, he couldn't save himself, he couldn't save his own wife. How could he have saved me?

'You could have saved me by leaving me alone,' I say, honest at last. 'I was fifteen when you first summoned me. I was frightened, and you were king. I had no business being your mistress, but you left me no choice.'

Malcolm opens his mouth, closes it. Across the fire, Keagan's eyes join Schuyler's, the pair of them watching us in mute fascination.

'It's not true,' he says finally. 'I invited you to my chambers, yes. But you were free to say no. You were free to go anytime.'

All I can do is look at him. Because the idea of me saying no to him, to any of it, is so impossible that I know not even he can believe it.

'I knew you were hesitant,' Malcolm admits. 'But I thought, at least at first, that you were simply nervous. I wanted so much to put you at ease, and I thought I did. I thought we were becoming friends. And then I thought –' He breaks off, swiping a hand across his jaw. 'It's something else I didn't see, isn't it?' He says this last part more to himself than to me.

'Your Majesty—'

'Don't call me that.'

'But you're the king.' He says nothing to this, so I add, 'You are the king.'

'Then as the king, I dismiss you,' he says. 'You're dismissed.' He gets to his feet and walks from the clearing into the rain, away from Keagan and Schuyler, and away from me.

EIGHTEEN

The next two days are a blur of walking at night and sleeping during the day. Since he dismissed me, Malcolm has said little, if anything, to me or to anyone else. He keeps to himself: sleeping alone, eating alone, walking alone. But his silence is a warning to me, and I'm always alert to where he is, what he's doing, what he might do next.

Through Fifer, Schuyler tells us that the Watch knows we're gone, but they don't know where. They suspect Keagan and Malcolm have made off for Cambria, and they've sent a contingent of men after them. Most of Harrow believes I've defected, that after what I did to John I saw my opportunity to leave Harrow and took it. They believe Schuyler simply deserted, and neither Fifer nor Nicholas stands to correct them.

By the morning of the third day, we've passed the barrier of Harrow, marked by a dozen signs graffitied with etchings of skulls and crossbones, flames and crosses.

From here it's a single day's walk southeast through Hainault and the southern tip of Walthamstow into the city of Upminster. We reach the outskirts just as the sun begins to dip below the horizon, and here we make camp for the night.

At dawn, we eat the rest of Fifer's carefully packed food, drink the last of the water. One by one we dash behind a copse of trees and change into clothing packed especially for this part of the trip.

For Schuyler and Malcolm there are coarse woollen trousers, muslin tunics, scuffed boots, and unshaven faces. For Keagan and me, threadbare brown woollen dresses and plain leather slippers, our hair stuffed beneath white linen caps. We look simple, as nondescript as servants. Specifically, Ravenscourt servants.

Underneath our clothing, though, we're anything but. All four of us are strapped with weapons: knives in our boots, tucked in belts beneath our dresses and tunics, and for me, the Azoth, secured in a sheath tied around my waist under my skirt. I can feel it calling to me, the invitation to violence hot and thrumming against my skin, not an altogether unpleasant sensation.

'We've been lucky thus far.' Keagan grimaces as she adjusts the ties on her cap. Without her short, wild hair on display, she looks more like a girl, a young girl at that, and she knows it. 'Since we left Harrow, we've seen and heard nothing. I don't mean to be alarmist, but this doesn't seem right to me.'

Schuyler, standing off to the side checking and

rechecking his weapons, looks to me. 'You think Blackwell knows we're coming?'

I consider it. I thought we had the element of surprise when we snuck into Greenwich Tower all those months ago, dressed as guests for the masque. I thought we had him fooled when all along, he knew. He was just waiting for the right opportunity.

'I don't know,' I admit. 'I thought we'd run into something, at least. Troops, guards…when I was a witch hunter, Blackwell had us patrolling every night, in every village within a fifty-mile radius of Upminster.'

'Well, the laws are different now, aren't they?' Schuyler says.

'Not that different,' I reply.

We pick our way through tiny hamlets, down the varying mud-soaked high streets lined with half-timbered buildings and stone cottages that grow progressively larger and more densely packed together the closer we come to the city. Still, nothing seems out of the ordinary. Men and women going about their daily lives: merchants pushing carts, laundry maids lugging baskets, doors and shutters open in each tavern and shop we pass. So far, it would appear that we're not being followed. But I think of the masque again, how everything seemed welcoming then, too.

Upminster seems the same as it was the last day I was here, the last day I walked free. A good deal better, actually, because today there are no protests, no crowds, no burnings. The air is filled with the scent of mud and dung, leather and livestock; the sound of shouts and laughter, wheels on cobblestone.

I glance at Schuyler. I know by the set of his shoulders, rigid and tall, that he's listening, picking through the minds of those around us, trying to pluck danger from the air as if it were petals on a breeze. Keagan, too, is on guard; her dress and her cap and her girlish, freckled face belie the hunt in her eyes, the way she looks to every corner as if she expects to be ambushed.

'I hear nothing,' Schuyler says, before I can ask. 'Everyone around us, they seem calm. No anger, no deceit, at least not above and beyond the usual. See that bloke over there?' He jerks his head at the merchant on the corner leaning on his broom handle. 'He's trying to figure how to tell his wife of twenty years that he's leaving her for a boy of twenty years. Meanwhile his wife' – he flicks his finger at a woman across the street lounging against an empty door frame, eyes closed and looking vaguely ill – 'she's working up the nerve to tell him she's fifteen weeks gone with her fifth baby, only this time it's not his.'

'Trouble won't appear before us,' Keagan says. 'It'll creep behind us, in shadows and around corners. It'll show itself the moment we look away, believing we're safe.'

'Where to, then?' Malcolm asks. 'If danger is everywhere?'

'A secret's safest place is in the open. So that's where we go: into the open.' Keagan lowers her voice. 'We're going to walk straight through the front gates of Ravenscourt.'

'Excuse me,' Schuyler says. 'I was listening for sound advice. But what I heard was the ramblings of a lunatic.'

'There's no sense in subterfuge,' Keagan says. 'There's

magical protection all over this palace, everywhere we turn. You don't see it because you're not meant to. The lanterns atop the gates? The flames are enchanted to flare green if they detect deception. The statues that line the promenade? They're hexed to come alive and attack.'

I think of them: the stone knights on horseback bearing swords, the gryphons carrying staffs, the horses fitted with horns on their heads as pointed and deadly as lances.

'I've seen them jump down and skewer men through the chest,' Keagan goes on. 'I've seen them take to the sky, only to plunge down and pluck men from the street, carrying them God only knows where.'

Schuyler and I exchange a rapid glance.

'You didn't tell us it was like this,' I say to her. 'You only told us about the gargoyles.'

'If I'd told you, would you have changed your plan? No.' She answers for me. 'It would have changed nothing.'

We walk along the Severn River, the waters frothy with activity: wherrymen carrying passengers on skiffs close to shore; fleets of larger ships clogging the deeper waterways, masts high, sails fluttering in the salty grey sky. Cut through the Shambles, a bankside maze of narrow, dark alleyways full of taverns and tabling houses, drunks and bawds. Malcolm draws his cap over his eyes to avoid recognition.

Finally, we emerge onto Westcheap Road, the large, main thoroughfare that leads directly to Ravenscourt, teeming with people and livestock, merchants and patrons. We pass the once-crowded square at Tyburn, now empty – no people, no scaffolds, no chains – all the way to palace gates, wide open but hardly welcoming.

Ravenscourt is large, the biggest of Malcolm's – now Blackwell's – royal palaces. Built from red brick and stone with depressed arches, elegant tracery, soaring stained glass windows, and its many flag-topped towers and spires, it sprawls across fifty acres alongside the banks of the Severn, a forty-bedroomed home to the over one thousand members of court.

The last time I stood here it was among men and women protesting, shouting against the king; they even had sledgehammers, breaking apart the stone tablets that hung from the iron posts, tablets that declared the laws of Anglia. Those tablets are gone now, along with the laws, along with the king, along with reason.

'Keep moving,' Keagan says without breaking stride. 'Don't slow down, don't hesitate, don't look around. Keep your mind blank, as empty as you can. Whatever you do, don't think anything violent.'

'What about the lanterns?' I look at them lining the promenade before us, the flames within stirring softly, each a different shade of yellow, pink, red. 'You said they turn green if they pick up deception. They'll change colour the moment we walk through.'

'If you're walking into Ravenscourt, your mind is already set to deceive,' Keagan says. 'It's the degree of deception it's attuned to. Cheating husbands thinking about their mistresses will get a pass. Would-be regicides posing as servants won't – unless they're not thinking about it. So think about something else. Anything else.'

'How do you know this will work?'

'I don't,' Keagan says. 'Now stop talking, stop thinking, and move.'

We pass through the gates, our pace quick with false confidence. Two red-bricked columns, each four feet wide and ten feet tall, are capped with a stone capital and, atop that, a stone lion. They're still; sentinel, all but for the eyes: They roam the crowd around us, all-seeing and unfeeling. Magic crackles around me everywhere I look. The flags atop the spires flap merrily against the grey sky, although there is no breeze. Ravens circle through the air, dipping and wheeling above us like storm clouds, their eyes not yellow but bloodred: hexed and knowing.

Keagan clenches her hands into fists, the only sign of her distress. Schuyler hums something off-key, a song I don't recognise. Beside me, Malcolm whispers. I can't make out the words, but something about their rhythm sounds familiar.

We reach the main entrance and step through the arched door into the central courtyard. The danger here is palpable. I can smell it in the air, sharp with smoke from the kitchens that smells like the pyre. I can hear it in the march of boots on cobblestone; the footsteps of courtiers, petitioners, pages, and servants that sound like the Inquisition. Trouble is everywhere, surrounding us. We are drowning in it.

A fountain lies in the middle of the courtyard, white marble and inset with spouts in the shape of lion heads. When Malcolm was king, the fountain poured red wine all of the day and night; he thought it would be amusing. And it was, with the crowds and the laughter and the constant merriment that surrounded it. Now the merriment is gone and the fountain runs empty, the lees of the wine dried into the marble like rails of blood.

Schuyler abruptly stops humming. Before I can think to wonder why, I hear it: shouts, a thunder of heels, a low murmuring of panic from the men and women around us that rises to a shrill. I whirl around to guards, a half dozen armed and in black, marching toward us, the crowd parting around them like ants before a boot.

Malcolm fumbles for his knife. Schuyler's song turns to a rapid litany of whispered curses while Keagan stands rooted to the spot, her fists curled tight. Only I can see their marbling: orange, red, white; fire at the ready.

The guards descend on a man beside the fountain standing not more than five feet from us. He starts to run. The men give chase but before they reach him, a cloud of the ravens I saw earlier pour from the sky in a swirl of oily feathers, the air rent with their shrieks and dusty, foul stench. They knock him to the ground, rending his navy robes to tatters before turning their claws and beaks to his eyes, his mouth, his face; his screams adding to theirs.

'Go.' Keagan's voice is a hiss in my ear. '*Now.*'

We walk – nothing draws more unwanted attention than a run – through the crowds who watch the scene before them in horrified fascination, to the archways that line the four sides of the courtyard, four to each wall. We pass through the third opening that leads into a dark shadowed hallway.

None of us speaks as we delve deep into the labyrinth that is Ravenscourt – past the lodgings, the offices, through the gate yard, and finally into the kitchen wing. We pass the cofferer, the wine cellar, the spicery, the pastry house, and the meat larders until we emerge outdoors again, into the narrow, dark, cold alley I was steering us toward: Fish Court. It runs directly beside one of Ravenscourt's many kitchens, where fresh fish caught from the Severn are brought and stored, hence the smell and the name. Schuyler and Keagan throw their hands over their noses, and Malcolm clamps a hand over his mouth to stifle a gag.

'Stop that,' I say. 'You're meant to be servants. You're used to this.' I turn to Malcolm, now slumped against the cold brick wall. His hand is no longer over his mouth, but he's bent over at the waist, staring at the ground. He looks as if he's going to vomit, but I don't think it's because of the smell of fish.

'That man the birds attacked,' I say to him. 'Was that who I think it was?'

'Uncle's chaplain,' he confirms. 'He's known him since he was a child. I don't know what he could have done to deserve that.'

'He got in the way,' I say, because that's all it ever comes down to with Blackwell. Malcolm nods, silent; he's beginning to know it, too.

'We're being circled.' Schuyler's watching the blur of black wings wheel above us, those hexed red eyes searching the shadows below. 'Where to next?'

I motion them down the alley, to a green painted door at

the end. On the other side of it is the flesh larder. It's where meat goes to be cured, and it's always, always empty. For good reason: It smells like a slaughterhouse in here.

In the centre of the room is a large grate set into the floor, where the blood drips from the butchered parts of at least fifty carcasses hanging from hooks in the ceiling. I lean down and unfasten it from its sticky moors. The smell that greets me from below is worse than the one that surrounds me.

'I knew you had a plan.' Keagan turns up her freckled nose, an expression that reminds me of Fifer. 'But I didn't think it would turn out to be so foul.'

'Not as foul as getting your eyes plucked out by crows,' I tell her. 'Now get inside.'

She reluctantly lowers herself down, Malcolm and Schuyler following behind, Schuyler spitting out obscenities at the smell. I'm unwittingly reminded of John then, of the way he would swear often and with glee, making me laugh. I wonder if he's still in Hexham, or if they let him out after our escape. I wonder if he is still free with his words, or if he tempers them for her. I wonder if he wonders about me; if he ever thinks of me, in hatred or at all.

'Sparrow.' Keagan peers up at me through the opening, breaking into my thoughts. 'Let's go.'

I fold myself through the grate. Inside, it's rancid. Sticky baths of blood stagnate beneath our feet; cockroaches scurry up the walls, maggots writhe in the dirt. The tiny space branches off into a network of tunnels, and I lead them down one after another – the four of us crawling on our hands and knees, filthy and damp – as we wind beneath the palace.

It is foul down here; Keagan is right. I've only ever been down here once, the night I crept from my room to the docks where I hailed a wherry to take me to the stews, to a ramshackle room in a narrow, timbered building set high above the river. There was a wisewoman there; I heard the kitchen maids talk about her. A woman who could speak to the dead, who could make a boy love a girl, who could bring a baby to a woman, who could keep one away.

She was the one who gave me the pennyroyal and silphium, told me how to stew them for three days under the darkness of a new moon, to mask the pungent smell with peppermint. The one who looked at me as I left and said, 'These herbs, they'll keep you out of trouble. But they won't keep trouble away.'

A wise woman indeed.

Soon enough light begins to squeeze through the darkness, a halo around damp edges. Voices and the sound of footsteps filter down to us: the roasted smell of meat, the sweet scent of pie, and the yeasty warmth of fresh bread as we pass beneath the main palace kitchen, just where we're meant to be.

We set our bags down and prepare to settle in for the night. Keagan warms our clothes with a quick blast of heat, but we don't allow her to start a fire for fear a current will waft its way upward, warming the air and alerting someone to our presence.

The evening hours stretch out before us, made longer by

the cold air, the damp, and the lack of food, made worse by the scent of dinner that lingers long after the kitchen closes. I whisper the plan laid out for tomorrow, every detail and amalgamation of it, nothing left to chance: for me to step into the tiny royal pew, no bigger than a closet, overlooking the chapel with its dark-panelled walls, lush red silk curtains, and richly painted ceilings. Where Blackwell takes matins every morning, where I will wait for him to arrive. Where I will pull out the Azoth and plunge it into his chest and watch his life's blood drain from him, along with his magic, along with the hold he's got on me, on John, on Anglia.

Rest comes uneasy for all of us. Keagan lies along the ground, shifting and turning for hours before finally going still. Schuyler sits against the wall, arms folded across his chest, eyes closed. He's not sleeping; revenants don't need to, but it's the closest thing to it.

Beside me, Malcolm fidgets: crossing and uncrossing his arms, pulling his cloak around his shoulders, raking his hands through his hair. He's shivering but I don't know if it's from nerves or cold. His distress puts me further on edge than I already am, and finally I can't take it any longer.

'What was it you were whispering?' I say. 'Earlier, when we passed down the promenade. It sounded familiar. What was it?'

At the sound of my voice Malcolm jerks his head toward me and, as I'd hoped, stops moving.

'It's the Prayer on the Eve of Battle,' he says. 'Do you know it? *To know you is to live, to serve you is to reign, be our protection in battle against evil…'*

He recites the words and at once, that cadence I recognised before becomes a pledge I wish I hadn't. Frances Culpepper, another of Blackwell's witch hunters, the only other female recruit and my only other friend besides Caleb, used to recite it before our tests. She said it brought her luck; she said it kept her alive. It was the last thing I ever heard her say: Frances didn't make it through our final test.

'I know it.'

'I used to recite it before meetings,' Malcolm continues. 'With the privy council, with parliament, diplomats, councillors, chancellors, pensioners, petitioners, parishioners…'

'So, everyone then.'

He laughs a little. Malcolm's always been free with his laughter, but his voice cracks on it this time, making him sound boyish and vulnerable, as if all his other laughs were just an imitation. Or maybe this one is the imitation.

'It gave me courage, I suppose, and I needed all the courage I could get,' he says. 'Those men, Bess. Elizabeth. They were awful, I can't tell you. Each meeting felt like a battle, it felt like they were after my blood. Who knew? Turns out they actually were.'

I don't say anything to this. Because it's true, because I don't know how he didn't see it before. Blackwell was expert at deceiving Malcolm, yes. But by then Malcolm was already expert at deceiving himself.

'How will it go tomorrow?' Malcolm cups his hands around his mouth, blows into them, rubs his palms together.

'Your plan. Do you think it will work? Or…' He breathes into his cupped hands again.

'It will work,' I say. 'Blackwell will die tomorrow, even if it kills me.'

By my side, the Azoth thrums its approval.

NINETEEN

Inside the distant clock court, a bell chimes three times.

Schuyler nudges my foot but I'm already awake. Three in the morning. Time for us to go. My stomach curls around itself, lurching and tumbling in a dance of anxiety and anticipation and finality.

We pull on our weapons belts and fill them, the sound of metal scraping on stone as we pick up dagger after dagger and stow them inside. They're all but useless against Blackwell, against his men and their magic, but it's all the protection we have.

Not all. I have the Azoth, but it's meant to be used only once: on Blackwell, to finish what I started. I don't need to use it any more than that; any more than that and the curse would set in more than it already has, and I would not be able to stop.

I slide the blade into the belt under my dress. Almost like a whisper, a call, words fill my head and my heart.

You will know the curse of power, it vows. *The curse of strength, of invincibility. The curse of never knowing defeat. Of flaying your enemies, of never knowing another one. As long as you both shall live.*

Schuyler jerks his head in my direction, his eyes wide in alarm. Shakes it once, hard. The voice and the warmth of the Azoth wink out, leaving me cold and uncertain.

'You're sure we'll be alone?' Keagan asks me the same question she asked at least a hundred times last night.

'We won't be alone,' I remind her. 'The scullions and pages will be there, stoking fires. Emptying chamber pots. Strewing rushes. They won't be paying attention to anything but that. Dressed the way I am, I'll blend right in.'

'Are you sure they won't recognise you?' Malcolm's voice, raspy with exhaustion and fear, cuts through the abject darkness.

'At this hour, they'll all be half asleep,' I reply. 'Plus, they're children. They've never seen me before. I haven't worked scullery in years.' Not since I was nine, not since I worked my way up to cooking and serving. The senior servants, were they to see me, would recognise me. But that's not the plan. The plan is to be long gone before they arrive.

'When it's safe for you to come up, I'll tap three times. We'll sneak up the back stairs, into the pages' chamber.'

'What about the pew?' Malcolm says. 'Are you sure Uncle won't be there already? And the magic. Are you sure—'

'I'm sure,' I say. 'And I need you to be sure of it, too. We can't have any doubt, any hesitation. That will kill this plan, and us, as sure as anything. Do you understand?'

The three of them nod in mute agreement.

With a small clank, Schuyler pops the grate open. He holds out a hand and I step into it; he boosts me up and through the opening with ease and at once, I'm in the kitchen. It takes a moment for me to adjust to this: *I'm in the kitchen*. Where I spent my childhood, where I met Caleb. Where this story began and where, if all goes the way I've planned, it will end. The sight of it – cold stone floors, warm brick fireplace, wide expanses of smoke-blackened, white plaster walls – combined with the smell – flour and spice, fire and hearth – is enough to fill me with happiness and sorrow, longing and regret.

It all looks the same. A row of low, rounded bread ovens. Stacks of pots and kettles. Cords of wood stacked high beside the fire. Trestle tables laid with food in various stages of preparation: loaves of bread draped with linen and ready to be baked; a boar carcass impaled with an iron skewer, waiting to be roasted.

I slip into my old morning routine the way I'd slip into an old coat. Sweeping the floors, collecting the old rushes and placing them in a basket beside the back door, dragging in a bundle of fresh ones. A maid no older than ten pokes her head in the door. She sees me doing the work she should be doing but if she's surprised, she's too sleepy to show it. She stifles a yawn with the back of her hand and turns away, off to another chore.

I tap my foot against the floor once, twice, three times.

There's a shuffle and a clank; the grate disappears and Schuyler, Keagan, and Malcolm reappear. I start for the darkened flight of stairs at the far end of the kitchen and gesture for them to follow me.

Upstairs, the pages' chamber. A long, narrow room with an unlit fireplace on one end, a single, closed door on the other. In the centre, a long wooden serving table stacked with goblets and trenchers, linens and cutlery, for the servants to use in preparing Blackwell's breakfast. The room is near black but for a blade of moonlight piercing the bank of square-paned windows, illuminating the pale plaster walls and turning them yellow.

As we pass the table, I run a finger along the rim of a cold pewter goblet and think, just for a moment, how easy it would be to drop in some poison. A salting of Belladonna in a cup or on a plate, just a single taste and it would be over in a five-minute show of spasms and screams, a slowing breath and a stopping heart. It would be easy. Easier, anyway, than what we're about to do.

Schuyler glances at me then, no doubt reading my thoughts. But he shrugs, knowing as I do that poisoning is a faulty plan. Firstly, because we don't have any. But secondly – and most importantly – Blackwell never eats without a page tasting his food first. A man like him knows his enemies, by nature if not by name.

One by one, we file out the door into a long, winding stretch of hall called the gallery. It leads from the pages' chamber on one end of the palace to the king's chambers – now Blackwell's chambers – on the other. I've walked this hall a hundred times, a thousand, when I was summoned to Malcolm, when I was summoned to Blackwell, and it was then as it is now: quiet, empty, dimly lit; only a few flickering torches set into brackets along the wood-panelled walls.

We creep into the silence. Forty, sixty, a hundred paces, passing portrait after portrait, gilded frames filled with oils not of Malcolm or his father or his father before him, not as it was before. Now there are only portraits of Blackwell. On the throne. On the battlefield. Sceptered, crowned, and ermined. I wonder: *When did Blackwell have those painted? And how many months did he store those paintings, so sure of his success that he dared to have them commissioned?*

The gallery turns right, and here we stop. Carefully, I peer around the corner. To the right, a bank of windows overlooks the courtyard below. To the left, a small fireplace with flames burning low, illuminating still more golden portraits of our tarnished king. Beside it, two closed doors lead into the royal pew, a dark-uniformed guard standing sentinel before them. Pike in hand, propped lazily against his shoulder. He's been on shift all night, and he's tired. Even now I see his eyes slip closed, stay closed for a beat, two; then crack open again.

He's easy prey.

I turn to the others. Hold up a hand. They nod; they know what comes next. I round the corner and at once, the guard sees me.

'Halt!' he shouts.

I pretend not to hear him. My eyes are downcast, focussed on the carpet, on the way my leather-clad toes peek from beneath the folds of my brown woollen dress. But my hand is restless, slipping beneath my apron to the Azoth beneath. I wrap my hand around the hilt, violence like the rush of fine wine warming me through.

'I said, halt!' The guard's voice draws closer and, finally, I lift my head. Slow, past his black uniform, past the strangled rose on his chest to his face, eyes now round with recognition.

'You!'

'Me,' I reply. And with that, Schuyler appears beside me. In an instant he's got the guard's head between palms pressed flat and, with a savage twist, breaks his neck with a snap. The guard slumps, Schuyler catches the body, I catch the pike.

Malcolm appears then, Keagan on his heels. He walks straight for the fireplace; Keagan to the portrait on the opposite wall, one of Blackwell on a coal-black steed in the heat of battle. Malcolm kneels before the hearth and, after wrapping his hand with a linen napkin filched from the pages' chamber, reaches inside. He slides his hand up the brick, feeling for a lever that, when released, will pop the latch on a panel hidden behind the portrait Keagan has lifted off the wall. It opens to a circular staircase that runs downstairs and opens into the clock court. This was Malcolm's contribution to our plan. Later, it will be our means of escape. Now, it's our means to hide the guard's body.

'It's stuck.' Malcolm rattles his hand inside the hearth. 'The handle won't lift all the way.'

Schuyler snatches the pike from my hand, rushes across the hall, and jams the tip of it into the crack of the panel's barely visible seam. With a snap and a creak, the panel swings open. He steps back, a grin on his face, his foot knocking against the heavy gold frame of the portrait resting against the wall.

It begins to fall. Keagan, in her haste to stop it from hitting the floor, shoves it back against the wall, but too hard, and the frame slams against the panelling. In the soft predawn silence, the sound travels the hall like a shot.

We freeze.

A beat passes; two, three. I start to relax, I almost do. But then I hear it: the tread of footsteps on carpet. Slow, then fast. The clink of pikes, the murmur of voices. Then they arrive: two guards rounding the corner, followed by two more.

Damnation.

I snatch two, four, six daggers from my weapons belt and send them flying, aiming for necks, eyes, hearts. Two hit, but two miss. Schuyler leaps forward, snapping necks one after the other. But he can't get to them fast enough, not before two of them shout a warning: the last thing they'll ever say.

Two more round the corner. One more dagger, one more snapped neck.

As fast as Schuyler and I kill them, Malcolm and Keagan drag the bodies to the passage in the wall, pushing them inside. But we planned for only two dead guards, maybe three. Not six, now eight.

We are surrounded by bodies and blood. It's everywhere: soaking into the carpet, black as ink, spreading among the rug's woollen vines. It spatters the gilded edge of the painting on the floor, of Blackwell in battle. Only now do I see that he's holding the Azoth, the emeralds in the hilt twinkling in the canvased daylight. As if in response, the blade of it fires hot against my leg, daring me to pull it out. Daring me to use it.

As the guards keep coming, the sounds of shouting, pikes clanking, necks snapping, and gurgled whispers of death filling the hall, I think of it. Think of moving past them down the hall to Blackwell's chambers, where he lies waiting – not sleeping now, not with this madness that's spun out of control – but rising, perhaps dressing, perhaps strapping on a weapon. Perhaps even knowing I'm here, readying to face me.

The Azoth whispers at me to do it, taunts me to use it. And though it is the bearer of curses and bad advice, I heed them anyway: pulling it from its bindings, the sing of the blade against leather more like a scream.

That's when it happens.

Keagan is locked in a fight with a guard, tangled together on the floor. The guard wrests the knife from Keagan's hand. But before he can attack her with it, she rolls toward the fireplace. With a sweep of her hands and a muttered incantation, the nascent flame in the hearth roars to life. It leaps from the brick and hurtles down the gallery, a fiery rope growing larger and larger, twisting and turning and suffocating. It crashes into the guard and sets him alight, his black uniform going up in black smoke.

She kicks him away from her. He smashes against the wall beside the windows and at once, the draperies catch fire. Flames devour the velvet and turn them to smoke that fills the hall, thick and noxious. Malcolm appears then, pulling me to the floor where the air is clearer but not by much.

'What do we do?' His words are barely audible through his coughing.

I think fast. This assassination attempt has gone well beyond even what I had planned for. But I refuse to retreat, refuse to walk away from what I set out to do. The Azoth won't let me and, besides, I won't let myself.

'You need to get out,' I say. 'All of you. Not through there,' I add, when Malcolm twists his head in the direction of the panel, lost now in the smoke. 'There's too much blood leading to it. Once the air clears they'll see it, and they'll follow you. Go through the kitchen. It will be chaos by now; no one will notice you.'

We paw our way back toward the pages' chamber, smoke obscuring our view and our breath. I snatch the cap off my head, press it against my nose and mouth before passing it to Malcolm, still choking and retching.

We're almost to the end of the gallery.

Five feet, four feet.

Three.

A fierce wind rattles down the hallway then, shrieking and whistling, a blast so frigid and cold it blows out the entire bank of windows above us. Glass explodes into shards, raining down on our backs, our necks, and our arms, splintered and sharp. Blood drizzles down my skin, hot and dire. Flames dance along their moorings, then begin to break, winking out one after the other like candles.

'What's happening?' Malcolm's voice is a panicked hiss in my ear.

'I don't know.' But it's not true. I do know. I'm just too afraid to say.

The smoke swirls above us, shifting into fog, then into clouds, lifting high into the coffered ceiling. They hover there a moment, a warning. Then a clap, a reverberation, that thunderous sound of a storm, and those clouds open up and begin to pour, a relentless lash of rain.

There's only one person I know who can manipulate the weather this way, who can summon a storm where there was none, bend the skies to his will, bring down rain and wind and dark and light. The way he did the last time I saw him, at the masque I nearly didn't return from:

Blackwell.

'New plan.' Schuyler's voice appears somewhere above me. He yanks me to my feet, the force so great it nearly dislocates my arm. Keagan grabs Malcolm. They push us back the way we came, toward the panel in the wall. Through the receding smoke and the rain, through my hair that's come loose from its knot and streams into my eyes, I see it: wide open and beckoning.

And then…

And then…

And then.

I hear it. Music. Dirgelike, the strains of it leaking beneath the door to the royal pew from the chapel below. It's coming from the organ, all music and no words but I know the lyrics anyway:

Sleep and peace attend me, all through the night.
Angels will come to me, all through the night.
Drowsy hours are creeping; hill and vale, slumber sleeping,
A loving vigil keeping, all through the night.

The song I sang to myself in my final test, the lullaby my mother used to sing to me. The song that kept me alive inside the tomb that tried to kill me; the one that broke the spell before it could kill me.

I turn around, face the sound. Raise the Azoth.

Schuyler is before me in a moment, his blue eyes wide, his grip on my arm fierce. I'm in awe, just for a moment, at the power Blackwell wields, so strong that it could cast fear into someone as fearless as Schuyler.

'Forget it, bijoux. It's too much. He's too strong—'

'I know.' I twist out of Schuyler's iron grasp. 'And that's why I have to do it.' I push Malcolm toward Keagan. 'Get him out,' I tell her. 'If you're caught, you won't escape this time. They will kill you on the spot. It's the Order's job, it's your job, to keep him safe.'

But Malcolm jerks away from her and rounds on me.

'Don't do this.' He takes my shoulders, grips them hard. Leans into me, his face inches from mine. For a moment, I forget to be afraid of him. 'As king, I ask you – no,

I command you – to come with me.'

'You are not king,' I say. 'Not unless I do this.'

'*Goddammit.*' I've never heard Malcolm swear before; the word comes out a frustrated groan.

Moon's watch is keeping, all through the night.
The weary world is sleeping, all through the night.
A spirit gently stealing, visions of delight revealing,
A pure and peaceful feeling, all through the night.

A shadow appears through the smoke then, dark and looming and figureless: a spectre in a foggy cemetery, a boggart in a dusky swamp. I can't see who it is, but then, I already know.

'Go,' I say. 'Let me do this. I need to do this.'

Schuyler growls one last curse before tearing Malcolm away from me, nearly lifting him off the ground with the force of it, shoving him toward the passage in the wall. Through the fog and the driving rain I can just make out Keagan hauling him inside and the final look Schuyler gives me before crawling after him. The panel door closes, a spark in the smoke as Keagan fuses it shut, the three of them making their way down the winding stairs into the clock court and the still-dark skies and, I hope, to safety. I am alone.

Not alone.

He walks toward me, and even in the swirling coalescence I know his height, his strength, his black clothes; I know the wink of the weapon he holds in his hand. How long has he been waiting for me? Since yesterday? All night? He knew I would come. He knew what I would do.

And deep down, I knew it, too.

The Azoth fires hot in my hand, the energy and the strength, the latent curse and the manifest hate coursing through me: sparks before a bonfire, drops before a storm. It is dangerous ground. But I don't care about drowning, and I don't care about burning. I only care about ending him, ending it all, once and for all.

Like a monstrosity lurking from the depths of the dark lake surrounding Rochester Hall, he emerges, and at last I see him. But it's not Blackwell, as I was expecting: It's someone – something – else entirely.

Dark blond hair, falling in waves above his eyes. Tall, pale, dressed in black with that damned strangled rose fixed to his sleeve. And the scent of him: a hint of earth and loam, mould and decay.

I never thought I'd see him again. I thought I had killed him. Yet here he is before me; the shock of it would bring me to my knees if terror weren't holding me up.

Caleb.

He is alive.

He is dead.

He is a revenant.

'Hello, Elizabeth.'

TWENTY

The Azoth goes wild in my hand. Searing, coursing, trembling, cursing; the power of it threatening to unhinge me if the sight before me doesn't. All I manage is his name: 'Caleb'. The music has ceased, and my voice echoes through the destruction of the gallery, a haunting moan.

He steps toward me. His gait unsteady, his eyes fixed not on me but on the Azoth, the emeralds in the hilt dull and lifeless now, as if they know they're caught. He doesn't reach for it but he looks at it, something like distaste but also fear crossing his cold, white face.

I should say something. I should do something. I should thrust the blade into him and I should run; I should find Blackwell and do the same to him. But all I can do is stand there and look at him.

Caleb a revenant. He didn't die after all, didn't die after I sliced him in the chest with the Azoth, spilling his heart and his blood and his life onto the ground, didn't die, didn't die…

'I did die,' he says. His voice is strange, murky. It's his but it isn't, the tone the same but the tenor gone. Not gone: *dead.* 'I died. I'm dead. Because you killed me.' Caleb tilts his head, an odd, unnatural angle, and fixes me with those eyes. Once blue and sparkling with life and mischief and ambition, now lifeless, pale, and grey, no soul behind them at all.

'I didn't want to kill you,' I whisper. 'I didn't mean to, I didn't. I cared about you. I loved you—'

'Funny things happen to the people you claim to care about,' Caleb says, and I freeze. He's reached into my head, plucked out the very thing John said to me inside his cell, the very thing I can't stop thinking about, can't stop turning over and over in my head.

'Caleb,' I whisper again. I think to plead with him, to ask him to spare my life when I know he stands before me to take it. But as soon as I think it, I dismiss it. Caleb didn't spare me when he was alive. He will not spare me now that he is dead.

This is what I know about revenants: I know that they are more dead than alive. I know they have no connection, no anchor to this earth. I know that they are little more than ghosts, the person they once were now just a wisp of cloud in a storm.

Revenants can learn to be human again, a facsimile of their former selves. They can learn to feel, to love; they can even begin to appear human again, the way Schuyler has – the soul he's rebuilt evidenced by the colour regained in his eyes. But it takes many years and an unwavering desire to attain it, along with an unshakable connection to someone, such as the one Schuyler has with Fifer. Revenants need a living, breathing being to keep them in the light, when their very nature is to live in the dark.

This is what I also know: Caleb has always lived in the dark.

'You knew I was coming to Ravenscourt,' I say. 'You read my thoughts, and you heard me coming. You told Blackwell, and that's how he knew to do this.' I wave my free hand at the rain-soaked gallery, at the pew in which I meant to meet him, in which I meant to end him.

Caleb nods, once.

I think of Malcolm then, and of Keagan and Schuyler. If Caleb knew I was coming, he must have known they were with me. Did they get free? Or did they simply wind down that staircase and into greater danger than they left?

Caleb only shrugs, a wholly human gesture, stiff and awkward now in the replicate.

'Blackwell doesn't care about Malcolm,' he says. 'If he did, he wouldn't still be alive. Malcolm can't stop Blackwell from becoming king. Nothing can. He *is* the king.' Caleb gazes at me, eyes hard and unfeeling as flint. 'You know what he needs.'

I nod, because I do. He needs the Azoth for its curse and for its power, and now he needs me, for reasons I still don't understand, to take back what he believes is his: my stigma. It flashes through my mind then – a thought so swift it takes flight again before it can land, before Caleb can seize on it – how can I give Blackwell what I no longer have?

With a confidence I very nearly feel, I squeeze the Azoth's hilt, long since gone cold, and I step toward Caleb, surrendering myself to him. His blank grey eyes go wide just for a moment, and I feel a fierce jolt of pleasure. Caleb may be able to read my thoughts, but I won't let him read my deeds.

'Take me to him.'

Down the wet, smoky, bloody hallway we weave around bodies: guards in black with twisted necks and punctured eyes, one charred and black and unrecognisable. Blackwell knew we were coming and he sacrificed his men to us anyway. For the sport of it, for the game of luring us in to see what we would do, how we would play it.

And I don't know how to play it. Not yet.

The hallway ahead ends in a row of double oak doors, closed. I can just make out the shadows of two men standing in front of them. Not guards, no, because they're all dead, but as I get closer and I see them – one tall, black-haired, brutish; the other medium height and reddish, from his hair to the freckles that spatter like blood against white skin – I see that they, too, are dead:

Marcus and Linus.

Witch hunters once, now both Knights of the Anglian Royal Empire. Both revenants. I feel their grey, dead gaze track me with a hate that turns to wariness as they catch sight of the glittering blade in my hand, the very one that brought them to the ground before Blackwell hauled them out of it. As Caleb steers me past, I turn my head. As with any monster, it's best not to look it in the eye.

Through the doors, the privy chamber. Where the king receives petitioners, where courtiers gather in sycophantic attendance, where musicians come to entertain. Now, it's empty; bare of everything save the throne, upholstered and canopied with a rich crimson cloth of state bearing the royal coat of arms: a crowned lion and a chained steed on either side of a red-and-gold quartered shield. Etched below, in Latin, a motto. Not Blackwell's old, steadfast motto: *What's done is done, it cannot be undone.* A new one now, for a new ruler and a new kingdom: *Faciam quodlibet quod necesse est.*

I will do whatever it takes.

In my wet woollen dress, I shiver.

Next, the presence chamber, the king's innermost private room. Bare and dark, just one shuttered window and one small fire burning in one small grate. No tapestries and no throne, only a desk in the centre flanked by two chairs, with a single book lying page-up on the surface. And there, sitting in the chair closest to the fireplace, facing the flame, his back to us, is Blackwell.

Whatever calm I'd forced myself into, whatever illusion of control I once had, now threatens to abandon me. My heart begins to race, my stomach to churn, my palms to sweat. That old feeling of dread, the one I always feel when faced with him, rushes toward me like a tide. Beside me, Caleb shifts; he must feel my turmoil. But I take a breath and push it down, as far as I can, away from his grasping intrusion.

Finally, Blackwell speaks.

'Elizabeth.'

This is all he says. He doesn't rise, he doesn't turn, he does nothing but stare into the fire in front of him, the flames crackling and spitting in the grate. At once, I know something is wrong. Maybe I should have known it when he didn't greet me in his privy chamber, on his throne, for me to witness the spectacle of his power.

Keagan's words come back to me, what she said in Hexham: *He hasn't made a public appearance since he was crowned. No one has seen him.*

'You didn't make this easy, did you?' Blackwell goes on. 'Coming here. You ruined my gallery, my paintings; you killed my guards.'

'You knew we were coming,' I say. 'If you'd wanted to protect your men, you could have.'

He shrugs, dismissive. But he doesn't reply.

'You want your power back from my stigma,' I continue, going straight to the point. 'It's why you sent Fulke and Griffin after me, why you sent the others the day of my trial.' I pause. 'I killed them, you know. All of them.' It's a lie, but it's what he would expect me to say if I were still who he thought I was. 'If you wanted them to bring me back to you, you should have presented a real challenge. I'm almost insulted.'

A strange huffing noise, something between a hiss and a laugh. Then: 'You always were one of my best witch hunters.'

Abruptly, Blackwell rises from his chair, the legs scraping against the wooden floor. He looks every inch the king:

dressed in crisp navy trousers and a matching coat embroidered in rich gold thread. Knee-high black boots, a black velvet cape around his shoulders, the collar and sleeves trimmed in ermine. Moments pass and, still, he will not turn around. My neck prickles in warning: a distant rumble of thunder before a storm.

'Do you know what you did?' he says. His voice is measured. But beneath the calm I hear a note of something else: an undercurrent of fury.

Blackwell turns to face me, and I see what I have done.

He is every inch the monster.

TWENTY-ONE

His face – what's left of it – is completely ravaged. A scar runs a diagonal path from his temple, across his right eye, and over his nose and lips, ending at his jaw. His right eye is useless, frozen half open; the eyeball underneath it white and cloudy and unseeing. His nose is split in two, his mouth ripped and twisted, half his jaw visible. Someone stitched him up – someone tried – and did a sorry job. The scar is raised and raw and horrible, and I can see the crooked marks of the needle and the indentations in his flesh where the sutures were tied. This is the damage I did, the damage the Azoth did.

Unflinching, I stare at the horror. As if it recognises a job well done, the blade fires to life in my hand.

'Caleb said that you, too, were injured by the Azoth.' A pause. 'I assume it doesn't look like this.'

I don't reply. The wound I received was terrible; I would have died were it not for John. But after he was sure I wouldn't die from every other injury I received the night of the masque, he made certain I wouldn't be scarred by them, either. He spent weeks applying herbs, making tisanes, doing everything he could for me. It was a labour of love, I know that now. But now that love is gone, just like my scar.

Blackwell lets out a short, barking laugh, that twisted, gaping mouth glinting in the room's dim light. 'Perhaps I should have spared myself a healer after all.'

I shift toward the fireplace. If I'm to do it, it's to be done now. Can I do it now? Are the Azoth and his fear of it enough to repel Caleb, enough to keep him away to do what I came here for?

In one fell motion this could all be over.

'Taking my stigma back won't heal you.' I inch forward another step. 'Its power is no match for the Azoth.' I remember the way the blade sliced into me, the way it hurt, the way it bled. The way my stigma did nothing. 'It won't do anything.'

Blackwell's mouth twists into a shape that almost passes for a smile. 'And I'm sure your warning is in my best interest and has nothing to do with self-preservation.'

I adjust my grip on the hilt. Fingers curled loosely, firm but not tight, my thumb pressed against the cross guard. All the while the Prayer on the Eve of Battle marches through my head, keeping my thoughts engaged so Caleb can't besiege them.

I'm almost to his desk now, almost halfway to him. I slide to the far side of it, putting as much distance between me and Caleb as I can, as if a mere wooden desk could keep him from me.

As I do, the book on the surface catches my eye. Red leather-bound with gilt-edged pages, open to a page dense with scrawling text surrounding a single image, an image I know well but didn't expect to see here. A glyph used in the Reformist symbol, representing unity, infinity, wholeness: a snake devouring its own tail.

'The circle closes its end.'

The words slip from my mouth; I didn't intend them to. It's a line from the prophecy given to me all those months ago by a five-year-old seer, her recitation holding the cryptic instruction that opened the gate to the path I stand on now, between one dead man and another cursed one, holding a sword.

'The Ouroboros,' I continue. 'It's a symbol of resurrection, continually reborn as it sheds its skin. It represents the cycle of birth and death, the eternal harmony of all things. The unity of opposites.'

Blackwell raises a ruined eyebrow. 'Been studying alchemy, have you?'

Not really, no; but in a way, yes. For a moment my thoughts slip from the battle prayer to the alchemy books at Rochester, the ones I brought to John at Hexham. How I flipped through page after page to choose one he'd like. Studying the words to try to get close to him, to try to understand what he was going through when Nicholas told me the magic I gave John was at war with his own.

'The stigma is a manifestation of invincibility.' Blackwell

speaks the words as if they were wine, something to savour. 'While the Azoth is pure destruction: the opposite of invincibility. Alchemists believe that if you were to combine a single element together with its opposite, uniting them, you could transcend them. Move beyond the power of either in order to become the power of both.'

I can almost picture the pages before me in that dark and shadowed library. The words etched on yellow parchment, the drawing of the serpent devouring its tail, the words *One is all* scrawled beneath it.

'The power of both,' I repeat. 'What would that power be?'

Blackwell watches me, his expression hungry. 'I think you already know.'

I don't answer right away, because he's right. I do. But if I say the words, if I allow them to form shape, then they become real: an abdication of sanity.

'Immortality,' I whisper at last.

That is when the fire goes out.

The room falls dark. And the air around me, once warm and still, drops by degrees and begins to swirl, great gusts of wind from nowhere whipping my hair around my shoulders, into my face, flaring my skirts around my knees. A cloud of breath snakes from my mouth, and I feel it against my cheek: the first flake of snow that within moments turns to a blizzard.

My dress freezes in place, the skirt ballooned around my knees in statuesque attitude. My hair freezes, too, strands sticking to my cheeks and my lips and eyelids that feel at once numb and sharp and heavy. The wind howls around my ears, bringing with it still more snow; the presence chamber has become a winter wasteland.

Blackwell appears before me, untouched by the cold, as if it exists for me only – *does it exist for me only?* – his coat and his face and his skin bear not a trace of it. I will myself to move. To pull away, to hold fast to the sword, to raise it and to lay it into him, to finish what I set out to do. But my commands fall on the deaf ears of my immobile body. Blackwell reaches forward and with a twist and a tear of metal against hardened skin, he pries the Azoth from my hand. I'm frozen solid as winter: I can do nothing but watch it go.

At once, the snow and the storm disappear, swirling upward into the pale plaster ceiling and into nothingness, a terrible silence descending on the room. Just the sound of Blackwell's strange, whistled breath, the dawn chorus of birds in the eaves outside the window.

'Take her away.'

Away: to Greenwich Tower. Where I am to be held until Blackwell can assemble his retinue of alchemists in preparation for the spell. When he will take the Azoth and run me through with it, when he expects my stigma, his power, to be absorbed by the blade. For the power of both to be transferred into him, making him whole before uniting those opposites, transcending them, allowing him to live forever.

These are the words he uses to describe what will occur

next. I use but one word, simple but final.

Execution.

I sit shackled in a wherry, floating down the murky Severn River. The waters are quiet at this hour, save for a few idling ships not wanting to risk getting moored in the morning's low tide. They wait in the middle, still as a raft of mallards. I find myself watching them, allowing myself to hope, just for a moment, that one of them is Peter's. A galley, maybe, with a hundred rowers at the helm to chase us down, pull up alongside us and whisk me away, saving me again the way he saved me before. But as we drift on by and there are no shouts, no anchors pulled, no row men and no pirates, I know that I am on my own.

Ahead, Upminster Bridge. Two dozen brick archways spanning the length of the water, topped by rows of leaning shops and taverns and lodging, some nearly four stories high. Like the waters, the bridge is nearly empty now, too early still for buildings to open their doors. But by noon, it will be madness: the pathway clogged with pedestrians and carts and carriages, stinking of mud and filth and people and waste. Caleb and I attempted to pass, just once; it took us an hour to get halfway. That was when he suggested we take to the river and swim our way across.

I wonder if he still remembers. How he jumped onto the low wall and stood teetering on the edge, arms wide as if he were flying, laughing. I laughed, too, because it didn't matter if he fell. He thought nothing could touch him then; we all did.

I glance at him, sitting behind me. I half expect to find

his muted grey eyes on me, watching me the way Schuyler does when he's listening to me, hearing my every thought. Instead, he's looking above me. I turn to follow his gaze, and I see it: them. A dozen heads impaled on a dozen pikes, set on top of the southern gatehouse, their faces frozen in a mask of defiance, fat carrion crows with their black legs tangled in bloody hair and Keagan's shredded pamphlets, pecking away at what's left: skin, sinew, eyeballs. I don't recognise them but that doesn't matter; they are traitors and this is what happens to traitors. If I do not find a way out, it is what will happen to me.

Greenwich Tower looms into view, casting a long, dark shadow, black with ever-present mould. Beyond that, the castle itself, four flag-topped spires marking each corner. The iron gate slides open as we approach, as though it were expecting us. The boat slips through and bumps against the bottom of a set of stone steps, the same steps I climbed the night of the masque, the night John danced with me, the night he first kissed me.

Today no footmen take invitations, no roses bloom in the gardens, no guests arrive dressed in finery or wearing masks. It's only Caleb and me standing at the top of the watergate, staring across the landing, across the now-bleak landscape to the park beyond. Guards in black teem from a nearby tower and make their way toward us, their footsteps crunching in the gravel. They pull me from Caleb's grasp, make a show of checking my bindings around my arms, my feet.

While the Prayer on the Eve of Battle continues to run

through my head, I tick through my options of escape.

I think of unshackling myself, but I can't without my stigma: I don't have the strength to break through the iron on my own. I spy a rock, two, scattered along the path. Consider snatching one up, smashing the guards with it before smashing my chains, then reject the idea immediately. It would take too long and be too loud.

I could try to escape the grounds. But how? I could probably outmanoeuvre the guards; they've never been much of a challenge. Then what? The river? I could scale the wall; even chained, I could still manage that. I'd have minutes – ten at most – before the other guards were alerted to my absence. It would be better to hide somewhere on the grounds, wait for cover of darkness to sneak away. But by then they'd have every guard, revenant, and Knight of the Anglian Royal Empire after me. And they would find me.

Of course, then there's Caleb. He would stop me before I could take the first step in any one of these plans. But I've got to figure out something. Because when Blackwell comes for me, when he tries to retrieve my stigma and discovers I don't have it, he will turn Caleb on me. He will turn Marcus and Linus on me, he will force me to tell him what happened to it. I will never tell him; I swear it on my life. But it is not only my life I am concerned about.

We pass the guards' station, the servants' quarters, and the lieutenants' lodgings, built back when Greenwich Tower was a defensive castle only. They could almost be mistaken for Upminster town homes: white plaster and dark-timbered facades, thatched roofs, rough-hewn wood doors painted in a charming shade of robin's-egg blue.

We reach the house at the end. I've never been inside before – I had no reason to be – but unlike the others, this one is no lodging: I know this by the heavy, barred door. The guards unlock it, and Caleb pushes me inside and up a set of circular winding stairs, through another and yet another locked, barred door into what looks like a holding room. It's strangely large, bright, and clean: high walls inset with leaded glass windows, fresh rushes strewn along the floor, a wide wood bench along one wall, and a fireplace along the other, though it's unlit.

The door shuts on me; the lock clicks into place. The guards turn and leave. Only Caleb remains: standing at the door, hands wrapped around the bars, watching me. It's a familiar scene, so reminiscent of the time I stood behind bars at Fleet, when I still believed in him, trusted him; when I still believed we could get through anything as long as we were together.

I start to turn away when Caleb's strange, murky voice breaks the silence.

'I have to tell him everything now,' he says. 'Everything he asks. I have to do everything he demands.'

This is typical. Revenants are always beholden to the witch or wizard who returned them from the grave. The magic that binds them together requires it. I don't know why he's telling me this, but perhaps there's a way I can use it to my advantage.

'Yes,' I say cautiously. 'You will have to do everything he

demands as long as he is alive. And once he has my stigma, he will always be alive.'

'Don't manipulate me.' Caleb's words turn quick, sharp; maybe I'm imagining it but I think I see a flash of blue behind his cloudy grey eyes, but then it's gone.

I nod, acknowledging the accusation. 'Even so, it's the truth. You know it is.'

He says nothing, at first. Then: 'You don't know what it's like.' His voice is quiet, hesitant; a whispered secret in a barred confessional. 'I feel nothing. I know everything. I exist, yet I do not. I am no one but who he tells me to be. I want to escape. I don't know how to escape. I don't –' Caleb stops himself. 'I have to go. He needs me.' He releases the bars and backs away. 'I would not,' he adds, 'turn your back.'

'What?'

Caleb shifts out of sight. And in his place Marcus appears: black cloak, black hair, those grey eyes black with hate and want for revenge.

TWENTY-TWO

I spend the next four nights in a cold, dark, tomblike room in the presence of the dead.

I don't sleep for long; I don't dare. Instead I sit perched on the edge of the bench, pinching myself to stay awake, succumbing to five-, ten-minute snatches of rest when I can't. Every waking moment is devoted to the Prayer on the Eve of Battle, a liturgy on a loop, keeping Marcus from my thoughts. He finds them anyway – not all of them but some – taunting me with carefully buried memories of childhood and of training, of my time spent with Malcolm, my parents' deaths and Caleb's, whispered in his loamy, rotting voice.

Not once does he mention John.

Not once do I turn my back.

I don't have to wonder why Marcus was given the job of guarding me. Caleb could have kept me from escaping just as well, but he would not have kept me awake for the purpose of unhinging me. He would not have stared at me all through the night, unblinking, seeing everything. Almost everything.

The only thing left to wonder is what will happen.

Days pass slowly, murky light breaking through quilted clouds each morning, escaping on dust motes through leaded glass each evening. I'm light-headed with exhaustion, my limbs and eyelids heavy with vigilance. The only sounds in the room are Marcus and his malignant mutterings, me and my mitigating prayer.

In the tower outside, bells chime out the hours. Then, on the fifth chime of the fifth day, Marcus finally stops speaking. Rises to his feet. I still don't move, rooted to the bench with manifest fear, watching how he cocks his head, a lupine gesture, toward the window. Listening to something I can't hear. Then he turns to me, a slow, sly grin crossing his face.

Today is the day.

I have to escape.

I don't know what to do.

I hear the echo of a clank, a key in an iron lock, the creaking of a door hinge. Footsteps on a stone staircase. Guards appear at the window of my door then, two of the same men that escorted me here. They let themselves in. It's not difficult to spot the caution on their faces; I don't know if it's directed toward me or toward Marcus.

The guards don't give an order, they don't have to: Marcus lurches for me, rips me off my spot on the bench. I struggle against him, against the chains still bound around my ankles and wrists; useless. Then, with Marcus on one side of me and the guards on the other, they march me out the door. My heart taps fast against my rib cage. I've got to do something, and time is running out.

We wind down the stairs until we reach the door at the bottom. One guard pulls out a key and unlocks it, the other holds it wide for Marcus to step through, keeping a wide berth. For a moment, just a moment, I'm left alone with them.

But a moment is all I need.

I swipe my hand through my hair, snatch the hairpin from the knot at the nape of my neck, still tucked there from nearly a week before. Jam it into the locks in my bindings, feel them catch, hear them snap open. Marcus hears it, or senses it; he spins around just as I reach forward and slam the door shut, jamming the bolt into place.

The guards advance. I throw my elbow up and back, hard, catching one in the nose. It cracks, breaks; blood spurts onto the floor as he bends over, groaning. I take him by the back of the head and slam it into my knee; he drops to the ground. The other guard turns to run, but he's not fast enough. I grab his arm, whirl him around, my fist is at his mouth before he can utter a sound. He joins the other guard on the floor in a heap.

Marcus batters himself against the door like an enraged wild animal.

I run like hell.

Up the twisting stairs, back to my cell again. Throw myself through the door, slam it shut, and lock it, yanking more pins from my hair and cramming them into the latch so it can't be opened from the other side.

I've got seconds, if that, before Marcus escapes and reaches me. I snatch the apron from my soiled woollen dress, wrap it around my fist as I've done before, and smash it through the window that overlooks the back of the lodging house, the opposite side from where Marcus still hammers on the door. Shards of glass fall from the frame and crackle to the floor. I move around them carefully in my worn leather slippers; I cannot cut myself, I cannot bleed.

I step onto the narrow window ledge, peer into the dawn and the darkness below. I don't know what might be down there; I didn't get a chance to scout it before, not with Marcus watching my every move. Likely it's a stone path. But what if it's an iron gate? A pitched roof? I could impale myself, I could hit the heavy, shale slats and knock myself unconscious; roll to the ground and break a leg, condemning myself to capture.

I'm willing to take the chance.

I don't get it.

The door to my cell explodes open, and Marcus is through it like a battering ram. He's fast – I cannot get used to his speed – and he's on me, fisting the collar of my dress with an iron, unforgiving hand. I'm yanked from the ledge, hard, thrown to the floor. I land on my stomach, the wind knocked out of me. I scramble to my back but immediately wish I hadn't. To look him in the face is to be terrified: He looks furious, vengeful, and worst of all, amused.

He grabs me, grasps my head between both palms, and begins to squeeze. The pressure of it lifts me off my feet;

it splinters my vision, at once going white, then red, then black. He's going to crush my skull. He's going to kill me with his bare hands. He mutters obscenities at me; his breath is in my face and it is not human. It is dark and black and oily; it smells of dirt and death and decay.

'Marcus.' Caleb's voice breaks into my screams. He stands at the door, hands curled into fists, either in anger or restraint. 'Release her.'

Marcus starts like a scolded dog, pulling his hands from my head. I don't expect it and I slump in a heap to the floor, my head knocking against the stone.

'Now go.' Caleb points to the door, blown open on its hinges. 'I'll have to tell him of this. You know what will happen when he hears.'

'I was told to prevent her escaping,' Marcus says. 'Using whatever means necessary. That is what I did.'

'Make your excuses to him,' Caleb replies. 'I don't have the time or the use for them.'

Marcus glares first at Caleb, then at me before stalking from the room. I don't know what to say to him: Thank him for stopping Marcus from killing me? Rail against him for it? Because wherever he's taking me, it's no better than where I am now, and the fate is the same.

But I don't get to decide because in an instant Caleb is beside me, pulling me to my feet. In the space between one breath and another my wrists are bound once more, a blindfold strapped over my eyes. He marches me back down the stairs, no chance of escaping this time.

Outside, the sound of gulls wheeling overhead, the gust

of cool wind on my face, and the brackish scent of the Severn River are my only sensations. I begin to struggle, but I know it's no use and I stop. Whatever strength I have left for whatever happens next, I'm going to need it.

The scent and the damp, velvety feel of grass give way to the crunch of gravel; the gravel gives way to pavers, then the dank smell and sudden coolness of a tunnel. I try to sort out where he's leading me. It could be any number of places, none of them good: This is Greenwich Tower, after all.

A slight stumble as we cross a threshold, the creak of a door, then the sensation of falling. Stairs. They go on and on. I've counted sixty, yet we keep going, deep beneath the Tower, into the ground. Into the earth.

The earth.

I begin to struggle again, bucking and twisting against his grasp. But it's as though I'm wrestling with a stone pillar. My skin chafes and burns, and I wind up nowhere.

Finally, we reach the bottom of the staircase, hitting solid floor. I start a little at the cold smoothness of it, at the ringing echo of our footsteps.

'Where am I?' I don't bother to hide my fear; Caleb knows it anyway. 'What is this place?'

Instead of his reply, there's a low rumble of chuckles in the room, not from just one man but from many. It makes the hair on my neck stand on end, the kick of buried fear taking flight in my chest. Caleb's hand fumbles to the back of my head, pulls away my blindfold.

I'm in a small circular room that I've not seen before. The floor underfoot is marble, the same that lines the walls and the ceilings. Brown, veined with white; an elegant tomb. Glittering stones inset into the floor form a star with eight points, marking the cardinal and inter-cardinal directions. In the middle, a table. Narrow, long, shining wood.

It's a ritual room.

I've seen them before, rudimentary versions of this. Dirt or brick walls, never marble. Twigs or rocks to mark the directions, never inlaid with precious gems. Rough-hewn candles made of tallow and stinking of fat instead of elegant oil lamps, cut glass hung from brass brackets along the walls. Eight men stand in a circle around the edge of the room, surrounding me. I spin around, looking at each of them in turn. They're cloaked and hooded, so I can't see their faces or tell who they are. They all look the same. But I know one of them by his height, his presence; I know him by the sword at his side, emeralds on the hilt glittering like a pulse.

I know it's useless, but I run anyway. Spin on my heel and sprint toward the door that Caleb just led me through, the door that not sixty seconds ago was there.

Only now it's gone.

At once, the eight men converge on me. I duck past one, knock into another. Jam into one with my shoulders, get past him only to run into another. I kick him, my hands useless and bound before me.

Someone grabs me from behind. I buck and I twist, gnashing at his arms, his hands, my teeth sinking into his flesh and drawing blood. He thanks me for it with a slap to my face, hard enough to rattle bones.

They throw me onto the table, face-up. Someone procures a length of rope and wraps it around me, around the table, binding me to it. I'm completely immobile. I twist my head around, side to side, watching as the men produce candles from beneath their cloaks, lighting them from the oil lamps before setting them along the edge of the eight-pointed star. A small wooden bowl of salt is set on the cardinal point north. A larger candle, also lit, set on the point south. A bundle of herbs east, a chalice of water west. Four directions, four elements, four virtues, four phases of time, all leading to a single, final end.

There's a rustle, then a squawking sound. A rattle of bars. A tall, hooded man steps forward; in his hands is a small black cage holding a huge black raven. He pulls out the bird as Blackwell holds up the Azoth. There's a flash of green, a caw, a rustle – then silence. A dripping noise, the scent of iron, a wet thud as the dead bird is thrown into the centre of the star. A sacrifice.

It all happens fast now. Blood smeared on the wall, shapes and figures I can't decipher. Herbs held over the flames, catching fire, then quickly put out, still smoking, the scents mingling with the blood. The swish of robes. All the while murmuring, chanting, an incantation.

I twist against the rope, my head whipping from side to side, when suddenly the room disappears. No marble, no glittering compass, no candles. No dead raven and no hooded men. Only a dark room. A hole, a tomb. No way in, no way out.

The room flickers back to marble, then back to dark.

Over and over again. The chanting grows louder, drowning out my shouts that give way to my screams. Marble, dirt. Men, no men. Light, no light. Faster, faster.

Blackwell appears before me then, the Azoth held high. Something flares inside me at the sight of it, the heat and pull and desire of the curse.

My pulse thunders now.

A swish of air as the blade is lifted. I take a breath, likely my last, wait for the point to impale me, for me to bleed onto this table, to die; the only solace is knowing that if I do, Blackwell will never get what he wants.

He pauses. I think, maybe, wildly, that the blade recognises me, knows who held it these last weeks, refuses to turn against me. But the Azoth has no loyalty. It would just as soon kill me as anyone else, as long as it kills someone.

'What is this?' Blackwell's voice in my ear; his palm to my head, twisting it this way and that. 'And this?'

I don't answer, because I don't know what he's asking. Then he answers for me.

'Bruises.' The room falls silent, all chanting stopped. 'On your face. Neck. How, Elizabeth, do you have bruises?'

I go still. Witch hunters do not get bruises. That is, witch hunters still protected by their stigmas do not bruise. All the care I took not to be cut, the care I took not to allow my secret to leak, now undone by the smallest of things: the imprint of Marcus's palms against my face as he tried to squeeze the life out of me.

'Where is your stigma?' Blackwell leans forward. Presses

the tip of the Azoth against my cheek; it's still dripping with raven's blood. 'What have you done with it?'

'I'll never tell you.' Somehow I find the courage to look into his ruined face, one last defiance. 'I will never tell you what happened to it.'

This, to him, is no threat. He simply looks to Caleb, who steps toward me, hood lowered and eyes narrowed. He will try to read me, he will burrow into my head and he will try to find the answer to Blackwell's question. Once again I recite Malcolm's prayer, over and over, I fill every crevice of every thought with it; I will not let him in.

After a moment, Caleb shakes his head.

'There are other ways to retrieve this information.' A smile crosses Blackwell's split face but it shouldn't: He does not know the lengths I will go to in order to keep it from him. He jerks his head at his men. 'Take her.'

The same tall, hooded figure who held the caged bird now clamps his hand around my wrist; unseen hands fumble with the rope. I stop my prayer long enough to direct one to Caleb to end me first, before they do. Blackwell has many avenues of making me talk; roads littered with the dungeon and the rack, eye gouging and tongue cutting, split knees and sawed limbs and irons and screams.

But Caleb remains still, mute to my pleas.

The rope slithers to the floor. I'm hauled to my feet, wrists still shackled, and dragged to the door that has now reappeared. I begin to imagine the things they will do to me, but I don't imagine this: a scuffle, a startled shout; a squeeze of my arm and a flash of light before the room once more goes dark. I'm being crushed, my lungs don't draw breath. I can't see. I'm moving, flying, yet immobile, going nowhere.

Then, finally, silence. Vast. Endless.

Complete.

TWENTY-THREE

The first thing I notice is warmth.

The smell of carbon: flames, but not ritualistic or stinking of oil, or of death. These flames are friendly: the rosemary-scented fire of holiday and family and life. The grip on my arm is still there, joined now by a hand on my shoulder, firm but gentle. This, too, feels friendly, but I'm unsure. Too many things that started out as one thing have too quickly turned to another, and not for the better.

'Elizabeth.' A whisper in my ear then, a voice I know. Quiet, reassuring. Fatherly. 'You're safe now. You can open your eyes.'

I do.

I'm kneeling on a soft rug, and I know it, too: flowers and vines woven in yellow, orange, and green. The fire I smell roars in a familiar hearth; woodland tapestries draped across white plaster walls, wide-open ceilings.

Before me: Peter, crouched on his knees, smelling faintly

of tobacco and something sharper – whiskey; brandy, maybe. He fumbles with the bindings around my wrists, my ankles, they unlock and he throws them aside; they land across the room with a clatter. Then he pulls back to look at me, his eyes dark and red-rimmed, his skin pale, his clothes rumpled. He looks so much like John I have to turn away.

Someone hovers beside me. Slowly, I turn to face him: a tall, dark-robed figure from the ritual room, no longer holding a candle but a stone. A lodestone, still giving off a faint, pulsating glow, a thin veil of white smoke. Slowly, he lowers his hood.

Nicholas.

'You,' I say. My voice is hoarse from screaming. 'How?'

'Keagan,' he replies. 'And Schuyler. They told me what happened at Ravenscourt, then Schuyler told me where you'd been taken. Keagan helped me devise a way in; Fifer helped me devise a way out.'

So Keagan made it back from Ravenscourt alive. 'And what of Malcolm?' I say. 'Is he safe, too?'

'Yes,' Nicholas replies. 'They are both alive, and they are both well.'

'They're at Rochester.' This from Fifer, standing in the shadows by the fireplace, Schuyler by her side. She's wearing a dressing gown pulled over sleep clothes, but she doesn't look as if she's been sleeping. 'Waiting to hear word of you.'

I don't say anything to this. I shouldn't be here, I shouldn't be alive; there should be no word of me because I should be dead. But I can think of none of this now, not after what I know.

'Blackwell's plan.' I look to Nicholas. 'What he intends to do. Is it possible?'

Nicholas discards that hateful hooded robe, carried off by Hastings's unseen hands, and doesn't answer right away.

'Perhaps,' he says finally. 'If you'd told me before, I would have said it was but a lark, a far-fetched scheme on his part. He required the Azoth to achieve it; he never would have gotten to it. Not hidden behind my walls, not protected by my spells. Now he has it.'

He says this not in accusation but in fact; guilt sickens me anyway.

'And now he needs but one thing to reach his goal, this one far more attainable.'

He means John, of course.

'We've got to get to camp,' I blurt. 'Fitzroy needs to know what's happened so he can rally his men. Protect John. I need to tell him; it's my fault, I'll go –' I get to my feet but stumble as I do, exhaustion pinning me to the floor.

'You will not.' Peter takes one arm; Schuyler steps forward to take the other. Instinctively I flinch from them; their grasp like those of the guards, and of Marcus and Caleb. At this thought Schuyler releases me, but Peter holds fast. 'Let's get you upstairs,' Peter continues. 'Cleaned up. Rested.'

'I can't rest,' I tell him. 'Not now. Not after what I did.'

I look to Fifer then, remembering how angry she was with me before I left, how she tried to stop me, how I all but blackmailed her to help me. How she was a friend to me and I was no friend back. To Peter, for once again failing to save his son. To Nicholas, because he put himself in great danger – once again – to save me. This after I lied to him and stole from him, after I lost the Azoth, a great asset that has now become a great threat.

'I'm sorry,' I say finally. 'I thought I could end this. I thought I could kill Blackwell, but I was wrong. I overestimated my abilities,' I add, and it shames me to admit it.

'Perhaps,' Peter says with a squeeze to my arm. 'But not as much as you underestimated his.'

'I don't know what to do,' I whisper, as much to myself as to them.

'You are going upstairs with Fifer, as Peter suggested,' Nicholas says. 'Get some rest. We will speak later, after I've had time to piece through all that has happened.'

I don't argue with him; I don't dare. But before I turn from him I say, 'Thank you. For coming after me. For risking yourself to save me. Again.'

Nicholas rounds on me, swift. Places his hands on my shoulders, his expression grave as he looks at me. For a moment, I fear his anger, his recrimination, all of which I deserve but none of which I want to hear, at least not right now.

'If I have any wish for you,' he says, 'it is that you understand the value of what you risk. What you do is no longer about you alone. There are no longer people who will simply turn their heads if misfortune were to befall you, no matter how true that may have been in the past. You are not,' he adds, in that way of his that makes me think he can read my mind, 'replaceable'.

Fifer's hand appears on my elbow then, soft and guiding, Schuyler close behind. Peter murmurs to me in a low, comforting tone as Nicholas's words burrow into me, finding their way to truth.

They lead me up the stairs: more plaster and wood, soft floors and tapestries, the occasional oil portrait of rough seas and prancing horses and vases of blooms – no painted kings or battles or weapons here – until we reach a door and the bedchamber beyond, welcoming in pale green and white, too bright for the darkness in my heart.

In the centre is a tub already filled with water, steam floating from the top. Beside the bath is a chair stacked with bath sheets, a nightdress, a blanket, and a bowl of what looks like bath salt. That was fast. *One of the benefits of a ghost servant*, John said to me once.

'I'm going to see about food,' Peter says. He smiles, but the strain still shows. 'I'll be back soon.' Then he and Schuyler step into the hallway, closing the door softly behind them.

'Fifer, I don't—' I start.

'Save it,' she says, but there's no malice in her voice. 'I'm still angry with you, but I'm more relieved you're not dead. You could have died. You should be dead.'

'I know.' I drop into a chair beside the fireplace, warm and crackling, and press my head into my hands. 'I know.'

'Yes. Well.' She goes quiet and when I look up at her, she's watching me with an expression I'm not used to seeing from her: worry. 'Let's get that dress off you,' she says finally, extending a hand and pulling me to my feet. 'The stench and the sight of it are unbearable.'

It takes a moment; five days of accumulated filth sticks the fabric to my skin. I watch as Fifer drags it to the fireplace and shoves it inside. With a savage thrust of a fire poker, the grimy brown fabric goes up in flames.

I step into the bath. At once, the water turns dark and murky with dirt. Fifer tosses in a handful of bath salt – what I thought was bath salt – and the grime disappears, winding backward in the water in tendrils before vanishing entirely. Magic. Then she reaches into the neck of her robe and pulls out her necklace: brass chain, ampoules filled with salt, quicksilver, and ash.

'I think it best we keep Caleb out of your head from now on.' She slips it over my head. 'Or anyone else who might be poking around in there. Schuyler told me about that prayer you kept reciting,' she adds. 'I figure you might be tired of saying it.'

I lean back in the bath then, sinking into the warm soothing water. The fatigue I've held off for days rushes back in force and it's a struggle to keep my eyes open.

'What happened?' I ask after a moment. 'After Caleb found me and everyone else got out? Did they run into trouble?'

'Schuyler said it was chaos.' Fifer clears off the chair and pulls it beside the tub. 'Guards pumping water from pipes in the courtyards, staff running around with buckets, people screaming. Everyone thought it was a kitchen fire, so no one was suspicious, at least not at first. But once they saw the blood and then found the bodies…' She pulls her robe against her, tight, as if warding off a chill. 'By then, they were far enough away to avoid being caught. They ran full tilt for nearly two days to get here – Malcolm was near vomiting when the Watch found him.'

'Were they arrested again?'

'No, although it was close. Malcolm, he was completely out of control. Demanded they go back for you, shouting at people, ordering weapons, horses; he even ordered Fitzroy to give him his army.' Fifer tsks. 'You'd think a deposed king would be less demanding, but you'd be wrong.'

I nod. I don't find this behaviour surprising, on or off the throne.

'Eventually, Nicholas had to give him something to calm him down. He slept for twelve hours, only to wake up and start his demands all over again.' Another cluck of displeasure. 'After you broke in and out of Hexham so easily, Fitzroy and Nicholas decided it was potentially unsafe to send him back, so they put him in Rochester under house arrest.'

'What about Keagan?' I say. 'Is she being detained, too?'

'Not entirely,' Fifer says. 'We thought she might be, but the council decided there was no cause to keep her. They released her to go home, back to Airann, but she asked to stay on to help us fight. But she's still an outsider, and a dangerous outsider at that. The council thought it best to restrict her to the grounds at Rochester. She's turning out to be a good ally,' Fifer adds. 'She's already sent word to the rest of the Order, asking them to join us. Keagan says they're as powerful as she is, if not more. We could use that.'

I nod but say nothing, my thoughts already moving on to another prisoner at Hexham. Wondering where he is, if he's safe.

'John is at Rochester, too.' Fifer guesses at my silence. 'He's being held in a room somewhere in the west wing, but I don't know where. They're not allowing visitors. I haven't seen him, not even Peter has seen him. Only Nicholas and—'

She stops herself, but I already know what she was going to say. The only visitor John has besides Nicholas is Chime.

'Do you know if he's any better?'

Fifer looks down, her long, pale fingers plucking at the hem of her dressing gown. 'I don't know.' She shrugs. 'I keep asking to see him, but Nicholas says it's best if I don't. So I assume not.'

I shake my head. At the utter failure of my plan, at the danger I've put everyone in again: even more danger than they were in before.

'I should never have stayed in Harrow.' I close my eyes. I don't want to see Fifer's face, her acknowledgment of this truth. 'If I'd left, Blackwell would never have found out I didn't have my stigma. I could have kept the secret, and I could have kept John safe. I could have kept Blackwell on the run until the curse and his weakness eventually killed him.'

'Do you really believe that?' Fifer's tone is so fierce I have to open my eyes and look at her. 'Do you really think it would have been that easy? Knowing Blackwell's goal now, do you really believe you would have been able to outrun him on your own? Alone? With no power? That Caleb wouldn't have picked your mind clean and eventually led Blackwell here?'

'I don't know,' I say.

'I think you do.'

I take a breath then. Everything I know, and everything I don't, war with each other until I'm left with the casualty of knowing nothing at all.

'What now?' I say. 'What happens now?'

'I think you know that, too.'

I do. Blackwell will learn the truth about my stigma, he will come after John, after Harrow. He would have anyway, but now, with this provocation, it will be different. The attacks we've had, they were coquettes compared to what's coming. They will not be skirmishes; there will be no delay.

'It was always going to come to this,' Fifer says. 'And there's nothing you can do to stop it.'

TWENTY-FOUR

I move back to Rochester. Nicholas wanted me to stay in his home, for a few more days at least, to recover. But you don't recover from Blackwell's devices. You absorb them. Shuffle them around, make room for them within a catalogue already full of horrors until, eventually, you find a place for them. A place that is never hidden, but one day you hope will be just out of reach.

Nicholas escorts me back to camp, a silent guard against the stares and whispers of the others who fall still when they see us. Me, wrapped in a long green velvet cloak but still shivering under a cloudless blue sky; and Nicholas, a soothing but stalwart presence in robes of gold and ivory, threading us through the grounds.

Despite efforts to contain them, the details of my disappearance – and subsequent reappearance – spread like a virus through the camp. Everyone knows where I went, what I did, what happened to me, how I was brought back.

News travels fast in Harrow, just as Gareth said.

Rings of white tents stretch out before me, flapping in the breeze like canvas sails. I veer toward mine, inner ring five, when Nicholas holds out a hand to stop me.

'Malcolm has requested your presence,' he tells me. 'It is your choice to refuse, of course, and I have made him no promises either way. We have passed along the message that you are here, and you are safe, but I think part of him won't believe it until he sees it for himself.'

I hesitate. It was my plan to install myself back in my tent, then back in the pits; to run myself ragged with training both to atone for the things I've done and to prepare for the things Blackwell is about to do. But a visit to Malcolm is inevitable, and a small part of me wishes to see him for myself, too, to make sure he is as well as I've been told.

'Yes,' I say. 'I'll see him.'

Nicholas takes me to the west wing of Rochester Hall, even grander than the east. Golden coffered ceilings, red-and-gold-brocaded walls fixed with miles of gold-framed oil paintings. Marble busts of Cranbourne Calthorpe-Goughs stare at me from pedestals, all of them awash in light from floor-to-ceiling windows framed by swaths of rich red velvet.

Guards line the many doorways, but I already know which door leads to the room where Malcolm is being held: Five men mill before it, none of them looking pleased. They snap to attention as we approach, pikes clanging to let us through.

Inside, Fitzroy and Malcolm sit at a small table by the window overlooking a garden and the lush forest beyond. Silver trays, crystal goblets, and pewter plates filled with food line the surface. Malcolm looks up from his untouched plate, sees me, and scrambles from his chair.

'Elizabeth.' His linen napkin flutters from his lap to the floor. 'You're here.'

In the past, when he would greet me this way, I would always curtsy. I almost do at present. But the impulse passes and I dip my head instead.

'I was told you wished to see me,' I say. I'm aware of every eye in the room on us both.

'I did. I do,' Malcolm says. He seems unaware of anything but me. 'Would you care to eat? You must be hungry. Or perhaps drink…' He looks around as if he's expecting servants to leap forward to do his bidding, still surprised they don't.

Fitzroy saves us both from embarrassment. 'Today is Sunday.' He untucks himself from the table and turns to Nicholas, standing firmly by my side. 'I understand they're roasting boar today. Not just one, mind, but an entire herd caught only last night, a spectacle I wouldn't mind seeing for myself. Perhaps you'd care to join me, Nicholas?'

Fitzroy gestures toward the door, but Nicholas smiles, apologetic. 'Would that I could say yes! But I am Elizabeth's servant today, and I wish to see her settled safely in her tent.'

'It's all right,' I tell him, warming at his protection. 'I can see myself there shortly. Or perhaps I'll meet you at the boars? I'd like to offer my thanks – and condolences – to the cooks who had to dress them.'

Nicholas smiles at this, then glances at Malcolm. His dark gaze holds Malcolm's pale one, and if I'm not mistaken, I see a flash of warning there. Then he and Fitzroy step out into the hall. The door slips shut and Malcolm turns to me.

'You're here.' A faltering smile. 'I know, I said that already. Are you well? Do you care to sit?' He rushes to Fitzroy's chair, holds it out for me.

'I'm fine,' I say, a slender and abridged truth. 'I'll stand.'

Malcolm nods, his smile disappearing. 'It was a frightening moment, there in Ravenscourt. So much magic. And to see Caleb like that…' He shakes his head. 'I get news slowly here, you know. No one is rushing to tell me anything, which is understandable, of course. But Fitzroy told me everything regardless. Everything you went through…' Malcolm breaks off and I break in; I don't wish to relive it, not at all, but especially not with him.

'I see you and Fitzroy are on a first-name basis.' I change the subject. 'Is that because you're familiar, or because you've grown tired of saying his surnames? Or perhaps you've forgotten them.'

'As someone with three given names, I understand what a disadvantage that can be. But to answer your question, we settled on first names mostly because Fitzroy didn't know what else to call me.' His smile is back. 'Although I suppose he could simply call me captain.'

'Captain?' I repeat. 'You?'

'Indeed. Of my very own fledgling army.' Malcolm steps

back, sweeps a hand toward a table on the other side of the room. It's covered in maps and parchment, chess pieces scattered across both. 'Turns out a deposed king can come in handy, particularly when said deposed king learned battle strategy from the very king who usurped him.' A pause. 'That wasn't too maudlin, was it?'

I almost smile. 'Not at all.'

'Good. I've been working on it. Fitzroy said I was irritating when I got that way. Called me stroppy! He's as bad as Keagan. No respect.' He says this last part in a put-on, lofty tone, and now I do smile.

'He's taught me a great deal about Harrow, and the people who live here. I'm glad for the knowledge, more so than the embarrassment of not having it before.'

'Such as?'

'Reformists,' he begins. 'I thought they all practised witchcraft, or at least had magical leanings. Not so. I'd say half the troops at camp are without magic. Neutral, Nicholas calls them. Funny word. In any case, since they don't have any magic to rely on, and since half of that half have never held a sword in their life, they've offered them to me to train.'

'So you're in charge of all of them?'

'Oh, no. Half of that half doesn't want anything to do with me. That leaves just over one hundred men who can stand to be in my presence. Half of *that* half—'

'Malcolm.'

'Sixty.' Malcolm shrugs. 'Sixty soldiers out of one thousand. But it is, as they say, a start. All things considered,

I'm grateful for it. Fitzroy thinks if I do well enough by them, if I can turn metal into gold as the alchemists say, more will join in. That's what I'm planning right now.' Another gesture at the table.

'When do you run drills?' I ask. 'Maybe I'll come join you. Then you'd have sixty-one soldiers.'

His expression is sunshine. 'Yes. I'd like that. It would be nice to see a friendly face.' He pauses, considering. 'Well, a face, at any rate.'

I do something then I didn't think I could: I start to laugh.

In the early days of training, when Caleb and I were new to the tests, when even he couldn't have imagined what we'd be asked to face or the things we'd have to do, he devised a way for us to manage the toll it was taking on us.

He showed up outside my dormitory at Ravenscourt one morning, dressed for the outdoors and carrying a bag, but he wouldn't tell me what was in it or where we were going. The sun was still rising, but the streets were already crowded and Caleb pulled me through them, cobblestoned and wide until they became gradually narrower, the smoke- and dung-scented air giving way to cottages and trees and grass, the scent of a village.

We traipsed up a hill; at the top was a cemetery. The gravestones tumbled over one another like pirates' teeth, jumbled and cracked and stained. Headless statues scattered throughout, fighting for space among the trees. There were no people around, no paths, no flowers; it was a place that had been forgotten, just like the dead that lay there.

Caleb found a flat patch of grass nestled in the centre of a half-dozen tombstones and sat down. He pulled his bag off his shoulder and opened it, pulling out food wrapped in linen: bread, ham, cheese, fruit he'd filched from the kitchen.

'What are you doing?'

He looked up at me. I expected him to tease me, as it was obvious what he was doing. But for once, his blue eyes were serious. 'Eating,' he replied. 'It's been a while since you ate, hasn't it? I know it has for me.'

I thought about it. It had probably been days since I ate, but who could know? It had probably been days since I slept, but who could know that, either? I sleepwalked through them; it was the only sleep I would get.

'How did you find this place?' I settled onto the ground across from him. He tore off a piece of bread and handed it to me. It was still warm from the oven.

'I don't know,' he replied, chewing as he talked. 'It was sometime after the second test. You know, the one at the Serpentine.'

I swallowed. Blackwell had taken us to Serpentine Lake, a forty-acre lake inside Jubilee Park where the royal family spent their summers boating and fishing. He commanded us to swim across it – it was December; freezing and snowy – and none of us knew how. We were forbidden to help one another. It was an agonising day spent listening to two of the recruits slowly drown: their pleas rending the frozen air, then all at once silent. One of them was only twelve.

'I couldn't stop hearing their voices,' Caleb continued. 'So one night, after three with no sleep, I just started walking. I had no destination in mind; I just wanted to move. I found myself here after several hours. Ironic, no?'

I managed a small smile.

Caleb took another bite of bread. 'I sat here for I don't know how many hours. Looking out at all these gravestones, these markers, these people... They're all dead, Elizabeth. More than that: They're forgotten. When was the last time someone thought of them? Enough to come see them? Look around. It's been a while.'

Years, at least, by the look of it.

'It hit me then,' he said. 'No matter what's happened to us, what we've been through, what we've had to see, at least we're not them. At least we're not dead. We're not like them, Elizabeth. We're alive.'

It was a small comfort, but it was the only one we had. So we spent the afternoon in that cemetery, both of us eating, Caleb leaning against a tombstone and napping. When I got back to Ravenscourt, I slept for the first time in four days.

We were alive.

Despite the chain around my neck, the soft pallet beneath me, and the relative safety of my tent – guarded now, for I've made more than a few enemies – I still can't sleep: Visions of Blackwell and his ruined face, of Caleb and his ruined life, haunt my nightmares. After my third sleepless night, I rise, dress, sling my bag over my shoulder, and step into the cold predawn morning, silent and still around the edges. I stop by the food tent, still waking up; the pair of cooks inside yawning as they measure grain into a vast, bubbling kettle. When I appear in the doorway they say nothing. But after a moment the older cook, a woman dressed in grey, steps forward and presses a bundle into my hand.

'It's not much,' she says. 'The cheese is a little hard, the bread's gone a little stale. But you look as if you could eat.'

I thank her, place the food inside my bag, then thread my way through the sea of sleeping tents, across the field and over the bridge, out of Rochester.

Three hours later, I find myself in Hatch End, standing before the black gates of the cemetery that lies beside Gareth's home. They're locked, but only about seven feet high, and even as tired as I am I scale them with ease. I skirt along the side of the chapel, through the flat patch of grass with neatly lined gravestones. Then, just as Caleb and I had done so many times so many years ago, I tuck beside an obelisk, unpack the food from my bag, lay it before me. But it is not the same.

I am alive, yes. But Caleb is dead, and it is not the same.

I don't know how long I sit there, my back against the stone, a flat of bread in my hand, before I see him. He creeps toward me, silent as a ghost.

'You followed me?' I look up at him, his hair quicksilver-bright in the nascent sunlight. 'Why?'

Schuyler shrugs. 'Wanted to see how you were coming on. Haven't seen you around much, and Fifer's worried about you. You've been keeping busy.'

Since I returned to camp, I've spent much of my time with Malcolm, as promised, helping run his men through exercises, showing them things I've never shown anyone: things no one should see. Ways to injure, ways to maim, ways to kill. We managed to add some twenty-odd soldiers to Malcolm's retinue after a demonstration in which I took out a band of wolves – magically conjured by Nicholas – with nothing but a pair of knives and a handful of coniferous tree branches.

'You think it's a good idea?' Schuyler continues. 'Coming here?'

'Why not? Gareth isn't here.' I shrug. 'He's been locked up in council meetings. Malcolm said he's not left Rochester in a week.'

'Not what I meant.' Schuyler brushes aside a pile of leaves and settles down beside me, leaning against a mossy tomb. 'You sure it's wise, convening with the dead like this?'

'I'm convening with you, aren't I?'

'Point.' Schuyler raises a hand.

I glance at him. At those almost unnaturally bright blue eyes, slightly dimmed today by worry or trouble or both. My thoughts run to Caleb again.

'He told Blackwell I was coming,' I say. 'Caleb. He said he has to tell him everything he knows, everything he thinks. He said Blackwell demanded it of him.'

'Yes,' Schuyler says. 'Blackwell is Caleb's pater – the one who brought him back – so Caleb must do what he orders. Everything he orders.'

'But he didn't tell Blackwell I didn't have my stigma.'

Schuyler shrugs. 'He probably couldn't hear you clearly enough to figure it out. I had a hard time hearing you through that damned prayer, and I've got years of practice. Caleb is new. It's hard to focus on a single person's thoughts, when there are so many others to hear.'

'I suppose,' I say. 'But in the ritual room, I wasn't saying the prayer. Not at first. I was too tired, too worried about what was about to happen. Caleb could have dug in, he could have heard everything. But when Blackwell asked him where my stigma went, he said he didn't know.' I pause. 'Do you think he did, and that he lied to Blackwell about it?'

'I don't see why he would.' Schuyler breaks off a piece of bread, tosses it into the grass. A pair of birds flutter to the ground beside us and begin pecking at the crumbs. 'He didn't do anything to stop what was happening to you. At any rate, it's not a matter of choice. A revenant's will is completely subordinate to that of his pater. He doesn't—' He stops, abrupt.

'You don't have to talk about it,' I say quickly.

'It's not that,' he says. 'It's just that it's hard for me to recall. It's been a few hundred years since I thought about it. I don't even remember how long it has actually been. Do you know I don't even remember my surname?'

'You don't?' I don't know whether to be amused or horrified. I decide on the latter. 'I'm sorry.'

'I'm not.' Schuyler grins, wicked. 'Feels rather legendary, having only one name.'

I fall silent a moment, recalling the way Caleb spoke to

me, the way he whispered to me through the door, as if he were telling me a secret. The way he seemed at turns angry and defiant, then almost contrite.

'Caleb cannot physically disobey Blackwell.' Schuyler interrupts my thoughts. 'But it doesn't mean he has to be loyal. There are a thousand ways to show disloyalty besides disobedience.'

'Such as?'

Schuyler shrugs again. 'Revenants are very base creatures,' he says. 'The word itself means "to return". When they do, they're like infants, in a way. They know only base desires.'

I note his use of the word *they*, as if revenants are a separate entity from himself.

'It's an indelicate balance,' he continues. 'They are beholden, but they don't want to be held. Some – most – simply bide their time, obeying in simmering resentment until their pater dies, until they can finally be free. Others, shall we say, take matters into their own hands, inasmuch as they can.'

'How do you know this?'

Schuyler fixes me with his bright, knowing gaze. 'Because I had my pater killed.'

I open my mouth; nothing comes out.

'He asked me to buy a ship; I bought him a ship,' Schuyler says. 'What he didn't ask was for me to buy him a sound ship or a competent crew. The ship was full of weak timber and shoddy sails; the crew not a crew at all but beggars and vagabonds looking for coins and drink; they didn't care how they got it. Nor did he ask me to ensure the weather would be clear when we sailed. So when we did, we hit a storm, the ship fell apart, every last man on board died. Except yours truly.'

I swallow a lump of bread that's somehow turned to stone.

'It's the things a pater doesn't ask that can be taken advantage of.' Schuyler throws me a look, a half smile on his face. 'You can exorcise a revenant with salt all you want, bijoux, but the devil inside still remains.'

He stops then, his hand frozen midthrow, the bread still poised between his fingers. Then he's on his feet in a blur, snatching my cloak and hauling me up. The bread tumbles from my lap; the birds converge. He hauls me behind the obelisk.

A second later, the door along the side of the cathedral opens – the same door I let myself out of the day of my trial, the day Blackwell's attacks came – and Gareth steps out. He's accompanied by another man, dressed in all black like a councilman, only I don't recognise him at all.

'I thought you said he was at Rochester,' Schuyler whispers.

'I guess I was wrong,' I whisper back. 'But does it really matter? He won't like our being here, but it's not as if he'll arrest—'

'*Shh.*' Schuyler clamps his hand over my mouth.

'I understand things have changed. But I cannot be expected to settle all my affairs in one week,' Gareth says.

'And what affairs would those be?' asks the man.

'I –' Gareth stops. 'My home.'

'Provided you have one left,' the man says. 'At any rate, there are plenty of fine homes to be had in Upminster.'

'That was not the plan,' Gareth says.

'Ah, but that should not faze you.' The man holds up an appeasing hand. 'You are, if nothing else, a master planner. I should think this is nothing to you. Even so, it is our role, is it not? To do whatever it takes?'

Gareth considers this, then nods. '*Faciam quodlibet quod necesse est.*'

Blackwell's motto.

Schuyler's hand is back over my mouth, stifling the gasp and the realisation:

Gareth is the spy.

TWENTY-FIVE

The man in black vanishes then – disappears into nothing, seemingly into thin air. Gareth glances around, furtive, before striding down the path, out the gate, and onto the road leading toward Rochester. Schuyler keeps his hand pressed to my mouth, waiting for him to pass out of earshot. Minutes pass. Finally, he lets go. Snatches my bag from the ground and darts out from behind the obelisk.

'One week?' I say. 'Does that mean Blackwell and his men will be at Harrow in one week?'

'I presume.' Schuyler's on his knees, stuffing my things into my bag, ruffling the ground to scatter the bread crumbs, erasing evidence of our presence.

'What are we going to do? Schuyler.' I grab his arm to stop his frantic and pointless tidying. 'Stop that. You need to listen to Gareth. Find out what else he knows.'

'I can't.' Schuyler rounds on me. 'I already tried. Can't hear a thing. My guess is they were both wearing a barrier.

Mercury, ash, like that damned necklace Fifer has. But I don't need to listen to know what they mean. One week until Blackwell sends his men to take Harrow, to take John, to take that stigma, and to go through with his bloody insane plan.'

One week.

'We're not ready,' I say. 'The troops from Gaul haven't arrived yet, the Order hasn't arrived yet, Malcolm's men aren't trained yet… What are we going to do?'

'Tell Nicholas. Fitzroy. Prepare.' Schuyler throws my bag over his shoulder. 'It's all we can do.'

'Do you think we should—'

'Kill Gareth? No.' Schuyler picks up on my thought before I can voice it. 'Can't go around killing councilmen, bijoux, even if they are traitors. No, we need to tell Nicholas and let him decide. After that, if he's looking for volunteers, I'll be first in line.'

We start back toward Rochester. I wanted Schuyler to go ahead of me, to try to reach the camp ahead of Gareth. But Schuyler doesn't know the path he'll take, and neither of us can risk being seen.

Walking at turns fast and cautious, we reach Rochester sometime before noon. Smoke rends the air, the scent of food being readied for supper. People cluster in groups at the tables; stand in line at the bathing tents, the laundry tents, the weapons tents; sit around multiple fires that spring in rows along the ground. In the distance, men scatter along the jousting pits, either sparring or watching, some at the archery butts, others running drills in the adjoining fields.

Schuyler and I look through the crowds, searching for one man taller than everyone else, one man dressed better than everyone else, and one man more traitorous than everyone else.

We don't see Nicholas, Fitzroy, or Gareth anywhere.

'Let's split up,' I say. 'I'll stay here, search the tents. You go inside. Check Malcolm's quarters, too,' I add as an afterthought. 'Fitzroy may be there.'

Schuyler nods. 'I'll fetch Fifer first. She needs to know what's happening, and she can help me look. If we don't find them, or even if we do, we'll meet you in an hour in the chapel.'

He slips into the crowd then, and I turn and make my way toward the tents, flipping the hood of my cloak over my head as I go, pulling it down low. I don't want to be seen, I don't want to be stopped, and right now, I don't want to speak to anyone but Nicholas or Fitzroy.

The crowd thins as I reach the ring of officer tents. Men in uniform, men carrying weapons, men poring over maps and endless lists of inventory. I'm spared a glance, two, as I thread through them, but still no Nicholas, and no Fitzroy.

I leave the relative safety of the inner ring and make my way to the jousting pits. Nicholas won't be there, but Peter might, and he might be able to tell me Nicholas's whereabouts. I'm squinting under my hood into the bright sun, and I don't see him until I'm nearly on top of him: a boy in a navy-blue cloak standing beside a girl bright as a winter rose in a crimson gown, her hand clutching his arm.

John.

'Elizabeth.' His eyes, still shadowed but not as deeply as last I saw him, grow wide at the sight of me. My heart, running rapid before, launches into a sprint.

'You're back,' Chime adds, when John falls silent and I don't reply. 'I was so pleased to hear you were safe,' she adds, but the pique behind her words tells me different.

'Yes.' I dart my eyes left, right; I look for an escape but there is none. Not from John's intense, searching gaze, and not from the three other boys, John's friends – some I recognise, some I don't – who walk up and encircle me. I feel vaguely hunted.

'I see you've returned,' one of them says. 'Returned, recovered, and now helping one king to try to kill another.'

'Yes,' I repeat. I think if I don't speak too much, they will grow tired of whatever game they're setting up for me and leave me be.

'Speaking of kings, I heard you faced Blackwell.' Seb, the ginger boy, looks me over, that unpleasant smirk I've seen before crossing his face. 'What was that like?'

I remember Marcus's hands against my skull, Blackwell's scarred face, the dead raven in the centre of the ritual room. Caleb and the legion of dead guards; the prowling, all-seeing lions, the vengeful, red-eyed crows.

I look away and don't reply.

'I heard you lost the Azoth, too,' another boy says. He's attractive, very much so, blond, blue-eyed, and tall like Caleb and Schuyler, though this does little to endear him to me. 'You went through a lot of trouble, didn't you, only to create more.'

I don't reply to this, either. Instead, I look at Chime, the only one of this company I can stand to look at, and then only barely.

'I'm looking for Nicholas. Have you seen him?'. The courtesy in my voice, you could choke on it.

Chime opens her mouth, but John steps forward and answers before she can. 'I have. He's in the solar, but you'll need an escort to the west wing. I can do that, if you wish.'

I don't wish it. But I've asked for Nicholas, John knows where he is, and at the very least it leads me away from this uncomfortable gathering.

I turn away from them without replying and make my way to the yew alley and Rochester Hall beyond. I think, for a moment, John has decided against going with me, or was talked out of it. But then a fall of footsteps and the flutter of a dark cloak beside me tells me I was mistaken.

I reach the exterior hallway and the guarded door leading to the west wing. John nods to the men; they move to let us pass. Soon enough I'm standing in the solar – a place I have no fond memories of – looking around at the settees, the fireplace, the window embrasure, and the round mahogany table set with chairs.

It's empty.

I push the hood off my face and whirl around. John steps before the door, blocking my exit. His eyes are trained on my face, watching me closely.

'What are you doing?' My confusion mingles with apprehension. 'Where is Nicholas?'

'I don't know,' he confesses. 'But I heard you were back at camp, and I wanted to talk to you. I've been looking for you all day.' John pushes his hair back in a gesture that's familiar, his dark curls longer than when I saw him last. He looks more like himself.

But he is not himself.

'I tried the tiltyard, the archery, the training meadow, and the park, which is a mistake too early in the morning. I was almost trampled by a herd of deer.'

'I'm sorry to inconvenience you,' I say. My words are casual, indifferent, but the tremor in my voice betrays me.

'I don't care about that.' He shakes his head. 'It's not what I meant. I just meant I wanted to see you.'

Latent anger flares up inside me. 'The last time I saw you, you said you never wanted to see me again,' I fire back at him. 'Do you recall that? I do. You said you wanted to put this – me – behind you. And then you told me to leave, and to never come back.'

'Elizabeth—' He steps toward me.

'While I appreciate the heroic effort you went through to find me, it wasn't necessary,' I go on. 'You don't need to tell me not to bother you, or get in your way. You're on your own now. Just like you wanted.' Then, out of spite, I add, 'But from what I saw, you're not so alone, are you?' Seeing John, talking to him, it's more painful than I thought it would be. I start for the door.

'Elizabeth, please, just listen.' He reaches for me, but I pull away.

'Don't touch me.' My eyes begin their telltale burning;

my voice cracks. I am dangerously close to tears now. 'Get out of my way.' I push past him for the door again.

'Goddammit, listen to me!' John snatches my arm, turns me around. I start to tear away from him again, until I see his face. Pale skin, eyes red, brows creased in an expression I know, or at least I used to: part pleading, part sadness, all misery.

'I was angry with you,' he says. 'I said things I wish I hadn't said. Stupid things I didn't even mean. And when I thought those would be the last words you ever heard from me – ' John releases me and turns to the door. For a moment I think he's going to walk through it; I don't know if I'll stop him or let him go.

'The stigma.' He turns back to me. 'It does things to me. It makes me violent. Irrational. Not myself. But you know this already.'

I nod, cautious.

'If I was unstable before I was put into Hexham, I was even worse after,' he continues. 'I got into fights with guards. Repeatedly. After you left, after you broke Malcolm and the other one out and you left, I was so angry. I injured one of them so badly they had to take him to a healer.' He winces at that. 'I was completely out of control. But you know this already, too.'

I nod again.

'Nicholas came to release me from Hexham,' John goes on. 'Told me Fitzroy petitioned the council for custody of me, that he needed me to tend to his mother. It was a lie; I knew that much. I was told I'd be kept under house arrest, but that was a lie, too: Nicholas and Fitzroy had me quarantined. I was not allowed out. No visitors were allowed in, except Nicholas. I was allowed nothing but herbs and tools, books and potions. He wouldn't even give me an alembic at first; he was afraid I'd burn the house down.'

John allows himself a rueful laugh, but I don't laugh at all.

'Within days, I started to feel better,' he says. 'I understood why they shut me away. Because the more I practised my own magic, the more the magic of the stigma seemed to go away. And the more I returned to myself, the more I thought of you. I wanted to know what happened to you, if you were safe. But Nicholas wouldn't tell me anything, and I thought…' He flinches, stops. 'The day he brought you back, he came to see me. And he told me everything.'

'Why did he finally allow you out?'

John reaches out a hand for me, then lets it fall.

'Because he said you needed me,' he says. 'But if you don't, tell me. I'll do my best to understand. But I need you. And I'll never stop trying to prove that to you.'

With that, my resolve breaks. I take a step toward him; he closes the distance between us in three strides. I reach out and he crushes me to him. His arms around me, his hands in my hair, his lips on my face and his words in my ear: *I love you, I love you, I love you.*

Nicholas is silent as Schuyler and I tell him about Gareth.

The chapel is empty but for the five of us seated in the

front pew: John to my right; Fifer, Schuyler, and Nicholas to my left. Light from the flickering candles set along the wall casts our blue shadows onto the marble floors.

'One week.' Nicholas looks skyward, to the stars painted on the ceiling. 'That will be because of the moon, of course.'

I frown; everyone else nods.

Nicholas turns to me. 'The day of the ritual, and of your rescue, the moon was in first quarter. Half light, half dark; in balance.'

I think back to that morning – up until now I've tried not to – and I remember it as I perched on the sill of the window in my holding room, on the edge of my escape: hanging low in the still dark sky, striking in its half light.

'A moon phase is not required for his spell; the magic he is attempting is far beyond that of the sky,' Nicholas continues. 'But Blackwell is leaving nothing to chance, and that explains the timing. The next half-moon, the third quarter, will be in—'

'One week,' Fifer says.

Nicholas nods. 'It is likely Blackwell now knows John has the stigma. If not from Caleb, then from Gareth, who has no doubt pieced it together by now.' A pause. 'I would not have believed it was him. That Gareth would turn to Blackwell, that he would sacrifice all he held dear for what I can only assume is an elevated position in a new regime.'

'He has always been ambitious,' John says.

'Yes,' Nicholas says. 'And it will be his downfall.'

Once again, I think of Caleb: of his unwavering ambition, how it drove him onward and upward until, eventually, it drove him into the ground.

'I don't understand,' I say. 'If Gareth has aligned himself with Blackwell, why then, at the trial, did he order me to kill him? And why did he send his scouts into Harrow? The information they were looking for, Gareth could have given him. He tipped his hand. If his men had never arrived, we wouldn't have known there was a spy within Harrow. Not until it was too late.'

'When Gareth ordered you to kill Blackwell, he was no doubt following orders,' Nicholas says. 'Blackwell knew you would rise to the occasion; what better way to get you in his path? As for the scouts, I believe they were sent to confirm the information Gareth passed on to him. Traitors cannot be trusted, as Blackwell himself knows.'

'What do we do?' Fifer says. 'Do we alert the rest of the council? Have Gareth arrested? Detained at Hexham, or somewhere else within Rochester?'

Nicholas steeples his fingers together. 'I think not,' he says after a moment. 'I think that would only hasten Blackwell's arrival into Harrow. If Blackwell discovered we knew the truth about Gareth, he would have no cause to delay his attacks. As I say: The quarter moon is not required for his magic, simply preferred. I do not believe he would sacrifice his military advantage for it.'

'You know that I would never question you,' Fifer says. 'But the idea of Gareth walking freely around camp, listening to our strategies, hearing our secrets – more of our secrets – I can't stand the thought of it.'

Nicholas looks to Schuyler. 'Will you monitor him? As

closely as you can? I know you said you cannot hear him, but I wish to make certain he has not ensnared anyone else, councillor or soldier, in his plans. And I wish to know who else he meets with, and who else he allows inside Harrow, within these next seven days.'

Schuyler nods. 'I'll shadow his every step.'

Nicholas turns back to Fifer. 'I know it is difficult to imagine, but sometimes it is best to let a plot run its course until the full extent of involvement is known. On both sides.' He gets to his feet. 'In the meantime, all we can do is prepare. John, I ask that you tell your father; he will know to keep it silent, and he will want to know the danger you are in. I am going to find Fitzroy. He'll need to begin preparing his troops in a way that doesn't alert Gareth. The sooner, the better, I think.'

TWENTY-SIX

Rochester springs into action. Troops begin arriving from Gaul, a thousand in the last twenty-four hours alone, another thousand due in the next twenty-four, over the safe, protected borders of neighbouring Cambria and through the tunnels hewn beneath the Hall. Fitzroy leads drills. Malcolm spends dawn until dusk with his men, running them through exercises. And I've begun training again, too: mornings at the archery butts, drills in the afternoons, sparring with Schuyler in the evenings.

On the morning of the fourth day – three days until Blackwell's troops begin their attack – I slip from my tent and into the deep grey, cloudy morning light, eager to get started. Already I hear the trumpets in the distance, calling us to order. The sight of three thousand men marching in uniform over the hills sends a thrill through my veins.

Halfway to the training yard I spot John walking toward me. He stops before me, offers me a quick, tentative smile.

Unlike me, he's not dressed for drills. He's in brown trousers and a black cloak, the strap of his worn brown leather bag thrown over his shoulder. He takes me in, his eyes warm but also a little wary. We stand there a moment, looking at each other but saying nothing.

'How are you?' I say finally.

'I'm well,' he says. 'You?'

'I'm well, too.' I shift a little at this awkward exchange.

I'm unused to being around John now. Unsure of how to act, what to say, or how to be with him. It was easy when he first came back to me, in the way that a crisis can charge down walls between two people. But in the days that followed, those walls were built up again, every word and every action calling attention to what raised them in the first place: the betrayal and the lies, the things he said, the things I didn't. I don't know how to knock them down again.

'Are you going somewhere?' I nod at his battered bag.

'I...yes,' he says. 'The apothecary. I haven't been in a while.'

Of course he hasn't been in a while, because he was in prison. Because I put him there.

'What I mean to say is, my stores have run a bit low.' John tries again. 'So I thought I'd go in, pick some up. Do you – ' He stops. Clears his throat. 'I know you're busy and have things to do. But I'd love your company, if you're up for it.'

I hesitate. If I don't report into drills, I'll have to answer to Fitzroy. He'll assign me to a menial task for punishment, dishes or laundry or weapons detail. But it's not just that. It's that I need to keep training. I don't have room to step back, not even a little. I start to say no, but then I see John's hands clenched into fists at his sides, the set of his jaw. The way his eyes dart around the camp, watchful and wide.

'Yes,' I say. 'Of course I'll come with you.'

He reaches for my hand, cautious; I take it. Together, we start toward Rochester Hall, to the only entrance left open for us now, the heavily guarded and magicked front gate.

If we were trying to leave the camp unnoticed, we chose the worst time to do it. The trumpets sound their final, frantic call as men stagger from their tents, tugging on coats and tunics and boots, and leap to their feet in the meal tent, knocking over goblets and snatching the last of the food from their trenchers, spilling into the grass around us.

I don't miss the stares levelled in our direction, or the whispered disapproval as we pass. John sees – he's far too astute not to – but he holds on to me as if he might protect me from whatever they might say or do. And when he smiles at me and squeezes my hand, I know his protection is a promise.

The wall edges down.

Until I see Chime in the courtyard, sitting on a stone bench, the brightest thing under today's dull grey sky. She's surrounded by friends: The girls in rainbow-hued gowns I recognise from that day in the meal tent when John was arrested, and some of the boys, too; the same ones he sparred with, who encouraged his violence while at the same time discouraging me. The girls are playing some sort of dice game, the boys choosing sides and placing bets. But when they see us they stop: A roll of black dice hits the stone and stays there, no one bothering to pick it up.

'John.' Chime greets him, ignoring me completely. 'Are you leaving camp?'

'Just for a little while,' John replies. 'To pick up some supplies.'

Chime arches a perfectly shaped eyebrow, then looks away.

'Back to healing, are you?' the boy beside her says, the blond one who harassed me a few days ago. 'If you ever get tired of nursing old women and delivering babies, you're always welcome to join us again. Well, one of you is.' He glances my way, nose flaring in distaste.

John lifts his finger to the air a half second before the trumpets blast their final call. The boys scramble to their feet, yanking on cloaks and holstering weapons.

'Enjoy wash duty,' John says, tugging me from the courtyard.

The apothecary lies in the centre of Harrow's high street in Gallion's Reach, nestled between the cobbler and the baker. It's nearly empty today: one or two merchants pushing carts along the road, a few standing in vacant doorways, watching as we pass.

John steers me into a side street that leads to the alley behind the shops. We cut through the mud and puddles of stagnant water until we reach a narrow, unassuming wooden door. He fishes a key from his cloak and unlocks the latch.

'The lock on the front door is broken,' he says. 'I've been meaning to fix it, but never got around to it.'

We enter the back of the apothecary, into what looks like a storeroom. It's dim inside, the light from the one small window set high beside the door just enough to see by. There are great wooden barrels, baskets on shelves, crates in the centre of the room. Set into a nook on the other side of the room is a bed, somewhere between a cot and a pallet. It's made up with clean white linens, unruffled and smooth, as though it hasn't been slept on in some time.

'My mother put that there,' John offers. 'She thought it might be useful to have an infirmary. It's not terribly welcoming, but it's away from the street, and quiet. Though as far as I know, no one was actually infirm enough to make use of it.' He smiles, gestures to another door. 'This way.'

I've never been inside an apothecary before, but it's just as I imagined. The back wall is lined with shelves, crowded with bottles in all shapes and sizes, murky glass of green, amber, and red, wrapped in labels of yellowed parchment and scrawled with John's illegible handwriting. A few jars, presumably hazardous in some way – I smile at his elaborate rendering of a skull and crossbones – sit on the topmost shelf. A single large, opaque window of ochre glass bathes the room in a golden, almost otherworldly glow, and the battered door leading to the main street is bolted shut with a beam, the broken lock hanging by its hinge.

The rafters bristle with flowers and herbs in various

stages of drying. I recognise a few by scent alone: lavender and anise, rue and cypress, hazel and marigold. The shop smells exotic, a mixture of sharp spices and tangy herbs along with something softer, candles or soap. It smells like him.

'I would say have a seat, but…' John looks around. 'There doesn't seem to be one, does there? I don't usually have visitors, just customers. I could bring in a crate from the back for you to sit on, if you'd like.'

'That's all right.' I hop onto the countertop, littered with books and tools and parchment and pens, brushing aside a few as I do. 'I'm fine here. Comfortable. It's nice.'

He gives me a wry smile. 'It's a mess. I would say it's because I haven't been here in a while, but that's not really it. It pretty much always looks like this.'

'What supplies did you come for?' I ask him. 'Maybe I can help you collect them. I'm good at recognising things; if you just give me a list I can – what?'

John's face, arranged in a careful expression of control, falls. 'I didn't come here for supplies. I came here because I had to get away from camp. From the people, from training, from everything. I just…had to get away.'

He crosses the room to an enormous cabinet standing beside the front door. Inside are shelves lined neatly with volumes of leather-bound books. He runs a hand along the stack, pulls one out, and walks it back to me.

'Remember how I told you that when I first came back to Rochester, Nicholas gave me books and supplies, in the hopes I would start practicing magic again?'

I nod.

'What I didn't tell you is that at first, I refused to touch any of it. I told myself I wasn't interested, but in truth, I didn't want to know just how far gone I really was. But when I finally forced myself to pick up one of the books, I saw what they were. Remedial texts. For children.'

He smiles at me, but I can't bring myself to smile back.

'I went into a rage. Threw them at walls, I nearly threw them out the window. But before long, in the absence of anything else to do, I began to read them. There's not much to them, really: just pictures and descriptions of herbs, botanicals, flowering plants. It was magic I already knew, just buried inside the violence and the anger of the stigma.

'Now, when I feel it start to take hold, I go back to this.' He gives the book in his hand a little shake. 'Back to the beginning, to remind myself of what matters. It's starting over, I know that now. And I suppose, what I really brought you here for, is to ask if you would start over with me.'

I hold out my hand. He passes me the book; the title written in gold on the brown leather cover: *Phytologiae Aristotelicae Fragmenta*. A text on botanicals.

'What do I do?'

'Just read me the names of the plants,' he says. 'And I'll tell you their indications.'

I flip it open to the first page. 'Hawthorn.'

'*Crataegus laevigata*.' He pulls himself up onto the counter across from me. 'Parts used: leaves, flowers, fruit. Improves shortness of breath, fatigue, and chest pain. No known precautions.'

I turn the page. 'Skullcap.'

'*Scutellaria lateriflora*. Leaves, stems, flowers. Used to relieve anxiety, insomnia, nervous tension.' A muscle in his jaw clenches. 'Known precautions: May cause drowsiness, and when combined with germander; may cause toxicity.'

'Goldenrod.'

On we go. Page after page, herb after flower, plant after root. Eventually, John's posture begins to droop, his eyes begin to close. His voice grows softer, deep and hypnotic.

I flip the page one more time, and what I see makes me smile.

'Jasmine.'

His eyes fly open. They find mine and they hold them, so full of longing my breath catches in my throat.

'*Parsonsia capsularis*. Parts used: petals and stems. As a tincture for abrasions, a compress for headaches and fevers.'

He slides off the counter then. Steps in front of me. Takes a strand of my hair, coils it around his finger, tucks it behind my ear.

'Precautions: May cause rapid heartbeat, shallow breathing, nervous stomach.'

Being this close to him I finally see – really see – what the stigma has done to him: the toll the fight against it has taken. The sleepless nights in the redness of his eyes. The worry in the dark shadows beneath them. His face, shaven though not carefully, a quick swipe with a razor to say it's done but not with much care. His shirt, too clean and too unwrinkled to be of his doing.

In that moment he lets his guard down: He places his

hands on the counter on either side of me, leans forward, rests his head on my shoulder. He's still, so still, as if he expects me to pull away, to tell him no. I feel the sweep of his lashes on my cheeks as he closes his eyes, the weight of his chest as he takes a breath and lets it out, a slow, long exhalation.

There are different kinds of strength, I know this now. The kind that wields swords and slays monsters but there's another kind, too; one that comes in quiet but in the end is stronger and harder and more powerful: the kind that comes from inside. For all the time I've needed him, I never understood the extent to which he needed me, too.

I slip a hand into his hair, thread my fingers around his curls. Lean forward, brush my lips against his, soft. I linger there a moment, my lips on his, but he doesn't kiss me back. He's gone still, and I know he's thinking if he moves, breathes, speaks, anything, this spell will be broken and I will be gone.

But I keep going.

I'm pressed against him now, and I can feel his heart hammering beneath his shirt, the tension in his arms as he grips the edge of the counter. My lips move back to his then away again, feather-light, across his cheek to his ear, then down his neck. I flick my eyes to his just for a moment, just long enough to see them close.

'You don't know what you're doing.' His voice is a whisper, a breath against my skin. Not an admonishment: a warning.

I allow myself a smile, just a small one, my lips curving

into the warm, spicy skin on his neck, kissing it once, twice, before slowly trailing my way back to his ear only to whisper:

'Yes, I do.'

He yanks me toward him then, one hand in my hair, the other gripping my waist before sliding me off the counter and onto his hips. I let out a little gasp of surprise and then his lips are finally, fiercely, on mine. I'm breathless, but he's not through. He kisses me again, still. My feet slip to the floor; we stumble away from the counter.

It's him who pushes me against the door; it's me who pulls him through. It's him who yanks off my coat; it's me who takes off his. It's him who slips off my tunic; it's me who unfastens one button on his shirt, then another, before sliding it off his shoulders. It's him who pushes me into the room with the small bed in the corner, me who pulls him on top of it, wrinkling the smooth, carefully made sheets.

When the only thing left between us is a question, he pulls away from me, as far as I'll let him, enough to look me in the eye and say without saying it: *Are you sure?*

It's not enough to say yes. It's not enough to answer not with words but with a kiss. I do both of them but I do something else, too: I say it. After feeling it for so long, I finally find the courage to say it.

'I love you.'

He twitches the blanket over us both, then he kisses me.

And the walls come down.

TWENTY-SEVEN

I wake to the feel of John's hands in my hair, running the ends of it through his fingers. I crack open an eye to find him watching me, his eyes half closed and half asleep, but the smile on his face wide awake.

'What time is it?'

He rolls to his back, lifts his head up, and glances out the window by the door. 'I'd say around seven or so.'

'Oh.' I think a moment. 'That's later than I thought. We'll have to come up with some excuse why we were gone all day. Maybe we can say we ate in town.'

John rolls over to face me, his grin now a smirk. 'Seven in the morning.'

I let out a gasp; he starts laughing.

'I'm in so much trouble,' I groan.

'You are,' he agrees. 'You'll be washing dishes for a week.'

'Just so you know, I'm blaming it all on you.'

'You can blame me for whatever you want, any time you want.' He grins again. 'Even so, I suppose we should get back. My father will be frantic.' He pauses, considering. 'Although if he's figured out you're with me, frantic probably isn't the right word.'

We collect our things and step from the back door of the apothecary, John locking it behind him, then thread through the alley into the cobblestoned main street. It's grey and early still, the air cool and calm. It was quiet yesterday, too, but today it feels almost abandoned. The doors to all the shops are closed tight, the windows shuttered, no one to be seen at all.

'Do you think something happened?' I whisper. No one is around, but it seems important to whisper.

'I don't know.' He releases my hand, moves down the street. Tries the door for the cobbler, lifting the shoe-shaped brass knocker and letting it fall once, twice. Next he tries the bakery, the fishmonger, the bookseller, then the tavern, aptly named the Shaven Crown. Knocks on their locked doors, waits for them to be opened.

They don't.

'I don't like this,' I say. But there's nothing not to like. No sounds of an attack, no screaming, or smoke, or horses whinnying. No stomping of boots or clashing of swords. No copper-scented wind, the smell of fresh blood hanging in the air.

'Let's go.' John is by my side again. 'If something's happened, someone at Rochester will know.'

We make our way past the apothecary again and the rest

of the empty storefronts. We're nearly to the end when a man appears around a corner, rushing past as if he were being chased.

'Ho!' He throws up a spear, a shoddy-looking thing, the rusty rough-hewn arrow broken from its shaft and lashed onto a knobby stick by a piece of leather. His eyes go wide when he sees John, and he lowers his weapon immediately.

'John Raleigh. What're you doing here? And you?' The man looks at me. 'Our troops came through here and rounded everyone up last night, took us into Rochester whether we like it or not.' By his scowl it's clear he doesn't. 'Blackwell's men got in again.'

'What happened?' John demands. 'Was anyone hurt?'

'Don't know.' The man shrugs. 'It's chaos. Rumour is people have gone missing, but it's hard to say who just yet. They're doing a head count now.'

John and I exchange a rapid glance.

'Best get back,' the man continues. 'Your father's no doubt worried.'

'If they took everyone to Rochester, what are you doing here?' John says.

The man nods toward the cobbler. 'Realised I forgot to lock up shop – stupid, really—'

The arrow pierces his eye before he can finish. The man sways on his feet, blood pouring down his face, before slumping to the ground, facedown. Dead.

It all happens in less than a second.

From the corner of my eye I see the archer. Black-cloaked, his hood up so I can't see his face, poised at the corner of the same side street the cobbler came from. He's reloading, and he's aiming right at us. John snatches the pitiful weapon from the man's death grip, takes my hand, and we run.

An arrow chases us; I can hear it whistling through the air. We don't dodge it; instead John grabs me and throws us both to the ground. We fall, hard, onto the cobblestones as the arrow sails by us. John's up before I am, pulling me to my feet again, and we run, again.

More arrows. They fly at us from every direction now: front, behind, from the side. We're surrounded. An arrow grazes John's shoulder; I gasp as he pitches forward, clutches his hand to his arm; it comes away with nothing but a small smear of blood: It's already healed.

We skirt into the alley, back to the apothecary. We reach the back door, the key already in John's hand. He jams it into the lock, flips open the latch, pushes me through.

'We need to hide.' I look up, down, around. 'Can we get into the attic somehow? Climb onto the roof?'

'We're not hiding.' John pulls me into the front of the shop. Pushes me behind the counter, then dashes around the room, opening drawers, turning in circles, muttering to himself. Then he drops to his knees and throws open a cabinet.

There's a crash, then a shower of ochre glass as a rock flies through the window. They've found us. After a moment John leaps to his feet holding two masks; they look like executioners' masks. He hands me one.

'Put it on.'

'John, I don't—'

'Put it on!'

I do. It's tight, with only slits for eyes and nothing for my nose. Just a tiny hole where the mouth is, not enough to speak, just enough to breathe. Barely.

John ducks down, his head disappearing into the cabinet again. When he reemerges, he's holding a small leather pouch. He quickly unties the leather strings and upends it onto the counter. Inside is a white block, only slightly larger than a sugar cube, wrapped in parchment. It's stamped with a red skull and crossbones, this one not drawn in his hand.

'John…what is that?' My voice is muffled.

Another crash; another rock sails through the window. The shouts out front grow louder. John turns to me, his face pale under his dark hair.

'It's *Ricinius communis*. Derived from the castor bean plant. Heard of it?'

I shake my head.

'It's poison. A single breath of it kills instantly. It's not just outlawed in Harrow, it's outlawed everywhere. I keep a bag for patients who are dying and don't want to prolong it, who want a quick end. If anyone knew I had it…' He doesn't finish the sentence; he doesn't need to. If the council had known about this, it wouldn't have meant prison: It would have meant death.

'I'm going to use it on them,' he continues. Even his lips are pale now. 'I'm going to blow it into the air, they're going to breathe it, and they're going to die.'

I feel sick. All the time he's spent to gain control over the stigma will now be undone in a single breath. I step forward, place my hand on his.

'Let me do it.'

'No. It needs to be me.' His voice is quiet but sure.

I nod.

'Keep that mask on, you hear me?' His words come fast. 'You're okay to breathe through it, but don't take it off until I tell you to. Don't touch anything, either. Don't do anything until I tell you to. Got it?'

I nod again.

He slips on his gloves: thick, heavy black canvas. Yanks the mask over his own face, pulling it tight around his nose and mouth. Plucks a long glass pipette off the counter. One end broad, the other narrow, like a trumpet. He unwraps the block of poison from the parchment, pinching and crumbling it between his fingertips before shoving it into the widest end of the pipe. He presses his thumb against the other end, creating a vacuum to hold the powder inside.

There's an enormous crashing noise. The front window has shattered, shards hanging by the frame, yellow and glinting like cats' eyes in the weak morning sun.

John points to the corner of the room, to the left of the door.

'Get down. Wait for them to come in,' he says. His voice is muffled behind the mask.

Another smash and they're here; they're inside the shop. Two, six, eight of them crawl in through the open window, and they converge on us, all black cloaks and choking roses, their arrows pointing right at us.

'Your armour won't do you any good,' one says, taking aim at John's forehead.

'Neither will yours,' John says.

And he blows.

Powder fills the air like mist. Finger-shaped white tendrils coil from the pipette, almost predatory, floating their way toward the men. For a second, the air is filled with the sounds of their laughter, but between one breath and the next, that laughter stops.

Their skin turns white; it's as if they've been doused in powder. Eyeballs turn red, veins dilating wider and wider until they're nothing but crimson. They jerk and shake like puppets until the strings are cut and in unison, all eight men slump to the floor in a bloody heap, a catastrophe of a grotesque tragedy.

I'm hauled to my feet. Elbowed, none too gently, over and out the broken window and into the street until we reach the other side. John shakes off his gloves, then spins me around, fumbling with my mask, pulling it off before ripping off his own.

He looks at me closely. 'You didn't touch anything?'

I shake my head. 'No. Nothing.'

John tugs me toward the water pump in front of the fishmonger's. Draws it a couple times until the pipe runs clean, then rinses his hands and face, sucking in mouthfuls of water and spitting it onto the cobblestones.

'Your turn,' he says. 'Even if you didn't touch anything, it won't hurt to make sure.' I reach down and cup my hands beneath the cold stream, rinsing my mouth and splashing water on my face until my cheeks are numb.

I dry my face and hands on the folds of my cloak, then look to him. I fear I'll see hostility in his face again, the violence from the stigma swirling through his veins, wreaking unseen havoc. But instead of aggravation, I see only caution.

'You're all right?' I say.

John glances back at his ruined apothecary, at the shards of yellow glass littering the cobblestones, the heap of black cloaks visible inside.

'Not quite,' he says. 'But I will be.'

I don't want to ask him, but I do. 'What about the bodies?'

John offers a grim smile. 'They'll take care of themselves. In six hours or so, they'll be nothing but bones.'

We keep a quick pace back toward camp, our heads swivelling right to left and back again, searching the meadow, the forest, watching for more archers in black lurking behind trees.

I barely see Rochester as we approach, hazy and blurry behind what must be a new barrier. I almost don't see the man standing just behind it, either; a figure in cloudy grey, a blaze of orange triangle on the lapel, a man of the Watch. He sees us coming and waves his hand; the air around us turns opaque, like fog, a clear opening in the centre.

'Were there more behind you?' He waves us through. 'Theirs, or ours?'

'Theirs, yes,' John says. 'But we took care of them. There was one of ours, too, but he didn't make it. He told us there were people missing. Have they been found?'

'Two of them have.' The guard nods at us. 'Best be off so they know you're safe.'

We continue down the road into Rochester, across the bridge into madness. Horses, men, soldiers, pages running everywhere; voices shouting orders. John and I push through it all, looking for Peter, for Fitzroy, for Nicholas, for anyone we fear has gone missing, for anyone who could tell us what's happening.

Soon enough there's a roar and Peter appears, wrinkled and dishevelled. He tackles John, pulls him into a rough embrace, ruffling his hair. He mutters in his ear; I can't make out the words but I can hear the tenderness behind them. Then he turns and does the same to me.

'I thought the worst.' Peter pulls back, his dark brows furrowed. 'Blackwell's men, they got in again. We rounded up all of Harrow, but people are still missing. I thought you among them.'

'We know,' John says. He fills Peter in on the archers, on the man they killed, on the poison and what happened afterward.

'God's blood,' Peter exclaims. 'You were at the apothecary? I went there myself after I couldn't find either of you here. The lights were off and the doors were locked. I didn't have a key, but when I knocked, no one answered.'

'We were there,' John says. 'We just…didn't hear you.' I flush a little at this and so does he, but he doesn't look away.

'But why – *oh*. Ah. I see. *Ah*.' Peter swipes a hand across his beard, looking discomfited.

'You mentioned people were missing.' John swiftly changes the subject. 'Who?'

'A few soldiers. A woman and her son from the Mudchute. From what you saw in town, we can add the cobbler to the list. And Gareth.'

'Gareth?' John and I exchange a rapid glance. 'Was he taken against his will? Or were Blackwell's men meant to be his escort out of Harrow?'

'There's no way to know for certain,' Peter says. 'But Nicholas believes he was abducted. Fitzroy went to Gareth's home and his door was unlocked, his belongings where he left them.'

'Why would they take him?' John asks.

'Hard to say,' Peter says. 'Could be because Blackwell discovered we know he's the spy, could be because Gareth had a change of heart about defecting, and we know what Blackwell does to traitors.' A pause. 'It doesn't much matter. He's gone, and though it's a small consolation, it saves us from having to arrest him ourselves. At any rate, we've got a larger issue at hand. A few members of the Order of the Rose arrived last night. Said Blackwell's men were beginning to mobilise in Upminster, earlier than expected. We believe they'll be here sometime tomorrow.'

'How many?' John asks.

'A conservative estimate is ten thousand.'

Ten thousand. Against our four thousand.

'Some of Blackwell's army – perhaps as many as half – are fighting under duress,' Peter continues. 'They will defect the moment battle begins. They'll either escape, or Blackwell will waste his troops to hunt them down. Even if this leaves us more evenly matched, he's still got his revenants. The strength of one is equal to that of ten ordinary men, and they'll be loyal to him.'

I think of Schuyler's words and wonder if that's not entirely true.

'Let's get you to your tents,' Peter says finally. 'You'll need to pick up your uniforms, and your weapons, and we're doing a last rally tonight. Tomorrow will be – ' He breaks off. 'Tomorrow will be here soon enough.'

John places his hand on Peter's shoulder, but there's nothing he can say that will ease the worry on his father's face. Peter knows there's a chance John won't make it through this battle. I know it, too, despite everything I will do to make sure he does.

We start across the crowded field, weaving through the circle of white tents toward mine when I hear it. A shout, a laugh, and then I see him, bounding toward us in a streak of stripes and feathers and smiles:

George.

TWENTY-EIGHT

'OI!'

He bounds across the grass toward us, bright as the afternoon sun in a green-and-blue-striped coat, blue hat with a yellow feather, and matching yellow cape. He hurtles into John, nearly knocking him over. They're both laughing and shoving each other; then finally George steps back and looks us both over, a smirk on his face.

'Well, well. If it isn't my favourite star-crossed couple.' He looks from John to me, then back to John again. 'Though it looks like the stars have finally aligned, conspiring now to blind us all.'

George steps forward and pulls me into a tight embrace.

'I really am glad to see you.' He looks me over carefully, his smile faltering for a moment. 'Fifer's been writing me, telling me what's been going on. All of it. You…' George trails off, uncharacteristically at a loss for words. 'You're going to be all right. I think we all are.'

He falls into step beside us as we thread through the crowds.

'When did you get back?' John asks him.

'Last night, late. It was a bit rough crossing the channel. But we're here now, and just in time, too. They came for a fight; it seems they're going to get one.'

John nods, then turns to his father. 'What's the plan for those not fighting?'

'After midnight tonight, the women and children will be inside.' Peter waves his hand at Rochester Hall. 'George has been placed in charge of them, and of their evacuation into Cambria, should it come to that. Regardless, they'll be safe. Nicholas and some councilmen are working on the spells now. No one will be allowed out until the council – minus Gareth, of course – gives the instruction.'

I don't ask what will happen if none of the council is left to give that instruction; I know I don't have to.

We look around the grounds at the thousands of Gallic men, their tents decorated with a fluttering flag of Gaul in stripes of red, blue, and white, chatting and laughing, some sparring, others reclining on the grass smoking pipes or drinking deeply from crystal goblets.

'I see they're making themselves comfortable,' John notes wryly. 'By the looks of it, you'd never know they were going to war.'

'They brought their own wine and their own glasses,' George says. 'They're the damnedest. Deadly as hell, but terribly high-maintenance. I can't tell you how many of them asked me where the ladies' tent is. We're at war, and they want a ladies' tent.'

I roll my eyes. John and George laugh.

'Not that it would be difficult to do,' George continues. 'Anglian women always did have a thing for Gallic men, and the women of Harrow are no different. So later tonight there'll be music, wine, food, no doubt as much flirting as when I was at court. And speaking of court…'

I look up just as Malcolm comes striding in our direction. He's dressed in Reformist colours: black tunic, black trousers, the orange-and-red Reformist symbol blazing in a crest along the front, a sword at his side. To see him dressed this way, free and armed and walking through the camp as if he owns it, is both a shock and an expectation.

George steps forward, sketches a quick bow. 'Sir.'

Malcolm waves it off, a smile crossing his face. 'I told you to call me Malcolm. I think we're well beyond formalities now.'

George turns to us. 'He's a rounder, this one, as I discovered last night. He took all my money in a single game of cards. Then, after ensuring I was thoroughly distraught, lost it all in one hand. A hand I do believe was skilfully thrown.'

'The skill was not mine but yours,' Malcolm says graciously. 'But I'm happy to arrange a rematch, if you'd like to test your theory.'

'I've got no plans tomorrow evening,' George says.

'You do now,' Malcolm says.

George laughs and extends his hand; Malcolm takes it, grinning. His eyes flick to me then.

'Glad you're back. We were worried.' He looks at John and nods. 'For both of you.' The silence hangs a moment. 'Elizabeth, may I speak to you?'

John turns to George. 'You seen Fifer?'

George nods. 'Last I saw her, she was terrorising some poor Gallic soldier. Cursing at him before *actually* cursing him. She gave him some kind of rash and now it's spread. All over the man's face and lips and tongue.'

John laughs. 'Why, what did he do?'

'He called her "*un peu fig mignon.*"'

A cute little fig.

John rolls his eyes. 'Mind leading me to them both? I want to let her know we're all right. And it sounds like I've got a pox to treat.' He turns to me. 'I'll find you later?'

'Of course,' I say.

John nods at Malcolm, squeezes my hand, then he and George walk away, the breeze carrying George's chatter and John's laughter back to me. It makes me smile.

Malcolm turns to me. 'How are you?'

'I'm fine,' I say. 'Had a run-in with some of Blackwell's archers, but they came out of it worse than I did.'

'Good. But I didn't mean just that. How are you feeling about tomorrow?'

Tomorrow. It stands on a knife's edge: victory and defeat, life and death, joy and sorrow. It will be one or the other; there will be no half measures.

'I'm ready,' I say, and this is the truth. 'I've lived beneath the shadow of your uncle's rule for so long, I'll do whatever it takes to overthrow him.'

He surveys the field, his eyes squinting against the setting sun in a way that makes the wrinkles around them deepen. I think of how he became heir at twelve after Blackwell killed his parents and unsuccessfully tried to kill him. How at sixteen he became king. Then, at twenty, how he went into a Yuletide masque a king and came out a prisoner, stripped of his title, his wife, his country, his life. He's experienced enough life for a man twice his age, and now, for once, he looks it.

Malcolm looks back at me, his mouth curving into a smile as if he knows exactly what I'm thinking. 'Did I ever tell you what I did my first day as king of Anglia?'

I shake my head.

'I turned the country over to someone else to rule.' He grimaces. 'To Uncle. I told him I didn't want to do it, that I couldn't do it. I should have known then, how quickly he agreed, that something wasn't right. He said he'd hand the reins back when I was ready. But drinking, gambling, roistering, hunting, well.' Malcolm laughs, a short, derisive sound. 'I thought I was doing the right thing, turning my head from whatever Uncle felt was his duty to do. Apathy became a habit; now it's all I'm known for.'

'You're here. You're fighting,' I say. 'You're helping to save the country, and you're putting yourself at risk to do it. That's what you'll be known for.'

'If I do this right, I won't be known for anything at all.'

'You're the king,' I say. 'You can't die.'

'I can, I might; I will, I won't. That's not what matters. What matters is that I'm ready. Like you, I'm ready to be out from underneath his shadow. I'm going to get Anglia back.'

He extends his hand to me. 'May I?' he says, and I nod. Then he presses my fingers to his lips; a formal, courtly kiss.

'I'm glad you're here with me,' he says. 'I don't trust a lot of people; I don't trust anyone. But I always trusted you. And now I need to apologise to you.'

I wait.

'I knew you didn't feel about me the way I felt about you. I simply chose not to listen.' He lets my hand drop as his expression falls; he looks as vulnerable as a boy. 'It was selfish and wrong, and I am sorry. I know they're just words but they're all I have. Can you forgive me?'

And on this, the eve of the final battle from which we may not return, I know that it's too late to withhold forgiveness, too late to hold grudges. Too late to punish him for playing by the rules when the rules were stripped from both of us, turned inside out before being served back to us on a poisoned platter.

'I can,' I say, and I'm not at all surprised to find I mean it.

'Now I've got a battle to win.' His grin is back; it lights up his face and that's the Malcolm I know: loud, brash, confident, the world at his feet and everything to hope for. 'This time tomorrow, we'll be celebrating. Mark my words.' He spins on his heel, throws me a wave.

I watch him go. As he walks off into the last of the dying light, it swallows him. And I think he'll come out brighter, untarnished, or the blaze will devour him, as it will all of us.

* * *

Night comes. And with it, a celebration. The Gallic soldiers insisted on it – to their way of thinking, it was the only thing to do. If the battle was to go poorly, if we were to fall, if they weren't to return to Harrow tomorrow, at least they'd have had tonight. Better than the alternative, they said: huddled in their tents, alone and afraid.

George was all for it. And no one can organise a celebration better than he: Within the hour we had wine, both from the soldiers who brought their own from Gaul, and from Lord Cranbourne Calthorpe-Gough's private reserve. Someone conjures fairy lights, tiny and white and nestled in the trees surrounding the camp, twinkling in the moonlit night.

Music fills the air: pipes and tabors, harps and drums. People laugh and they dance; they chatter in Gallic and flirt in Anglian. And none of us talks about it at all. The chance we won't return, the chance that this will be it. The very real chance that come tomorrow, there will be nothing left.

At midnight, the music ends. The fairy lights go out; the laughter stops. With little fanfare and even fewer words, the celebration disperses. The women and children are led inside Rochester Hall. The Gallic soldiers retreat to their side of the grounds, drunk with laughter and wine not moments earlier, now sober and stoic.

The armourers retreat to finish the task of preparing weapons for the three thousand that make up our army. We don't have many horses, a few dozen, perhaps. A handful of coursers to lead the initial charge, some palfreys for signalling. But this won't be a cavalry charge; it never was going to be. This will be an infantry battle: face-to-face and hand-to-hand, bloody and vicious and personal and deadly.

As abrupt as the others, John steers me back to my tent. Wordlessly, we huddle together on my narrow camp bed, his arms around me tight, my head pressed against his chest. I breathe him in, that same, soothing scent of him: lavender and spice; the same warmth and comfort I always feel around him.

I don't tell him I'm afraid of tomorrow. I'm afraid of what will happen if we lose, what will happen if we win. I'm afraid of the heartache and the loss and the wait, the interminable pause between the start and the finish to know how it ends. I don't tell him any of this. But by the way he holds me and kisses me and says he'll always love me, he tells me he already knows.

TWENTY-NINE

In the morning, the air is cool and still. Muted sunlight filters in through the white canvas, bathing it in a yellow glow. Outside, the rustle of activity has already begun, frantic and loud. The knot, already coiled tight in my belly, turns tighter.

John and I dress in silence, both of us in the same thing: brown trousers, white tunic under a thin layer of mail, blue-and-red colour-blocked surcoat – traditional Anglian colours in a battle to restore Anglia – topped with a breastplate of armour. I help him fasten the leather straps at his shoulders and sides. When I'm finished, he does the same for me. And for a moment we stand there, face-to-face. I can read the look of dark finality in his face, hear the men shouting outside the tent, their footsteps and the thundering of hooves, and I know it's time to go.

But still, we don't move.

Finally I step away from him, reach for my bag stuffed

beneath my cot. Pick through it until I unearth it: the dark green length of ribbon I pulled from the bodice of the pale green linen nightgown Fifer gifted me with, the one I wore the night I climbed up the trellis into John's bedroom, the last time we were together before everything went terribly wrong.

I hold it out.

John's eyes skim the length of it, then flick back to me. 'I never thought you were one for ribbons,' he says. 'But I remember this. I remember everything about that night, including what you wore. I wondered why that colour. Why green when your best colour is easily blue. Then I wondered where you got it, and if you had others like it.'

'You thought a lot about it,' I say.

'I think a lot about you,' he corrects. 'Most of the time, though, it's not about ribbons.'

That makes me smile, but only for a moment.

'I want you to wear it,' I say. 'And I want you to think of me when you do. Whether green is my best colour, or whether you'd rather be thinking about something else.' My words are coming fast, but we're out of time and I need him to hear them. 'But however you think of me, I need you to know that I need you. I need you to come back to me.'

I hold up the ribbon, and with a shaky hand I tuck it inside his armour. It's something a maid would do, giving a knight her favour as he enters a joust. But this is no joust, and I am no Queen of the May. I am what I am: A killer and a traitor, a sometime liar and a forever troublemaker, but he somehow found a way to love me anyway. 'Please think of me,' I repeat. 'Please come back to me.'

John reaches for me, captures my hand in his. There's nothing left for us to say so he kisses me, hard, crushing me against him, maybe forgetting we're wearing armour, maybe not, not caring either way. We kiss to the sound of drums, to the sound of trumpets and hoofbeats and heartbeats, we kiss until there's nothing left but to stop or go on, so we go on. He tugs at my armour, impatient, and before I know it it's on the ground, his hand sliding beneath my tunic as I start to pull on the fastenings of the armour I only just put on him.

There's a flash of sunlight and a cool draft of air and from the corner of my eye I see Schuyler, standing in the mouth of the tent, shaking his head and smirking.

'You're about six hours too late for this kind of send-off,' he drawls. 'You should have done this last night, along with the rest of camp.' A pause; another smirk. 'Did you know there's a twenty per centum increase in the number of children born in wartime than in peacetime?'

'Get out,' John murmurs against my lips. He doesn't turn away from me, doesn't release me. But Schuyler continues.

'It also nearly doubles the average number of infants born to a single couple. Frightening, considering this one' – he jerks his head at John – 'already wants six.'

I push away from John then, my mouth dropping open. 'You want six children?'

'Quit that,' John snaps at Schuyler.

‘I’m not listening in. I swear it.’ Schuyler holds up his hands. ‘Fifer told me.’

‘Six?’ I repeat.

‘I thought it sounded like a nice, even number.’ John shrugs. ‘Maybe we can talk about it later? Because as much as I’d like this to be a group discussion, I really don’t think now is the best time.’

‘That’s right,’ Schuyler says. ‘Because ten minutes before going into battle is the best time to unsheathe your sword and—’

John fires off a stream of curses, all of them aimed at Schuyler. But they’re both laughing, and so am I.

‘Save your endearments for the bedroom,’ Schuyler says with a grin. ‘It’s time to go.’

John plucks my armour off the ground, helps me back into it. He starts to lead me out of the tent, but I stop him.

‘I’ll catch up with you in a moment,’ I say. ‘I’d like to speak to Schuyler first.’

John leans forward and presses his lips against mine, holding them there. Then he leaves, mouthing something to Schuyler as he pushes past. I catch the gist of it, and it isn’t pleasant. It makes Schuyler laugh anyway. The tent flap falls, blocking out the sun, a shadow falling across us both.

‘How is this going to go?’ I say. ‘Are we marching into victory or into defeat?’

‘I’m no seer, bijoux.’ Schuyler’s voice is uneven with honesty. ‘I don’t know what’s going to happen. And I wouldn’t dare try to read what anyone else thinks will happen, either. I'm prepared for it to go any way. I've made my arrangements.'

Revenants rarely die; rarely die again, that is. But it can be done: most often a savagely broken neck, something only another revenant can do, or by fire, something anyone can do. And I know that somewhere, ensconced inside Rochester Hall, Fifer waits with the knowledge that he may not come back.

'What about John, then?' I say. 'I'll do whatever I can to keep Blackwell from finding him, we all will. But what if John decides to go looking for him first? He says he's got the stigma under control. Does he?'

'He thinks he does,' Schuyler says. 'And as much as he's thinking of that, he's thinking of you. That's all I get from him, and it's all I want to know. Don't ask me to listen for any more.'

'Schuyler—'

'You can't stop what's going to happen,' he interrupts. 'For all that you tried, you never could. It was always going to come to this.' Fifer's words in Schuyler's mouth.

We slip outside into the bright sunlight. Make our way across the green while a thousand others do the same: filing from their tents, armour glinting in the sun. Squires number in the hundreds, boys in white scurrying behind weapons masters, fitting men with longbows and quiver belts, spikes and knives, axes and swords. A dozen or so men and women, members of the Order of the Rose, carry no weapons. Their magic is enough for them.

I spot Keagan standing in a small group near the jousting

pit, her long white tunic bearing the black embroidered outline of a rose. She sees me and waves me over.

'This is Odell and Coll,' she says, introducing the boy and girl standing beside her.

'We heard about you.' The girl, Coll, looks me over and smiles. She's small, like me, with short dark hair, dark skin, and a bright smile. 'Keagan says she calls you sparrow. I like that. It's fitting.'

'What magic can you do?' I ask.

'Oh, me?' Coll holds up a hand, wiggles her fingers. Within seconds a red-crested bird alights on her shoulder. It cocks its head and watches her closely.

'You can summon animals?'

'And speak to them.' Keagan glances at Coll, who seems to blush under her gaze. 'We're so lucky to have her. Power like that is exceedingly rare. It comes along only once every ten years, and only to a tenth female born from a tenth female.'

'You have nine sisters?'

'Twelve, actually.' Coll's grin is as white as her tunic. 'There's one now.' She points to a girl no older than ten ducked behind the yew alley, half her face poking out from behind a tree. 'Her name is Miri. You should see what she can do.'

The bird careens from Coll's shoulder into the air just as a wall of water from the nearby lake rises up, twisting and turning and hurtling toward us. It slams to a stop, hovering above our heads like a shimmering pane of glass, then squirts a single stream of water into Coll's face.

Keagan flicks her wrist and the entire wall of water explodes into mist. Across the field, soldiers break into laughter and applause.

'I haven't seen you around,' I say to Keagan.

'Rochester's a big place, is it not? Thousands of people, only fifteen of us. At any rate, they've kept us sequestered. Thought it best for others not to know too much about what we do, so it wouldn't get out.'

The trumpets begin blowing then. Calling us to ranks, calling us to orders. The noise stills the air, dissolving the tense exuberance of three thousand men and women armed with magic and weapons into silence.

'See you on the field.' Keagan turns and strolls away, her cropped red head held high.

'Keagan,' I call after her, but I don't know what to say. I want to tell her to watch out for herself, to watch out for the Order. For Malcolm, who I know despite everything she's grown fond of. 'Be careful.'

'I will.' She turns around. 'You be careful, too.'

I dive into the crowd, make my way to my company. Soldiers fall into formation around me, bright in their red-and-blue surcoats and Reformist badges, burning yellow and orange against the bright blue sky and looming walls of Rochester, the browning hills and greening trees. Horses and shields, pennants and pikes, courage and fear, all of it stretching in front of me, farther than I can see. It's so much more than I thought it would be.

But when John appears by my side, the brightness of his armour tempered against the shadow in his eyes as he surveys the men around us, I know he's wondering, like me, if it will be enough.

We see Nicholas then, cutting through the swath of men, dressed not as a soldier but as a wizard: ivory robes to distinguish him from Blackwell, who will surely be wearing black. Nicholas has no armour, no weapons. He pulls up short before us, glancing at each of us in turn.

'He's vulnerable,' Nicholas says. I know without asking he means Blackwell. 'But he is still powerful. And he is desperate, which makes him formidable. He needs only one of you, but he will be looking for you both. If he finds you' – Nicholas looks to me – 'he will not let you go.'

'I know.'

Nicholas looks to John then. For a moment they look at each other, something passing between them, something I'm not privy to.

'He will not hesitate,' he says. 'He will not take you back to Upminster, he will not risk the time because he does not have it. He will kill you as quickly as he can.'

Caution and premonition tug at me: Nicholas's words don't sound like a warning as much as they do an instruction. But John only nods.

Nicholas steps away from us then, takes his place along the front, between the line of men and the barrier. John and I find our place along the middle, behind the spearmen, in front of the bowmen. Between the formations, each of the councilmen sits atop a horse, sheathed in armour, ready.

We march under the Reformist banner: a small sun surrounded by a square, then a triangle, then another circle;

a snake with its tail in its mouth. Each symbol has its own meaning: the sun the dawn of a new existence; the square to represent the physical world; the triangle is for fire, a catalyst for change; and the snake – an Ouroboros – for unity.

Today, we fight for all of it.

We march to the barrier, to the edge of it all. I can't see Blackwell's men, but I know they're there. I can feel it the way you can feel an oncoming thunderstorm. The air, still and pregnant with tension, waiting to crack open and rain destruction on us all.

At once, the councilmen raise their hands and begin whispering an incantation, no more than a breath, but then it happens. Dissolving like mist, like clouds in the morning, thick then thin, there then gone.

THIRTY

At once, there's sound. Like a curtain that's been lifted, I can suddenly see and hear everything: every leaf on every tree, every bird in every nest, every man on every horse.

Every enemy in front of me.

They stretch for miles, ten thousand of them in all black, an endless, roiling midnight sea. *God, they're everywhere.* The darkness on the ground stretches into the skies: rolling clouds of black, swirling with unleashed menace and peppered with murders of crimson-eyed crows. They press down on us, dissolving the sun and the blue above Harrow.

I don't know who draws first. But someone does, a blade pulled from a sheath, steel singing against leather, a roaring command, a rustled footfall, a shout. And then, with a booming roll of thunder and a flash of lightning, the battle begins.

I lose John immediately. Men push between us and I shout his name once, twice, but my voice is engulfed by the chaos unfolding around me. The skies open up and freezing rain floods the air, pouring in sheets around us, obstructing our view like a veil.

For a moment I freeze, overcome by what's unfolding in front of me. The enormity of it; the finality of it. But then something takes over: years of training, years of anger, years of fear. I plunge into the seething mass of bodies, knives yanked from the belt at my waist. I fling one after the other, the scent of blood filling the air around me, red and hot and copper, the sound of men dying.

I need to find Blackwell; it's the only thing I need to do. I know he's here, somewhere. Too cowardly to show himself now, he'll hold back until we're weakened, until half his army is dead and we begin to grow tired and weak, until he can take our advantage and turn it into his.

I don't see her, but Miri makes herself known: The rain abruptly stops, holds unmoving in the air, and with a sound like an incoming tide, roars up and back across the plain. I can't see it, but I hear the water hitting, crashing onto the sea of men in black.

The reprieve isn't long and the rain starts up again, this time coupled with streaks of white-hot lightning. It strikes where the water falls, at the feet of men on both sides: black and blue and red. I watch as they jerk and sizzle, rooted to the spot before slumping to the muddy ground, charred and unrecognisable and dead.

I keep moving, threading through the mass until I see Malcolm, his dark hair plastered to his face, his skin covered in blood and mud. He's surrounded by his men, locked in battle with the crows that rain and swirl around them, lashing out with beaks, talons, and beating wings, knocking them one by one to the ground.

'Coll!' My shouts disappear into the rain and the screams, but somehow she hears me. In an instant, a mob of owls appears as if from the clouds, a hundred of them feathered in tawny brown, inky black, snow white; each with blazing yellow, enchanted eyes. They dive into the crows, their bodies flapping and screeching; the noise is deafening.

Malcolm rolls away from the fray, gets to his feet. Blood mixed with rain runs down his face; he snatches his blade from the mud and plunges into the fight again. I move alongside him and his men, an eye on what's in front of me and always, always an eye on what's not.

Arrows fire indiscriminately around me, some iron-tipped, others blazing with fire, the latter no doubt Keagan's. They slam into man after man, all of them in black, their cloaks catching ablaze and the stench of burning wool and skin adding to the miasma already in the air. Malcolm, clashing swords with someone, is caught in the crossfire and gets hit: the arrow slicing into his unprotected forearm, the sleeve of his tunic turning into flame.

Malcolm twists to try to put it out, the distraction opening up an opportunity for his attacker to end him. He doesn't get it. I yank another dagger from my belt, take aim, and let it fly. The blade impales the man's eye; he drops to the ground in a heap.

I'm at Malcolm's side in an instant, slapping the flames out, examining his wound. It's deep, but it's clean.

'Hold still,' I say. 'I'll pull it out on three. One, two – ' I yank the arrow out. Blood soaks his tunic, but he'll live. 'Go,' I say. 'Your men need you. They – ' My words are cut off, along with my air.

I can't breathe. Malcolm pulls at his armour, at his mail; his mouth is open and he's gasping for air but there's none for him, either.

A soldier in black stands before us, his index finger twirling idly in the air, his face twisted in a grin as all around us men drop to their knees, to the mud, holding their throats, gasping, their faces turning blue. Dizziness overcomes me and I stagger to one knee, then the other, my lungs screaming. I claw at my throat, fall to the ground and into the soft, cold mud. I can't breathe, I can't breathe...

Keagan appears from nowhere, and it happens before I blink: the flash of a knife blade, a line drawn across the throat. A fountain of blood and a gargled moan and the wizard slumps to the ground, eyes open, staring unseeing into mine.

'Get up.' Keagan reaches down, snatches my arms, pulls me to my feet. 'Elizabeth. Get up now.'

Malcolm is already on his feet, pale and breathing hard. Men lie all around us, some gasping for air, some so still I think they've died. The owls and the crows have all taken flight, only a few feathered bodies strewn in the mud. Rain continues to pour around us, all of us soaked down to the tunics beneath our mail, cold and rough against our skin.

'Let's move.' Keagan grabs the back of my tunic, shoves me across the field. Malcolm's men fall in beside us, still breathing hard but weapons out.

At once, a pack of soldiers step in front of us – no, not soldiers, revenants – weapons and malice bared. Caleb, Marcus, and Linus are not among them, but still I know that's what they are. I can tell by the grey in their eyes and the ferocity on their faces. I can tell by the way the human soldiers in the field give them a wide berth, pouring around them as if they were stones in a river.

But for all I don't know them, Malcolm does. He steps in front of me, hand out as if to shield me. His other hand holds out a sword, useless against them.

'Majesty.' One of the revenants dips a clumsy, false curtsy; the others laugh, deep and throaty.

'Bray.'

Now I remember who this is, was. Bray, a nickname for Ambrose Courtenay, once one of Malcolm's most trusted courtiers. Malcolm told me he was banned from court after his gambling and drinking and violent behaviour became too much for even Malcolm to bear.

'I'm not called that anymore. At least not by you.' He breaks from the pack, begins to circle us. He's not armed – doesn't need to be – but his hands, flexing in and out of fists at his sides, promise as much violence as a cannon.

'When did this happen?' Malcolm gestures at him with his sword. 'When did you come back to court? When did you…' He trails off. I don't know if Malcolm knows how revenants are created.

'I returned when he summoned me. The king.' The other revenants shift around him as he speaks. I know their movement and posture well: They're falling into formation; they're preparing to attack. 'The true king.'

He's baiting us, I know this. But I can't stop myself from saying, 'Summoned you, then killed you.'

'Do I look dead to you?' Bray was handsome once, this I can tell. Not by his looks, no; I can tell by the way he is like Malcolm, the way Malcolm was. Confident, as if the answer to everything simply lay around every corner, under every stone, just waiting to be discovered. 'We are all very much alive.'

'We?' I say. 'And how many would that be, exactly?'

'One hundred.' Bray grins, his teeth flashing in the dark grey air. 'More to come. More every day. Men line up to serve, to serve an eternal king for all eternity.'

My heart sinks. One hundred revenants, with more to come.

'*Ach.* I've had enough of this.' Keagan throws up her hands. Palms out, skin already red.

'Down!' Malcolm shouts to his men before snatching the back of my armour and throwing me facedown into the mud. I hear it, even before I lift my head to see it: twin ropes of fire blazing from Keagan's hands, coiling and twisting into knots around the revenants. Their robes erupt into flames, black into red. The rain, still falling, has no effect on them: the water turns to steam around us, the air filled with white fog and grey smoke and unending fire.

But the revenants, they don't scream, they don't fall to the ground, they don't cease. They continue walking, aflame and charred, skin melting into bone, hair singeing from their scalps. They hold their weapons high, and they keep coming.

'Goddammit.' Malcolm pushes himself away from me, onto his feet. Pulls his sword. Swings. The blade slices through one revenant's burning neck, then another, then another.

Keagan drops her hands, the fire sputters out. The air is a cloud of burning stench, like Tyburn, smuts floating around like charred snowflakes, the scent of burning skin so sickly sweet I could gag on it. A few of Malcolm's men do, retching into the mud.

'Well done, Your Highness,' Keagan says.

Malcolm nods by way of acknowledgment, but he's not looking at her, nor is he looking at the heap of smoking bodies around us. His focus is on the field, at the battle that still rages all around.

'Those men. Those revenants.' Malcolm glances at his sword, the revenants' black blood dripping into the mud. 'The birds. The elemental magic.' He looks into the air. 'They keep appearing. One thing after the other.'

'As things do in battle,' Keagan replies, sarcastic.

'No.' Malcolm turns to face us. 'Look around. Look at what's happening. Look closely.'

I do. All around us, battles wage. But I cannot see what's happening, I cannot see who is making ground. I cannot see retreat, I cannot see advance. All I see is chaos, but now I see that it is orchestrated chaos.

'We are fighting in place.' Malcolm continues, 'It's as if he's trying to keep either side from moving. Uncle. It's as if he's throwing one thing or another at us to keep us from looking beyond the battle – to distract us.'

'Misdirection,' Keagan says, sharp.

Malcolm nods. Turns to me. And there, in the field around us full of men and revenants and hybrids, the sky full of black, seething, impenetrable fog, is my clue.

'Blackwell once told us the best way to achieve one objective is to make your opponent believe you're trying to achieve another.' Realisation drops my voice low. 'In a battle, this means chaos, disorder, feints, misinformation. You're so preoccupied with what's in front of you that you don't see what's happening around you. He called it the fog of war.'

'What is his objective, then?' one of Malcolm's men says.

'Rochester Hall.' Keagan jerks around to look at me, her eyes wide.

I should have sensed it, known it; as soon as I saw Blackwell's men, his creatures, all here in front of me: It was a diversion. A way to concentrate all our men here, too, so he could reach the one place he really wanted.

But not only that.

I think of how John disappeared the moment the battle began.

I think of Nicholas's warning to him, the one that felt more like instruction.

And I think of Blackwell's constant advisement: *Warfare is based on deception.* This time, I wasn't deceived by Blackwell, someone I expected. This time I was deceived by two people I didn't, people I trusted.

Maybe Keagan can see it in my face; maybe she's realised

it, too. But she turns to me, her blue eyes wide, the black smuts from the burning revenants stuck to her face.

'Let's go.' She gestures to Malcolm, his men. 'Stay behind me. All of you. If he's trying to keep us away, he'll try to stop us. I'll burn what I can, but keep your weapons out.'

With only a precious few knives left, I yank my bow from my shoulder, an arrow from the quiver at my waist. Malcolm readies his sword. The three of us plunge into the organised disarray, dodging men and arrows and rain, running back the way we came. We don't get more than a few hundred feet before a flapping noise, like wash on a laundry line, fills the air. Dark shapes fill the darkening sky: winged, oily, sharp. I remember them, these hybrids, from training. We killed them once but now they live again, this time en masse. Five, ten, then fifteen of them assault the sky.

At once, they swoop. Onto the fields, claws out, pointed, deadly, snapping up man after man indiscriminately, slashing them open, some of ours, some of his. But I know Blackwell doesn't care. He won't be satisfied until we're all dead and he's the last one standing, because a king over nothing is still a king over everything.

They come with a caw, dipping and wheeling and grasping, picking up men the way birds pluck worms from the ground, wriggling and trying in vain to escape. Keagan holds up her palms and at once the air is filled with threads of fire, wrapping around three of the hybrids, consuming them in flames.

I raise my bow and take aim. As with most of Blackwell's

hybrids, their eyes are the weakest spot, and that's where I fire. Once, twice. I miss the first but land the second, then the third. The thing shrieks and plummets to the ground in a jumble of leathery black wings and purplish-black blood. Malcolm finishes it off with a clean slice of his blade to its neck, severing the head from the body.

I reload; Keagan readies her fire. But for every hybrid we kill, three more appear and descend on us, as if they've been sent straight for us. That's when I see it: a mass of white across the sky, as thick as a cloud but faster, denser. And then I see her, sitting in the highest branch in the highest tree, a silhouette of a girl in white against the marbled black sky. Coll, the girl who can control animals.

She sees me watching her and grins, cocky and sure. Coll raises her hand skyward and curls her fingers slowly, as if beckoning. I see her lips moving, muttering, speaking an incantation to that mass in the sky. Then she slices her hand through the air, a blur.

The birds dive. Into the mass of blood and limbs and screams, and unlike Blackwell's hybrids, they attack only black: pecking at faces, ears, mouths, gouging out eyeballs. The air is filled with the sounds of flapping wings, screeching beaks, feathers and leathery skin and death.

We start to run again, Keagan beside me, Malcolm and his men behind me. I need to get to Rochester. I need to find Blackwell, I need to stop John, to stop Nicholas, from whatever it is they think they're doing, from whatever mistake they are undoubtedly making.

We make it a couple hundred yards, maybe, when

suddenly the ground begins to buckle and jerk beneath us. It trembles and rumbles, as if something from far beneath is pushing its way through, shaking the trees from the ground, me from my feet, my weapon from my hand. Keagan spins one way, I fall the other, plunging face-first into a damp smear of leaves, Malcolm skidding beside me. There's a crack like thunder, a sway I can almost feel. I snatch my bow with one hand, Malcolm with the other, and roll us both over as an oak tree smashes to the ground with another earth-shattering tremble, where the pair of us lay not a half second before.

'That was too goddamned close.' Malcolm's lying beneath me, his mouth pressed against my ear. 'How is he seeing us? How does he know where we are?'

'Don't you know this yet, about your uncle?' I jump to my feet, pull him to his. 'He always knows everything.'

Keagan screams at us to keep moving, her voice dampened by the smoke that rends the air; somewhere, something is burning, from her magic or from Blackwell's. She directs us away from the trees, into the open field. I turn to follow but as I do, I catch a glimpse of him. Malcolm sees him, too, and then he's at my side, his sword raised as we look at him, standing at the mouth of the forest, alone, as still and rooted as the trees around him.

Caleb.

THIRTY-ONE

He watches me – only me – his eyes as grey and restless as the Severn. And, as the Severn, there is no telling what may lie beneath the surface. I hesitate a moment, studying him as he does me, wondering what he plans to do. I can feel Keagan beside me: the heat shimmering around her, ready to attack him, to kill him before he can kill us.

But I don't think he will. Caleb can hear me, he can feel me. He's known where I've been ever since this battle began. I didn't wear Fifer's necklace, not today; I needed Schuyler to be able to hear me. If Caleb wanted me dead, he would have done it by now; there's nothing or no one that could stop him. So what does he want then, standing there, staring at me, if not to kill me?

I start for him.

'No.' Malcolm steps in front of me, to try to stop me.

'It's all right,' I say. 'I don't think he'll hurt me. I think' – I glance at Caleb, see his slight, almost imperceptible nod

– 'he wants to talk to me.'

Malcolm and Keagan exchange a rapid glance.

'Revenants aren't much for talking, are they? No.' Keagan answers her own question. 'But if he's got something to say, it might be worth hearing. As long as he doesn't get any other ideas.'

A burst of flame leaps from Keagan's palm; she lobs it across the field toward Caleb. He's fast but the fire is faster; he spins out of the way but not before the flame grazes the side of his head. He turns back to us, eyes gleaming with malice.

'Antagonising a revenant,' I say. 'That wasn't wise.'

'It's wiser than you think,' Keagan replies. 'Now go, before I change my mind and set him alight like St. Crispin's Day fireworks. We'll be watching from the woods.'

I cross the ruined field to where Caleb waits for me. He's dressed in uniform, as the last time I saw him: black tunic, black trousers, Blackwell's badge on his sleeve and the insignia of the Knights of the Anglian Royal Empire on his chest. His blond hair is singed black over his left ear, smoking slightly.

'Elizabeth.' Those grey eyes flick over me, empty, but not with hostility. 'You're alive.'

'Yes.' But then, because I can't help it – I never can – I add, 'Are you planning to change that?'

Something then, a glimmer behind his cold expression. If this was the Caleb I knew, I'd almost think it was amusement. Then it's gone.

'No,' he says. 'I don't plan to hurt you.'

'What are you doing here?' I say. 'You should be fighting. Killing. It's what he wants, isn't it? It's what he would order.'

A pause. Then: 'That's not what he's ordered me to do.'

It's the things they don't ask that can be taken advantage of. Schuyler's words play in my head.

'What did he order you to do?' I ask, knowing as I do he can't tell me.

'Your friends,' he says instead. 'They know what has to be done. They all do.'

'My friends?' I want to ask Caleb what he means, but I know he can't tell me that, either. Instead, I think about why he's here. It's not to help me; Caleb has always only wanted to help himself. It is as Schuyler said: He is beholden, but he doesn't want to be held. He is disloyal without being disobedient. But all of these things are in service of a goal that, for once, is the same as mine. So I try and frame my words in a way that will help us both.

'If I go to Rochester Hall,' I say, 'what will I find?'

Caleb's eyes flash, an acknowledgment of my guile. 'What you are looking for.'

I turn then, and I run. I don't wait to see if Caleb follows me, or if Keagan and Malcolm and his men do. It scarcely matters. All that matters is reaching Rochester Hall, to find what Caleb wants me to find, to play my part even though I don't know how it's written.

To confront whatever is happening there before I'm too late to stop it.

I thread through the woods, through the trees until the smoke ends and fire dies and the rain runs out, until I reach the other side, plunging into the open rolling valley and heading north toward Rochester. Now that the battlefield is behind me, I see how little progress was made. So much destruction for so little direction.

Thirty minutes of hard, flat-out running and I finally reach Rochester. Whatever magic Blackwell used to keep us corralled in battle doesn't exist here, where the air is pale blue and clear, sweet and silent. The barrier does not exist here, either: It was altered before the battle to allow our side in but Blackwell's side out in the event of a retreat. But no magic can stop Blackwell, I knew that even then.

And now I know it was never meant to: that the plan all along was to bring him in.

Rochester Hall stretches in front of me, that bastion of red brick and beauty and safety: the safest place in all of Harrow. The surrounding grounds are empty of men, the lake serene and smooth. No shrieking from the monsters above, no crying from the bodies below, only the third-quarter moon, half black and half white, hanging low in the horizon. Even my footsteps across the road sound muffled, a tiptoe instead of a crunch, a sigh instead of a groan. This is a relief to me; it means the women and children – and Fifer and George – remain safe inside. But then, they are not who Blackwell is after.

I peel yet another arrow from the quiver at my waist, and nock it into place before stepping from the main road onto the footpath, then to the bridge that leads across the lake. I'm vulnerable – too vulnerable – and it's in every move I make. My slow, careful footsteps; the way I swing the bow up, down, left, right; the way I control my breath in an effort to contain my careening pulse.

The path ends at the massive iron door, barred shut. There are only three ways, that I know of, to access the grounds from the outside: across the lake on boats, through the main door, and through the tunnel specially allowed for John.

But the tunnel will be closed to me, because John is not with me. I need to find another way. Rochester is so highly protected magically that I think there may be no other way. I turn left, walking along the parapets, searching. Nothing, just an endless stretch of red brick. Then I see it: a tiny stone monkey crouched on a parapet, its head cocked to the side, staring at something directly below it. I remember the gargoyles at Ravenscourt, how they marked secret entrances, passages that led into and out of the castle.

I run my hand along the surface and soon enough I feel it, buried in the tracery, the intricate lacework of stone that decorates the wall. A latch. I hook my finger into it, pull. There's a low, echoing click and a shifting of brick: a door. It creaks open, leaving just enough room for me to slide through.

Inside is a tunnel, perhaps an adjunct to John's, perhaps different; it's hard to tell in the dark. But I push my way through it, a thousand twists and turns and dead ends, until I find another panel that slides open behind a marbled bust, one of a dozen I passed in the east wing on my way to visit Malcolm the week before.

Where could Blackwell be? Nicholas said he would not

hesitate. That he would not risk the time to go back to Upminster to perform the ritual. Once he has John he won't need much to perform it: a ritual room and four elements; an eight-pointed star and a sacrifice.

My footsteps are muffled by the thick carpet underneath as I dash through the west wing, forgoing bedchambers and solars for great halls and music rooms: spaces that are bare enough to allow for adornment, private enough to discourage discovery.

Even disallowing half the rooms in Rochester as options, it takes ages to search them all. There are so many floors, so many hallways, so many twists and turns that I lose my way, only to search the same spot twice.

Still, nothing.

I stop and I think. Try for a moment to put myself into Blackwell's frame of mind, his insane desperation. He's in a place he doesn't know. He doesn't have time to learn about it, to walk from room to room and risk getting lost, as I have.

I walk to the window, staring out at the late afternoon sky. From here, I cannot see the moon, the trees blocking my view of the horizon. Nicholas said it was not necessary for the ritual, only preferable. But he also said that this time, Blackwell would not take any chances. If I were the gambling type – I'm not, at least not with lives that aren't my own – I would wager that Blackwell will want to see it; to be close to it. He will want the security it brings him, when he's in a place and a position that gives him none.

I turn in place, trying to align myself with the direction

where it will be visible. If the sun is to the west, the moon will be directly north. A room facing north could be both in the east wing and the west, but those in the west face nothing but hills; I remember seeing them the day I visited Malcolm. Besides, they're all chamber rooms there, and carpeted: difficult to draw a star upon. The east wing, then.

Keeping an eye on windows as I pass, I race through the massive entryway into the east wing until I reach the stretch of rooms Fitzroy kept open for his troops to visit. I pass the library – a too-crowded space for a ritual; the chapel – too holy; the dance hall – too windowless. Finally, I reach the dark, polished door at the end. Small, quiet, facing due north and banked with windows for visibility: the music room.

I hesitate, just a moment. I fear what I'll find when I open the door; I fear what I will not find. Raising my bow, I shoulder open the door.

Inside: wood-panelled and tapestried walls, a grid of parquetted floors, a bank of stained glass windows casting around fractured, jewel-toned light from the fading sun. In the centre of the room stands a group of figures, gradually coming into focus as my eyes adjust to the darkness.

The first I anticipated, tall and deadly and dressed entirely in black: Marcus. The second I expected, slashed and twisted and stitched back together, dressed as a king in crimson and gold, ermine and jewels, sewn with his coat of arms and always, always, that damned strangled rose: Blackwell.

But the third I neither expected nor anticipated, standing

sacrifice in the centre of the room, his ivory robes ripped and pulled apart as if by a beast, blood blooming fast against his chest: Nicholas.

If they're surprised to see me, none of them shows it. Marcus regards me with gleeful malice; Blackwell with feigned disinterest. But Nicholas doesn't regard me at all, eyes fixed intently at a spot somewhere over my head, as if he doesn't even see me.

I blurt out his name, start toward him, but stop when Blackwell pulls a knife from nowhere and holds it to Nicholas's throat.

'Let him go,' I say, a useless plea.

'You found me,' Blackwell says. 'Although it's not me you're looking for at all, is it? You came for your healer, didn't you, to bid him one final goodbye before I take back what is rightfully mine? I have to say, Elizabeth, I'm surprised. Giving up your power, your own life, to save his?' He shakes his head. 'A pity you didn't show me half that loyalty.'

By way of response, I raise my shaking bow and aim it at the gaping hole that holds the remains of a milky, ruined eye.

'Charming, as always.' The s whistles serpentine through his cavernous cheek.

I glance at Nicholas once more, to try to get a sense of how injured he is, if he can move, if he can help me somehow rescue him. But he still does not meet my gaze.

'Set down your weapons,' Blackwell commands. 'All of them.'

I don't.

'Do it,' he says, 'or his blood will be on you.' As if to illustrate his point, he slides the tip of the knife into Nicholas's bare, vulnerable neck. A line of blood dark as ink appears, joining the rest on his tunic.

'Don't!' I throw out my arm, the one holding the bow, and it drops with a thunk to the parquet floor. One by one I lay down my sword, my knives, my quiver of arrows, and back away.

'You forgot the one in your boot,' Blackwell says.

Unwillingly, I reach into my boot and toss my knife – my last – into the pile. Before Blackwell, before Marcus, I am completely, utterly vulnerable.

Blackwell releases Nicholas then, throws him to the ground. He lands on his stomach; there's blood on the back of his cloak, too. He's injured worse than I imagined; he may even be dying. Marcus – I suspect this is his work – could have so easily finished the job. Why didn't Blackwell order him to?

A breeze of a warning makes the hair on my neck stand on end.

'Nicholas.' I keep my voice low to disguise its trembling. 'Listen to me. Look at me. Don't let him—'

'That's enough of that,' Blackwell barks. 'He cannot hear you. Even if he could, he would not reply. Nicholas is under my command now, and he must do what I say. Exactly what I say.' Blackwell snaps his fingers and Nicholas rises, puppet-like, to stand by his side. Another snap and his eyes shift to mine, finally seeing me. They narrow to hard, obsidian slits.

Blackwell circles around him, the hard soles of his polished boots a staccato against the floor.

'We have some unfinished business, you and I,' he says to me. 'And I thought it fitting that the one who once saved you' – a dismissive wave at Nicholas – 'should be the one to end you.'

Another snap, and Nicholas raises his arm, points a finger in my direction. And with the unseen force of a battering ram, I'm lifted off my feet and thrown backward across the room. I slam into the hard, panelled wall, my breath and half my consciousness knocked out of me.

I drop to my knees, try to breathe. Try to stand. Another snap and I'm thrown forward to the floor. Another snap: backward into the wall. My head rings from the force of the blows, I cannot breathe, and I cannot think fast enough to know what to do. So I do the only thing I know how: I lunge for the pile of weapons on the floor.

I don't make it.

Yet another snap of Blackwell's fingers propels Nicholas once more into action.

He turns to the window, throwing his arms wide, conducting the bank of stained glass panels as they bow and crackle and then, with an explosion like thunder, a kaleidoscope of deadly shards hurtles toward me.

I run – I almost don't make it – to the wall and the tapestry before me, diving beneath it just as the glass shatters around me, a dull thud against the thick, dense wool. A few larger pieces pierce the fabric like daggers, stabbing my cheeks and my arms, drawing hot drops of blood I don't bother to wipe away. Because the warning I felt before, the slight breeze of a caution, has now turned into a torrent with understanding.

In the first, failed ritual attempt, Blackwell offered up a raven as sacrifice: its death an oblation for his own, to be forever withheld. Now, in his second attempt, Blackwell needs another sacrifice. He could have chosen anyone or anything, another humble raven, perhaps; it needs only to be a living, breathing thing. Instead, Blackwell chose Nicholas. An act of revenge, perhaps, or twisted symbolism: to extinguish Nicholas's light in order for Blackwell to shroud the world in dark.

But for him to risk capturing the only man with power to rival his own at a time when he cannot risk anything, that tells me the real reason:

Blackwell is out of magic.

Just as the Azoth gives power, the way it gave to me when I used it, it takes power, too, from those it injures – and from those it curses. *A curse can deplete magic*, Nicholas said. And while Blackwell's got enough power left to control Nicholas, it's not enough to carry out the ritual. Not with whatever magic he used up to be here in Rochester, to control his army, his creatures, his revenants.

Caleb must have known this. It must have been why he sent me, at least in part. Because maybe – maybe – if I'm able to bypass Marcus's malevolence and Nicholas's capitulation to get to my weapons, I can take advantage of Blackwell's weakness. Before he sacrifices Nicholas, before he finds John, before he can carry out his insane plan of immortality.

To do the impossible. Again.

I throw back the tapestry. Yet another snap and Nicholas advances on me, lips curled in something that looks like amusement. I don't look at him, I don't acknowledge him. Instead, I turn to Blackwell.

'Is that all?' I taunt. 'You're the most powerful wizard in Anglia, and that's all you can do? Turn puppeteer before blowing out the windows?' I allow myself a wide, feigned smile. 'First you send Fulke after me, now this. Once again, you insult me.'

Engaging him is a gamble, a liability. But if I can tempt him into using his power, it will show me what he's got left, using up what he's got left. I may be empty of weapons, but I'm not empty of wit.

Blackwell gleams at me. 'You always were one of my best witch hunters.'

'Yes,' I say. 'I was.'

There's no snap. No ministration. He throws his own arms up this time.

And the sky comes down.

The vaulted ceiling of the music room cracks; massive shards splinter and plummet to the floor. Falling lumber tears the tapestry from its moorings; the heavy cloth falls on top of me and I hold it over me like a shield. Marcus and Nicholas stand watching me, unharmed: The air around them is clear.

I run through the room, dodging falling timber to try

to reach my discarded weapons. My tapestry snags on something along the floor; it's yanked off my head. I free it but not before a splinter of wood, sharp as a knife, slices through my forearm, through skin and bone, all the way through to the other side. I gasp, stumble to one knee, rip it out. Blood pours down my arm, drips through my fingers. I press my hand to staunch the wound; press down my feelings to stanch the pain.

The roof is open to the sky now, no longer blue and clear as it was when I arrived, but choked with a swirl of black rumbling clouds rolling in like a band of horses. Blackwell flicks his hand and with a clap and a roar the clouds open up, a waterfall of rain pouring in through the open roof.

I spot a gleam of steel beneath the tinder. A knife or a sword, I can't tell. I drop to my hands and knees, scrabble through the dust, the wood, until finally I reach it. It's a knife, but only one. I grasp the hilt. Spin around. Through the rain I see his outline, as black and thunderous as the clouds above. I pull back, take aim: the space right between his eyes.

I will not miss.

Then: an earsplitting crack, a blinding flash. Lightning. It tears into me, spears me to the floor; I feel as if I'm on fire. In the middle of the pyre at Tyburn, heat and smoke and lit from within by searing-hot pain that rain does not abate, and I begin to scream.

'Stop.'

At the sound of his voice, the recognition of it, everything ceases. The rain, the lightning, but not the pain. I'm pinned

THIRTY-TWO

'Stop,' John says again. He starts toward me, but Caleb holds him back. 'Let her be.'

'You don't command me.' Blackwell's voice has taken on a clipped edge, one of authority and triumph.

'I have something you need,' John says. 'If you want it, then you'll do what I say.'

Blackwell chuckles. 'Rather ridiculous request, don't you think? But I'll acquiesce. I'll let her be, until the time it takes to kill you. What I do to her after that will no longer be your concern.'

'If you think she'll allow you to do anything to her, you don't know her as well as I do.'

A lewd, twisted grin. 'I'm sure I don't.'

John's eyes haven't left me since he entered the room. To others, his careful expression may read as fear. But only I know him enough to know it's determination. He's determined to do this. To give himself to Blackwell, to die for him, to allow him to become immortal. I don't understand, and I don't want to.

I turn from him to Blackwell. Get to my feet, slowly. Raise my arm, the one still holding the blade, and once again take trembling aim.

'Elizabeth.' John's voice, a whisper, rings through the room like a shout. 'Don't make the end harder than it has to be.'

This: the end. What John planned for all along, what Nicholas planned. Never mind what I planned: scheming and lying and stealing to make sure it didn't. Even so, I drop the knife and it falls to the floor, a thud among the rubble.

Blackwell's tangled, destroyed eye flicks to John. 'Confidence, determination, fearlessness.' His voice is a drawl. 'You possess all the qualities I value in my men, despite your allegiance. At the very least, you appear to have been a competent steward for my power.' A pause. 'I'm curious. What did it do for you? This power?'

There's so much John could say to this: too much. But his reply lies only in his disdain. 'Nothing,' he says. 'It did nothing for me.'

The levity drops from Blackwell's face, and he turns back to Caleb. 'Did he put up a fight?'

'He was trying to escape,' Caleb replies. 'With the rest of their army. They're retreating.'

'Retreating,' Blackwell repeats, his voice a satisfied purr. 'And my nephew?'

'Dead.' Caleb shrugs. 'I saw to that myself. He is dead, and you are king.'

I expect Blackwell to revel in this news. To eat it, to drink it. Instead, his eyes narrow and he says in a voice full of silent rage, 'I am king. I have always been king.'

A pause. Then Caleb sketches a deep bow. 'Majesty.'

John, escaping. Malcolm, dead. None of this rings true to me. John wouldn't turn from a fight; he would die before he would do that. As for death, Keagan would never have allowed Malcolm's. Not without some sign of a fight, of blood or of fire, and Caleb shows neither, nothing more than the singed hair he wore earlier.

But then I see the skill in Caleb's reply to Blackwell's questions. He gave him an answer, but he didn't tell him what he really wanted to know. And Blackwell never commanded him to be truthful. *It's the things a pater doesn't ask that can be taken advantage of.* Once more, Schuyler's words echo in my head.

Something is happening, I don't know what. I turn to John, then to Caleb to try to glean something from their faces. But they both look away, ahead, anywhere but at me.

Blackwell snaps his fingers and on command, Nicholas steps to his side.

'Begin the preparations.'

Nicholas holds out a hand, murmuring under his breath. Embers begin to glow beneath the rubble strewn along the floor, and as Nicholas waves his hand, his movement coaxes the nascent flame until it begins to roar, cracking and spitting and smoking.

Marcus steps forward, reaches into his cloak, passes the contents to Blackwell. A scattering of salt, a clutch of herbs, a skin of water set to mark the cardinal points north, east, west. A bundle of thin, rough-hewn candles lit from the fire on the floor. A single one set south, four more to mark the intercardinal directions: an eight-pointed star.

I know what happens next.

And it happens so fast.

Nicholas, now immobile in Marcus's grip, dragged to the centre of the star. Blackwell beside him, a knife in his hand. A glint of steel, a repressed grunt of pain, and blood – still more blood – to flood the rest of his ivory robes. Nicholas slumps to the floor, dead. A sacrifice.

I'm too horrified to even make a sound.

Blackwell reaches for his scabbard, and with a song against the leather he slides it out, the same damned blade that's etched in duplicate on the badge on his sleeve: The Azoth. This time, it doesn't call to me. This time, it repels me. I want nothing more than to see it – its curse and its power – destroyed.

Blackwell begins chanting. His voice, the only one in the room this time, is clear, and I can hear every word:

I am old, weak, and sick; fire torments me;
Death rends my flesh and breaks my bones.
My soul and spirit have abandoned me;
In my body is found salt, sulfur, and mercury.
Let them first be distilled, separated, purified;
That they will be transmuted and reborn,
Through Opus Magnum; the greatest of all works;
The circle closes its end.

The emeralds embedded in the Azoth's hilt begin to wink brightly, frantically, as if they understand the change that is about to occur.

'You.' Blackwell gestures to John, still in Caleb's grip.

'Don't!' I shout, finding my voice. 'Don't do this. Don't—' I lunge for him, for them, just as Blackwell raises his hand, and a shard of glass flies across the room and slices into my face.

'Elizabeth!' John shouts my name as I gasp, pressing a hand to my face. The glass, it's only skimmed me: a long cut across my cheek that stings and bleeds but a little, though it stands as a warning. 'Don't,' he says. 'Please.'

'Okay,' I say. 'Okay.' I try to be as brave as he is but I am not. Everything I did, all of it, was for naught. Saving Nicholas, only to have him killed in front of us. Saving John, only to have him offered up like a lamb for slaughter. The both of them saving me – not once but twice – but without the charm of the third.

Caleb brings John forward, to the centre of the star. John doesn't hesitate; he doesn't stumble. He walks straight to Blackwell, stops in front of him. They stand eye to eye: John's armour is missing, his surcoat is tattered and battle-worn, his face is shadowed with dirt and his hair plastered with sweat. But his posture is ramrod-straight and his gaze is direct. He does not flinch from Blackwell's horror.

'You will not fight,' Blackwell says. 'If you do not want to see her throat slit, slowly, agonisingly, in front of you. You will not fight,' he repeats, 'if you wish for her end to be merciful.'

'What do you want me to do?' John's voice is steady.

'You?' Blackwell scoffs. 'You do nothing.' Then, without warning or ceremony, he holds up the Azoth.

And he thrusts it into John's chest.

For a moment, nothing happens. Then, a glow: It begins, like the embers in the fire beneath our feet, spreading from John's chest outward, down his arms into his hands, up his neck into his face. John's eyes go wide, he opens his mouth; nothing comes out but a gasp. His body goes rigid for a beat, two; then he begins to convulse as if someone's shaking him. The light around him turns from white to yellow to red as he burns up with the force of the magic, the force of the stigma leaving his body.

I know this pain; I finally remember it. The heat, the burning, the feeling of being carved inside out and thrust back together. I remember the pain of it, the surety that I was going to die, the pleading because I wanted to die.

Once more I lunge for John, to try to stop this. Caleb is beside me in a blur, his hand clamped around my arm, pulling me back. He's saying something to me but I don't listen, it's drowned out by my screams.

Then, like a torch that's been plunged into water, the light goes out. Red fades back to white and John drops to the floor in a heap, lifeless, his hazel eyes open wide to the ceiling, seeing nothing.

Caleb releases me and I run to John, drop to my knees beside him. I shake him, because that is what you do. I call his name, because that is what you do, too, hoping that somehow this is all a joke, a cruel joke but one nevertheless, that they somehow might groan or cough or roll over or sit up, that they might have cheated death after all.

But this is not what John does. I run my hands across his face, his neck, his pulse points on his wrists, his chest: They are all empty, silent. He is empty. He is silent.

He is dead.

And I have nothing to save him with. I can do nothing for him. Nothing at all. I knot my fists into the front of his shirt, already gone cold, and I begin to sob. But even as I do, I cannot take my eyes off Blackwell, off what happens next.

Blackwell raises the Azoth to the sky, swirling charcoal above us, faster and faster. The blade is coated in blood, dark red and nearly black. But the hilt, the emeralds…they are no longer green. They are yellow and bright as the sun, not twinkling but flashing, growing brighter and brighter with every passing moment. He continues chanting, his words picking up speed, pulsing in time with the sky and the light from the Azoth.

A hole opens in the centre of the clouds, a window into the now-deepening sky. There, in the centre of it: the moon. Half light and half dark, heavy and guiding, luring the spell to its completion.

The Azoth explodes into sunlight. It engulfs us, it fills the room with brightness so white and suffocating I close my eyes, bury my head in John's chest. I can feel it pouring into me, filling me with a heat so intense I feel as if I'm being burned from the inside out. I grip John's body tighter, shielding him with my own as if I can protect him from this, even when I could not protect him before, even though he does not need my protection anymore.

As quickly as the room filled with light, it goes out. Black. Silent. I open my eyes, but I can see nothing before me. Not John, not my own arms around him, not anything or anyone. Just the sound of ragged breathing: mine, perhaps Blackwell's. The others do not breathe at all.

Moments pass. I don't move; no one around me moves, not that I can hear. Then, slowly, the room begins to illuminate: gently around the edges at first, a ring of purple and red fading inward, giving way to lavender and rose until the room is bathed in a haze of pink. It should be beautiful but there is something horrible about it, as if the air itself is drenched in blood. And in the middle of it all, Blackwell.

He stands stiffly, the way John did. His eyes open wide, an expression of something – pain? Fear? I don't know, I've never seen Blackwell anything other than composed – etched into his face, his arms held stiffly before him. The Azoth, held in his hand just moments before, is gone. All that remains is a scattering of stones along the floor, green again now, but a dull green of decay, as if whatever illuminated them before from within is now dead.

It is as if I'm watching time run backward: Blackwell's skin knits together, growing and stretching over his face; his black veins fading to grey before disappearing altogether. The spell is working. The destruction of the Azoth has combined with the invincibility of the stigma. It is repairing him.

This is the end.

And we are all finished.

There's a shuffle beside me then. I turn to see Nicholas moving toward me, a slow laboured crawl. I hold John tighter, shield his body with mine. There is nothing more Nicholas can do to him now, I know. But that doesn't matter.

Nicholas ignores me, he keeps moving toward me, toward us.

I pull back my leg, the same way I did in Fleet prison all those months ago. When Nicholas came to rescue me and I almost didn't trust him, when I almost didn't go with him, when I almost killed him.

I stop.

Look at him closely – really look at him. His dark eyes – blank and unseeing before – are now focussed on me, full of clarity and pain and desperation and the closest thing I've seen to fear ever come to pass along his face.

Whatever spell Nicholas was under, it's gone now. I don't know how: Maybe Blackwell released him; maybe Blackwell's transformation severed the magic. I reach for him again but he shakes his head – once, hard, and once more I pull away. He crawls closer, close enough for me to see how pale he is, how he trembles, how he's left half his blood on the floor behind him. Close enough to John to touch him, his hand fluttering along his neck.

'He's dead,' I say, and I could scream with the grief of it. 'This wasn't part of your plan, was it? It couldn't be, not this.' The sobbing that never really stopped starts up again.

'Elizabeth. Listen to me. Listen.' Nicholas's voice is a

rattling breath, a choking cough full of blood. 'The unity of opposites.'

Abruptly, I stop crying. 'What?'

'Everything must have its opposite. Up to down. Black to white. Destruction to invincibility.' He speaks quickly, his voice urgent; he wants me to understand something I do not. 'Everything has an opposite.'

'Yes.' I lean toward him. His hand is still pressed to John's neck, his trembling fingers cupped behind it as if caressing him. 'I know this. I understand—'

Another sharp jerk of his head. 'Immortality. It has an opposite, too. Do you hear me? Elizabeth.' More coughing, more blood. 'Immortality cannot exist without its opposite.'

I turn back to Blackwell, still standing in the centre of the room, his empty hands still held before him. He presses them against his chest, a frown crossing his now-pale, unscarred face. He looks as if he was expecting to see something he does not, to feel something he does not. How should immortality feel? What is the shape of it, the breath of it?

Or does it not exist at all?

'Immortality has its opposite, too.' I whisper it as I finally begin to understand it.

The Azoth, now dead and dusted and gone, gave up its destruction, just as Blackwell planned. The destructive power of it combined with the invincibility of the stigma to transcend them both, just as Blackwell planned.

But what he did not know, what John and Nicholas somehow did, was that immortality does not exist. That it cannot exist: not without death alongside it. That the powers of both became the power of neither, and here Blackwell stands, empty of it all.

Mortal.

'The circle closes its end. That end is for you to make. His end. Do you understand? Do – ' Nicholas slumps to the floor then, his hand still clutched around John's neck. His eyes close, and he falls terribly, horribly still.

The end is for me to make.

I wanted to make it mine, when I swore I would protect John from his. This is not what I would have chosen, but it has been given to me to carry out, to finish what was started too long ago to remember, a history that started without me but somehow entangled me and is now left to me.

Does that still make it mine?

Does it matter?

As if he can hear my thoughts, Blackwell turns to me, and by the look on his face he blames me: for what happened to him, for what didn't happen to him; for not understanding what happened at all. He stands there and he stares at me, the haze of pink still surrounding him like a halo of blood, his eyes dark and his expression even darker.

'You did this.' Blackwell flicks a hand and at once Marcus is by his side, drawing his own sword and placing it in Blackwell's hand. Blackwell advances on me, waving the blade before him, a slow, sluggish movement. 'You. And him.' I don't know if he means Nicholas or John; it doesn't matter.

I climb to my feet. Slowly, painfully; through broken

bones and bleeding wounds and burnt, torn flesh. Pull myself from the rubble, from the carnage, from Nicholas and from John, releasing him the worst pain of all.

'You told me once we create our own enemies.' My voice is determined, but it is weary: as weary as the end of every battle I've ever fought. 'I was never your enemy, nor were they.'

'You conspired to deceive me; you colluded to deceive me. You stand here before me, deceiving me still.'

'I said I *was* not your enemy.' I reach down and gently slide John's sword from his scabbard. It is dirty, stained with blood, ordinary. But if Blackwell is ordinary, if he is mortal, it needs to be nothing more. 'But I am now.'

'You think you can kill me?' Blackwell's voice, it's different. Not just in tone or timbre but in tremor: the slightest shake that alerts me to the truth: He is afraid. For once, he is like me; he is like all of us. And for a moment, just a moment, I almost pity him.

'You should have left me alone,' I say. 'If you'd left me alone, I'd be nothing to you. But by pursuing me, you created your own worst enemy. And for that, for what you did to them, to all of us, I'm going to pay you in kind.'

I raise John's sword. At once, Marcus starts for me, jerky, hesitant steps as if he's moving against his will, against Blackwell's will. Caleb does not move at all. Blackwell waves a hand to dismiss them both, exerting his control as a pater, the only power he's got left.

Blackwell tries to circle me, tries. But I match his every step. He throws up his blade. It's slow, it's unsure, it's the swing of a mortal man and a frightened man at that. I meet the blow, deflect it, the clash of silver on steel echoing off bare wooden walls, the empty wooden floors.

He strikes again; I deflect again. I can hear him gasping for breath as we whirl across the floor, lunging, parrying, attacking. But he's not landing the blows he should, and he knows it. So he does something I don't expect:

He throws his weapon down.

It spins end over end across the slick wood floor, skidding to a stop against the panelled wall. The shock of him disarming himself is enough to stop me, enough to divert my gaze, only for a second. But a second is all he needs.

Blackwell leaps forward. Snatches my right arm, the arm carrying the sword, thrusting it away from him. With the other hand he grabs a hank of my hair, then kicks me hard, harder than I thought possible, along the side of my knee: a move I learned from him now turned against me.

I crumple to the floor, a sharp shriek of pain escaping my lips. The blade tips from my grip, skittering along the floor into a heap of rubble. I scrabble for it, my leg tangled beneath me, but I cannot reach it.

Blackwell turns to Marcus. 'Finish her.'

Marcus snaps to attention. Those grey eyes alight on me as he starts for me, grin as bright as his gaze, his steps smooth: commanded. Caleb stands in attendance beside Blackwell, both of them watching, waiting, for the end.

My fingers search wildly in the dust and the timber, and finally they find something: cool, smooth, a handle; not of a sword but of a dagger. I unearth it, twist to a crouched position.

Blackwell's eyes go wide as I pull back the blade, wider still when I fling it. It hits where I mean it to: his chest, two inches right of centre, straight to the heart. He grunts, falters to his knees. Blood blooms against his surcoat, flushing the red rose of his house – that twisted, snarled, thorned rose – black and drenched with it.

A roar of anger and Marcus leaps for me, wild as any animal, hate and revenge in his eyes. He never makes it. Caleb reaches him before Marcus reaches me; it happens so fast. A scuffle, a curse – the savage snap of a neck and Marcus slumps to the floor, dead once more; his face frozen in a twisted snarl of surprise.

Blackwell reaches for the blade in his chest, pulls it out. More blood, a stifled gasp of pain, a shocked look at Caleb for allowing this to happen. Yet he is still breathing, still alive, and I have no time. No time until Blackwell turns his command to Caleb, commanding him to turn on me.

I get to my feet. Pitch under the weight of my shattered knee, of the wounds scattered like petals along my skin. Spot Marcus's sword, the one Blackwell so carelessly flung away. A quick glance at Caleb: I know he hears my thoughts, knows what I intend. Blackwell knows, too; he must. I've got seconds before Blackwell orders him to finish me and this time, there's no one to stop him.

I rush forward to grab the weapon. And before I can consider the fear beginning to etch itself along Blackwell's face, the fear of defeat and of death, the fear that defined him and now defies him; before I can stop to regret it or allow sympathy to temper it, I plunge the sword into his chest. It screams into his flesh, smooth; no hitches, as easy as a hand into warm water. And there it stays as his life ebbs out.

There is no pomp in killing a king, only circumstance: no magic, no fire; no ceilings thundering down like rain. The end comes for Blackwell the same way it came for Nicholas, and for John; the way it does for any man: quickly, silently, painfully.

Finally.

THIRTY-THREE

It is over.

The magic Blackwell took and twisted to his own purposes – before it twisted against him – is gone. At once, the room is lighter. The clouds, black and ominous before, have scattered, giving way to muted, early-morning skies. It throws the destruction around me into sharp relief: the blood, the piles of rubble, the discarded weapons, the shattered glass. The broken bodies: John's and Nicholas's.

I don't move, I don't speak. Not even when Caleb shifts into motion, moving slowly across the room, footsteps dragging through the ruin. He stops before Blackwell, his body as lifeless and still as the others', but unlike the others', his face is twisted into a grimace of pain and defeat. There's no peace for him, even in death.

'He's dead,' Caleb says. That gleam, the one I saw earlier in the field, in the heat of battle, flares once more into his face. 'I feel as if I can breathe again.'

'You knew.' My voice is dull, emotionless. I have no emotion left. 'You knew this would happen. You helped make it happen.'

Caleb shakes his head. 'I didn't know, not at first. But Nicholas and your healer, they figured it out. They knew what the unity of opposites really meant. It's why they sacrificed themselves to allow Blackwell to attempt it. Your other friend, Schuyler, he knew it, too. He called to me, told me I could help. Him. Nicholas. You.'

'Yourself.' The word is bitter enough to choke on.

'Yes. Myself.' Caleb acknowledges the truth. 'But Blackwell is dead now, and we are all free. That's what you wanted, isn't it? To be free?'

Free. Without John, and without Nicholas, the word feels more like *forsaken.* But I know what Caleb wishes me to acknowledge. His role in this, the risk he took; the part he played that no one else could. John, Nicholas, they are not the only ones who had to die in order for Blackwell to die, too.

'Anglia is grateful,' I say, 'for what you've done.' It's all I can manage, the only thing I can manage.

'Maybe someday, you will be, too.'

I nod, but I'm already backing away. I don't want to talk to Caleb and I've already stopped listening. I want to sit with John until I cannot sit with him anymore, and then I need to figure out a way to tell Peter his son is dead. It's nearly enough to make me wish Peter were dead, too, so he wouldn't have to bear it.

Caleb glances toward the open, shattered windows.

Frowns, purses his lips, shakes his head. It's a gesture I've seen Schuyler do before, one he does when he's piecing something together from the fragments of thought around him.

'They're retreating,' he says after a moment. 'Blackwell's men. They're leaving. I can feel them.' Another crunch of glass as he moves toward the open window. 'I should leave now, too.'

I don't ask where he'll go. But when Caleb steps through the window, half in light, half in dark, he turns to me and says, 'Do you think we'll meet again?'

I look at him. Watching Caleb leave – again – holds nothing for me this time. There are too many wrongs that have passed between us that can never be set right.

'I don't know,' I say. 'But I think it's best if we don't.'

Caleb says nothing to this, only nods. Then he's gone, slipping through the window like a ghost. And I am alone.

Slowly, as if in a nightmare from which I will never wake, I walk to John's body, resting pale and motionless before me. Nicholas lies prone beside him, looking younger in death. His face is pale, marblelike in its placidity, but arranged in a peaceful expression that looks almost as if he's smiling. His hands are clasped over his chest; he is so, so still.

I kneel beside John, take his hand, cool in my own fevered grip. His eyes, open before, are closed now; Nicholas must have done that. His body has shifted slightly, his head listing toward the window. Nicholas must have done that, too. Unlike Nicholas, John doesn't look younger in death. Nor does he look peaceful. His brow is slightly furrowed, creased between his eyes. He looks as if he's asleep and not having a particularly good dream, he looks as if he could open his eyes at any moment and tell me all about it. But he can't and he won't and the simple, sharp finality of that is more than I can take.

'I'm sorry.' I repeat it over and over, curling into him, grasping his tunic and rocking back and forth, whispering and sobbing until my voice gives out and I'm limp with exhaustion and grief.

That's when I feel it: a hand on the back of my head, cupping my neck, fingers feathering my hair. I don't move, not right away. Because when I do, I know I'll see Peter standing beside me, grief etched in his face the way I know it's etched in mine, and I can't bear it. But then, when I hear him say my name, '…beth,' in a voice that's not a whisper as much as it is a breath, I jerk my head up.

John. He's turned his head, he's watching me through one eye, barely open, his hand that was just on my head poised in the air. His other eye cracks open and he blinks, dropping his hand to my side, his fingers grasping for the hem of my tunic.

I'm too afraid to say anything. Too afraid to do anything that might take this moment away, that might lift the spell, that might take the possibility of what I'm seeing and turn it back into what it really is: impossible.

But when he says my name again, clearer and louder this time, I'm finally able to utter a single word. 'How?'

John doesn't speak. He just turns his head and there, on the skin along the side of his neck where Nicholas had laid his hand, is a tiny fleur-de-lis, no bigger than a thumbprint, no darker than a sunburn. It's all that's left of Nicholas, of his power: given to John, healing him as they both lay dying.

'Oh.' It's all I can say. I tuck my head back onto his chest and wrap my arms around him and bury myself into him again. John presses his head against mine and whispers in my ear, his words unintelligible from the tremor in his voice and the tumult in my breath, but I feel the love and relief in them anyway.

Slowly, eventually, I help him sit up and then to his feet. He's unsteady, and he holds to me tight. 'How do you feel?' I don't know if I mean without the stigma, or with Nicholas's magic, or after having died. Perhaps I mean all of it.

'It's hard to say.' He offers up a tentative smile, as if he knows what I'm thinking. 'I'm tired. A little dizzy. But for the most part, as far as I can tell, I feel like me again.'

'Caleb said you planned this,' I say. 'You and Nicholas. When?'

'While I was sequestered in Rochester,' John replies. 'Nicholas brought me the books I needed to figure it out. It was part of the reason he shut me away. He needed me to know what my part in this was. What I would need to do. What we both would need to do.'

'Did anyone else know about this? Your father? Fifer?'

'Fifer knew,' John says. 'She figured it out even before I did. Even so, she had a hard time accepting it. Especially toward the end.' I remember how she was nowhere to be seen the night of the celebration before the battle, how Schuyler was absent, too. 'I waited until last night to tell

Father, though,' John continues. 'I almost didn't. But I didn't want him to think I went into it unknowingly.'

'But you didn't tell me.'

He nods. 'Because I don't know if I could have gone through with it if I had.'

John takes my hand and we pick our way through the destruction of the music room, out into the hallway. It's quiet and calm here, as is the neighbouring chapel. With care, we carry in Nicholas's body, laying it in the chancel and draping it with the heavy, embroidered altar cloth before making our way outside into the courtyard.

It's clear here, unharmed, but that doesn't mean it's safe. And it isn't: As we emerge from the yew alley into the meadow, the battle that began in the fields and farms outside Rochester is before us now, spilling into the tents and the grass, the jousting pits and the training yards. Men running everywhere: men in black, men in blue and red, a few in white.

I yank John's arm, pulling him back into the alley.

'Wait.' He peers around the tree line. 'They're not invading. They're retreating. Look.'

We edge out into the field, cautious. But John is right, and it seems Caleb was, too: Blackwell's men, what's left of them, are rushing across the grounds, desperate in their attempt to escape. The skies above us are clear now, empty of dark clouds and hybrids with wings, a landscape of nothing but dawn and green.

'I want to find my father,' John says. 'I need to let him know I'm all right. And I want to help, if I can, people who need it.'

We make our way toward the bridge that leads away from Rochester, never straying too far from each other, never letting our guard down. We search the scattered felled bodies for those we recognise, but they are mostly Blackwell's men and a handful of Gallic soldiers. We cross to each one, to see if there's anything John can do to help them. But they're all past saving.

The other side of the bridge is a far different story. The road here is littered with men wearing both colours; some of them alive and injured, but most of them dead, including two in white, members of the Order. The first, a boy I don't know, the second a girl I do: Miri, the one who could manipulate water. I feel a stab of sorrow at that: She was only ten years old. John goes to them to see what he can do to help, and I continue roaming the field, searching the maze of men dashing around, looking for Peter.

That's when I see Malcolm, lying in the clearing. He's alone, and I know he's hurt by the way he moves, twisting from side to side, slow; his back arching, his hand splayed beside him, grasping at the wispy, flattened grass. But more than that, I can tell by the pool of blood beneath him, creeping outward, rusty and bright.

'Malcolm!' I sprint toward him, drop to the ground beside him and take his hand. It's slick with blood, his or someone else's. His armour is missing, his blue-and-red surcoat shredded and torn.

'How'd we do?' He squints at me through one half-opened eye, grey and pale against the blood on his face. 'Did we win?'

John appears then, slow and a little out of breath. He kneels beside Malcolm, lifts up his surcoat to reveal what's left of the tangled mail beneath. It looks as if it's been chewed away. Carefully, John peels the rest of it off, piece by piece.

'We won,' I say.

Malcolm closes his eye, breathes in. When he exhales, he's looking at me again.

'What of Uncle?' He holds my stare. 'How did he fare in all of this?'

I debate telling him I don't know. But I know he already does. I can tell by the resigned look on his face, the way he looks at me, holding me to the truth.

So I tell it.

'He's dead.'

Malcolm nods, slow. 'Did he hurt you?'

'No,' I say. 'Not today, and not anymore.'

He closes his eyes again. When he opens them and looks to me, they're full of sorrow and light, relief and darkness, all of those things all at once, impossibly opposite, like the Azoth but impossibly human.

'I can't say I'm sorry for it,' he says. 'But I can't say I'm glad of it, either. Ironic, isn't it? He was all I had left, and he wanted me dead, and now he's gone.'

'He's not all you have left,' I say, only I don't know if that's true. I don't know what waits for him back at Rochester, or at Upminster, what waits for him at all.

'You're only saying that because I'm dying,' he says, as if he's reading my mind.

'You're not dying,' I say.

'Try not to talk,' John says. He reaches forward and gently rolls up Malcolm's tunic. I hiss in a breath. His skin is sliced across the middle in a diagonal line from hip to armpit. His entire chest is coated in blood.

John slides a knife from Malcolm's belt. 'I'm going to cut your tunic off, all right?'

Malcolm gives a tiny nod, and John begins slicing the fabric. He examines it before tossing it aside; it's nothing but a bloody rag. John slips off his surcoat and mail before pulling his own tunic over his head, naked now from the waist up.

'What are you doing?' I can feel my eyes go round.

'I need to stop the bleeding.' John presses his shirt into Malcolm's chest, the white linen quickly blooming red. 'Hold this here,' he says to me, climbing to his feet. He darts across the meadow in a stop-start motion, looking along the ground. He disappears into the trees, then after a moment reemerges clutching a handful of bell-shaped white flowers with spiky dark green leaves. I'd laugh if I weren't so confused.

'You really know how to woo a lady,' Malcolm says when John drops beside him again. 'The bawd in the battlefield, shirtless, dodging certain death to pick flowers…'

John shoots him an exasperated look, plucks the leaves from the stem, then shoves a handful into his mouth and begins chewing.

'I take it back,' Malcolm says. '*That's* how you woo a lady.'

'Comfrey,' John says, his voice muffled. 'It'll help stop

the bleeding.' He spits the leaves into his palm, an enormous green glob.

'That's disgusting.' Malcolm looks genuinely distressed.

'If you prefer, I can let you bleed to death,' John replies calmly. 'Leave you here for the gulls to peck out your eyes, the boars to tear you up, and those red-eyed crows to finish you off—'

'By all means, carry on.'

John jams the wad of leaves into the wound, holding them in place with the flat of his palm. Malcolm lets out a stream of curses, twisting in pain under John's hand.

'It'll hurt only a minute,' John says. After a moment he pulls his hand away. It's bloody and sticky with green, but just as he said, the bleeding has slowed. John takes the knife, quickly slices his own discarded shirt into a bandage, and wraps it tight against Malcolm's chest.

'We'll need to get you out of here.' John glances around. The field is littered with bodies, soldiers still darting around, weapons held high. 'We can try to cut through the woods back to Rochester, though we don't know what could be lurking inside – oh, only you.'

I look up to see Schuyler step from the trees into view. He's got a sword in one hand, a bundle of grey fabric clutched in the other. He pauses a moment, takes us in.

'It's a good look.' Schuyler eyes John's half-naked body. 'Bit like a republic gladiator, strutting about the arena. Shall I bring you a loincloth? A pair of sandals? A lion, perhaps?'

John flips him an obscene gesture, and then, to my surprise, he laughs.

Schuyler tosses him the grey bundle – a shirt. 'Found this lying around. Thought it might come in handy.' John takes it with a word of thanks, then yanks it over his head. 'He going to die?' Schuyler jerks his head at Malcolm.

I shoot Schuyler a look.

'No, he's not,' John says. 'It's a nasty cut, to be sure, but it's not fatal. Jagged, though – it'll be hell to stitch up.' A look of mild distress crosses his face; at once I know why. John may not recall how to stitch him up, not anymore. He looks back to Malcolm. 'What was it? A serrated knife?'

Malcolm shakes his head. 'It wasn't a weapon. It was talons.' He points overhead. 'One of those bloody winged things picked me up and flew me a hundred feet straight up before someone shot it down. I was still fifty feet in the air when it dropped me.'

'You're lucky you didn't break something.' John pauses, considers. 'Unless you did. Can you move your arms and legs?'

'I can move everything but my left leg,' Malcolm says. 'I can't bend it. I already tried.'

John looks up at Schuyler. 'You'll have to carry him.'

Schuyler reaches down, scoops Malcolm into his arms. He pauses, then nods. 'I'll warrant you didn't,' he says, and I can guess what Malcolm's thinking: that he never imagined himself to be injured in a battlefield, fighting against his family, tended to by a Reformist, helped by a revenant. 'And you're welcome,' Schuyler adds.

THIRTY-FOUR

Fifer and Peter greet us at Rochester Hall. Fifer rushes up to Schuyler like she doesn't even see anyone else. She looks at him as if she wants to laugh and cry at the same time. Then she turns to John, throws herself in his arms.

'Nicholas.' It's all she says; it's all she needs to say. John shakes his head, and Fifer ducks her head into his shoulder again. He whispers to her, his voice drowned out by her sobs.

'Put me down,' Malcolm says to Schuyler, cracking open an eye. His voice is barely a whisper. 'I can walk – hop, rather – and you should go to her…' He wriggles in Schuyler's grasp, breaks off with a gasp of pain.

'No talking,' John tells him. 'And no more moving.' He glances at Schuyler. 'I need to get him to the infirmary. Do you mind taking him? I'll come along. You can drop him off but I'll stay.' John turns to me as if to explain, but he doesn't need to. He's going to stay with Malcolm to make sure he's taken care of, because although one enemy is gone, there are still many others who would see him gone, too.

Schuyler starts off across the field, Malcolm still in his arms, Fifer beside him. John tells me he'll be back for me soon, and then he's gone.

It's just me and Peter alone now, alone save for the thousands of men running around us, shouting and screaming, cursing and laughing. I watch them as they pass, some in chaos and in pain, some in triumph and in relief. Perhaps they never expected to win but now we have, and it's a strange, heady sensation to rejoice when so many others have died, to feel that we've won when we've still lost so much.

Before I can say anything, before I can begin to say or even think what it might mean for us, for them, for everything, Peter snatches me in an embrace, patting my back as if I were a child, murmuring words of comfort I didn't know I needed. I let myself sag in his embrace and cry until I'm weak with release and his shirt is wet with my tears.

The battlefield continues to clear off; men continue to stagger back to camp at Rochester, coming in steady streams through the gatehouse. After seeing Malcolm safely installed and heavily guarded in an infirmary tent – with the promise that he would return to check on him soon – John finds me again, Schuyler and Fifer in tow. There were a panic-filled few hours when we couldn't find George, but finally Schuyler finds him huddled around a tent with two dozen Gallic soldiers, all of them drunk as choirboys. We're angry for all of one minute, until one of the soldiers tosses John a bottle of wine. John takes a drink before passing it to me, grinning. The four of us sit down beside them, and we spend most of the night drinking and laughing and feeling something I've not felt in a long time:

Relief.

Much later, Gareth is found. Back in Harrow, hiding in the cathedral of his own home, huddled beside the pulpit where he denounced me and ordered me to kill the very man he renounced his own side for, a sword in his hand, dead.

Peter reasoned that at some point during the battle he'd had a change of heart, a traitor turning traitor once more. Perhaps he was injured before; perhaps he took a hit on the way back. It wasn't a deep wound, something a healer could have fixed had he returned to Rochester. Instead, he bled to death; he hadn't even bandaged it to try to stop the blood. But perhaps he didn't know how injured he was, not until it was too late.

In the days that follow, Nicholas is laid to rest in a plot beside his home, a home that now belongs to Fifer. Shortly afterward she disappeared from camp alongside Schuyler, keeping to herself and working through her grief in private.

With Blackwell's death, Anglia falls into crisis: We are a country without a king. Upon their surrender, Blackwell's councilmen – once Malcolm's – meet with Harrow's council, led by Fitzroy, the newly appointed Regent of Anglia. And for days they table the unprecedented question: Who is to take the crown? By right, it should revert back to

Malcolm. Only, he won't take it.

'I can't do it,' Malcolm says. We're inside Rochester Hall, in one of the hundreds of plush bedrooms, most of them filled now with recovering soldiers. I sit in a chair beside his bed, John on the other side, checking him over. It's been seven days since the battle ended; six since Malcolm was installed in a fine room, far different from the room he was imprisoned in. He could have had any one of a dozen healers attend to him, but to my surprise, he only wanted John.

'I couldn't do it the first time. You saw what happened. It led to…all this.' He waves his hand vaguely out the window. In the distance, soldiers still mill about the camp. 'I thought about what I'd do, if we won. I was going to hand the crown to Margaret, but that was before…' He trails off, turning his gaze to the floor. John and I exchange a glance.

Malcolm was not a good husband, not at all. But when he learned of the death of his wife he took it hard, more than I imagined he would. Her death was not a repercussion of war, but one of neglect: Three days ago she was found abandoned in a cell at Fleet, left to a pitiful death by starvation and cold.

'Someone's going to have to do it, and soon,' I say. 'Fitzroy can't continue ruling; his claim isn't strong enough. Great-grandson to Edward the First, three times removed—'

'Four times,' Malcolm and John say at the same time.

'Fine. Four times removed. He can hold it now, but once someone starts digging – and you know they will – they'll find someone with better lineage. If it's someone the council doesn't like, and whoever it is doesn't give up his claim, there could be another war. We can't have that.'

'Were I to claim the throne, there would be a war anyway,' Malcolm says. 'I'm still the enemy to some. To many. Don't make me do the math again.' He hisses in pain as John presses down on his broken leg.

'Sorry,' John says. 'Your leg looks good, though. You should have full use of it within six months. Your days of jousting and hunting and dancing might be limited for the next year, but that's not too bad, all things considered.'

'I was thinking of taking up painting,' Malcolm says, his face still a grimace. 'Or maybe lute playing.'

I don't say anything for a moment. The sight of John and Malcolm talking as if they don't hate each other, as if they aren't enemies, holds me to silence.

There's a knock at the door, then it swings open.

We get to our feet, John and I, nodding our heads in deference. Fitzroy nods at us, then glances at Malcolm.

'Forgive me for not standing, Lord Regent.' Malcolm smiles at him, and there's no malice in his voice at the deference. 'I seem to be at a disadvantage at the moment.'

'No apology necessary.' Fitzroy smiles in return. 'Do you have a moment? I thought we could talk.' He flicks his hand, and a handful of servants appear from behind him carrying trays laden with food and wine; pewter plates and crystal goblets; fine silverware. A feast for a king. He glances at John. 'I know this isn't on the approved list of physics, but if you could allow it just for today…'

'It's fine,' John says, then looks at Malcolm. 'I think I can trust you not to overindulge?'

'I think my days of indulgence are over,' Malcolm replies.

We leave Malcolm and Fitzroy alone and make our way down the long, light-filled hallway, out one of many doors and into one of the many courtyards. There's a ring of benches around a fountain, splashing and gurgling in the warm sun, the bushes and hedges around it beginning to show bloom. I sit down on the one closest to the water; John sits beside me.

'You and Malcolm,' I say after a minute. 'It's an odd thing to see you by his side. Helping him.' I pause. 'Why did you? Not just here, today, but before on the battlefield. Why did you do it?'

John smiles. 'Well, I wouldn't be much of a healer if I left him to die, would I?'

'That's not what I meant,' I say.

'I know,' he says. 'But I don't know if I've got a better answer. Part of caring for people is to try to see past what it is they're showing you. Malcolm was in a cell beside me at Hexham. He showed me a lot about himself there, most of it having to do with you.'

I pull a face. I don't want to know the things he said.

'I'll spare you the details,' he says. 'But if I thought for a second Malcolm ever meant to harm you, that he acted out of malice instead of ignorance, I wouldn't have stood by him. I would have healed him, but I wouldn't have helped him.

'He's spoiled and he's flighty,' John continues. 'He's ignorant, too, but not about things. About people. He's lived so long with people telling him yes that he can't imagine a world where they say no.' A pause. 'You forgave him, didn't you?'

I nod. 'He asked it of me, and I didn't think I could put it behind me if I didn't. It was right before we went into battle, and I didn't know if I'd ever see him again. At the time, it seemed pointless not to.'

'And now?' he says. 'How do you feel about the possibility of him being king again?'

'I think it will be different this time,' I reply. 'I think he's different. I think we all are.'

John cups my face with his hand, skimming his thumb along my cheek. 'Not that different,' he says. And then he kisses me.

'The Gallic king offered his daughter in marriage to Malcolm,' Peter says. We're loitering in yet another courtyard outside yet another hall where yet another council meeting is taking place: the fifth one in as many days. John, Schuyler, Fifer, George, and me.

'Not three weeks ago they wanted to ransom him to the Berbers,' I say.

'Three weeks ago he was a prisoner,' George replies. 'Now he's the victor of a battle, the heir to the throne of Anglia. The heir who abdicated to a commoner.'

'Fitzroy is hardly a commoner,' I say

George shrugs. 'To Gaul he is. His line is impressive, to be sure. But it's too removed. Great-grandson to King Edward, three times removed—'

'Four.' I correct. 'Four times removed.' George raises his eyebrows. 'Sorry. Go on.'

'Not much else to say,' Peter continues. 'The Gallic king offers his daughter, along with a sizable dowry, including a hundred thousand livres to help rebuild Anglia.'

John lets out a low whistle.

Peter nods. 'A marriage like that would strengthen our ties to them, unite us against attacks from Iberia, against the Low Countries, should they ever decide to move against us. As it stands, they see us both as weak. One country without a king, the other with only a daughter to be queen.'

'He doesn't want to do it,' I say. 'He told us.'

'Doesn't matter.' George shrugs. 'Kings don't get much of a say in how they were born, do they?'

Peter shakes his head. 'They don't. It's coming to a vote tonight. Fitzroy is prepared to step aside, if he has no one to contest him. If the majority say yes, it's down to Malcolm to refuse. And I don't think he'll refuse. Do you?'

I don't imagine everyone's eyes on me, as if I could guess what Malcolm might do. But I do anyway. And I shake my head.

In the end, I was right.

Malcolm agreed to the council's wishes and he's to be king of Anglia once more, but ruling Anglia in a way that's never been done. He will have a privy council, as before. But he will also have two additional regional councils – the Council of the North and the oddly named Council of the Marches – to oversee the northern and southern outlying counties of Anglia. The divine right of kings – the law that allowed kings to rule as gods – has been abolished. The Twelve Tablets, already abolished, would remain so, new laws drawn up and voted on.

It was all but done.

When the Gallic princess arrived with her courtiers, her ambassadors, her advisors, her plate and her jewels and her livres, I wasn't there. When Ravenscourt opened back up, the gates and the courtyards scrubbed clean of all signs of war and death, hybrids and revenants, I wasn't there.

The week after Malcolm was reinstalled as king, the privy council was installed inside their apartments inside Ravenscourt, now being lavishly redecorated and refitted to erase all signs of ever being inhabited by Blackwell. Once again, I wasn't there.

I can't go back to court; I don't think I'll ever want to.

John helps his father load the last of his trunks onto the wagon that sits in front of their cottage, waiting to take him to Upminster. As a member of the Council of the Marches, his presence is required monthly at court, and although he doesn't need to be there more often than that, he's taken a house along Westcheap, a short walk from the palace.

We watch the wagon tip its way down the narrow lane, the wheels kicking up mud. There would be a wagon for me, for us, if we decided to go. Half the girls in Harrow have already left, eager to be ladies-in-waiting in the court of the soon-to-be-queen. I could do it, too, if I wanted. I could be part of it all, just as I was before.

But I know how close power comes to corruption, how

fast good intentions turn bad. I know that despite promises and declarations and even laws, things have a way of turning on their own, of starting down a path, trespassing so far that redress becomes impossible.

I turn to John. He's watching me and I know he's waiting – in that way he does – for me to tell him what he already knows. That I can't be part of Malcolm's court, no matter how much I'm asked, no matter how much it's changed. Because there are some things that never would change, just as there are some things I don't want to remember.

'I can't do it,' I say.

He closes his eyes for a moment and for a moment I think I've disappointed him, that I've read his looks and his words wrong, until he opens his eyes, a grin on his face.

'Thank God.'

I blink back surprise. 'You don't want to go, either?'

John shakes his head. 'No. I never did. But I would have, if that was what you wanted. I just want to go where you go.' He watches me carefully. 'But I wanted you to make up your own mind. For once, I wanted you to do what you wanted, without anyone deciding for you.'

'Are you sure?' I say. 'You won't mind being alone?'

'I'm not alone,' he says. 'I'm with you.'

I smile. 'You know what I mean.'

He grins. 'We'll hardly be alone. Schuyler is staying. Keagan is staying, too; she and Fifer are starting a new branch of the Order here in Harrow. As for the rest, we can see the others anytime we want. Upminster isn't that far.'

'It's far enough,' I say.

John smiles. 'It's far enough.'

He takes my hand and tugs me toward the cottage, the bright blue door still open to the sunshine and the breeze, welcoming us in. It's a good place to start over.

And a good place to continue on.

ACKNOWLEDGEMENTS

Ah, the second book. It's a thrill, a challenge, a stressor, and a triumph: it is, much like all of publishing, all the things people tell you it will be but you don't believe until you reach the other side. This book is dedicated to everyone who helped me push through.

My agent, Kathleen Ortiz. I feel like I could thank you every day and it still wouldn't be enough. For your patience, for your perseverance, for always having my back, and for knowing me well enough to know when I need *that* phone call to say, 'I think we should talk.' (And for always starting those calls with 'You aren't driving, are you?' followed by, 'Don't freak out.') You are a BAMF, and I adore you.

My editor, Pam Gruber. We made it! I consider this book your accomplishment as much as mine: all those calls, all those emails, all those conversations ('Do you really think she would?' 'Maybe, but I don't think she *should*.') and spreadsheets (yes, we plotted spells using spreadsheets). Thank you for your endless patience, guidance, intuition, for making me better at what I do, and for making this story something I am truly proud of. I feel like we are forever bonded in magic.

My agency, New Leaf Literary + Media. You are still the coolest kids on the block, and I'm so proud to be part of your ranks. Special thanks to Joanna Volpe, Danielle Barthel, Jaida Temperly, Dave Caccavo, Jackie Lindert and Mia Roman.

My publisher, Little, Brown Books for Young Readers. Not a day goes by that I am not profoundly grateful to be part of this imprint. Immeasurable gratitude to my incredibly talented team: Leslie Shumate, Kristina Aven, Emilie Polster, Victoria Stapleton, Jenny Choy, Jane Lee and everyone at The NOVL. Marcie Lawrence for the most gorgeous cover I've ever seen, Virginia Lawther and Rebecca Westall for making me a book, Annie McDonnell for making it shine and Emily Sharratt for your spot-on, London-specific notes. Thank you also to Megan Tingley, Alvina Ling and Andrew Smith. The support, kindness, respect and enthusiasm you've shown me and my books is in everything you do.

My foreign publishers. Thank you for your support, your beautiful covers, and for giving Elizabeth & Co. the best home in all corners of the world.

Alexis Bass. I could not do this publishing thing without you. Thank you for our long, hilarious, insane conversations, inappropriate crushes, and for sharing the same brain and taste in just about everything. You are the bestest, and I am so grateful for our friendship.

My Secret Society. The ranks have closed, and we are it. KL, JMT, LK, I love our corner of the universe where things are dark, funny, truthful, and supportive. Of all the groups in all the towns in all the world, I am so happy you walked into mine.

Stephanie Funk. For being there from the beginning.

Melissa Grey, critique partner extraordinaire. We're like those two things in chemistry class you should never mix together, yet somehow when we do it shines. Here's to cupcakes, Freixenet, sushi, crying over puppies, hot gay mages, and Mexican Al Rokers. I love the alchemy of us.

April Tucholke. Thank you for your friendship, your mentorship, and for making me laugh so hard it hurts. May we always have stormy coastal writing retreats and Liberace Panel Resting Faces™.

The writing community. Readers, reviewers, bloggers, booksellers, teachers, librarians: thank you for taking the time to read my words, writing about them, telling your friends about them, and coming to see me talk about them. Thank you for your support. For all my fellow authors: you're all so talented, and such an inspiration. I'm so grateful to know all of you.

My friends and family. You are proof that magic exists. Thank you for your endless patience and understanding with 'this writing thing'. Special thanks to my intuitive daughter Holland, when she sees me looking less than happy, for saying, 'You didn't go on Goodreads again, did you?' My clever son August, when he sees me deep in thought, for saying, 'Do you need a magic spell? How about one where a wizard steals oxygen from the air?' (Thanks, buddy! That one I used!) And to my husband Scott, whose words of wisdom could fill an entire book. Thank you for always believing in me no matter what. Because of you I am, quite simply, the luckiest girl in the world.

PENGUIN BOOKS

Little Boy Blue

M. J. Arlidge has worked in television for the last fifteen years, specializing in high-end drama production, including prime-time crime serials *Torn*, *The Little House* and *Silent Witness*. Arlidge is also piloting original crime series for both UK and US networks. In 2015 his audiobook exclusive *Six Degrees of Assassination* was a number one bestseller.

His debut thriller, *Eeny Meeny*, was the UK's bestselling crime debut of 2014. It was followed by the bestselling *Pop Goes the Weasel*, *The Doll's House* and *Liar Liar*.

@MJArlidge

Little Boy Blue

M. J. ARLIDGE

PENGUIN BOOKS

PENGUIN BOOKS

UK | USA | Canada | Ireland | Australia
India | New Zealand | South Africa

Penguin Books is part of the Penguin Random House group of companies
whose addresses can be found at global.penguinrandomhouse.com.

First published by Michael Joseph 2015
Published in Penguin Books 2016
001

Typeset by Jouve (UK), Milton Keynes
Printed in Great Britain by Clays Ltd, St Ives plc

A CIP catalogue record for this book is available from the British Library

B-format ISBN: 978–1–405–91923–4
A-format ISBN: 978–1–405–92062–9

www.greenpenguin.co.uk

I

He looked like a falling angel. His muscular body, naked save for a pair of silver wings, was suspended in mid-air, turning back and forth on the heavy chain that bound him to the ceiling. His fingers groped downwards, straining for the key that would effect his release, but it remained tantalizingly out of reach. He was at the mercy of his captor and she circled him now, debating where to strike next. His chest? His genitals? The soles of his feet?

A crowd had gathered to watch, but *he* didn't linger. He was bored by the spectacle – had seen it countless times before – and moved on quickly, hoping to find something else to distract him. He always came to the Annual Ball – it was the highlight of the S&M calendar on the South Coast – but he suspected this year would be his last. It wasn't simply that he kept running into exes that he'd rather avoid, it was more that the scene had become so *familiar*. What had once seemed outrageous and thrilling now felt empty and contrived. The same people doing the same old things and wallowing in the attention.

Perhaps he just wasn't in the right mood tonight. Since he'd split up with David, he'd been in such a deep funk that nothing seemed to give him any pleasure. He'd come here more in hope than expectation and already he could feel the disappointment and self-disgust welling up inside him. Everybody else seemed to be having a good time – and there was certainly no shortage of offers from fellow revellers – so what was wrong with him? Why was he incapable of dealing with the fact that he was alone?

He pushed his way to the bar and ordered a double Jameson's. As the barman obliged, he ran his eye over the scene. Men, women and others who were somewhere in between paraded themselves on the dance floors and podiums – a seething mass of humanity crammed into the basement club's crumbling walls. This was their night and they were all in their Sunday best – rubber-spiked dominators, padlocked virgins, sluts-who-blossom-into-swans and, of course, the obligatory gimps. All trying so hard.

As he turned back to the bar in disgust, he saw him. Framed by the frenzied crowds, he appeared as a fixed point – an image of utter stillness amid the chaos, coolly surveying the clubbers in front of him. Was it a 'him'? It was hard to say. The dark leather mask covered everything but the eyes and the matching suit revealed only a sleek, androgynous figure. Running his eyes over the concealed body in search of clues, he suddenly realized that the object of his attention was looking straight at him. Embarrassed, he turned away. Seconds later, however, curiosity got the better of him and he stole another glance.

He was still staring at him. This time he didn't turn

away. Their eyes remained glued to each other for ten seconds or more, before the figure suddenly turned and walked away, heading towards the darker, more discreet areas of the club.

Now he didn't hesitate, following him past the bar, past the dance floor, past the chained angel and on towards the back rooms – heavily in demand tonight as private spaces for brief, fevered liaisons. He could feel his excitement growing and as he picked up the pace, his eyes took in the contours of the person ahead of him. Was it his imagination or was there something familiar about the shape of the body? Was this someone known to him, someone he'd met in the course of work or play? Or was this a total stranger, who'd singled him out for special attention? It was an intriguing question.

The figure had come to a halt now, standing alone in a small, dingy room ahead. In any other situation, caution would have made him hesitate. But not tonight. Not now. So, entering the room, he marched directly towards the expectant figure, pushing the door firmly shut behind him.

2

The piercing scream was long and loud. Her eyes darted left just in time to see the source of the noise – a startled vixen darting into the undergrowth – but she didn't break stride, diving ever deeper into the forest. Whatever happened now, she had to keep going.

Her lungs burnt, her muscles ached, but on she went, braving the low branches and fallen logs, praying her luck would hold. It was nearly midnight and there was not a soul around to help her should she fall, but she was so close now.

The trees were thinning out, the foliage was less dense, and seconds later she broke cover – a svelte, hooded figure darting across the vast expanse of Southampton Common. She was closing in fast on the cemetery that marked the western edge of the park and, though her body was protesting bitterly, she lurched forwards once more. Seconds later she was there, slapping the cemetery gates hard, before wrenching up her sleeve to arrest her stopwatch. Forty-eight minutes and fifteen seconds – a new personal best.

Breathing heavily, Helen Grace pulled back her hood and turned her face to the night. The moon was nearly full, the sky cloudless and the gentle breeze that rippled over her was crisp and refreshing. Her heart was beating out a furious rhythm, the sweat creeping down her cheeks, but she found herself smiling, happy to have shaved half a minute off her time, pleased that she had the moon at least to bear witness to her triumph. She had never pushed herself this hard before, but it had been worth it.

Dropping to the ground, she began to stretch. She knew she made an odd sight – a lone female contorting herself in the shadow of a decaying cemetery – and that many would have chastised her for being here so late at night. But it was part of her routine now and she never felt any fear or anxiety in this place. She revelled in the isolation and solitude – somehow being alone made it feel like *her* space.

Her life had been so troubled and complex, so fraught with incident and danger, that there were very few places where she truly felt at peace. But here, a tiny, anonymous figure, dwarfed by the immense darkness of the deserted common, she felt relaxed and happy. More than that, she felt free.

3

He couldn't move a muscle.

Conversation had been brief and they had moved quickly to the main event. A chair had been pulled out into the middle of the room and he had been pushed down roughly on to it. He knew not to say anything – the beauty of these encounters was that they were mysterious, anonymous and secret. Careless talk ruined the moment, but not here – something about this one just felt right.

He sat back and allowed himself to be bound. His captor had come prepared, wrapping thick ribbon around his ankles, tethering them to the chair legs. The material felt smooth and comforting against his skin and he exhaled deeply – he was so used to being in control, to being the one thinking, planning, doing, that it was gratifying to switch off for once. It had been a long time since anyone had taken him in hand and he suddenly realized how excited he was at the prospect.

Next it was his arms, pushed gently behind his back, then secured to the chair with leather straps. He could smell the tang of the cured hide – it was a smell that had intrigued him since he had been a boy and its aroma was pleasantly familiar. He closed his eyes now – it was more enjoyable if you couldn't see what was coming – and braced himself for what was to come.

The next stage was more complicated, but no less tender. Wet sheets were carefully unfurled and steadily applied, from the ankle up. As the minutes passed, the moisture began to evaporate, the sheets tightened, sticking close to his skin. Before long he couldn't move anything below his waist – a strange but not unpleasant sensation. Moments later, he was bound to the chest, his lover for the night carefully finishing the job by securing the upper sheet with heavy-duty, silver duct tape, winding it round and round his broad shoulders, coming to a halt just beneath his Adam's apple.

He opened his eyes and looked at his captor. The atmosphere in the room was thick with expectation – there were many different ways this could play out: some consensual, some less so. Each had its merits and he wondered which one he, or she, would choose.

Neither spoke. The silence between them was punctured only by the distant thump of the Euro pop currently deafening those on the dance floor. But the sound seemed a long way away, as if they were in a different universe, locked together in this moment.

Still his captor made no move to punish or pleasure him and for the first time he felt a flash of frustration – everyone likes to be teased, but there are limits. He could feel the beginnings of an erection, straining against its constraints, and he was keen not to let it go to waste.

'Come on then,' he said softly. 'Don't make me wait. It's been a long time since I had any love.'

He closed his eyes again and waited. What would come first? A slap? A blow? A caress? For a moment, nothing happened, then suddenly he felt something brush against his cheek. His lover had moved in close – he could feel his breath on the side of his face, could hear his cracked lips parting.

'This isn't about love,' his captor whispered. 'This is about *hate*.'

His eyes shot open, but it was too late. His captor was already winding the duct tape over his chin, his mouth . . .. He tried to scream but his tongue was forced back down by the sticky, bitter adhesive. Now it was covering his cheeks, flattening his nose. Moments later, the tape passed over his eyes and everything went black.

4

Helen stared out into the darkness beyond. She was back in her flat, showered and swathed in a towel, sitting by the casement window that looked out on to the street. The adrenaline and endorphins of earlier had dissipated, replaced by a relaxed, contented calm. She had no need for sleep – she wanted to enjoy this moment a little first – so she'd taken up her customary position in front of the window, her vantage point on the world beyond.

It was at times like this that Helen thought she was making a go of her life. The old demons still lurked within, but her use of pain as a way of controlling her emotions had eased off of late, as she'd learnt to push her body in other ways. She wasn't there yet – would she ever be? – but she was on the right track. Sometimes she suppressed the feelings of hope this engendered in her, for fear of being disappointed; at other times she gave in to them. Tonight was one of those moments when she allowed herself a little happiness.

Cradling her mug of tea, she looked down on to the street below. She was a night owl and this was one of her favourite times, when the world seemed quiet, yet full of mystery and promise – the dark before the dawn. Living high up, she was shielded from view and could watch undetected as the night creatures went about their business. Southampton has always been a bustling, vibrant city and around midnight the streets regularly fill with workers, students, ships' crews, tourists and more, as the pubs empty out. Helen enjoyed watching the human dramas that played out below – lovers falling out and reconciling, best friends declaring their mutual affection for each other, a woman in floods of tears on her mobile phone, an elderly couple holding hands on their way home to bed. Helen liked to climb inside their lives, imagining what would happen next for them, what highs and lows still lay ahead.

Later still, when the streets thinned out, you saw the really interesting sights – the night birds who were up at the darkest point of the day. Sometimes these sights tugged at your heart – the homeless, vulnerable and miserably drunk ploughing their lonely furrows through the city. Other times they made you sit up – fights between drunken boys, the sight of a junkie prowling the derelict building opposite, a noisy domestic incident spilling out on to the streets. Other times they made Helen laugh – fresher students pushing each other around in 'borrowed' Sainsbury's trollies, clueless as to where they were or how they would find their way back to their digs.

All human life passed before her and Helen drank it in, enjoying the feeling of quiet omnipotence that her elevated view gave her. Sometimes she chided herself for her voyeurism, but more often than not she gave in to it, wallowing in the 'company' it afforded her. On occasion, it did make her wonder whether any of the night stalkers were aware they were being watched, and if so whether they would care. And occasionally, in her darker, more paranoid moments, it made her wonder if somebody might in turn be watching *her*.

5

The panic shears lay on the floor, untouched. The heavy-duty scissors were specifically designed to cut through clothing, tape, even leather – but they wouldn't be used. There would be no deliverance tonight.

The chair had toppled over as the panicking victim attempted to wrestle himself free of his bonds. He made a strange sight now, bucking pointlessly on the floor, as his fear grew and his breath shortened. He was making no headway loosening his restraints and the end could not be far away now. Standing over him, his attacker looked on, wondering what the eventual cause of death would be. Overheating? Asphyxiation? Cardiac arrest? It was impossible to say and the uncertainty was quietly thrilling.

His victim's movements were slowing now and the leather-clad figure moved away. There was nothing to be gained by enjoying the show, especially when some sexed-up freak might burst in at any minute. His work here was done.

Turning away, he walked calmly towards the door. Would they get it? Would they realize what they were dealing with? Only time would tell, but whatever happened there was one thing that the police, the public and the freaks out there *wouldn't* be able to ignore: the lovingly bound figure lying on the floor nearby, twitching slowly to a standstill as death claimed him.

6

Where was he?

The same question had spun round Sally's head for hours. She'd tried to go to sleep, but had given up, first flicking on the radio, then later switching on the light to read. But the words wouldn't go in and she'd reach the end of the page none the wiser. In the end she'd stopped trying altogether, turning the light off to lie awake in darkness. She was a worrier, she knew that, prone to seeing misfortune around every corner. But surely she had a right to be worried? Paul was 'working late' again.

A few weeks ago, this wouldn't have been a cause for concern. Paul was ambitious, hard-working and committed – his fierce work ethic had often meant him returning to cold dinners during the course of their twenty-year marriage. But then once, three weeks ago, she'd had to contact him urgently, following a call from his mother. Unable to reach him on his mobile, she'd called his PA, only to be told he'd left the office at 5 p.m. sharp. The hands of the kitchen clock pointed mockingly to 8 p.m., as Sally hung up in shock. Her mind had immediately filled with possible scenarios – an accident, an affair – but she'd tried to quell her anxiety and when he returned home safe and sound later that night, she said nothing.

But when he next called to say he'd be late home, she plucked up courage and visited him in person. She'd gone to the office armed with excuses, but they proved unnecessary, as he wasn't there. He'd left early again. Had she successfully hidden her distress from his PA? She thought so, but she couldn't tell. Perhaps she already knew. They say the wife is always the last to find out.

Was Paul the kind of man to have an affair? Instinctively, Sally thought not. Her husband was an old-school Catholic who'd promised to honour his marriage vows and meant it. Their marriage, their family life, had been a happy, prosperous one. Moreover, Sally had kept her looks and her figure, despite the birth of the twins, and she was sure Paul still found her attractive, even if their lovemaking was more sporadic these days. No, instinctively she rebelled against the thought that he would give his love to someone else. But isn't that what every scorned wife believes until the extent of her husband's duplicity is revealed?

The minutes crawled by. What was he up to so late at night? Who was he with? On numerous occasions during the last few days, she'd resolved to have it out with him. But she could never find the right words and, besides, what if she was wrong? Perhaps Paul was planning a surprise for her? Wouldn't he be devastated to be accused of betraying her?

The truth was that Sally was scared. One question can unravel a life. So though she lay awake, groping for the correct way to bring it up, she knew that she would never ask the question. Not because she didn't want to know. But because of what she might find out if she did.

7

It was nearly 2 a.m. and the seventh floor was as quiet as the grave. DS Charlie Brooks stifled a yawn, as she leafed through the cold-case files on her desk. She was exhausted – the twin pressures of her recent promotion and motherhood taking their toll – but she was determined to give these cases the attention they deserved. They were unsolved murders going back ten, fifteen years – cases that were colder than cold – but the victims were all someone's daughter, mother, father or son and those left behind craved answers as keenly now as they did at the time of their bereavement. There was so much going on during the daily grind that it was only at night, when peace finally descended at Southampton Central, that Charlie could get to grips with them. This was just one of the extra duties required of her now that she'd made the leap from Detective Constable to Detective Sergeant and she was determined not to be found wanting.

She had Helen Grace to thank for her elevation. Although Helen already had DS Sanderson to act as her deputy, she'd demanded that Charlie be promoted, following her good work on the Ethan Harris case. Helen had met resistance from those who worried that the chain of command would be compromised, but in the end Helen had got her way, convincing enough of the people who mattered that Charlie deserved promotion.

DC Charlie Brooks had thus become DS Charlene Brooks. Nobody called her that of course – she would always be Charlie to everyone at Southampton Central – but it still felt good when she heard her full name read out at the investiture ceremony. Helen was on hand that day, giving Charlie a discreet wink as she walked back to her place among the other deserving officers, trying to suppress a broad grin from breaking out over her face.

Afterwards she'd wanted to take Helen out, to say thank you to her personally, but Helen wouldn't have it – ushering her instead to the Crown and Two Chairmen for the traditional 'wetting' of the new sergeant's head. Was this to avoid any charges of favouritism, or simply because she wasn't comfortable accepting Charlie's thanks? It was hard to say and in any event the booze-up that followed had been a good one. The whole team had turned up and everyone, with the possible exception of Sanderson, had gone out of their way to tell Charlie how pleased they were. Given the dark days she'd endured getting to this point, Charlie had been profoundly grateful for the vote of confidence they'd given her that night.

Charlie was so wrapped up in her recollections – dim memories of a very drunken, late-night karaoke session with DC McAndrew now surfacing – that she jumped when she looked up to see the duty sergeant standing over her.

'Sorry, miles away,' she apologized, turning to face him.

'Justice never sleeps, eh?' he replied with his trademark wink. 'This just came in. Thought you'd want to see it straight away.'

The piece of paper he handed her was scant on details – a suspected murder with no victim ID and no named witness – but there was something that immediately leapt out at her. Listed at the top of the incident sheet was the address – one she'd never been to, but which was notorious in Southampton.

The Torture Rooms.

8

Helen walked towards the chaos. The club had been packed to the rafters and the partygoers now spilled on to the street, ushered there by the harassed bouncers. It was an arresting sight – a dozen police officers in their high-visibility jackets drowning in a sea of PVC, chain-mail and naked flesh. In different circumstances it would have made Helen smile, but the fear and shock on the faces of those present banished any such thoughts. Many of the clubbers lingered outside despite the management's attempts to move them on, clinging to each other as they speculated about the night's events.

Flashing her warrant card, Helen pushed through the throng towards the entrance. The uniformed officer gave her an awkward nod, embarrassed to be found standing guard over a notorious S&M club, then heaved open the vast leather doors that kept its members in and the world's prying eyes out. Helen had never visited the Torture Rooms, and as she stepped across the threshold, she was immediately struck by the gaping staircase that descended in front of her. Deep crimson from floor to ceiling, flanked by walls studded with ingenious instruments of torture, it looked like the entrance to Hell.

Helen descended quickly, clinging to the rail to avoid slipping on the stairs that were uneven, sticky and cast in shadow. The club was comprised of a series of brick-arched vaults and Helen made her way to the largest of them now. An hour or two earlier, this had been a scene of wild abandon, but it was deserted now, save for Charlie, DC McAndrew and a number of junior officers. Only the smell lingered: sweat, spilled lager, perfume and more besides – a sweet, pungent cocktail that was at odds with the lifeless feel of the club.

'Sorry to have called you so late. Or early. I'm not sure which it is.'

Charlie had spotted Helen and was walking towards her.

'No problem,' Helen replied warmly. 'What have we got?'

'Lover boy over there found the body,' Charlie answered.

She indicated a pale, blond youth who was giving his statement to McAndrew. The police blanket he'd been given couldn't completely conceal his skimpy LAPD outfit and he tugged nervously at it now, seemingly embarrassed by the presence of genuine police officers.

'He and a friend were looking for somewhere to be intimate. They barged into one of the back rooms and found our victim. We've separated the pair of them but their accounts tally. They swear blind they didn't go into the room – Meredith's taken samples from them to check.'

'Good. Any sign of the manager?'

'DC Edwards is in the back office with Mr Blakeman now.'

'Ok. Let's do this then, shall we?'

Charlie gestured Helen towards the back of the club and they walked in that direction.

'Any witnesses?' Helen asked.

'We've no shortage of people who want to talk, but I wouldn't call them witnesses. It was dark, noisy and crowded. Half the punters were in costumes or masks. We'll be lucky to get anything useful and no one is saying they saw anything "unusual". According to the bouncers, a few punters scarpered as soon as the police turned up. We've asked Blakeman for a full list of their members, so we can try and track them down but –'

'They're unlikely to have used their real names,' Helen interjected. 'And I can't see them willingly coming forward to help us. Keep on it anyway, you never know.'

Charlie nodded, but Helen could tell her mind was also turning on the peculiar complications a case such as this might offer. Given the paucity of eyewitnesses, they would probably have to rely heavily on forensic evidence, CCTV and the post mortem results if they were to make any tangible progress.

Upping her pace, Helen now found herself in the company of scene-of-crime officers. They had reached the murder scene. Slipping sterile coverings on to her shoes, Helen nodded to Charlie and, bracing herself, stepped into the room beyond.

9

The small space was a hive of activity. Meredith Walker, Southampton Central's Chief Forensics Officer, was already on her hands and knees, diligently searching the floor space. The club's owners clearly didn't spend much on cleaning and it was going to be a mammoth job for Meredith and her team to bag all the detritus. The foot-fall in this room was evidently large – Helen feared it might be easier to work out which of the club's members *hadn't* been in this room than pin down those who had – further complicating the task that lay in front of them.

Helen caught Charlie looking at her and, putting these defeatist thoughts aside, moved cautiously forward. The victim lay in the middle of the room, bound to a metal chair with duct tape and wet sheets. Helen presumed he was a man, given the height, but it was hard to be sure. The victim's entire head was encased in silver tape, not a strand of hair or patch of skin visible anywhere. The wet sheets clung to him, bolstering Helen's sense of the paralysing immobility the victim must have felt. It was a horrific way to die.

There had been S&M deaths before of course – auto-eroticism and sex games gone wrong – but this one felt different. A pair of sturdy panic shears lay on the floor next to the body, circled by Meredith's team and tagged for inspection. Whoever did this then had the means to release their victim, but had *chosen* not to. Instead, they had left the room, closing the door behind them and walking away without once attracting anyone's attention. This was no accident then. This was a deliberate, calculated attempt to kill.

The police photographer gave Helen the nod and she now moved forward. Slipping her gloved hand beneath the victim, she raised him from the ground. The chair wobbled a little, then righted itself, settling into position in front of her. The victim's head lolled downwards, eventually coming to rest on his chest.

'Could you give us a couple of minutes, guys?' Helen said quietly, but firmly.

Meredith and her team withdrew, leaving Charlie and Helen alone with the deceased. It was time now to reveal the victim and begin the process of trying to identify him – a task that didn't require an audience.

Gripping a pair of sterile scissors, Helen snipped through the wet sheets that bound the legs and torso. She was unlikely to be able to ID him from the sight of his feet, but she wanted to release his arms and legs from their constraints. This would allow her a better line of attack on the duct tape that bound him from the chest up. She knew she could ill afford to inflict any post-mortem injuries on him by hacking blindly at the tape, so though every instinct urged her to remove the tape from his eyes, nose and mouth, she resisted for now.

Patiently, Helen cut through the stiff sheets, releasing

his body from its purgatory. The sheets fell away, revealing the ribbon that secured his ankles to the chair legs. Helen untied this, bagging it along with the sheets, but the body didn't respond at all. Rigor mortis was setting in – their victim looked like a man frozen in time.

Pressing on with her unpleasant task, Helen stripped off the upper sheets, passing them to a rather pale-looking Charlie. Now she slipped one scissor blade underneath the tape on his chest, sliding it over the soft leather of his suit without marking the surface. She slowed her progress as she cut upwards towards his neck – every mark, every bruise on his body, might provide them with vital clues and Helen was determined not to stymie their investigation through human error.

The tape covering his throat came away easily – only his head remained covered now. Downing the scissors, Helen decided to finish the last, most delicate stage by hand. Teasing her fingers along the top of his head, she soon found what she was looking for. The end of the tape had been stuck down firmly, but with a bit of coaxing, it came free.

This was the moment of truth then. Grasping the loose end, Helen began to unwind the tape. Slowly at first, then faster and with more confidence, until finally it fell away altogether.

The sight that greeted her took her breath away. Not because she was disgusted by the victim's waxy, lifeless face, but because she *recognized* him. This poor wretch was her friend. Her dominator.

It was Jake.

10

Helen stumbled up the stairs, her hand clamped over her mouth. She could feel the vomit rising in her throat and she needed to be *away* from this underground hell. The green exit light could be glimpsed up ahead and she took the final steps at speed, barrelling through the exit and out into the night.

Ignoring the startled looks of the uniformed officers on guard, Helen hurried over to the chain link fence that bordered the club and clung on to it. Her breath was short, her heart was racing and the waves of nausea just kept coming. She gulped in huge lungfuls of air, desperate to avoid drawing attention to herself, but to no avail. She vomited now, hard and loud, her stomach cramping over and over again until there was nothing left inside.

Nobody made a move to help her, so Helen remained staring at the ground, empty and drained. It *couldn't* be Jake. A small part of her was tempted to return to the crime scene, to prove to herself that she'd made a stupid mistake. But in her heart she knew it *was* him. His face was distinctive and familiar and, besides, the tattoo on his neck sealed it. The man whose company she'd paid for on numerous occasions over the years, who'd beaten her dark introspection from her many times during their S&M sessions, was dead. Jake was the only person who knew the real Helen, and his sudden death left her feeling disoriented and confused.

The last time she'd seen him he was happy and settled. He was dating a new boyfriend, had relinquished his crush on Helen and seemed to be making a decent fist of his life. What had gone so terribly wrong that he had ended up here, in an after-hours club, falling into the clutches of a brutal and pitiless killer? Helen would have given anything to be able to turn back time, to step into that small room as Jake was being attacked and drag his assailant away.

'Are you ok?'

Helen looked up to find Charlie standing nearby, framed by the darkness. No one else would have spoken to her so informally or with such affection and it knocked the stuffing out of her now. Normally she would have blustered a response and sent them away, but she and Charlie had been through too much together for her to be dismissed like that. A large part of Helen wanted to blurt out that she knew the victim, that he was a friend. But as she opened her mouth to speak, her tongue refused to obey.

'What is it, Helen? What's wrong?' Charlie persisted.

Still Helen said nothing. To admit that she knew the victim would mean confessing how they met. Instantly she recoiled from this – she didn't want to offer Jake up to them like this – and, besides, how could she look any of her colleagues in the eye once the details of her private life were laid bare? She'd be a laughing stock, the butt of endless ribald jokes, but more than that they would *know*. Her sessions with Jake had always been private, discreet and special – a space where she could reveal her historic wounds and confront her feelings of guilt. If she opened herself up like that she'd be exposed, humiliated and in all likelihood taken off the case – and that was something that Helen was not prepared to countenance.

'I'm fine. It was just a shock,' Helen replied, straightening up.

'Not a pretty sight, was he? If you want me to handle this –'

'It's ok. I'm good now,' Helen said quickly. 'Let's get it over with, shall we?'

Her jaunty tone sounded forced, but Charlie didn't comment. So swallowing down another wave of nausea and putting her best foot forward, Helen walked back towards the club's gaping entrance to perform her grim duty.

11

He slipped into bed and turned his eyes to the wall. He could tell Sally wasn't asleep – though she was pretending to be – and he wondered what she was thinking. Could she hear his heart beating sixteen to the dozen? Could she sense his excitement?

He had taken his time returning home, hoping that he would be in a calmer state of mind on his arrival. But the adrenaline coursed through him still, and even though he had taken a long shower, he felt sure the stain of the night remained on him.

He sometimes had the sense that Sally wanted to say something, as they lay together. That his increasing absence from her life had been noted, that her patience was reaching breaking point. If he was honest, he wanted her to ask. Not just so that he could apologize and make amends for the cruel way he'd treated her. But also because he wanted to explain – to make sense of his wanton, self-destructive actions. He was playing with fire, risking everything and everyone he held dear, and he wanted to share this burden with her.

Should he seize the initiative? Tell her himself? As soon as the thought entered his head, he dismissed it. Where would he begin? What would he say? Sally was no doormat, she was an intelligent and spirited woman – why couldn't *she* tackle him on it, demanding an explanation for his actions?

She wouldn't, of course. Theirs was a marriage sustained by silence now. So nothing would change, while with each passing night *everything* changed. He was slowly becoming a different person – someone new and unfamiliar. It thrilled and scared him in equal measure, such was the strength of his obsession. And this was why he wanted someone to talk to him, challenge him. Because he knew instinctively that, left to his own devices, he would never, ever stop.

12

It was only 7 a.m. but Emilia Garanita had been working for several hours. Journalists are often up at odd times, but crime reporters have it particularly bad – murderers, rapists and kidnappers having no respect for those who have to chronicle their deeds. Emilia was used to it and, if she was honest, rather enjoyed her lifestyle. She loved her bed as much as the next girl, but the buzz of her mobile phone in the middle of the night always presaged something exciting, something new.

She had been called at 4 a.m. by PC Alan Stark, a tame officer who was happy to accept cash payments for information. There had been a murder during the night – an unusual one – which is why Emilia was now ensconced with him in a transport café near the Torture Rooms, huddled over a bacon sandwich.

'Did you see the body?' Emilia asked, cutting to the chase.

'No, but I spoke to a mate in SOC and they gave me chapter and verse. This place is something else.'

'Meaning?'

'It's a fetish club and tonight was their "Annual Ball". So they were all out in force – poofs, dykes, gimps, devils, angels –'

'Did you recognize anyone?'

'I'm sure they were all there,' he laughed grimly. 'City councillors, BBC folk, vicars, but you can bet your bottom dollar they scarpered before CID turned up. Those that did hang about were wearing masks, helmets and such, so –'

'Did you pick up anyone with a criminal record?'

'We're still processing them.'

'And who owns it – the club, I mean?'

'Pass. But the manager – if that's what you can call him – is talking to CID now. Sean Blakeman.'

Emilia wrote the name down.

'Tell me about the victim.'

'White guy in his early forties. Tied to a chair, before having his head taped up from chin to crown. I'm guessing the poor bastard suffocated.'

He continued to describe the scene, giving what details he could about the victim and the clientele of the club. Emilia was only half listening, writing his testimony down in her crisp, efficient shorthand, her mind already spooling forward to the story she would write. Sex, murder, torture, titillation – this case was kinky with a capital 'K' and would go down a storm with her editor. It had everything going for it and the icing on the cake was Stark's confirmation that the case would be handled by Emilia's erstwhile friend, now nemesis.

DI Helen Grace.

13

Helen walked briskly along the corridor, her heart sinking lower with each step. She'd been up all night, heading straight from the crime scene back to the incident room. She'd secretly hoped that the team might have made some quick progress, but in reality she knew it was too early for that – the peculiarities of this crime meant that they would have to be patient. Eyewitness reports were thin on the ground, and with no surveillance systems in the club they would have to garner amateur shots from mobile phones and piece together some kind of timeline. This might yield something and, of course, Meredith was still working her team hard on the forensics. Meanwhile, there was one very valuable piece of evidence that was as yet untapped – Jake's body.

Helen reached the mortuary doors and buzzed herself in quickly. If she hesitated, she would lose her nerve and turn back. Jim Grieves, the pathologist, turned as Helen now approached. He didn't offer much of a greeting and Helen was glad of it. She hadn't the mental capacity or emotional strength for small talk. She just wanted to get this over with.

'He's a Caucasian male, late thirties to early forties, with a keen interest in body art, piercing and masochism. Lots of old injuries associated with the use of restraints, including a fractured wrist sustained a few years ago and a dislocated ankle that has never fully healed. Some evidence of STDs and I also found historic semen residue – not his own – on parts of his clothing.'

Helen nodded but said nothing – it was upsetting to hear her friend dissected in such a cold, clinical way.

'We've done preliminary bloods – alcohol, ketamine and a small amount of cocaine, but that's not what killed him. He died of asphyxia. You can tell by the petechial haemorrhages on his cheeks and eyelids and also the cyanosis, which is what gives his face that blue discoloration. There are no bruises or marks on his torso, so we can assume that the duct tape around his head was sufficiently tight to cut off oxygen to his airways and that his killer had no need to apply any pressure to his throat or neck. The bleeding and bruising to his lips suggest that he was trying to bite his way through the tape when he lost consciousness.'

Helen shut her eyes, overwhelmed by the horror of Jake's predicament.

'He suffered severe dehydration thanks to a massive rise in his body temperature, which eventually led to a cardiac arrest, but he wouldn't have known much about it. His brain was starved of oxygen – it was this that did for him rather than anything that came after.'

'How long?'

Helen's voice sounded brittle and tight.

'Four to five minutes to lose consciousness, a little longer to die.'

'Would he have known what was happening?'

'Until he blacked out. Perhaps that was the point. There was no attempt to torture or harm him physically, even though he was at his killer's mercy. Which might suggest your attacker wanted his victim to be cognisant of what was happening, to *feel* his helplessness as his oxygen failed.'

Helen nodded, but said nothing in response. She was riven with emotion – anger, despair, sickness – as Grieves laid bare the brutal details of Jake's death. *Did* his assailant stick around to watch him die? Was being there at the point of death important to him? Beneath her fierce outrage, Helen now felt something else stirring – fear. Fear that the darkness was descending once more.

'Anything else? We're light on hard evidence at the moment,' Helen went on.

'Given the environment his body was found in, his clothing is surprisingly clean. I did find some fresh saliva on his cheek and right ear, however. I doubt it's his own, given the position of it.'

'Can we fast-track the analysis?' Helen said quickly. 'We need something concrete we can work with –'

'I'll do what I can, but I've got three other cadavers to process and everyone wants things yesterday, don't they?' Grieves grumbled.

'Thank you, Jim. Quick as you can, please.'

Helen squeezed his arm and turned on her heel. Grieves opened his mouth to protest, but he was too slow. Helen was already gone.

14

Helen walked back to her Kawasaki, lost in thought. Barring one occasion, she had only ever encountered Jake in his professional guise. They had met at his flat, where the lighting was dim and conversation kept to a minimum. Over time they had got to know each other better, but they were still playing roles during their sessions and Helen now realized how little she knew her friend. She had certainly never seen him as she had this morning – naked and unadorned, under the powerful glare of the mortuary lights.

She'd remembered that he had an eagle's head tattooed on his neck, but had never asked him what it signified. She knew he didn't speak to his parents, but had never asked who they were or where Jake was brought up. She knew he had an eye for the boys as well as the girls, but didn't know which came first or whether he was looking for the same things as everyone else – commitment, security, a family. She wished now that she had asked more questions of someone she considered a true friend.

He had in the past thought of her as more than that. During the Ben Foster case, Jake had taken to following Helen, such was the level of his romantic obsession with her. She had put a stop to that, cutting off their relationship for a while, and to her surprise it had worked. When they had last met, by chance in a city centre bar, he'd been seriously dating a guy he'd recently met. He seemed happy and together, so much so that when he texted Helen a few months later, asking if she wanted to resume their sessions, she'd been sorely tempted. In the end, caution had won out, however, and she'd made alternative arrangements, keen to avoid messy emotional entanglements. But she still often thought of him.

Could the boyfriend be involved? It would be interesting to find out the status of their relationship and whether he frequented the Torture Rooms too. Had their romance been one long seduction, building up to this savage murder? It was tempting to head round to Jake's flat now, tear it apart in the hunt for concrete leads, but to do so without an official ID of the victim would be foolish in the extreme. It was agonizing to have to wait – it felt like she was deliberately letting his killer off the hook – but she knew Jake had been picked up for drugs offences previously and that, once his tissue samples had been processed, his identity would be swiftly established.

Then the investigation would begin in earnest. The thought cheered and chilled Helen in equal measure. She knew her team would leave no stone unturned in their hunt for Jake's killer, but what might their interrogation of Jake's life mean for her? Had he kept records of their meetings? Any tokens of her? Had she left her mark on him? It was over two years since she'd used his services, but it was very possible that gaining justice for Jake would result in her exposure.

Part of her wanted to run from this, but her better part knew she had to run *towards* it. Whatever the possible consequences for her, she had to find his killer. She owed that – and a whole lot more – to her old friend. So climbing on to her bike, she fired up the engine and kicked away the brake. Her heart was thumping, she felt sick to her stomach, but there was no point delaying the inevitable, so, pulling back the throttle, she sped away from the mortuary in the direction of Southampton Central.

15

Detective Superintendent Jonathan Gardam stood by his office window, looking out at the world. It was not the finest view Southampton had to offer, but it afforded him a discreet vantage point on the station's car park below.

Helen Grace had just arrived and was now dismounting her bike. She was a creature of habit, always choosing the same spot, always removing her helmet and leathers in the same precise order. Whether this was driven by logic or superstition, Gardam couldn't tell. He knew that her passion for motorbikes was a legacy of her childhood – in one unguarded moment she had confessed to stealing mopeds as a teenager – but beyond that he knew little. The inner workings of her mind were as much a mystery to him as they always had been.

So he watched her from afar. He had a pretty good idea of her routine now – when she went to the gym, when she went running – and he timed his arrival at the station to coincide with hers. He would be stationed at his window by the time she walked away from her bike, running her fingers through her long hair to breathe new life into it after its temporary constraint. She was always so focused on the business in hand that she never looked up, never clocked his face at the window. He often wondered how she would react if she did. Would she be alarmed to see him there or would she offer him a smile and carry on? He had pictured the situation many times and in his head it was always the latter.

She was later than usual today, following an early-morning trip to the mortuary. Gardam had had to delay his first meeting by half an hour, so he could be in place to receive her. It had put his PA in a mood, but it had been worth it – Helen looked particularly beguiling this morning. She was unfailingly attractive – he had always been captivated by her Amazonian figure, pale skin and fuck-you attitude – but as he'd got to know her better, he had seen a deeper beauty. There was a vulnerability there that was hidden from all except those closest to her. This fragile quality was very much in evidence today. Pale, distracted, deep in thought, his best DI looked utterly haunted.

Gardam pressed his fingers to the glass. As so often these days, he wanted to reach out and comfort her. But she remained beyond his reach. He hoped in time to change that, but for now all he could do was watch.

16

This was better than she could possibly have imagined. She had heard the stories about the Torture Rooms before of course, but had never had the inclination – or the bottle perhaps – to investigate further. Seeing the club now for the first time, she felt a surge of excitement – you couldn't have dreamt up a better backdrop for a gruesome murder. The moral majority out there would hoover this up, scared and titillated in equal measure.

Emilia pulled out her Nikon and got to work, snapping the exotic instruments of torture and restraint. Her time here was limited and she knew she had to work fast. Gaining access had been harder than usual – the manager and most of the bartenders had gone to ground – so she'd had to track down the security company who usually provided the muscle on the doors. The first two guys she'd contacted had told her to sling her hook, but the third one was twice divorced, with a drinker's thirst, and needed the money.

'You can have twenty minutes, but that's it. I need this job and I'm not going to get fired on your account.'

Emilia had agreed, knowing that once she was in there, she could push it to half an hour. Once people have your money in their pocket, they become a bit less grand.

Having photographed the dance floor area, she headed swiftly down the corridor to the crime scene. But it was taped up and the door firmly secured. So, feigning a weak bladder, Emilia scurried back down the corridor, making her way to the small box room at the back that served as the club's office.

The room was nearly bare – a decrepit desk, a small filing cabinet and naked light bulb. Emilia got to work, but the drawers were empty, the files uninteresting, and there was little here to detain her. Emilia cursed – this visit wasn't proving quite as fruitful as she'd hoped.

As she turned to leave, her attention was caught by the photos that decorated the walls of the poky office. They were of past events – balls, fashion shows, photo shoots – that had been held in the club. They were full of exotically dressed revellers and deserved her careful attention.

'Gary, can you come in here a second?' Emilia shouted.

Moments later, he entered the office, looking flustered and annoyed.

'What you doing in here? I said front of house and the back corridor only.'

'I got lost,' Emilia said, smiling sweetly, 'but now that I'm here, could you take a look at these?'

She gestured towards the photos on the wall. But her partner in crime was already backing off.

'We're already over time as it is.'

'You saw the victim, right?'

'Not exactly.'

'Either you did or you didn't.'

'His face was taped up, but I knew the fella from the

way he was dressed. Can't tell you his name – we always used to call him "Twinkletoes" because of the gold boots he wore –'

'Look at these photos then and tell me if you see him.'

'No way. We need to be going –'

'You've had good money out of me, now you have to earn it. I know Sean Blakeman's mobile number,' she continued, lying, 'it would only take a minute for me to put you back on benefits.'

Grumbling, Gary pulled some reading glasses from his top pocket. Emilia suppressed a smile as he perched the owlish glasses on the fleshy folds of his red face. He really did make a comical sight.

'There. That's the fella.'

His finger was now pointing towards a figure on a podium who was dressed in gold lamé shorts and posing for the photographer. Emilia shot a look at the photo frame – 'Annual Ball 2013' – and moved in for a closer look. The man in the photo was half naked, muscular and seemingly having a very enjoyable time.

'But I've no idea who he is and you won't get anything more out of me today,' the burly bouncer added.

'No need,' Emilia said, straightening up. 'I know exactly who he is.'

Her guide was stupefied for a moment, before replying:

'Who? Who is he?'

Emilia was already walking to the door, but turned now. Smiling coyly, she answered:

'Read the paper tomorrow and you'll find out.'

17

'The victim's name is Jake Elder.'

Helen's voice held firm. It was the first time the full team had gathered together and she was determined not to reveal her distress to them, despite the emotions that churned inside her. She *had* to be strong.

'Forty-one years of age, he's been living in Southampton for the last fifteen years. His DNA matched samples taken following an arrest for possession of a Class B drug three years ago. He's got a couple of other charges on his file – nothing major, but we should chase them down anyway. See if he owed anyone any money, whether he was consorting with known dealers. DC Lucas, can you coordinate that?'

'Of course.'

'His family have been informed and are on their way over from Taunton now. I'll field them, but in the meantime I want us to climb inside our victim's life. Did he have a boyfriend or girlfriend? Was he invited to last night's ball by anyone? The victim had fresh saliva on his cheek – was it left there by a companion or by someone more casual? Also, it appears from his online activity that Elder was a professional dominator. Who did he meet? Who were his regular clients? Let's interrogate his phone records, email, bank accounts, credit card statements . . .'

The team were busy scribbling down Helen's instructions, so she paused now to gather herself. It was strange and unsettling to be talking about Jake as if he were a total stranger, to be deliberately withholding vital information from the team. Helen took a deep breath, before continuing:

'Jake Elder lived his life online and via his phone – he is not your usual office worker. So check his web history, the chat rooms he used, his text messages, Snapchats, his Twitter followers . . .'

'Do we think he was specifically targeted?' DS Sanderson piped up.

'Impossible to say, which is why we have to dig,' Helen resumed evenly. 'His killer may have a personal motive or Elder might just have been in the wrong place at the wrong time. There are numerous DNA traces at the scene of the crime – cigarette butts, items of clothing, discarded fetish gear. We'll need to run them all down, but I'd like us also to pay particular attention to the equipment our killer employed. You can't buy wet sheets and panic shears in your local Tesco's – they are specialist equipment with only one purpose. So let's contact local bondage retailers – I'd like a list of all outlets situated within a twenty-mile radius of Southampton. Many of these operations are online only, meaning you *have* to pay with a credit card. So let's interrogate their transactions, find out who's been buying this stuff. Edwards, are you good for this?'

'It's my natural home,' the handsome young officer replied, earning a few wry smiles from the rest of the team.

'Let's also make ourselves visible in the immediate environs of the club,' Helen carried on, ignoring Edwards's joke. 'People heading to the Torture Rooms presumably cab it, rather than taking the bus. Find out if the local cabbies saw anything. Our victim was probably killed sometime between midnight and one a.m. – we should follow up on anyone seen leaving the club around this time, particularly if they appeared distressed or agitated.'

'Perhaps they stayed to party?' Lucas interjected.

'Possibly, but we've got a lot of lines to run and my instinct is that they would probably try to leave the scene before the body was discovered. But you're right, we should rule nothing out.'

Helen paused, picking up a file from the desk. She was finally getting into her stride, but the most difficult part was yet to come.

'Alongside this, I want us to look at mummification.'

A ripple of nervous laughter spread through the team.

'Also known as total-enclosure fetishism. It's at the extreme end of the S&M spectrum and involves somebody getting a sexual kick from being completely reliant on another for their liberty, their movement, even their life.'

Visions of Jake – bound and taped – punched through Helen's mind. Flicking through her file to buy herself a moment, Helen swallowed and pressed on:

'There are many different ways to do it – straitjackets, wet sheets, bandages, rubber strips – but one thing that's crucial to every method is *trust*. You have to trust the person doing it to you or you wouldn't even start –'

'So he *knew* his attacker?' Charlie suggested.

'It's very possible. There are S&M groups who meet regularly to discuss, socialize and occasionally play. Their meets are called "Munches". I want us to investigate them, see what we can dig up about the scene. Have there been similar incidents that we haven't heard about? Is there anyone out there who is known for taking things too far? I don't think a head-on attack is going to work, so I'll be looking for a volunteer for undercover work.'

More nervous laughter, but as Lucas jokily tried to raise Edwards's arm against his will, Sanderson stepped forward:

'I'd like to take this, unless anyone objects?' she said firmly, scanning the team for dissenters.

'Thank you,' Helen replied quickly. 'Run down a list of forthcoming meets and then let's discuss which ones to target.'

'I'll have it for you within the hour.'

'Good.'

Helen paused, her ordeal nearly over, then said:

'I don't need to tell you how much coverage this murder is likely to get. So no talking out of school, no short cuts and any leads come *straight* to me. We do not rest until we have found Jake Elder's killer, understood?'

The look on the faces of the team showed that they had got the message and they now hurried off to do her bidding. Helen was aware that her tone had been a little harsh, but she was not prepared to soft-soap anyone while they still lacked any tangible leads. The investigation was starting to take shape now – the victim identified, multiple strands of enquiry set in motion – but there was one key element of this killing that remained as impenetrable and mysterious as ever.

The motive.

18

He was rooted to the spot. He knew it was coming, but even so it was a shock. The newscaster was only relaying information that had been buzzing around internet chat rooms for hours, but hearing it relayed in her professional monotone was still disquieting.

Nobody else in the office seemed to be paying attention to the radio bulletin, but he drank in every word: 'A popular S&M club . . . appealing for witnesses . . . the victim has not yet been formally identified.' He knew the victim's name of course, but did the police too? Was their 'failure' to identify him just a smokescreen as they pursued their enquiries or were they genuinely in the dark? He suddenly realized how much he needed to know.

He had been careful to conceal their connection, but who knew what they were able to access these days? Terrorism had a lot to answer for, providing the police with the perfect excuse to snoop on everything and everyone. He had never used the computer at home and had never contacted Jake via direct text, but even so he suddenly had the unnerving feeling that he hadn't been careful enough.

The newscaster had moved on to local traffic and travel, but still he didn't move. Things seemed to be moving fast now and he was suddenly aware of how much he had to lose. Would they suspect him? Or would his middle-class exterior and respectable job shield him from suspicion? He was too far into this, too stained by his actions, for this to unravel. There were two sides to him – but they were known only to him – and that was the way it *had* to stay.

He was so deep in thought that at first he didn't notice his PA marching across the room towards him. He might have remained there for hours were it not for her sudden intrusion.

'Your ten o'clock is here,' she said testily.

He didn't respond, didn't trust himself to. Instead, he gathered up his files, nodded at her and walked purposefully away towards the meeting room.

19

The silence in the room was suffocating. Helen had given Moira and Mike Elder the basic facts of their son's death, avoiding the more distressing details. She'd shouldered this unpleasant duty many times before and knew that if you hit people with too much too soon, you lose them. Assaulted by the shock, bowing under their grief, the bereaved just implode. It wasn't fair to treat them like that and, besides, it served nobody's purpose – she needed facts, not tears.

But, to Helen's surprise, Jake's parents had barely reacted at all to her carefully chosen words. Moira had shot a brief look at her husband, then joined him in staring at the floor. Their gaze remained doggedly turned in that direction and, though Helen provided a few gentle prompts, the couple stayed resolutely silent.

'We have a full team working on this. As I said, your son was discovered at a nightclub in Banister Park and, once you've formally identified him, we can make arrangements for you to visit it, if you feel that would be helpful. Relatives sometimes find that it's important to see the place where –'

'What sort of club was it?'

Mike Elder's voice was cracked and harsh. For a moment Helen wondered if it was a trick question – the news was already out there in radio bulletins and on the internet – then pushed that thought aside. They had probably driven all the way from Taunton in silence, their minds trying to grapple with their unexpected tragedy. It was no surprise that they were still processing the details.

'It was an S&M club,' Helen replied gently. There was no point dressing it up – they'd find out soon enough anyway.

Mike sniffed loudly, while his wife fiddled with the buttons on her cardigan.

'It wasn't a club he visited regularly, just somewhere he used now and then.'

'I bet he did.'

Now it was Helen's turn to be silent. Four words – four simple words – but they were said with such bitterness that for a moment Helen was speechless. She had encountered many emotions in the relatives' room – despair, denial, fury – but she had seldom seen such distaste. She felt anger flare in her but, aware that the eyes of the Family Liaison Officer were on her, swallowed it down.

'Can I ask you what you mean by that, Mike?' she said.

'I'm sure by now you know what my son was' was the curt reply.

'Obviously we're aware that Jake worked as a professional dominator. That's one of our main lines of enquiry, to see if he might have been attacked by someone he knew through his work.'

'His work,' Mike repeated, shaking his head ruefully, before casting a sardonic smile at his wife.

'Can you tell me how much you knew about Jake's professional life?' Helen continued.

'Too bloody much, but nothing that would help you.'

Helen was beginning to see why Jake had never got on with his parents, but resumed her questioning as patiently as she could.

'His life in Southampton, then? Did you ever visit his flat? Meet up with him?'

'This is our first visit to Southampton.'

Finally, Moira had spoken.

'He moved away from Somerset when he was a young man. He threatened to come back and visit us, but . . . but he never made it.'

Was the use of the word 'threatened' deliberate? Helen was so bewildered by this interview that she couldn't tell.

'And you weren't tempted to visit him here?'

'It's a long way to come and we can't leave the animals,' Moira replied quickly, trotting out her excuse with practised ease.

'I see.'

'Do you?' Mike Elder now said, suddenly turning to look directly at Helen. 'I can tell from your tone what you're thinking, but you've got no right to look down your nose at us.'

Helen stared back, refusing to break eye contact. He was right, however – Helen *was* allowing her feelings to affect her judgement and was behaving in a manner that was unprofessional and unkind.

'I've nothing but sympathy for you and your wife, believe me,' she said quickly.

'That may be, but it doesn't change things. You might feel our son's "lifestyle" was acceptable, but we didn't. I don't blame the boy entirely – we should have been tougher on him when he was small,' he resumed, his wife flinching slightly as that barb landed. 'But he made his choices and had to live by them. He was never interested in my opinion, but, for the avoidance of doubt, I'll give it to you anyway. I thought what he did . . . was perverted. For the life of me, I could never understand why he wanted to surround himself with degenerates and freaks – he could never explain it himself, just said it was "who he was". He thought we should accept him, but why should we accept something like that? He chose his path, we chose ours and, believe you me, they never met.'

It was said with something approaching pride and for a moment Helen thought she might actually slap him. She had never heard someone damn their own flesh and blood in such blunt terms.

'We haven't seen him in nearly ten years and we're not going to be much help now, so let's just get this over with, shall we? I don't want to be here any more than you do.'

He rose abruptly, clearly keen to get the formal identification of his son over and done with. Moira followed suit, hurrying after her departing husband.

As she left, she glanced briefly back at Helen. After her husband's harsh words, Helen had expected to see some embarrassment there, perhaps even contrition. But not a bit of it.

The look Moira now gave Helen was one of pure scorn.

20

Her fist slammed into the metal, rebounding off it violently. Without hesitating, she raised her arm again, ploughing her clenched fist into the unyielding surface. This time her impact was true and the metal buckled under the assault. Wincing, Helen withdrew her hand and stepped back to survey the damage. To her shame, she saw that she had left a large dent on the unfortunate locker door – a complement to the bloody knuckles on her right hand.

She turned away, furious with herself, but angrier still with Jake's parents. They seemed so dismissive, so fixed in their view of him, yet if they had known their son *at all*, they would have known that he was kind, generous and loving. They refused to see that, remaining blinkered to the bitter end. What must it be like to live your life that way, Helen wondered, to sacrifice so much on the altar of your principles? Would it bring them happiness in the end? She suspected not.

Helen hadn't trusted herself to return to the incident room straight away, so had been pacing the ladies' locker room ever since, trying to quell her growing anger. Helen knew that indignation and fury were sometimes positives, driving you to work harder and faster, but this wasn't like that. For the first time in years, Helen felt out of control. She hadn't slept at all, which didn't help, but still she was surprised at how upset and disoriented she was by the morning's events. She knew that, for Jake's sake, she had to find a way to contain her emotions. She couldn't run a major investigation in this state.

A sharp knocking sound made her look up. Seconds later, the door swung open and Charlie entered, clutching a thin file.

'Sorry to disturb you. I looked for you in the interview suite and Gardam's office but –'

'No problem,' Helen said quickly, slipping her grazed hand into her pocket. 'What have you got?'

Charlie pulled a sheet of paper from the file, but hesitated now before replying. The look on her face suggested she knew Helen was upset and was perhaps debating whether to say anything. In the end caution won out and, dropping her eyes to the paper, she said:

'We've made a bit of progress with Elder's communications. He sometimes used texts and emails to set up his appointments, but his favoured method of communicating with his clients was Snapchat.'

'Right.'

'Now, most people assume that when Snapchats disappear, they disappear for good, but actually the phone companies store them. We pulled Elder's this morning, along with his recent texts and emails, so we've now got pretty much every communication he sent or received in the last three months.'

'And?' Helen said, hurrying Charlie to the point.

'Well, we cross-referenced them with mobile phones

that were transmitting in or near the Torture Rooms on the night Jake was killed and we've got a list of about twenty numbers.'

Helen took this in – their first small lead in a difficult case. As she did so, she saw Charlie's eyes flit to the dented locker, before quickly returning to Helen once more. If there was a question implied there, Charlie hid it well.

'Any links to anyone with a criminal record?'

'Not yet, but we're still processing them.'

'Chase them all down,' Helen replied impatiently. 'Anything else?'

'One regular texter who *wasn't* in the vicinity was David Simons. He appears to have been in a serious relationship with Elder until fairly recently.'

Helen said nothing, her mind flitting back to the man she'd glimpsed in a city centre bar all those months ago.

'How recently?'

'Split up a couple of months back.'

'Why?'

'Lack of commitment from Jake, clinginess from David – judging by their lengthy emails on the subject.'

'Where is Simons now?'

'Los Angeles. He divides his time between the US and the UK. He's been there the last four weeks. I've been trying to get hold of him, but . . .'

'Get him over.'

'Of course,' Charlie replied, bristling slightly at Helen's tone. 'But I think we have to mark him off the list as a suspect, don't you?'

There was something challenging in Charlie's tone, but Helen decided not to rise to it. Instead, thanking her, she sent her on her way. Helen knew that she was being overly assertive, but the news that Jake's boyfriend was long gone had sent her mood plummeting still further. Jake had seemed so happy when they last met, but Helen was suddenly struck by how lonely his life must have been.

No lover or friend had come forward to claim him, his parents wouldn't have spat on him if he was on fire and even Helen had feigned ignorance of his identity to protect herself and her career. He had been abandoned in death by all those who should have cared for him and that was something those that remained would have to live with for the rest of their lives.

21

'The victim lived and worked in Portswood. We're still pinning down the precise details, but it appears that he earnt his living in the sex trade, working out of his flat as a professional dominator. Today we are asking anyone who's encountered Jake Elder – in whatever capacity – to get in touch and help us with our enquiries.'

Emilia jotted down the details, chuckling at Gardam's careful euphemism. Everyone present knew what he meant – he was appealing to the spankers to put aside their embarrassment and come forward.

'Good luck with that,' Emilia whispered to her neighbour, who raised a jaded eyebrow in response. Gardam was in cloud cuckoo land if he thought anyone in the BDSM community was going to willingly walk into a police station. A lot of them had criminal records, others had wives and families, and none of them would want to run the gauntlet of being judged by the small-minded sergeant on the front desk. Better let a killer walk free than endure that.

As Gardam continued, casually talking over his Media Liaison Officer's attempt to direct proceedings, Emilia's mind began to wonder. She already knew what her article would look like – she'd written it in her head on the way over – and there was little that Gardam could offer that she hadn't already been told. The real question – and the only reason she'd come to this briefing at all – was what role DI Grace would play in proceedings. She was not someone who embraced the fourth estate, preferring to leave that to her superiors, but still her absence from the press conference was intriguing.

Emilia was pretty sure she was the only person present who knew that Helen had used Jake's services. She had stumbled on their connection during the Ella Matthews investigation and had immediately tried to use it to her advantage, threatening the unfortunate DI with exposure unless she gave her exclusive access to the investigation. Not surprisingly, Grace had fought back, calling her bluff by revealing her knowledge of Emilia's illegal surveillance techniques. It had ended in a score draw, both relieved to have emerged unscathed, but it still stuck in Emilia's craw.

She had never been a good loser and perhaps it was payback time. Helen Grace had kept her on a short leash for a while, but the boot was on the other foot now. Had Grace confessed her knowledge of the victim to her team? Was that why she wasn't present? Or had she kept her secret close? Emilia intended to find out. Journalists always love an exclusive and this story – 'the copper and the bondage freak' – was going to be the best scoop she'd ever had.

22

Helen sped through the city streets, pleased to be away from the station. She found the incident room claustrophobic and unnerving – photos of a happy, carefree Jake staring down at her from the murder board – and there was little point being there just now. Charlie was chasing down Jake's clients, McAndrew was leading the house-to-house calls, and until something concrete turned up she was better used elsewhere.

As she slid past the stationary traffic, Helen felt her mood rise. Perhaps it was the fresh air, or the satisfaction that riding her bike always gave her, or maybe it was just that she was finally *doing* something. Her interview with Jake's parents had yielded nothing, so it was good to be on the road at last, taking the lead.

Jim Grieves was still poring over Jake's body, just as Sanderson, Charlie and the team were trying to climb inside his life. The items used to imprison and kill Jake, however, were only just being examined – Meredith and her team having recently returned from the crime scene – which is why Helen's first port of call was the Police Laboratory at Woolston.

Meredith ushered Helen into the viewing area. Lying on the table in front of them were the wet sheets, the loose reel of silver duct tape and the leather restraints – their killer's weapons of choice.

'Preliminary testing on the victim's clothing and the bondage items has shown up only one source of DNA – the victim's. We'll run them again, but I wouldn't bank on anything more on that front.'

Helen nodded, disappointed but not surprised.

'As for the rest of it, there's nothing particularly unusual about these items. The duct tape can be bought from any hardware store and though the wet sheets and restraints are specialist gear, they're the standard size, colour and design. They were probably bought off the shelf, rather than custom made.'

'Had they been used before? Was this gear the perpetrator already owned?'

'Probably not, given the lack of DNA traces. Plus, look at this.'

Meredith reached forward and picked up the leather straps, holding them up to the light. Intrigued, Helen leant in closer.

'The hole which the buckle prong penetrated to secure the victim has been punched through cleanly. You can see the light through it.'

'But the others haven't,' Helen replied, running a gloved finger over the sequence of closed holes. 'Which suggests that last night was the first time these straps had been used.'

'Your killer could have used them before perhaps, practised at home –'

'But he'd have to have known exactly which hole he'd

use. And unless he correctly guessed the diameter of the victim's ankle and the chair leg then –'

'Exactly, so let's assume they're brand new. That might narrow the field down a little?' Meredith offered hopefully.

Thanking her, Helen pulled her mobile from her pocket and headed on her way, speed-dialling Edwards back at base.

By the time she left the building, he'd already pinged her his list of local bondage outlets. And by the time she was on her bike, they'd divided up the list – split four ways between Edwards, Helen and a couple of broad-minded DCs.

It was time to take a walk on the wild side.

23

Sanderson sat perfectly still, as the brush caressed her cheek. As soon as Helen had asked her to lead the undercover work, her mind had been turning on how best to ingratiate herself into a scene that was utterly alien to her. She was a conventional, middle-of-the-road girl and now she wondered if she was a little bit 'vanilla' for the role. She was no prude, but humiliation, submission, restraint and punishment had never been part of her personal lexicon and she knew she would be on a steep learning curve. She had spent most of the day studying the scene, picking out the latest trends in the fetish world, while creating a new identity and personal history to carry into the operation.

She'd already coloured her hair and purchased the necessary bondage gear and now her good friend Hannah P. was applying the finishing touches to her face. Face painting and body art seemed to be a big part of the 'peacocking' that characterized a world fuelled by fantasy and role-playing. If she was honest with herself, it made her feel more relaxed, concealing her true identity beneath brightly coloured paint. If she could forget herself, she could more easily become her alter ego. And that was crucial for the task that lay ahead.

It was not just that she wanted to appear convincing

to elicit information from those attending the 'Munch' this evening. It was also a question of safety. Their perpetrator had already proven to be without mercy or scruple, proficient and artful in taking another's life. Sanderson was not easily scared, she could handle herself, but she knew she was out of her comfort zone here. This was the sharp end of the job.

Hannah had finished her work and now presented Sanderson with a mirror. Her older, more bohemian twin stared back at her. It was a good look and would serve her well tonight. Now was not a time for trepidation. If she could fashion a break in the case, it would play well with Helen. She'd always looked up to her superior, admiring her dedication, professionalism and bravery, and had felt well placed to be her deputy. Now, though, there was competition and if she was honest she feared that the personal connection between Helen and Charlie would hold her back. The only way to counter this was to prove to her boss that she was first among equals, the officer best suited to be her deputy. Which was why tonight was so important.

Thanking Hannah P. once more, Sanderson swept up her phone and keys, before sliding her baton carefully into her suit. She was ready and there was no point putting it off. It was now or never.

24

Paul Jackson was between meetings and resentful of Charlie's intrusion. He was a manager at the Shirley branch of Santander – a position of some responsibility – and was clearly embarrassed by her presence. His eyes kept flicking to the clock and his answers – when they came – were brief.

'So just to confirm, that phone number – 07768 057374 – belongs to you?'

'Yes.'

'And you had your phone with you last night?'

'I think so.'

'Can I ask where you were? Between the hours of ten p.m. and two a.m.?'

There was a moment's pause, before Jackson responded:

'I went for a drink after work. Watched the football. Then went home.'

'Oh, right, who was playing?'

Another slight hesitation, then:

'Saints versus Watford. Easy win.'

'And which pub was this?'

'The Saracen's Head, near the hospital.'

'Bit out of your way, isn't it?'

'There are pubs closer to the office, but the beer's better there, so . . .'

'And you went with colleagues?'

'No, I went by myself.'

'Right,' Charlie replied, making a note on her pad. 'And what time would you say you got home?'

'A little after midnight, I think.'

'That's pretty late for a school night, isn't it?' Charlie replied, smiling.

For the first time, Jackson seemed lost for words.

'Is it usual for you to be out that late?' she continued.

'Not really, but it's not one of those pubs where they kick you out after last orders.'

'Lock in, was it?'

'Something like that.'

'I didn't realize they did those on Tuesday nights.'

She smiled once more, but Jackson only gave her a tight grimace. He was nervous and uncomfortable and his answers were a little too stiff for Charlie's liking. There could be a perfectly innocent explanation – most people tensed up as soon as they saw a warrant card – but Charlie suspected that was not the case here. Fortunately there was one surefire way to find out.

'Your phone number has come up in our investigation into the death of Jake Elder. His body was found in the early hours of this morning at a nightclub in Banister Park. You probably heard the headlines on the radio.'

Jackson nodded, but said nothing.

'A series of messages were sent to Mr Elder from your phone. Snapchat messages organizing appointments with him –'

'I didn't send any messages.'

'So you don't know Mr Elder?'

Jackson shook his head.

'Have you ever visited the Torture Rooms?'

'No,' Jackson replied quickly. 'I'd never even heard of them until this morning.'

'And you've never used Mr Elder's services?'

'Of course not.'

'No contact with him whatsoever?'

'No.'

'Ok then, I know you're a busy man, so I'll get out of your hair . . .'

Charlie could see the relief on Jackson's face.

'But, before I do, I would be grateful if you'd consent to provide a DNA sample. Just so we can strike your name off our list.'

'Clearly my phone has been cloned or someone at your end has cocked up. As I've said, I didn't know the guy, I've never met him –'

'I know this seems intrusive, but as we've established that you were out last night and were in the vicinity of the club in question, we'll need to eliminate you from our enquiries and, believe me, this is the quickest way to do that.'

'I'm not sure. I'm already late for my next meet—'

'It is your right to refuse, but we could later compel you to provide one. So what do you say? I've got a swab here. It will only take a few hours to process and that will be that. All being well, I'll never darken your door again.'

Keeping up her breezy patter, Charlie pulled the swab

tube from her bag. Jackson stared at her, saying nothing. Before, he looked angry, now he just looked empty. He seemed determined to resist, to try and pretend this wasn't happening, but Charlie had done this many times before and knew that insistent good humour often overcomes the fiercest of objections. If you give them nothing to argue with, they have nowhere to run.

Which is why, despite his unmistakable hostility, Paul Jackson now opened his mouth. Slipping the swab in, Charlie extracted the necessary skin cells and sealed them in the clear plastic tube.

'That's me done. Thank you for your time,' she said, shaking Paul Jackson's hand and heading for the door.

Moments later, Charlie was out of the foyer and walking fast away from the building. As she went, she chanced a look back. Her suspicions had been raised by her interview and she wasn't surprised by what she now saw.

Paul Jackson staring right back at her through the window.

25

'I'm not a snooper, but when it's paraded under your nose, what can you do?'

DC McAndrew sighed inwardly, but smiled as she took the cup of tea being offered to her. She had been knocking on doors all afternoon, working her way up and down Jake Elder's street. Elder was not a man who got involved in community events and he was seldom seen by other homeowners during the day. So far she had amassed precious little information about Elder or his activities. Now she expected she was about to get rather too much.

She was seated in Maurice Finnan's front room. His wife had passed away some years back but the 'good room' was still spick and span, in keeping with the standards the dear departed Geraldine had laid down. Pristine sofas, startling white lace, a faux Persian rug – the whole room had the air of a museum piece. It was the sort of set-up that made the naturally clumsy McAndrew nervous. A tea spillage here might herald the apocalypse.

'They were coming and going all hours and they weren't social calls, if you get my drift,' he insinuated knowingly.

'I see. Anyone in particular catch your eye?'

'Not really,' he replied. 'They don't come dressed up, you know? They're just ordinary-looking people – probably lawyers, accountants and the like. I imagine that kind of thing always attracts people with a guilty conscience.'

He winked at McAndrew, clearly pleased to have a young female to perform to. McAndrew sensed that Maurice was probably lonely and reminded herself not to judge him too harshly.

'Ever see Mr Elder with any boyfriends? Girlfriends?'

'Confused, was he?' Maurice retorted. 'Not really. There was a fella a few months back – tall chap, with short, chestnut hair, barrel-chested – but he didn't last long. Funny thing is I seldom saw *him* – this Jake, I mean – just his visitors going in and out. Quiet as you like during the day, but as soon as darkness fell you'd see them traipsing up to his front door. Three, four, sometimes more in a night. Say what you like about him, he was a hard worker.'

McAndrew smiled and this time it was genuine – despite his curtain twitching, verbosity and fastidiousness, Maurice had a nice sense of humour.

'I never worked out exactly what he did for them, though if you're as old as me you can hazard a guess. It was all very discreet, but they always came and went on the hour, see? Doesn't take much imagination, does it?'

McAndrew was about to butt in, but Maurice beat her to the punch once more.

'Each to their own, that's always been my motto. But we've all got to live around here, haven't we? Kids, pensioners, mums and dads. And you don't know who a place like that will attract. Then there's the house prices. Soon as it becomes common knowledge that you've got a brothel next door – Sorry, love, am I boring you?'

McAndrew realized her gaze had drifted out of the window towards Jake's flat. Snapping out of it, she turned to Maurice once more.

'Not at all.'

'You're very sweet, but you're not a good liar and I know you're busy. Now I did jot down a few number plates in case the police should ever get around to doing anything about it, let me see if I can find them . . .'

He hurried over to the dresser. McAndrew thanked him, grateful that her time here hadn't been completely wasted. It was tough doing door-to-doors – 'hit-and-hopes' – when you knew the real police work was going on elsewhere.

'Right, let's start at the beginning – this was from March 2013,' Maurice said cheerfully, seating himself and opening his large notebook at the first page.

McAndrew sighed again. Perhaps Maurice had important information for the investigation. Perhaps he didn't. Either way, one thing was clear – she was going to be here for a long, long time.

26

'Don't tell me. Let me guess. I've got a talent for these things.'

Helen said nothing. She had just spent a dispiriting couple of hours trawling industrial estates and wasn't in the mood for games. Two of the businesses on her section of the list had gone into liquidation, another had refused to talk without a lawyer and two more were dead ends, with nothing in their recent transactions that fitted the bill.

'I look at you and I see . . . nipple clamps, bondage mitts and perhaps a cock cage for that special someone in your life,' the bearded man drawled.

'Well, feast your eyes on this,' Helen replied, flipping open her warrant card. 'Is there somewhere we can talk?'

'You'll get nothing out of me without a warrant.'

They were seated on cardboard boxes in the back office. In truth it was little more than a storeroom, but Steven Fincher clearly felt it was his turf and was determined to press home the advantage.

'If that's the way you want to play it, that's fine,' Helen replied. 'But your lack of cooperation suggests to me that you have something to hide.'

'Bullshit.'

'And any formal investigation of your affairs would necessarily be quite wide-ranging. I take it you're up to date with your tax returns, national insurance and so on . . .'

Fincher's eyes narrowed, but he kept his counsel.

'So perhaps it would be easier all round, if you just do as I ask. Do you have an up-to-date list of recent transactions?'

'Of course. This is a legitimate business.'

'I'm very glad to hear it. And I take it you sell these items: wet sheets, leather restraints, duct tape?'

'Of course.'

'Have you sold any of those items within the last three months? Either individually or as a package?'

Grumbling, Fincher opened a nearby box file and pulled a tea-stained ledger from it. Helen watched him closely as he ran his finger down the columns. Edwards hadn't had any joy in his search; neither had the other DCs – they were fast running out of options here.

'This *might* be it,' Fincher said cautiously.

'Go on.'

'Three wet sheets, blue, two tan leather restraints with gold buckles and a roll of silver duct tape.'

Helen nodded, concealing the excitement rising within her. She had been deliberately vague in her description of the items so far, but Fincher had just described the murder weapons in perfect detail.

'Were they bought in store?'

'No, delivery.'

'Do you know the name of the courier company who delivered them?'

'Course I bloody do. It was me.'

'So you saw him?' Helen said quickly. 'The person you delivered them to?'

'No. The house was derelict. But it was definitely the right address and the order form had instructions to post through the letter box if no one was at home. I never heard any more about it, so I assumed everything was ok . . .'

'How did he pay for them?' Helen asked further, her tone hard with disappointment.

'Credit card.'

'And do you still have those details?'

'Sure,' Fincher replied, rummaging around in another box file. 'I've got the card number, the cardholder's name and' – he pulled a transaction receipt from the box with a flourish – 'I've got his home address too.'

27

'Who is this? What do you want?'

Emilia suppressed a smile. It was still early in Los Angeles and David Simons sounded bleary and half awake. His cracked voice and faltering speech suggested that he'd probably been out half the night. That wasn't ideal – he might still be drunk or high and was more liable to get emotional – but the key thing was to get to him before the police did. They would have been trying to contact him, but they were spread thin over what was already shaping up to be a major investigation. Simons was a freelance cameraman, whose website had all the relevant contact details, and she'd had his mobile number on repeat dial since early afternoon. It had been going to voicemail for hours, but finally he had turned his phone on and she had struck gold.

'My name is Emilia Garanita. I'm a journalist.'

'Is this about the film? You need to talk to someone in the publici—'

'No, it's about Jake Elder. I was wondering if you'd heard the news?'

Silence on the end. Emilia could picture the groggy Simons sitting up in bed, trying to process what he'd just heard.

'What news?' Simons eventually said.

'I'm sorry to have to tell you this . . . but Jake was killed last night.'

'I don't understand. Is this a joke?'

'It's a lot to take in and you have my sincere condolences. I know you and he were very close.'

Another long silence. Simons's breathing was short and erratic.

'Killed how?'

'He was murdered. At a nightclub called the Torture Rooms in Southampton. Do you know it?'

The first teaser question to see if he was going to lie to her.

'Yes, I know it. But I still don't understand. Was he involved in some kind of fight?'

'No, nothing like that.'

'Was it an accident? Did something go wrong?'

Even with the line as echoing as this was, Emilia heard the wobble in David Simons's voice.

'It looks like he was murdered. And, like everybody else, we're just trying to work out why. Can I ask when you last saw him?'

'Jesus . . . I . . . this is hard to take in.'

'I know and I'm sorry to be the bearer of such dreadful news. But I thought you'd want to know straight away.'

'Why? Who are you?'

'I work for a newspaper here, but I also knew Jake. Given how close you were to him, I thought you'd want to be told.'

Another long silence.

'Now I'm sure you'll want to get back here, but that'll probably mean you missing out on some work, not to mention the cost of the flight from LA, so I was going to suggest that we pick up your expenses.'

'I'm not sure . . .'

'And all I'd want in return is ten minutes of your time now. What do you say?'

The deal was already done – she could sense he wanted to talk, wanted to find out more about what had happened to his ex. Emilia made all the right noises, adopting a consoling tone and offering her condolences, all the while revelling in the doublespeak of it all. She said she was sorry to be the bearer of bad news but the truth was very different.

There was something exhilarating about being the harbinger of death.

28

'I haven't seen your face before.'

The man, dressed from head to toe in black leather, gripped Sanderson's chin, turning her head this way now that to admire her painted face.

'I'm new to town.'

'And what do we call you, new-to-town?'

'Rose.'

'A rose with thorns, no doubt. Come this way, I'll introduce you to the others . . .'

The burly man led Sanderson down a long corridor. The light sockets hung down from the ceiling without bulbs and only a couple of weak wall lights rescued the pair of them from total darkness. Sanderson was pleased to feel the hard steel of her baton on her flank, as they walked further and further away from the light.

They soon reached another door. Her companion – who'd introduced himself as Dennis – knocked on it and moments later a hatch in the door slid open.

'Fresh meat,' Dennis said, a thin grin on his face. Moments later, the door swung open and they hurried inside. Sanderson wondered if her mobile phone would work in here, especially as they now seemed to be heading down to some kind of basement, but she didn't dare look at her phone. Dennis's eyes were glued to her.

The Munch convened minutes later. Fifteen committed sado-masochists, hunched round in a circle, enjoying the subversion and secrecy of their gathering. Normally they would have been discussing best erotic practice and comparing case notes, but today there was only one topic of conversation. Less than twenty-four hours had elapsed since Jake's death but it had sent shock waves through the community.

Dennis sat Sanderson next to him, acting as her friend and sponsor, despite having only 'known' her for a few minutes. She had contacted him via a website – 'The Brother*Hood*' – and after a few exploratory messages he'd sent her a curt email including an address and time. She'd turned up five minutes early – time enough to check that her backup team was in place – then rang the bell for admission. Dennis had stuck close to her the whole time and Sanderson wondered if he did this to all new members or whether there was something special about her.

'Bloke I know from Bevois Mount had a similar thing happen to him,' a guy who appeared to be dressed as a satyr was saying. 'Took a bloke home he hardly knew. The guy taped him up and robbed him blind.'

'There was a girl I knew – right vicious little bitch she was,' added his female neighbour, covered head to toe in PVC, apart from webbing at the crotch. 'Used to advertise for partners, but as soon as they turned up, her boyfriend and his mates set on them. Beat a couple of people half to death.'

'One person you don't want to mess with is my ex,'

said another, to general agreement. 'You get him on the wrong night, he'd kill you as soon as look at you. If he wasn't doing a two-stretch, I'd have said this was him.'

'This is different though, right?' Sanderson piped up, dismissing all these suggestions out of hand. 'I think it was a hate crime.'

'No,' Dennis countered quickly, 'if it was a hate crime they'd have been more explicit. They'd be all over social media now talking about poofs, freaks –'

'What then?' Sanderson countered.

'This is someone *within* the community, someone who's into Edge Play.'

The thought was clearly not a welcome one and an angry debate now ensued. Sanderson said very little, glad of the cover the argument gave her. She knew Edge Play was at the extreme end of the BDSM spectrum, pushing the supplicant almost to the brink of death by starving them of oxygen, but she knew little more than that and was not keen to be drawn into the discussion.

'Do you have anyone in mind?' Sanderson butted in. 'You seem to know a lot about it.'

The comment was directed at Dennis with just enough mischief in her tone to provoke a response.

'Well, *I* was at home,' Dennis replied, pretending to bridle at the insinuation. 'My mother had had a funny turn, so you can count me out.'

There followed a few minutes' discussion about the welfare of Dennis's mother. Sanderson hid her frustration as best she could, waiting for a chance to steer the conversation back to where she needed it to be.

'Well, I won't be taking any risks until I know what's going on,' she said, as the conversation once more hit a lull.

'Like the rough stuff, do you, honey?' chipped in the PVC enthusiast.

'Not as much as Dennis, here,' she said leadingly, raising another half-smile from her new friend. 'Come on, you know the scene. Help a girl out who's new to town. I don't want to run into trouble the first time I hit the scene proper.'

Dennis thought about it for a moment, then said:

'There was one person. Everyone likes to push things a bit, but this one was cruel. Proper messed up, in and out of therapy, drugs, pills, didn't know if it was Christmas or Tuesday half the time. I've only ever been scared once in my life . . . and that was it.'

'Who was it?' Sanderson replied, keeping her voice neutral. 'Don't tease us, Dennis.'

He looked straight at her, then at the assembled throng, then back to Sanderson again.

'I'd love to share, but I'd need to trust you a little better first. And trust has to be *earnt*, doesn't it, Rosie?' he said, as fourteen pairs of eyes turned towards Sanderson. 'So why don't you tell us your story?'

'I show you mine, if you show me yours?'

'Something like that. And why not start from the very beginning,' he continued, reclining in his seat. 'I want to know *all* about you.'

29

Helen stood on the doorstep, pulling her coat around her in an attempt to keep warm. The sun had dropped from the sky and the air temperature had dipped sharply. Helen could see her breath dance in front of her, as she pressed the doorbell for a third time.

The credit card used to purchase Jake's instruments of torture belonged to Lynn Picket, a single mum living in a council house in Totton. The first couple of rings had gone unanswered, but Helen could now hear someone coming to the door and braced herself for what was to come.

'Do I look like I use that kind of stuff?'

Helen was now in Lynn's living room, balancing on the edge of a sofa that had seen better days. It was clearly not the best time to have called round – Lynn had three children, all of whom appeared to be in varying stages of outrage, distress or meltdown – but Helen was not going to be put off by this or Lynn's blustering response. She knew bondage practitioners came in all shapes and sizes.

'Well, I don't,' sniffed Lynn. 'I don't have the time and I don't have the money.'

'Do you have a computer, Lynn?'

'No, I bloody don't.'

'Tablet?'

'I've got a Chrome book that the kids use. If you want to take a look at it, be my guest. But all they use it for is watching CBeebies. There's nothing like *this* on it,' she said, looking at the list of S&M purchases Helen had given her.

'What about a smartphone?'

'Course, who doesn't? Knock yourself out.'

She tossed Helen her phone. It was badly dented and the screen was cracked.

'So you're sure you didn't purchase these items?'

'I know what I have and haven't bought. Besides, I don't even know what half these things are. What's a wet sheet for God's sake? It sounds like something I'd use to wipe my little girl's bum . . .'

'Does anyone else have access to your credit card?' Helen interrupted. 'Boyfriends, family, friends . . .'

'No, I wouldn't let it out of my sight. And I certainly wouldn't trust a fella with it.'

'Do you shop online?'

'Yes, I do, but not on sites like that and if you don't believe me you can see my statements. I've got them going back three, four years, maybe more.'

She bustled out of the room to get them, leaving Helen alone. Helen flicked through her phone search history, but in truth she was going through the motions. She believed Lynn. Which meant that someone had cloned her credit card.

It was an alarming thought, suggesting a level of

criminal sophistication that Helen hadn't been expecting. Their killer was clearly no amateur – he was methodical, tech savvy and adept at covering his tracks. Which made Helen wonder what his game plan was exactly – and what this elusive killer might do next.

30

Charlie's eyes were glued to the house. Paul Jackson had left the bank just as the sun was setting and Charlie had followed him. To her surprise, this proved far more difficult than usual – Jackson was on a bike, so she was constantly in danger of losing him in the busy city centre traffic. But something told Charlie it would be worth the effort, so she'd stuck with it, following him all the way home. They hadn't had the results of his DNA sample back yet, but Jackson had lied to her – Charlie was sure of that – and he had clearly been rattled by her visit.

Charlie stifled a yawn and pulled the last Dorito from the bag. It was pushing midnight now – she had been here over four hours already – and so far she had little to show for her patience. Jackson had returned home, greeted his wife, then sat down to dinner in front of the TV. They had remained together until just after 10 p.m., when Jackson had taken himself off upstairs. No lights came on at the front of the house, so Charlie had decided to walk round the block. The houses round here had long gardens, and by clambering on to a bin in the adjacent street Charlie could see a light burning in a small room at the back of the house. Was it a study of some kind? Attic storage? What was he doing there?

Charlie lingered there for twenty minutes, but it was

cold tonight and as the pubs began to empty, she'd abandoned her position and returned to the comparative warmth of her Renault Twingo. Minutes later, she'd been rewarded with the sight of Paul Jackson returning to the front room once more, kissing his wife goodnight as she headed off to bed. Jackson stayed where he was, watching the TV, but occasionally casting a glance upstairs.

Would he venture out tonight? Charlie looked at the clock. Her partner, Steve, had not been pleased when she'd called to say she wouldn't be home. She usually relieved him for bath and bedtime with Jessica and, even though he knew her job was unpredictable, he still got grumpy when she didn't show up.

She suddenly felt foolish to be stuck out here on her own, when she could be home in bed with her family. Police work was increasingly encroaching on her home life, but it was hard for it to play out any other way. She wanted to make a decent arrest, create a bit of a splash, if only to rid herself of the feeling that she was on probation. The odd look from Sanderson and a stupid sexist comment from a junior officer had been enough to make her feel as if she still had something to prove, despite her promotion.

Which is why she wasn't going anywhere yet. Even though it was well past midnight, she would give it one more hour.

31

'I knew it was time for a change. I mean, no one needs that abuse, do they?'

Sanderson was deep into her tale about a violent and neglectful boyfriend. Despite the fact that she had actually been single for nearly eighteen months, she was doing rather well, sprinkling her tale with lots of choice details.

'So what did you do, flower?' Dennis replied, his eyes still glued to her.

'I cleaned him out and moved on. He'd saved up nearly ten grand for some souped-up Mazda and I took *every* penny of it.'

One of those present whistled, earning a smile from Sanderson.

'You should have seen the texts he sent. Vile, they were. I replied a few times, then when I hit the M25 I threw my phone out the window.'

'A new life,' the PVC enthusiast said.

'Exactly.'

'And how long have you been doing *this*?' Dennis gestured at the dungeon they now sat in.

'Most of my adult life.'

'Why?'

'What's the point of walking in a straight line? Life's more fun if you deviate.'

'So what are you – top or bottom?'

'Bottom. I like to be disciplined.'

'Then you've come to the right place.'

Dennis rose now and crossed to the wall, running his finger over the heavy chains attached to the wall.

'Why don't I give you a little test drive, then? See how you like the Southampton touch . . .'

There were low chuckles from the group, as they turned their attention from Dennis to Sanderson. Was this what they'd come to see? Maybe Dennis hadn't been joking about his 'fresh meat'.

'All in good time. I'd need to know *you* a little better first.'

'What you see is what you get,' Dennis said, opening his arms to her.

'Uh uh,' Sanderson said. 'You're still holding out on me, Dennis. You were about to give me a cautionary tale before.'

'That's one way of putting it,' the satyr chuckled.

'You had someone in mind when you were talking,' Sanderson said, ignoring the joke. 'Someone I should steer clear of.'

'Why are you so interested in her anyway?'

'Because she obviously got to you.'

'Perhaps.'

'Why won't you talk about her? Are you scared of her?'

'Of course not,' Dennis responded sharply, but Sanderson didn't believe him.

'Well then?'

Dennis hesitated. Was he intimidated by this mystery person? Or was it just not the done thing to name names?

'Her name is Samantha. She's a mid-op she-male.'

'What did she do to you?' Sanderson enquired, banking the name.

'Half killed me is what she did,' Dennis replied tersely.

Sanderson nodded sympathetically, but said nothing. Dennis was going to elaborate – he just needed a moment to collect himself.

'She put me in hog ties and a deprivation hood. You shouldn't wear those things for more than an hour unless you want to go gaga, but she left me in it for five. I was panicking, couldn't breathe, but she just seemed to enjoy it. She abused me, told me I deserved it, she even laughed at one point.'

Dennis's voice shook as he said it. He was no longer the cheeky figure of fun he purported to be. It was clear that he had genuinely thought he was going to die during the experience.

'Is she likely to have gone to the Annual Ball?' Sanderson asked.

'Never missed it.'

'And where do you normally find her? Where does she live?'

'Well, that's the million-dollar question, isn't it?'

'Do you know?'

'Maybe I do, maybe I don't. But I think I've said more than enough already. I've got no love for Samantha, believe me, but I've got even less love for the police. So I think it's time you were going.'

As he said it, fourteen pairs of eyes swivelled towards her. Sanderson opened her mouth to respond, but Dennis quickly went on:

'You're going to have to work on your act a little, *Rose*. The look of terror in your eyes when I suggested a bit of slap and tickle was a dead giveaway. Missionary all the way with you, is it?'

Now he was looking at her with open hostility. The atmosphere had suddenly turned and Sanderson wanted to be out of this basement as quickly as possible. She had overplayed her hand, pushed too hard. There was nothing to do now but retreat, so Sanderson stood up and scurried towards the exit, watched all the way by thirty accusing eyes.

32

'I won't be able to come here again.'

Angelique looked up, pausing momentarily.

'Something wrong?'

'It's just work,' Helen replied. 'I'm going to be abroad a lot, so . . .'

Helen wasn't a liar by nature and it showed. Fortunately this was not an environment in which awkward questions were likely to be raised.

'Let's make it a good one, then,' Angelique replied. 'Something to remember me by?'

The slender dominatrix moved forward, taking Helen's wrist in her hand.

'No restraints tonight,' Helen said firmly.

Angelique paused. The look on her face suggested to Helen that there was much that could be said. Angelique was well-known on the S&M scene and had presumably heard about Jake's murder. Had she known Helen a little better she might have raised it – it had clearly rattled people – but they barely knew each other, so whatever it was it would remain unsaid. Helen had visited Angelique on a handful of occasions in the last three months. She had tried to wean herself off her habit, but when the need became too great, she had sought paid companionship. This time she had sought out female company, hoping it would remove any sexual attraction from the equation – this had been her undoing on more than one occasion before.

Overall it had worked pretty well and Helen was glad to be able to use her services when the need arose. But she knew this would be her last visit. She would have to absent herself from this world during the investigation. It was hard to know what would fill the void – she was already running three times a week and smoking far more than she should – and Helen wondered what other compulsions might rear up in Angelique's absence. As she'd biked home from Lynn's house, she'd tried to persuade herself not to come. But her head was full of darkness tonight and the news that Sanderson's cover had been blown so quickly had pushed her over the edge.

Nodding to Angelique, she relaxed her body and waited for the first blow. Today had been awful in so many ways and she couldn't rid herself of the unpleasant images swirling round her mind. The look of disgust on Mike Elder's face, his son's cold corpse on the stainless steel slab, and – shot through with these – images of her *own* past. Mike Elder's sneering face seemed to alternate with her father's, while the submissive Moira seemed to walk hand in hand with visions of her own mother, turning the other cheek as her brutish husband beat, tortured and raped his own flesh and blood. Helen had never been a parent – and she knew in her heart that she never would be – but still she felt a fierce, primal anger at those who visited such terrible cruelty on those closest to them. The events of today had taken her straight back to when she was a little girl, remembering the intense fear, impotence and terror that only a child can feel. It filled her with terrible rage, but also terrible sadness. This had been her birth rite, just as it had been Jake's.

The crop bit into her back, jolting her from her thoughts. This had always been the way – the endorphins flooding through her as she concentrated on the rhythm and power of her beating. She needed the release now more than ever on this darkest of days. Which is why, as Angelique raised her crop a second time, Helen shut her eyes and uttered a single word.

'Harder.'

33

Her boots clicked on the stone cobbles, as she walked away down the dark street. It was deserted and deathly quiet tonight. This was one of the reasons why Helen used Angelique – her flat was part of a converted warehouse down by the docks, away from the hustle and bustle of Southampton. It was discreet and off the beaten track, which is how Helen liked it.

Her session had been punishing, but still she couldn't settle. Usually she would have walked away feeling lighter, happier, more optimistic. Tonight though, she felt a weight on her conscience. Not simply because of what she had endured today, but because there was one task she had still to perform.

She had known it the moment she'd seen Jake's lifeless face, but her conversation with Charlie had brought it home to her. Callous as it was, she had to sever her connection with Jake for good. She told herself that by so doing she was just freeing herself to pursue his killer, but it still made her feel disloyal and unworthy, as if she was somehow embarrassed of her relationship with him.

Unzipping her jacket pocket, she pulled the battered Samsung phone from inside. She had bought it from a market stall in Portsmouth. It had clearly been stolen, but Helen didn't quibble, handing over the cash, before heading off in search of another stall that sold knock-off SIM cards. Putting them together, she had an unregistered phone from which she could send messages that would never be traced back to her. She had her own phone of course for everyday stuff, but this phone was purely used to arrange her appointments. First with Jake Elder, later with another dominator, Max Paine, and then finally with Angelique. A discreet way to organize a side of her life that Helen wanted to remain hidden.

Helen knew this number would come up at some point in the investigation, as the team investigated Jake's past communications. She had messaged Jake regularly in the old days, setting up their meetings, confirming times and occasionally cancelling their sessions when duty called. Recently their communications had been much more sporadic, but he had messaged her a few months back. It was innocuous enough – a request to resume their professional relationship – and Helen had been kindness personified in knocking him back. Still, it would be on the list of numbers to check out. Her team obviously couldn't place her at the club and there would be precious little to flag her number as one of particular interest, given how irregularly she'd used it. But it was just possible that they might try to trace its location and that could lead to some uncomfortable questions, as she often had the phone on her at work.

This was why this part of her life had to end tonight. Once more she had cleaved close to someone only for them to meet a horrifying end. On nights like these Helen genuinely wondered if she was cursed. Everyone she had feelings for, everyone she formed any sort of relationship with, ended up suffering for it. Her sister, Marianne, and her nephew, Robert, had suffered, as had her former lover, Mark Fuller, and now Jake. Was *she* the connecting factor here? Was it somehow her fault that these people should endure the horrors they did?

Helen suddenly realized she had come to a halt, lost in her own thoughts. Cursing herself for her self-indulgence, she scoured the surface of the road. She soon found what she was looking for and marching across to the gutter, pulled both the battery and the SIM card from the body of the phone. She checked the street was clear once more, then dropped all three parts down the drain.

And that was it. Brutal, short and definitive. The last rites on her relationship with Jake Elder.

34

Whose bright idea was it to put mirrors in the lifts?

Charlie was already late for work – she'd forgotten it was Jessica's 'Show and Tell' this morning – and her mood was not improved by the sight of herself in the floor-to-ceiling mirrors. Her clothes were ok, if a little tight – it was her face that depressed her. The lighting wasn't great in the lift but, even so, she looked washed out, with deep, dark rings under the eyes. She wasn't the greatest advert for being a working mum.

The doors pinged open and, turning her back on the accusing mirrors, Charlie strode down the corridor to the incident room. She paused by the door to smooth her hair down, then pushed through it with an energy she didn't feel. Her late-night stakeout had yielded nothing – Jackson had stayed put all night – and she was paying the price for it this morning. The only consolation – if you could call it that – was that Sanderson had lucked out too.

Charlie headed straight to her desk. As she approached it, however, she slowed her pace, surprised by the sight of two Media Liaison Officers talking to Helen in her office. They only turned up when something important had happened, and looking around the office Charlie noticed that there was something different in everyone's expression today. They looked optimistic and energized.

Waving Edwards over, she cut to the chase.

'What's going on?'

'Got the DNA samples back this morning.'

'And?'

'We got a match. Paul Jackson. He's the manager at –'

'Santander in Shirley. I know, I spoke to him yesterday.'

'There you go then.'

Edwards turned away, but Charlie stopped him.

'Someone should have called me.'

'I did, but it rang out. Then I thought I'd tell you when you came in – we were expecting you in a bit earlier.'

'I got held up,' Charlie responded tersely. 'Anyway, what are we waiting for, we should be down there –'

'It's under control,' Edwards replied crisply.

Charlie was already scanning the office. She had a nasty feeling where this was going and wasn't surprised in the least when Edwards concluded:

'DS Sanderson has just gone to pick him up.'

35

He knew it was coming, but still it was much more brutal than he'd expected.

He was in the middle of a divisional meeting – the heads of all the local branches gathered together for tea and biscuits. These sessions always ran over time, the various managers positioning themselves for promotion, while sharing tales from the coalface, but he still enjoyed them. In this environment, he was king. He liked the deference, the banter and, if he was honest, the power.

The meeting room was glass-walled, so everybody saw them coming. His PA – the redoubtable Mrs Allen – was trying hard to look professional – but in reality just looked shit scared, saying nothing as she opened the meeting room door and ushered the tall, serious-looking woman inside. He didn't recognize her – she wasn't the one who'd come yesterday – but he could tell by the way she carried herself that she was a police officer. A fact she now confirmed by presenting her warrant card to him.

'DS Sanderson. I wonder if I could have a word, Mr Jackson,' she said, her voice quiet, but clear.

'Of course. My office is just –'

'I think it would be best if you accompany me to the station.'

The walk of shame through the office was quick, but felt interminable – the eyes of every staff member glued to him. Colleagues shuffled out of the way in silence and moments later he found himself striding down the brightly lit corridor towards the exit.

Before long, he was in the back of a saloon car, moving fast down the road. As he pulled away from the bank that had been a happy home for many years now, he caught sight of his managerial colleagues staring out of the meeting room window at him.

This was it then. The end of his old life. And the beginning of something new.

36

'What do we say to the press?'

There was more than a hint of excitement in Gardam's voice, but Helen knew he was experienced enough not to get carried away.

'There's massive media interest in this case already and I don't want to whip them up any more,' he continued. 'I take it you've seen the early edition of the *Evening News*?'

Helen confirmed that she had, trying to put Emilia Garanita's lurid four-page spread from her mind. It was written as if in sympathy with the dead, but in reality was a hatchet job on Jake and everyone 'like' him. She could tell that Emilia was hoping that this story would be a long runner and felt a small sense of satisfaction that she might be about to cut her enjoyment short.

'I think we play it straight,' Helen carried on. 'We say that an individual is helping us with our enquiries and leave it at that.'

'They'll know he's in custody. DS Sanderson has made sure of that. What details are we prepared to release?'

'Gender, age if you want, but leave it at that,' she replied, making a mental note to talk to Sanderson. 'We don't want a witch hunt.'

'I think we're probably going to get one, come what

may, but I'm sure you're right. I'll give them enough and no more. If you want to come along to say a few words to start us off –'

'I think I'm better used in the interview suite, sir.'

'As you wish. I understand he's already downstairs, so don't let me keep you. I'll field the hacks and leave you to do what you do best. The sooner we nip this one in the bud, the better.'

Helen thanked him and headed for the lift bank. Paul Jackson was an unlikely suspect in some ways, but he had history with Jake, a taste for the exotic, as well as access to people's credit card details. Killers came in all shapes and sizes and Paul Jackson had a lot of explaining to do. Would he be able to tell her why her good friend had been so brutally killed? As she descended to the custody area, Helen felt a surge of excitement, a sense that they were finally getting somewhere. And unless her eyes deceived her, Gardam was feeling it too.

'Of course not.'

'We're equal rank, you can't steal leads from me. Just because your undercover gig was a bust –'

'You weren't here, Charlie,' Sanderson interrupted. 'What was I supposed to do?'

'You were supposed to *call* me. That's what any normal person would have done. But you're so busy trying to impress Mummy that you'd –'

'You're out of line.'

'Deny it then. Look me in the face and deny that you deliberately stole my collar to make yourself look good in front of –'

'Go to Hell.'

'You'd like that, wouldn't you? Be just like the old days –'

'What's going on?'

Charlie was almost nose-to-nose with Sanderson, but pulled away sharply on hearing Helen's voice.

'We have a suspect in custody,' Helen continued, approaching fast. 'We have dozens of leads to chase up. So why are my two senior officers going at it like a pair of fishwives?'

Neither Charlie nor Sanderson answered. They didn't dare, given the look on Helen's face.

'You've both been around long enough to know that any problems need to be settled in private, not paraded for the rest of the station.'

Charlie stole a glance at the desk sergeant who'd clearly been enjoying the show.

'DS Brooks, you will accompany me to the interview

suite. DS Sanderson, you will return to the incident room and lead the team.'

Sanderson opened her mouth to protest.

'And don't even think about answering back,' Helen said, silencing her before she'd begun.

Without another word, Helen turned, walking away fast towards the swing doors. Charlie sped after her. She didn't bother looking back at Sanderson – she could tell what she'd be feeling now. Not that this was any consolation – they were both in trouble now and had a lot of ground to make up.

Whatever way you looked at it, Charlie's bad day had just got a whole lot worse.

38

'You are making a monumental mistake and when this is all over, I will be expecting a formal apology.'

Helen Grace had already been surprised twice by Paul Jackson in the ten minutes they'd known each other. His agreement to field questions before his lawyer arrived was unusual, as was his decision to adopt such an aggressive tone. He was either extremely confident of his innocence or an accomplished liar.

'As I've said, you're here because your DNA was found on the victim's body,' Helen responded calmly. 'In saliva on his cheek and ear. It's highly unlikely that our laboratory got that *wrong*. They double- and triple-check their findings –'

'You hear about mistakes all the time in these places,' Jackson interrupted. 'Petri dishes that haven't been cleaned properly, evidence that has been cross-contaminated, your lot are constantly arresting the wrong people because of cock-ups at laboratories.'

'I agree that there have been mistakes, but the fact remains that it is your DNA. The only way cross-contamination could have occurred is if they had a sample of your DNA stored there from a separate incident. Is that the case? Have you ever had to provide a DNA sample for the police before?'

'No.'

'Then the only "mistake" that could have occurred was if your saliva was accidentally transferred to Mr Elder's face. Can you explain how this might have happened?'

'I've no idea. Perhaps our paths overlapped on the way to work, perhaps we use the same gym –'

'Mr Elder works from home, keeps very different hours from you and to the best of our knowledge didn't have a gym membership.'

'I can't explain it then.'

'You've never met him?'

'Never. I've said this three times to three different officers now. Perhaps if you tried listening to me, we could sort this mess out?'

Helen was about to respond when the door opened and Jackson's lawyer hurried in. Helen knew Jonathan Spitz to be an astute and experienced lawyer and he wasted no time in reprimanding her for proceeding without him. Helen ignored his protests and carried on:

'Mr Jackson has confirmed that he didn't know Mr Elder and can't account for the DNA samples we found on the victim's face.'

Spitz looked relieved that no serious damage had been done.

'I'd now like to ask your client about his phone history. I'm showing Mr Jackson a black iPhone. Can you confirm that this is yours?'

Jackson nodded.

'For the tape, please, Mr Jackson.'

'Yes.'

'When we spoke yesterday,' Charlie interjected, 'you said that you'd never contacted Mr Elder via email, message, phone –'

'Correct.'

'Yet dozens of Snapchat messages were sent from this device to Mr Elder. I have the dates of some of them here' – Charlie pulled a sheet of paper from her file – 'August the tenth, August the fourteenth, September the first, September the sixth, September the fourteenth. The list goes on.'

'I didn't send them. The phone must have been cloned or something –'

'It's curious though that the gap in messages in the second half of August coincides with the dates that you and your wife were on holiday in Santorini. The data roaming charges on your account give us a pretty good picture of your movements and, of course, we're double-checking this with Sally as we speak.'

For the first time since they'd started, Helen saw Jackson react. Clearly he was not keen on his wife being dragged into this.

'Furthermore, we've had a chance to look at some of the other messages and texts you sent from this phone. And it's interesting that the same grammatical tics that we see in your texts also crop up in the Snapchat messages that Mr Elder received. You always seem to leave a gap between a word and a question mark, for example, and you're pretty scrupulous about using commas. Not everyone is as fastidious in their messaging these days.'

It was said with a smile, but provoked a blank response from Jackson.

'This is all circumstantial,' Spitz butted in. 'Do you have any actual evidence against my client?'

'Apart from the DNA evidence, you mean?' Helen rejoined. 'I should point out that no other DNA was found on the victim, hence our interest in talking to your client.'

Helen let that settle before continuing.

'I'd like now to move on to your movements on the night of the fourteenth. You told my colleague that you left work at seven p.m. and went for a drink at the Saracen's Head.'

Jackson said nothing. He appeared to be waiting for Helen's next move before committing himself.

'That's strange, because your phone was transmitting in the Banister Park area of the city – very near to the Torture Rooms – at around eight p.m. that night and again at just after twelve thirty a.m. the following morning. I'm assuming that in the interim you were in the basement club and thus out of reception?'

'I don't know anything about the Torture Rooms or Banister Park. Somebody's obviously messed up –'

'Yet another mistake, you do seem to be unlucky . . .'

'I went to the Saracen's Head, I watched the game, had a few drinks –'

'Why the Saracen's Head, out of interest? You work in Lansdowne Hill, you live in Freemantle. Going to a pub near the hospital seems an excessive diversion.'

'For God's sake, I like the beer there, so –'

'What beer do they serve?'

'Shepherd Neame, I think . . . Adnams, a couple of local brews.'

'Actually they haven't served Shepherd Neame in over two years,' Charlie interjected. 'I went there yesterday afternoon, spoke to the bar staff. Nobody remembers seeing you there on Tuesday night. In fact, I couldn't find a single person to back up your version of events.'

Spitz looked at his client, hoping for more defiance, but none was forthcoming. Helen took over, adopting a more emollient tone.

'I know you're in a fix here, Paul. You're thinking of Sally, of the twins, of what this will do to them. But lying won't help. We have firm evidence you knew Jake and were active on the S&M scene. Your phone places you near the scene of the crime, yours is the only DNA on the body and I have no doubt that one of those present at the Torture Rooms *will* positively ID you as having been there that night. So let's start again, shall we?'

Helen looked Jackson straight in the eye.

'Tell me what really happened on Tuesday night.'

39

She didn't see her coming until it was too late.

Sally Jackson had been in the midst of a particularly difficult conversation when the call came. Paul's PA had seized the nettle, ringing Sally to tell her that her husband had been arrested and taken to Southampton Central. She'd been irritated when the phone rang – she worked at a local Family Centre and was busy explaining to an irate dad why his meetings with his estranged children had to be supervised. These discussions required finesse and patience, not interruptions, so she was tempted not to answer. But when the phone kept ringing, her curiosity was aroused.

She didn't know what to say at first, other than to check that it wasn't a joke and that she was *sure*. But the tone of Sandra Allen's voice – tight, sombre, with a hint of embarrassment – convinced Sally that she was. What do you do in these situations? Sally had extricated herself from her work, claiming a migraine, and hurried to her car. But once inside she just sat there, trying to process what was happening. Why hadn't Paul contacted her? Terrified, she'd considered calling a lawyer friend, then, discarding that option, decided to go to her sister's. In the end, she'd done neither, driving home instead. It was like she was on auto-pilot, heading to the place she felt safest.

'Mrs Jackson?'

She had just stepped out of the car when the woman approached. She was curious to look at – beautiful from one angle, but scarred on the other – and the situation was made stranger still by the look of concern on her face. How did she know so soon? Who was she?

'I'm Emilia Garanita from the *Evening News*. I understand you've had a terrible shock.'

She was so blind-sided by the woman's sudden approach – had she been lying in wait for her? – that initially Sally was struck dumb.

'There's no way you can be alone at a time like this, so why don't I sit with you until someone else comes?'

Sally was surprised to see that the woman had taken her arm and was now guiding her towards her own front door.

'Your hands are shaking, poor thing. Give me your keys and I'll do the honours. Then we can have a nice cup of tea.'

She stood there smiling, her hand outstretched for the keys. She seemed so confident of what she was doing that Sally now found herself rummaging for her keys. As she pulled them out, however, she spotted her key ring. On it was a small picture of her, Paul and the twins, taken about six months ago, at the top of Scafell Pike. They were all smiling – tired but exhilarated by their triumph in reaching the summit.

'I'm sorry, who did you say you were again?' she said, keeping the keys gripped tight in her hand.

'I'm from the *Southampton Evening News*,' the woman replied, her smile tightening a touch. 'I know you must be wondering what to do for the best and I'd like to help. Within the hour, you're going to have reporters, TV journalists and God knows who else camped on your doorstep. I can deal with them. Let me do that for you,' she said, casting an eye across the street as a van pulled up near by, 'or, believe you me, it's going to be a free-for-all. And nobody – least of all you – wants that.'

'I don't even know you.'

'Here's my ID,' she replied, thrusting a laminated press card into Sally's hand. 'You can call the office if you like. It's now or never, Sally.'

Sally now spotted a reporter she recognized from the local news heading up the road towards her.

'I'm sorry, I don't want to talk to anyone,' Sally said, finally finding her voice.

'You're going to have to talk to someone –'

'Please get off my property,' said Sally, cutting her short. She opened the door and bustled inside.

She turned to find the woman had a toe on the doorstep – where do these people get their cheek? – and slammed the door shut quickly. She hurried out of the hall, taking refuge in the kitchen, but before she'd even sat down, the doorbell rang. This time she heard a male voice, imploring her to answer. She said nothing in response. There was no way she could talk to anyone. She had the boys to think about and, besides, what could she tell them? She didn't have any information about why Paul had been arrested, what was happening or when he'd be back.

The only thing she did know was that their happy, ordered life was about to implode.

40

He grasped the metal bar and pulled down hard. The weights at the other end of the rope shot up and he held them in that position, his broad shoulder muscles taking the strain. He counted down the seconds in his head – thirty, twenty, ten – before easing the weights back down to base. They touched down without making a noise, bringing a smile to his face. It was stupid to revel in the finesse he brought to the job, but not everyone could do it, so why not?

Rising from the bench, Max Paine surveyed the scene around him. This was by far the most expensive gym in Southampton – complete with floor-to-ceiling views of the Solent – but you got what you paid for. It had the latest equipment, was quiet and full of professional gym bunnies. A particularly well-toned pair of girls wandered past now as he towelled himself down and he took the opportunity to scrutinize their tight backsides. They pretended to be deep in conversation, but they knew he was checking them out and loved it. Max made a mental note to say a few words to them before he left.

He was still following their progress towards the treadmills, when his attention was caught by one of the large plasma screens on the wall. There were TVs everywhere in this place, showing sports, lifestyle programmes, soaps and of course the ubiquitous game shows that clogged up daytime viewing. He generally ignored them – he was here to exercise – but this time what he saw stopped him in his tracks.

The news was playing, showing a press conference with Hampshire Police. Max didn't recognize the guy leading it and his headphones were switched off, so he couldn't hear what he was saying – but his eye was drawn to the headline bar at the bottom of the screen: TORTURE ROOMS MURDER. Dropping his towel on the bench, he hurried over to the screen, tapping his console to tune into the relevant channel.

'. . . in custody. We won't be releasing a name, but we can confirm that he is a male in his forties who lives locally.'

Max Paine listened intently. He had been to the Torture Rooms on numerous occasions and had been scouring local media for updates since he'd heard the news of Jake Elder's death.

'That's all I'm prepared to say for now. As you know, Detective Inspector Grace is leading the investigation, and I'm very confident that we'll make swift progress in this case. There is no need for members of the public to be alarmed as we are currently treating this as a one-off incident.'

Max stood still. Had he been hearing things? No, the guy had definitely said DI Grace. Suddenly he laughed out loud, provoking startled looks from the gym bunnies nearby. This was too good to be true. No, this was *priceless.*

All thoughts of his workout were now long gone. As he strode towards the exit, his mind turned on the possibilities this surprising development threw up. This was an opportunity to make some serious money. What he had to say would pay for his expensive gym membership and a lot more besides.

41

'So this was your third visit to the Torture Rooms?'

'Yes,' Jackson replied, without choosing to elaborate further.

Helen nodded, but didn't push it. He had clearly never spoken about this to anyone before.

'What time would you say you got there?'

'Around eight p.m.'

'Did you go with someone else or –'

'I was alone.'

The way he said it made Helen think he had been 'alone' for some time.

'This is not something I've shared,' he continued. 'It's not something I want shared. It's been a process for me.'

'You'd told Jake Elder though.'

Jackson looked up sharply at Helen, then lowered his gaze once more.

'How did you first encounter him?'

'I went to a Munch. They're –'

'We know what they are. Go on.'

'Well, I'd looked at some things online. I suppose I've always been attracted to men. But I've never told anyone, never done anything about it until recently. Maybe it's because the kids are older, because I've got more time on my hands. Don't get me wrong, I love my wife, but there's a part of me that's just . . .'

Helen nodded, but said nothing. There was more coming.

'I liked the S&M stuff. Can't say why. I've got a stressful job, a busy life . . . but maybe that's just excuses.'

'And Mr Elder . . . ?'

'Someone at the Munch mentioned him, so I got in touch. We had a session at his flat and well . . . that was pretty much it for me.'

Helen nodded. It was so odd to hear him articulating feelings *she* had felt, but she kept a poker face. She wanted more than this discursive preamble.

'I went as often as I could. Spent I don't know how much money. After a while, it became unsustainable so I thought I'd venture on to the scene to see if I could find some more . . . companionship.'

'That must have been risky,' Charlie interjected.

'Of course it was, given my position . . . but there's a kind of unwritten rule about these places. If you see someone you know – someone you recognize from normal life – well, you never mention it.'

'What happens on tour stays on tour.'

'Something like that.'

'And what about Tuesday night?' Helen said, inserting herself into the conversation once more. 'When and how did you meet Jake Elder?'

'I saw him on the dance floor. He looked bored. He looked . . . sad.'

'Why?'

'I've no idea.'

'What happened next?'

'I beckoned to him,' Jackson replied cautiously. 'I beckoned to him and he came over. I suggested . . . I suggested he might like to go somewhere with me.'

'Did you touch him?'

'A little. Just to get him in the mood . . .'

'Why was your saliva on his cheek and ear?'

Jackson sighed, fidgeting.

'Why, Paul?'

'Because I sucked his ear.'

'Ok.'

'I whispered a suggestion of what we might do and then . . . then I sucked his earlobe. I don't know why I did it . . .'

'Then what?' Helen persisted. She could sense Jackson retreating inwards. These confessions were taking their toll.

'He turned me down.'

'Why would he do that?'

'You'd have to ask him that,' Jackson laughed bitterly, earning a reproachful look from his lawyer. 'He said it was because he didn't want to blur the lines between the personal and professional, but who knows?'

Helen eyed Jackson carefully. It was a convenient excuse and Jake wasn't around to contradict him. Was his bitterness just an act?

'Did you go into the rooms at the back of the club?'

'No.'

'So we definitely won't find any traces of you – hairs, skin, prints – in those rooms?'

'I never got near them.'

'Why not?'

'I don't know, you tell me. Maybe it just wasn't my night.'

'A handsome guy like you?'

'There's no accounting for taste,' Jackson spat back sourly.

'Are you sure Jake didn't accept your invitation and take you backstairs?'

'Look, I've told you what happened. If you don't believe me . . .'

'Do you like the rough stuff?'

'Don't answer that,' his lawyer interjected.

'For God's sake, Paul, our guys are poring over the search history on your phone. We're picking up your computers – from home and work. We are going to find out what you've been looking at, so do *not* hold out on me now.'

'Yes, I like the hard stuff.'

'Paul . . .' his lawyer warned gently, but his client appeared not to hear him.

'Have you ever watched Edge Play? Online or in the flesh?'

'Yes.'

'Have you ever participated in Edge Play?'

'Occasionally.'

'Have you used wet sheets?'

'Yes, I have, but that doesn't mean –'

'Doesn't mean what?'

'That I did anything to Jake.'

'Why would it mean that? I haven't mentioned wet sheets in connection with his death. Neither has the press, so how would you know that?'

'I wouldn't . . . I was just saying that . . .'

'Did you kill him, Paul?'

'No . . .'

'Did you take him to one of the back rooms that night, tie him up –'

'No, a hundred times no . . .'

'Punish him as he deserved to be punished?'

'I would never do that.'

'Why?'

'Because it's not my thing.'

'You're contradicting yourself now, Paul. We've all just heard you say –'

'I like the rough stuff, but –'

'But what?'

'But I'm always the bottom, ok, never the top,' he finally said, glaring at Helen.

'Sorry, I'm a bit –' his lawyer began.

'Bottom means the submissive, the top is the dominator,' Helen interjected, keen to keep the focus on Jackson.

'I . . . I don't *like* to dominate.' Jackson's voice faltered. 'I want to be humiliated, abused, degraded. That's why . . . that's why I could never do something like this.'

Jackson raised his gaze to meet Helen's and she was surprised to see that tears were threatening.

'Please believe me. I didn't kill Jake Elder.'

42

'Is he lying?'

Helen and Jonathan Gardam were huddled in the smokers' yard, away from the prying ears of colleagues, lawyers and Gardam's PA.

'Hard to say for sure. He sounds genuine, but there's a lot that links him to Elder, to the scene. Also, Lynn Picket banks with Santander – it would have been the easiest thing in the world for him to lift her card details off the system and use them for his own devices.'

'Would he really shit on his own doorstep like that?'

'How could you link him to it? Nearly a hundred people work in that bank, thousands more have access to their system.'

'So what's our next move?'

'I'm going to go back to Meredith, see if we can link Jackson to the crime scene. They've got mountains of stuff – cigarettes, beer bottles, hair, spit, semen – if we can put him in the room, then we can prove he's lying.'

'And if we can't? What does your instinct tell you?'

'I don't really believe in the copper's gut,' Helen replied, dropping her cigarette to the floor. Nicotine was doing nothing for her today, but that still didn't stop her wanting another.

'You must have a view though,' Gardam persisted.

'I'd be tempted to believe him, in the absence of evidence to the contrary.'

'Why?'

'He was in the right place at the right time but . . . he just doesn't seem the type to me. This murder was unusual, elaborate and provocative. It's a statement killing – whoever did this *wants* our attention. Maybe he's a good actor, but my feeling is that Jackson doesn't want the world to know that he likes men, likes S&M . . .'

Gardam nodded, even as his eye was caught by the discarded cigarette on the floor. A smudge of Helen's lipstick was still visible on the tip.

'He's married, got twin boys,' Helen continued. 'He's leading a double life and my instinct is that he wants to keep it that way.'

The irony of this comment wasn't lost on Helen – this case just kept rebounding against her – and she toyed with her lighter to avoid looking directly at Gardam.

'Do you want to hold him?' Gardam said, interrupting Helen's chain of thought.

'I'm not inclined to. He's not a flight risk – he's too anchored in Southampton – and I don't want to put too much pressure on him, in case we're wrong. He seems pretty fragile to me.'

'Well, I'll back whatever you decide.'

'Thank you.'

Gardam offered Helen another cigarette, which she took without hesitation.

'I know they're not good for you,' he said, lighting Helen's cigarette before fixing one for himself, 'but I can't do without them. I have to smoke them here as Jane thinks I've given up.'

Helen nodded, but didn't play along. She'd never been comfortable with the way male colleagues deceived their wives, then enjoyed publicizing the fact.

There was a brief silence, then Gardam asked:

'Are you ok, Helen?'

'Sure. Why do you ask?'

'You look very pale, that's all. Is anything the matter?'

'I don't think so,' Helen lied. 'I'm always like this during a big investigation. I'm not a good sleeper at the best of times, so . . .'

'I'm the same,' Gardam replied. 'Thank God for cigarettes, eh?'

'Indeed.'

They smoked for a moment in silence. Then Helen said:

'I'd better get back.'

Gardam nodded and Helen walked off, squeezing the last vestiges of nicotine from her dying cigarette as she did so. Gardam watched her cross the yard, his eyes never straying from her, until eventually she disappeared from view and he was left alone.

43

She looked in the mirror and saw darkness staring back.

It wasn't the scratches on her arms or the faint shadow of bruising on her face. It was what she saw in her eyes that shocked her. Something dying, an emptiness taking hold. She had no idea how long she'd been sitting here, drinking herself in, but somehow she couldn't find it in herself to move. The last couple of days had taken so much out of her.

Draining the last drops of her vodka, she reached for her mascara and resumed her preparations. For most of her life she had been friendless, but if there was a staple in her life – apart from self-abuse, drugs and the dolls of course – it was this. Her war paint had been part of her for as long as she could remember and she never felt whole without it. There was something soothing, exciting and empowering about the ritual of self-improvement and she loved the feeling of the brushes against her skin. She had always been into this kind of thing – her mother had once said she was very intuitive about 'texture'. It was one of the few kind things she had ever said to her.

Putting the brushes down, she pulled the tub of hair gel towards her. Scooping up a large handful, she smeared it over her hair and scalp. She often wore her hair up – in a riotous, peacocking display – but not today.

Running her hands over her crown, she worked hard to flatten her hair. She liked the severe, asexual look it gave her – she was determined that there would not be a hair out of place.

Satisfied, she rose and walked over to the wardrobe. This was the most painful part and best done quickly. Pulling the whalebone corset from the wardrobe, she stepped into it and raised it up and over her chest. Grasping the strings, she pulled as hard as she could. The corset gripped her ribcage, punching the air from her lungs. She gasped but didn't relent, pulling still harder. She loved the feeling of breathlessness, of constriction, of pain. After thirty seconds, she finally relented, loosening the strings a notch and tying them in a neat bow. Surveying herself in the mirror, she was pleased by what she saw. She looked sleek, smooth, in control.

Time was pressing now, so she slid into her jumpsuit, reaching over her shoulder to zip herself up. Then marching into the bathroom, she applied the final touches. Coloured contact lenses, changing her irises from light blue to a deep chocolate brown. Her hair looked dark and slick, her face uncharacteristically pale and the eyes that stared back at her were those of a stranger. She didn't recognize herself. She hoped others wouldn't either.

Her preparations were complete now, so there was no point hesitating. Switching off the light, she walked quickly towards the front door. It was time to do battle again.

44

'I'm going to release Paul Jackson.'

Helen had dragged the entire team into the briefing room. They looked shocked at the news – Charlie in particular – but Helen wasn't in the mood for a discussion. Jackson might still have a role to play in the case, but in her mind at least he wasn't the elusive, sadistic killer they were hunting. Crushing though it was to have to admit it, they were back to square one.

'It's only on bail and he'll be under surveillance, but I want us to widen our search and consider other possibilities. We should assume for now that Jake Elder's murder was *not* an opportunist act. The careful choice of venue, the credit card fraud, plus the tactics employed by the perpetrator to conceal the purchase of the items used suggests a high level of planning.'

'Does that mean the perpetrator had a special grievance against Elder, that he'd been plotting his murder for some time?' DC Reid offered.

'Have we found anything in Elder's communications or recent history to support that? Has he angered anybody recently?' Helen responded.

'Nothing on the drugs or money front,' Lucas replied.

'Nor in his private or professional life,' Edwards said,

overlapping. 'His life seems pretty . . . empty, to be honest.'

Helen felt a sharp stab of guilt but, swallowing it, pressed on.

'In which case we have to consider the possibility that whoever did this has no personal animus against Elder.'

'Perhaps it's what he represents?' DC Lucas said.

'Could be a hate crime,' Sanderson added, overlapping. 'Anti-gay? Anti-BDSM?'

'Maybe, but if so I'd have expected someone to have claimed responsibility for the murder,' Helen replied. 'Or posted some kind of justification for their actions. Let's keep an eye on that – see if anyone surfaces in the next twenty-four hours.'

'Maybe they just get off on the thrill of it,' DC Edwards said. 'The sense of control, playing God. Maybe whoever did this *enjoyed* watching Elder die –'

'He'd be taking a chance when anyone could have walked in,' Helen interrupted quickly, keen not to dwell on this thought.

'Perhaps,' Edwards countered, 'but according to Blakeman there's a kind of unwritten rule in that club. If the door's closed, it means "do not disturb".'

'What about exposure?' Sanderson now offered. 'By killing him he's revealing to the world what Elder really was. A dominator, a "pervert" . . .'

Helen nodded, suppressing her alarm. She had seen this kind of thing before in the Ella Matthews case, a young prostitute who'd killed her male clients to expose them. Could this latest murder be a copycat killing of her awful crimes?

'But that would suggest that the killer isn't part of the BDSM scene,' Charlie objected. 'Which doesn't hold water for me. I think our killer knew the club, knew the scene and was very deliberate in his choice of target.'

Sanderson said nothing. Nor did her colleagues. As Helen had predicted, everybody knew about their earlier row and they were keen to avoid getting involved.

'In the absence of any specific pointers, we'll have to keep an open mind on the perpetrator's motivation,' Helen said, shooting a warning look to both Sanderson and Charlie. 'For now, let's deal with what we *know*. Our killer was calm, methodical –'

'Suggesting that he's done this before?' Reid offered.

'Maybe. We should certainly consider the possibility that our killer has a criminal past. Let's look for the obvious – hate crimes, false imprisonment – but I also want us to check out anyone who's been convicted of credit card fraud in the last five years and cross-reference their names against those already on our list. How are we doing with our Snapchatters?'

'Apart from Jackson, we've tracked down seven of the twenty – all of whom have alibis,' Charlie replied.

'Not good enough. That's twelve possible suspects who like to conceal their identities and who have a strong personal link to the deceased. Chase them down *quickly*, please.'

Charlie nodded but said nothing, so Helen continued:

'Edwards, I'd like you to do some further credit card digging for me. This is our killer's only footprint so far. How did he get Lynn Picket's card details? Check her friends, family, workmen who visited the house – anybody who could have gained access to her bag. Check where she shops, which internet sites she uses and ask the tech boys to investigate whether her card details could have been sold as part of a bundle on the internet or dark web. If our killer prefers anonymity, he may favour using a Tor browser.'

'I'll get them on to it straight away.'

'I've also asked DS Sanderson to draw up a list of names from last night's Munch. I'm sure word's spread about our presence on the scene,' Helen went on, 'and it's going to be hard for us to place someone else there, but we can at least follow up on the intel we *do* have.'

'I'll circulate the list to everyone,' Sanderson added quickly. 'Our main person of interest is "Samantha", a mid-op transsexual – male to female – who indulges in extreme BDSM and has a history of assault, ABH and so on.'

'Finally, I'm going to ask DC McAndrew to keep us all up to date with any forensic developments,' Helen concluded. 'In the absence of any other direct DNA sources on the victim's body, we'll need to interrogate the other traces found in the room and its environs. If there's a match to someone with a criminal past – however trivial – we need to know about it.'

There was a silence in the room as everyone looked to Helen once more.

'Well, don't just stand there,' she barked at them. 'There's a killer out there and he's laughing at us.'

And with that she turned, heading for the sanctuary of her office.

45

Helen pushed the door to and tossed her jacket on to the sofa. She felt drained and dispirited, her high hopes of the morning dashed. She needed time and space to gather her thoughts – gather herself – but she had only just made it back to her desk when she heard Charlie's angry voice:

'You could have spoken to me first . . .'

Helen turned to see Charlie shutting the door behind her. Helen stared at her, then at the door, irritated by this act of insubordination. She was not in the mood to be crossed today.

'I wasn't under the impression I had to run my decisions past you,' Helen replied, just about holding her anger in check.

'Jackson is a good suspect.'

'I agree, but you were in that interview room. Do you think he's guilty?'

'It's too early to say. We have to go at him again.'

'He's being released as we speak.'

'Why, for God's sake? We've interviewed him *once*. We can hold him for at least another forty-eight hours –'

'Because if he is an innocent man, I don't intend to ruin his life completely. He has already been the subject of some pretty vile speculation in the press –'

'I appreciate that –'

'Do you? There are people out there who, for valid reasons, want to keep the different parts of their life separate, who've committed no offence –'

'But Elder rejected him. Jackson told us as much. He wanted sex with him and he was rejected. He has a strong motive –'

'So strong that two weeks prior to this murder, he ordered a collection of bondage items with which to commit the crime. This was *not* a crime of passion and you shouldn't dress it up as one.'

'You don't know that for sure,' Charlie threw back at her, her anger flaring now. 'He could have bought those items discreetly, intending to use them recreationally, but on that particular night he was angry and rejected –'

'Put him in the room then,' Helen spat back, 'put him at the crime scene and then we can have this conversation.'

The two women had now squared off against each other. Helen's eyes flitted to her office window. She could tell the rest of the team were listening to their argument and she was keen to bring it to a conclusion.

'I think we're making a mistake,' Charlie said defiantly.

'Noted,' Helen replied. 'But ask yourself why you're so hot on Jackson as a suspect. Could it be because you want to prove something to Sanderson?'

'He was my collar and she brought him in.'

'And now he's "yours" again you want to see it through, one in the eye for your fellow DS.'

'That's not true. Yes, Sanderson was out of line –'

'*I* told her to bring him in – because you weren't here.'

This time Charlie said nothing in response, stung by the implication.

'You were late and I will not let anyone's lack of professionalism hamper this investigation.'

'That's completely unfair,' Charlie said, stunned by this personal attack. 'I work harder than anyone else –'

'It's a statement of fact. You weren't here when you should have been.'

Charlie stared at Helen, speechless.

'But I'll tell you what. As you're so convinced Jackson is guilty, *you* can take the surveillance detail.'

'Oh, come on, that's a DC's job at best –'

'It's yours now,' Helen asserted.

Charlie opened her mouth to protest, but Helen continued:

'Bring me evidence of his guilt. Show me I'm wrong and I'll eat my words.'

She crossed the room and pointedly opened the door of her office.

'But know one thing, Charlie. This case is not about *you*. You may think it is, but it's not. It's about an innocent man –'

Helen's voice faltered as Jake's lifeless corpse once more sprung to mind.

'– an innocent man who deserves justice.'

'Why are you being like this?' Charlie said, emotion suddenly ambushing *her*.

'Because it's my job. You'd do well to remember yours.'

Helen stared at Charlie, challenging her to respond.

But this time she didn't. Instead, she turned and walked straight out of Helen's office and towards the exit without saying a word to anyone. Helen retreated quickly to her desk, keen to busy herself with her case files. She could feel her face burning, as if she were the one in the wrong. She *needed* to regain her composure.

Silence reigned in the incident room beyond but Helen knew that that was just show. They were all trying very hard to look busy and engaged, but as Helen distractedly turned the pages of the case file in front of her, she knew instinctively that all eyes were on her. Everybody was watching her, but nobody was saying anything.

46

Max Paine flicked through the pages of the newspaper until he found what he was looking for. The *Evening News* was dominated by sensational reports of the Torture Rooms murder, but it was the centre spread he was after. There at the top-right-hand corner of the page was the journalist's mug shot and direct line.

Emilia Garanita was no looker, given the extensive scarring on one of her cheeks, but she was a famous face in Southampton – with a number of high-profile exposés already to her name. She was happy to walk where angels fear to tread, going anywhere and talking to anyone who might provide her with a scoop. Paine hoped to use that to his advantage now.

He would meet with Garanita and tell her in confidence the information he was prepared to sell. He would then ask her to make him an offer. Under the pretext of thinking about it, he would then contact Grace and see what *she* was prepared to pay. To the winner, the spoils. He wasn't on some moral crusade after all. He just wanted money.

He punched Garanita's phone number into his mobile and turned away from the café counter – he didn't want to be overheard. But the call didn't connect, going straight to voicemail instead. He decided to be short and sweet.

'My name is Max Paine. I have information about the Torture Rooms murder that you'll want to hear. Call me on 07977 654878. I'll be waiting.'

He rang off, pleased to have made the first move, but irritated not to have been able to speak to Garanita in person. Still, there was plenty of time for that. No point getting strung out this early in the game.

He finished his coffee, flicking carelessly through the rest of the paper, before heading on his way. It was getting late and he had work to do. He thought about taking the *News* with him, but he had Garanita's number on his phone now, so tossing it casually on to the table, he left. The waitress swooped, scooping up his empty coffee cup, pausing momentarily to take in the front page of the abandoned paper. Something approaching sympathy now creased her features as Jake Elder's smiling, happy face beamed out at her from beneath the screaming headline:

SOUTHAMPTON SEX MURDER.

47

They stood staring at each other, neither daring to speak.

The enormous relief Paul Jackson had felt on being told he was to be released swiftly turned to anxiety, when he realized what lay ahead. He didn't trust himself to call Sally – he wasn't even sure if she'd answer – so he'd texted her. His message was brief, saying simply that he was on his way home and would see her shortly. It was the kind of anodyne message he had sent a hundred times before. Now, however, it had a very different meaning.

He had hoped to avoid the press by sneaking out of the back exit of Southampton Central, but they were waiting for him there, as they were when he eventually pulled into his road. There was no question of heading in via the back door – the garden wall was too high to be scaled without a ladder – so getting out of the car he made a dash for the front gate. Immediately, he cannoned off one journalist, knocking over a photographer in the process. Nobody actually laid a hand on him but they all contrived to impede his progress. They wanted to provoke him, to get him to lash out, but he kept his head down until he reached the sanctuary of his front door.

His hand had been shaking when he'd put the key in the lock and the house seemed eerily empty when he finally succeeded in getting inside. The twins had been picked up by another school mum and were still blissfully unaware of what was happening. Sally, however, was waiting for him in the kitchen, seated at the table with her hands folded.

He was about to kiss her, then thought better of it. He pulled out a chair – the trailing leg made a sharp, squealing noise on the polished wooden floor – and sat down. He saw Sally flinch at the noise and looking at her he now realized that she was on the edge of tears. The sight made him feel sick. This was his fault. All this . . . hurt . . . was his fault.

'I haven't been able to go out,' Sally said suddenly. 'They've been ringing the doorbell, banging on the door. I pulled the phone out of the wall, but they got my mobile number from somewhere . . .'

'I'm so sorry, Sally. I never wanted any of this . . .'

'Please tell me it's a mistake,' she replied quickly, her voice wobbling. 'I heard the headlines, I know what this is . . .'

'Of course it's a mistake, my darling. I'm not a violent man. I would never hurt somebody like that.'

'And the rest of it?'

Paul was suddenly unable to look at her.

'That place. Where this man died . . .'

She didn't elaborate further, but the unspoken question was clear.

'Yes. I went there.'

'How many times?'

Paul said nothing in response.

'How many times have you been there? And please don't lie to me, Paul.'

'Six, maybe seven times.'

'What did you do there?'

For a moment, Paul was tempted to lie, to soften the blow. He could start by saying he went to drink, dance . . . But in the end, he simply said:

'I went there to meet men.'

Sally nodded slightly, then rose from the table. Paul rose too, moving towards her, but she held up a hand to fend him off. Turning, she walked from the room without looking back, running up the stairs to her bedroom. Paul heard the bedroom door slam shut and moments later the sound of her crying.

He walked over to the window, pulling the curtains round to block out the press photographers who were straining to see in from their vantage points on the wall opposite. It was a pointless gesture – it was too late to protect his family. He had never hated himself so much as he did in that moment. He hadn't heard his wife cry in years and now in one awful day he had destroyed her happiness, her peace of mind and her faith in him.

His very public arrest would cause her embarrassment both at home and at work. The revelation that he was bisexual would hurt her deeply too. But perhaps they could have worked through those things – for the boys' sake – were it not for the fact that he had betrayed her. He had lied to her night after night, as he slept with casual pick-ups. It was this that would damn him ultimately and he knew that Sally would never forgive him. Nor, if he was honest, would he.

48

From her viewpoint across the road, Charlie watched the horrible soap opera unfold. Charlie remained to be convinced that Paul Jackson was innocent, but she still felt for him and his family. Like her, they must have got up this morning with no inkling of what was about to befall them. They might even have been looking forward to the day. But in the time it takes the sun to rise and set again, secrets had been revealed, accusations made and a family's happiness shattered.

Thanks to her job, Charlie came into contact with many unsavoury characters, but few were as unpleasant and pitiless as the journalists now camped outside the Jackson house. In time, they would drift away, as new developments emerged, but the next forty-eight hours would be Hell. The family could take legal steps to protect themselves from intrusion, but these things took time and in the interim press hounds, radio and TV journalists, bloggers and more would be beating a path to their door.

They would claim that they were only doing their job – 'it's a free country' was the common refrain – but Charlie knew they enjoyed it. It was bullying pure and simple, the pack descending on whomsoever they deemed fair game. They would climb walls, scale lampposts, shout through letter boxes, bribe, threaten, cajole – all in the hope of getting a few words with the accused or a photo of his weeping wife. Many people out there thought the same of coppers – that they were only on God's earth to cause grief and upset – but in Charlie's mind, at least, the two professions were very different indeed.

The biting wind whistled round Charlie and, cursing her luck, she retreated to her car. Helen had sent her here as a punishment, knowing full well it would be a wasted journey. It was easy enough to blend in with the journalists and gawpers, but with such a crowd outside what were the chances that Jackson would actually do anything incriminating? If he was smart, he would stay exactly where he was, until the interest in him waned.

Charlie had the disquieting feeling that Helen had turned against her. They had exchanged some harsh words earlier – words that had shaken Charlie to the core – and even though she knew she deserved to be sent to purdah for rowing with Sanderson, she never expected to be publicly dressed down like that. Helen's behaviour was out of character – impulsive and erratic – and it unnerved her. Especially when she still felt she had so much to prove.

Charlie hoped her exile would be brief. She missed her family, hated the tedium of a stakeout and desperately wanted to be back in the heart of things. But this case was doing strange things to people – to Helen, Sanderson, even Charlie herself – and she wondered if she had permanently blotted her copybook with her boss. Truth be told, she had never felt so uncertain of her position as she did tonight.

49

'I like the look of this one.'

Sanderson was hunched over her desk, running Helen through a print-out from the PNC database. The atmosphere was tense following the latter's clash with Charlie, and Sanderson was working overtime to appear efficient, professional and productive. Like her rival, she still had a lot of ground to make up.

'There's a few on the list, but she seems the most likely, given Dennis's description. Real name Michael Parker, now a mid-op transsexual, living as a woman. She's used a number of different identities over the years . . .'

'Sharon Greenwood,' Helen replied, reading the details, 'Beverley Booker and most recently *Samantha* Wilkes.'

'Exactly. And look at her form. Affray, drugs, theft, obtaining money by deception, false imprisonment . . .'

'What have we got on that last charge?' Helen said.

'Questioned, but never charged, about an incident with a Julian Bown, a married man she took back to her flat. Parker said their acts were consensual, Bown said they weren't, wanted to press for GBH, but dropped it at the last minute.'

'And obtaining money by deception?'

Sanderson leafed through her file to find the relevant page.

'Credit card fraud,' she said, looking up at Helen. The excitement that always comes with a new lead was rising inside her, but she hid it well. Best not to get ahead of herself when her boss's mood was still so hard to read.

'Dennis said Samantha never missed an Annual Ball, so it's likely we can place her there . . .' she continued.

'Let's check her out,' Helen said decisively. 'Does this Dennis know where to find her?'

'I believe so.'

'Then I'd better pay him a little visit. In the meantime, let's contact gender reassignment clinics, starting in Southampton and rolling out from there. If Samantha's a mid-operative transsexual, then she shouldn't be too hard to track down. Also, can you locate Julian Bown? If he still lives locally, we need to talk to him.'

'Sure thing, boss.'

'Stay in touch. This is good work, Sanderson.'

'Thank you.'

'But that doesn't excuse what happened this morning.' Helen lowered her voice. 'I'm sure you know that, so I won't labour the point – except to say that I expect every member of my team to work *together* regardless of their rank, temperament or personal history. Is that clear?'

'One hundred per cent.'

'I'm very glad to hear it.'

Sanderson watched on as Helen scooped up her jacket and marched from the office, handing out a few last tasks as she did so. As reprimands go, it had been brief and to the point – Sanderson knew she had escaped lightly. But there was still work to do. The decision to release Paul Jackson may have angered Charlie, but it also reflected badly on her. Helen clearly didn't believe he was guilty and Sanderson's call in arresting Jackson so publicly now looked very misguided.

Charlie had been right about her motivation. Sanderson *did* feel threatened by Charlie and the chance to grab some glory and emphasize her rival's tardiness was too good an opportunity to miss. She had hoped it would play well for her, but in fact it had achieved the very opposite. But all was not lost and a new lead, and a possible breakthrough in the case, could change everything. She would do whatever was in her power to remedy the situation because through all the backstabbing, insecurity and confusion one thing remained true – she craved the good opinion of DI Grace.

50

Emilia Garanita hit the hands-free button and punched in the number. She was the last person in the office and this was her final duty on what had been a tiring, but satisfactory day. She always replied to phone and email messages before the day was out – it was one of the things she prided herself on as a journalist, one of the things that singled her out from her peers. Once she was done, she would head home, open a bottle of wine and read tonight's edition.

It was an indulgence but she never got tired of seeing her words in print. It was just a provincial paper in some people's eyes – but to Emilia it had always been more than that. It was a city paper – her city – and it still excited her to see her byline and photo at the top of the page.

Today's spread was particularly good. Everyone knew that people in stressful, high-pressure jobs often had unusual ways of relieving the pressure, but, still, a respectable bank manager was an absolute gift. This story had all the best ingredients – murder, sex, betrayal – and was guaranteed to run and run. Not just because the killer was still at large, but also because the main suspect, Paul Jackson, was clearly leading a double life. He was happily married with two kids and, judging by the look on his wife's face, the revelation about his involvement in the Torture Rooms murder must have come as a complete shock to her, not to mention to their friends and neighbours.

It was the kind of story that would have people all over Southampton speculating about what *their* neighbours were up to after hours, so the *Evening News* had gone to town on it – Emilia once more enjoying a four-page spread all to herself. They'd mocked up an image of the crime scene, constructed a possible narrative of events and gone large on the views of a psychologist about the attraction of hardcore BDSM. The latter element had been part of their wide-ranging profile of Paul Jackson. They'd initially run shy of using his name, but once he was released on bail the gloves were off. Maybe he was guilty, maybe he wasn't. In some ways it didn't really matter – it was still great news, packed with secrets, lies and depravity.

The phone was still ringing, so Emilia clicked off and tried again. But she was growing tired now, so after another fifteen rings she hung up, heading for the exit. Whatever Max Paine wanted would have to keep for another day.

51

'Always nice to see a fresh face,' Max said as he straddled the chair and sat down to survey her. 'I've not seen you before, have I?'

'I'm just passing through.'

'You seem very well kitted out for someone who's in transit.'

'Oh, don't let this fool you, I'm very *green* really.'

Max Paine smiled. He loved the tease of this job and always responded to clients who were prepared to make their time together more than just a soulless exchange. They were the ones who became regulars, the ones with whom the job was always fun and never a chore.

'Well, let me take you in hand,' he suggested, walking over to her.

She was tall and thin with slicked black hair and striking eye make-up. It was a classic Berlin look and suited her down to the ground. Running his finger up her arm, he paused to knead the flesh beneath her shoulder blades. She exhaled happily, so he carried on running his hands down her back, sliding them round to the front. Continuing his progress, he ran them over her chest, before bringing them to rest on her crotch. The soft, pliable bulge that now began to harden to his touch revealed that this was going to be even more interesting than he'd imagined.

'Aren't you the girl that's got everything?' he said, rounding her to face her full on.

'You better believe it' was the impish reply.

Smiling, Max walked away, towards the locked cupboards at the back.

'We have two hours ahead of us, so why don't you choose your weapon?'

He opened the double doors of the wardrobe to reveal his arsenal of crops, whips, paddles, bats, maces and more. There was nothing he couldn't provide for his clients, nothing he hadn't tried.

'You're very sweet, but I wonder if we might use a couple of things *I've* brought along with me. I've never used them and I might need a little help.'

Without waiting for an answer, she now walked across to the drawstring bag she'd dropped by the door on arrival. Max watched, intrigued, as she drew a series of restraints and a large Zentai suit from within. The tight-fitting suit looked brand new, the spandex glistening in the beams of the ceiling spotlights.

'I know we've only just met, but I'd like us to push things a little tonight. I want Edge Play. Can you stretch to that?'

Normally Max wouldn't rush to do this on a first meeting, but she seemed to know what she was taking on, so, nodding, he moved forward to pick up the Zentai suit. But, as he did so, she laid a gloved hand on his arm.

'The thing is, Max,' she continued in a whisper, 'I want *you* to be *my* bitch tonight. Are you willing to be my bitch?'

Max paused, turning to her. She was attractive and commanding and didn't seem like a psychopath, but you could never be sure.

'That's a bit rich for a first date,' he said. 'Maybe when we know each other a little better.'

'Pity, but have it your own way,' she replied, putting the suit down. 'These are troubled times. Everyone's running scared at the moment, which is why I was willing to pay so much. But, as you say, another time –'

'How much?'

Paine hated himself for asking, but he couldn't resist. He hadn't paid his rent in over three months and lived in daily fear of eviction.

'Five hundred pounds if you're a bad boy. A thousand if you're a very bad boy.'

His client removed a wedge of twenty-pound notes and placed them on the table.

'What do you say, Max? Can I tempt you?'

Max looked her up and down – there wasn't much to her – then, shrugging his shoulders, he relented. Walking towards her, he smiled warmly and said:

'I'm all yours.'

52

'You can't barge in here like this.'

'I didn't barge in anywhere, Dennis. I rang the doorbell and your mum let me in.'

The mention of his mother provoked a visible flinch. Dennis was pushing fifty, overweight and underemployed and clearly had mixed feelings about living at the family home. Geraldine Fitzgerald was a slim, punctilious septuagenarian, who could now be heard preparing tea in the kitchen. Helen imagined she would do it the proper way – warming the pot, using leaf tea – and wondered if her domestic regimen was as meticulous and old-fashioned. Did she still ask her adult son to tidy his room?

'Haven't you people done enough already?'

'"You people"?'

'We don't do anything illegal, we don't do anything *wrong*. You've no right to send spies to our gatherings –'

'Well, if people don't talk to us, what can we do?'

Dennis eyeballed her, but said nothing.

'Everyone in the BDSM community *says* they are shocked by Jake Elder's murder,' Helen told him. 'Yet nobody has come forward to help us. Which makes me wonder how deep their concern is.'

'Fuck you.'

'Careful now, Dennis, mother might hear . . .'

Dennis shot her another venomous look, but said nothing. The sound of clinking crockery drifted in from the kitchen.

'I think you're rather more interested in protecting yourself. You can dress it up as suspicion of the police, but I think it's more about keeping your little secret safe. Don't get me wrong, I understand that and I have no desire to make your life difficult so –'

'How did you find me?' he interrupted.

'The Brother*Hood* website. IP address of the site runner is registered to this address. Electoral register has a Geraldine and Dennis Fitzgerald living here. It took one of our data officers less than five minutes to locate you. Hardly a secret society.'

'And are you harassing the others too?'

'No, just you, Dennis. Because you have something I want.'

Helen took the photo of Michael Parker from her bag and handed it to him.

'Do you recognize this person?'

Dennis took a cursory look at it, then handed it back.

'Look at it, Dennis. Or I swear I'll arrest you for obstructing police business.'

As Helen raised her voice, the clinking of crockery in the kitchen stopped. Helen could see small beads of sweat appearing on Dennis's forehead.

'We know he's got form, Dennis. Was this the person who hurt you? Is this "Samantha"?'

Dennis said nothing, but Helen noted that his hand was shaking slightly as he held the photo.

'If you're worried for your safety –'

'It's not that –'

'Or concerned about giving up a fellow member of your community, then I'm happy to make this an anonymous tipoff. But a young man has died here and we need to talk to anyone who might be connected.'

Dennis's mother was on the move now, so he spoke quickly.

'I don't know where she lives. But, yes, it's her.'

'You never went to her flat, a place of work?'

'She got in touch over the internet, we only ever met in neutral spaces. Clubs, hotel rooms –'

'Come on, Dennis,' Helen cajoled, 'give me *something* here.'

'But I do know that she sometimes performs at The End of the Road.'

Helen breathed out, relieved. The End of the Road was a gay bar in central Southampton that specialized in drag acts and cabaret.

'She's a performer?'

'Sometimes she works behind the bar, other times she performs. Calls herself "Pandora" when she's on stage. To be honest, I've avoided her since . . . you know . . . but she probably still works there.'

'And do you think she could be responsible for Jake Elder's death? Does she have it in her?'

Dennis thought for a moment then gave her back the photo.

'Yes, I do.'

Nodding, Helen took the photo from him. Right

on cue, his mother appeared in the doorway. Thanking Dennis for his help and reassuring the curious Geraldine that there was nothing to worry about, Helen took her leave.

As she walked briskly to her bike, her eyes remained glued to the photo still in her hand.

Was this the face of their killer?

53

'There, that didn't hurt now, did it?'

Her voice was soft, but had an edge. Max could tell she was excited by what they'd done. And what was still to come.

He had stripped for her – much to her evident pleasure – then slipped on the Zentai suit that she'd brought with her. It was a snug fit – she was clearly far more experienced than she let on – and it covered him from head to toe. Max hadn't done much Zentai before, the oriental stuff wasn't really his bag, but he liked the way he looked. He was like a kind of depraved Spiderman, every inch of him covered in black spandex.

It was an odd thing to be inside. You could still hear, but the sound was muffled, you could still see, but everything was a little darker. You felt different, not like yourself, the strangeness of the situation underlined for Max by the fact that he was the one taking the beating, rather than handing it out. This was not the norm and given recent events he had been tempted to refuse. But she seemed in control of herself and the blows she was giving him were mild. Besides, he wasn't inclined to believe the fevered tabloid speculation about there being a killer at large in their community. He wouldn't be at all surprised if Jake Elder's death turned out to be an accident with the press turning it into something it wasn't.

Max suddenly realized that she had stopped. He was still bent over the wooden horse and, straightening up, he saw that she had retreated to her little bag of tricks once more.

'Hog ties,' she said, holding up the leather and chain contraption triumphantly. 'I think we've both had enough of the nursery slopes, don't you?'

Max crossed the room to where she was now pointing.

'No more talking from now on. Just do as I say,' she ordered.

Max nodded, enjoying the game.

'Get down on your knees. Good, now arms behind your back.'

Max did as he was told. He felt her secure his ankles in the leather restraints then, pulling his arms sharply down and back until his fingers were almost touching the upturned soles of his feet, she secured those too. All four restraints – two wrists, two ankles – were joined by a series of short, metal chains, making it virtually impossible for him to move.

He was on his knees now and utterly at her mercy. His mouth was dry and he could feel his heart beating fast. She'd said she was into Edge Play – he suspected he was about to find out exactly what her version of that was. He heard her move towards him and seconds later she lowered herself to his level. Her cheek brushed against his and he couldn't conceal his growing excitement when she finally whispered:

'Let the games begin.'

54

Paul Jackson stepped into the garage and closed the connecting door firmly behind him. He had tried to talk to Sally three times now. The first couple of times she'd just shut the bedroom door on him, but on the third she'd finally found her voice – telling him to pack his bags and go.

He hadn't been expecting that. He had thought she would let him stay, as they tried to work out what to do next. He'd wrongly assumed that that was partly why the boys were being looked after elsewhere – to give them time to talk.

But she didn't want him in the house. In fact she barely seemed able or willing to look at him. The last twenty-four hours had been beyond awful but this was the straw that finally broke the camel's back and he'd sobbed as he'd begged for her forgiveness. He *loved* her – in spite of everything he'd done, he loved her now more than ever.

But she was deaf to his pleas, refusing to engage with him. And though the thought of facing the assembled journalists filled him with dread, he had eventually complied, pulling the small suitcase from the shelf in the wardrobe and throwing a few odds and ends into it. He never went away, never travelled for his work and it all seemed like a ghastly pantomime as he tossed his socks, shirts and toiletries into the suitcase, heading off on a journey that he had no desire to make.

Zapping the car open, he raised the boot and dropped the suitcase inside. It fell with a dull thud, the sound echoing off the brickwork that surrounded him. They'd only had the garage done a few months ago. It was supposed to be his space. What a pointless waste of money it seemed now.

He climbed into the driver's seat and picked up the remote control for the garage doors. Was this it then? His departure from the family home? Inside was nothing but desolation and despair. And outside? A mass of prurient journalists, idlers and neighbours keen to enjoy his disgrace, not to mention two innocent boys who would never look at their dad in the same way again. It was hideous to contemplate.

Which is why he put down the remote control without pressing it, reaching instead for the car keys. Then, winding down all four windows, he sat back in his seat and, closing his eyes, started up the engine.

55

She hurried along the street, taking care to avoid the fast-food wrappers, empty pint glasses and the occasional pool of vomit. It was Thursday night in Southampton and the drinkers were out in force.

The End of the Road was in the heart of Sussex Place and Helen pushed her way through the post-pub crowds to get to it. There was a long queue snaking from the entrance, but Helen bypassed this, heading straight for the bouncer and presenting him her warrant card.

Inside, the party was in full swing. The cavernous bar was a sea of peacock feathers, sequins and elaborate eye make-up – punters and staff alike dressing to impress. Sleekly dressed in her biking leathers, Helen fitted in pretty well, receiving several complimentary catcalls as she jostled to the bar. But she ignored them – something told her that speed was of the essence tonight.

She had to bellow to be heard at the bar. The bartender looked unimpressed by her enquiries but sloped off anyway. Cursing under her breath, Helen turned away to examine the scene. Her eye was immediately drawn to a poster for 'Pandora', frayed round the edges, but still in pride of place on the far wall. Helen drank in the face – even with the deep-gold eye shadow, and generously applied rouge there was a coldness to the face that was unnerving.

'Can I help you?'

Helen turned to find a short, bald man looking at her across the bar. Craig Ogden owned The End of the Road and was clearly unnerved by the presence of a police officer in his bar on a busy Thursday night.

'I need to speak to Samantha. You may also know her as Pandor—'

'Both.'

'She works here?'

'She does the late shift. Can I ask what this is about?'

'When are you expecting her?' Helen replied, ignoring the question.

'Well, she was due in at ten. But she called in sick.'

'When?'

'Just as we were opening,' he replied, his frustration clear.

'Where can I find her? Do you have an address?'

'We did, but she moved a few weeks back. Hasn't told us where she is now. She might be living in a skip for all I know. She's not the type to encourage questions and God alone knows where she ends up at night . . .'

'A phone number then?'

'I can see if we have anything on file, but to be honest I inherited her from the last manager and the record keeping at this place has never bee—'

'But she phoned you earlier,' Helen insisted. 'You must have her –'

'Number withheld. Fuck knows why . . .'

'What about friends then?' Helen said, increasingly exasperated now. 'Or colleagues? Is there anyone here who might know where I can find her?'

'Ask around, by all means,' Ogden replied, shrugging. 'To be honest, I kept well clear of her. Sometimes you can just see it in the eyes, right?'

Ogden was in full flow now, but Helen was scarcely listening, turning to look at the hundreds of revellers who were packed into the club. It would be like looking for a needle in a haystack.

Helen ended the conversation and pushed through the crowds, keen to escape the din. She wanted to get back to Southampton Central, touch base with Sanderson and see if the team had made any progress. Helen had been in an optimistic frame of mind after her chat with Dennis, pleased to have a lead on the elusive Samantha at last. But now she was leaving The End of the Road empty-handed and frustrated, plagued by the feeling that Samantha was vanishing from their radar for a reason. She had vowed to get justice for Jake but she was still no closer to catching his killer.

A promising lead had just gone up in smoke.

56

The sweat was oozing down his forehead, creeping into his eyes. It was incredibly hot in the Zentai suit and his discomfort was increasing by the second. What had started out as a tantalizing, transgressive game was now becoming unpleasant and unnerving.

He shook his head to dislodge the sweat, but only succeeded in making himself feel dizzy. His heart was racing and the clinging material of the suit was making it hard to breathe. For a moment, he thought he might faint, something he'd never done before. That could be disastrous in a BDSM situation, so gathering himself he said:

'Liberty.'

This was their safe word, but his voice was cracked and his resulting call weak. He wasn't surprised she hadn't heard it, so he said it again, louder this time.

'Liberty.'

Still nothing. He knew she was still here – he could hear her moving. So why wasn't she responding? It wasn't done to tease someone in this situation. If you heard the word, you stopped everything.

'Liberty,' he screamed, fear suddenly getting the better of him.

He heard her moving towards him now and tears

sprang to his eyes. He was still furious with her, but if she let him go now, then . . . He heard something tearing now. What was that? Was she cutting him out of this suit? Cutting his bonds? Then suddenly he felt something strike his face. He jumped, shocked by the impact, and too late realized what was happening. The tearing sound had been her ripping off some duct tape – tape which she had just stuck over his mouth.

'Let me go.'

He bellowed the words, but the tape held, muting his cry.

'I'd love to, sweetheart, but we've only just begun.'

The last word was said with such emphasis that for a second Max thought he was going to vomit. Fear now mastered him completely – he suddenly realized that he had made a terrible mistake in playing her games and that because of this misjudgement he was about to die.

57

Charlie stifled a yawn and looked at the clock. It was nearly midnight – she had another two hours before she was relieved. If Helen wanted to punish Charlie, she was doing a good job. Steve had complained about being dragooned into emergency childcare yet again and Charlie was irritated too – with Sanderson, with Helen, but mostly with herself. When had she become so brittle? She used to be the fun, cheeky officer who everyone got on with. Now she was exhausted, short-tempered and *paranoid*. She didn't regret starting a family for one second, but there were a lot of hidden costs that nobody told you about and she was feeling those now.

Outside, the press pack's enthusiasm was starting to wane. It was cold and a thin drizzle floated down the street, saturating all those still out and about. Most of the journalists had retreated to their vehicles, experience teaching them that you can catch your death on a night like this. Those that remained outside were swathed in thick North Face jackets, praying that the weather would clear. They would have gone home some time ago, but for the light that stole underneath the garage door. Somebody had turned it on a while back and, as the family car was stored in there, everyone present was expecting Jackson to make a break for it.

Charlie assumed it was Paul Jackson, as she'd seen his wife head upstairs a few hours ago. The gaggle of photographers that haunted the property was hoping to grab a through-the-window shot of him fleeing his home. There was something about the angle and context of those shots that always made the subject look guilty. Editors loved them, which is why people were prepared to brave the elements to get them.

Charlie flicked through the radio stations again. If Paul Jackson was smart, he'd turn the light off and head to bed. The best way to deal with journalists was to starve them of what they craved. By hanging about he was just raising their hopes. Finding little to divert her, Charlie switched off the radio and stole another look at the clock. Ten past midnight.

Had Paul Jackson been banished to the garage? Surely not. There were plenty of bedrooms in the house, so even if his wife didn't want anything to do with him . . . Charlie looked over at the garage again. Paul Jackson's sons were elsewhere and his wife had stormed off upstairs, meaning he was in the garage alone. And had been for thirty minutes or more.

Charlie now found herself opening the door and stepping out into the rain. It settled on her face, gentle and cold, but she didn't bother pulling her hood up as she marched towards the garage. If she was wrong, then she wouldn't mind getting a little wet. But if she was right . . .

She walked straight up to the metal garage door and put her ear to it. A motorbike roared past in the road and a couple of news hacks now shouted at her, ribbing her for doing their job for them. She waved at them to shut up but it made no difference. Furious, Charlie dropped to all fours, her knees soaking up the moisture from the ground. She placed her ear at the bottom of the metal door, where the narrowest chink allowed a little light to escape. She was listening for the sound of the engine, but it wasn't the noise that struck her first. It was the smell.

Now Charlie was on her feet, yanking at the garage handle. But it was locked from the inside and refused to budge. She re-doubled her efforts, but still nothing.

'Get over here now,' she roared at the startled photographers.

The look on her face made them comply.

'Get that open now.'

As they grappled with the door, Charlie raced up the steps. She rang the doorbell once, twice, three times, then opened the letterbox and yelled through it. There was no time for hesitation, no time for caution. This was a matter of life and death.

58

He was straining with every sinew, but getting nowhere. The fabric of the suit was smooth and the wooden floor so perfectly polished, that the more he moved, the more he spun in pointless circles. He couldn't get any purchase and his attacker watched now as he exerted himself in vain. It was strangely moving to behold. *This* was what somebody looked like in their death throes.

It had all gone to plan. The only moment of danger had come when Paine had screamed to be liberated. That had been a surprise – a testament to his instinct for danger or perhaps his innate lack of trust in his new 'client'. It was a mistake, but a small one. Duct tape had been quickly applied to the mouth and the danger had passed.

The foreplay had been completed, the preparatory work done – now it was time for the coup de grâce. Had the thrashing figure on the ground made the connection to Jake Elder's death or was he as clueless as the rest? By the looks of things, he was still in denial, desperately trying to belly-slide towards the door. What was he going to do when he got there? Open it with his feet? It was a crazy last throw of the dice, but there was a possibility that his banging might alert a neighbour. So, crossing the room quickly, the figure lowered the rope from the ceiling pulley and slipped it through the hog ties, tying them together in a secure, grapevine knot under Paine's wrists.

Alerted by the sound of the pulley, Paine bucked even more wildly, but, in the end, what could he do? His attacker yanked the rope tight and Paine lurched up into the air. He was only a few inches off the ground but this sudden development clearly alarmed him – he swung back and forth on the rope, as he made one last, desperate push to escape. It was hard to hang on, but his assailant moved steadily backwards, pulling sharply with each step, until Paine was safely suspended in mid-air. Securing the rope firmly to a wall hook, the figure then stood back to admire its handiwork – Paine, covered from head to toe in spandex, spinning in the air like an obscene mobile.

This had been more arduous than expected but the hard graft was done. Moving quickly, the figure now walked in and out of the bedroom, lifting a tablet and smartphone from the bedside table and popping both of them in a zip bag.

Satisfied, the figure headed for the doorway, flipping down the white plastic flap on the thermostat by the entrance. Casting a last look at Paine, his attacker punched the central heating up to the max, then quietly slipped out of the door.

59

The doors burst open and the medical team hurried through in the direction of the intensive care unit. Paul Jackson lay on the hospital trolley next to them, an oxygen mask secured over his mouth and nose. His ashen wife ran alongside, occasionally laying a hand on his, but he didn't react. He had been unconscious when they found him.

Charlie followed a few feet behind, keen to see what was happening, but anxious not to get in anybody's way. Paul Jackson was dying and every second counted. She had eventually roused Sally Jackson, who seemed stupefied at first, barely believing what the desperate police officer was saying. When she had finally unchained the front door, Charlie had raced straight past, navigating her way by instinct towards the internal door that connected to the garage. Jackson had locked it from the inside, so Charlie had had to kick it in.

As soon as she had done so, great clouds of noxious fumes swept over her. Visibility had been poor, but the smell even worse. Clamping her scarf over her mouth, Charlie had pushed through the lethal haze, feeling her way towards the car. Fortunately, Jackson hadn't locked the doors – if he had, it would have been all over for him. As it was, she had managed to manoeuvre the comatose figure on to the floor, just as the journalists on the other side finally levered the garage door open.

Putting her hands underneath his armpits, Charlie had dragged him out of the garage, laying him in the recovery position in the fresh air outside. Moments later, the ambulance had arrived and Charlie's leading role in events was over. Leaving Sally to join her husband in the ambulance, Charlie had hurried over to her car, receiving a few respectful nods from journalists as she went – their mutual hostility suspended for a few hours at least.

The paramedics had done their best, but Jackson remained unconscious as the medical team now pushed through the double doors and into ITC. Sally Jackson hesitated, aware that this was as far as she was allowed to go, turning to Charlie as if looking for guidance. Charlie knew from experience that family members in this situation always wanted to do something to help, but the truth was that there was very little they could do. It was in the hands of the doctors and surgeons at South Hants Hospital now. Putting her arm around her, Charlie shepherded her towards a vacant chair. Greater tests lay ahead and she would need to preserve her strength.

As she did so, Charlie reflected on her earlier irritations. She realized now how unworthy those thoughts were, how petty her complaints. Life had its frustrations, but in reality she was blessed. She possessed one thing that Sally Jackson might never experience again – a happy, healthy, loving family. And for that she was eternally grateful.

60

Helen laid down her flowers and kissed the headstone in front of her. It was gone 2 a.m. and the driving rain raked the lonely cemetery, but still Helen lingered, pressing her forehead against the cool stone. She had been on her feet for nearly forty-eight hours, but was too wired and upset to return home. She would rather be doing something – anything – than pace her flat, and, besides, this was a duty she never shirked. Marianne was family, so every Thursday night after hours Helen came here, to tend her graveside and leave flowers for the sister she had loved and lost.

Offering a few final words of love, Helen turned and walked down the path. She had hoped a simple act of kindness, of remembrance, might dispel the darkness growing within her – but her conscience weighed heavily on her tonight. She had only just got back to base when Charlie rang. She was racing to the hospital, panicking and upset, and her news had hit everyone hard. Paul Jackson had been a decent suspect, but now he was fighting for his life.

Had they driven an innocent man to suicide? The press had to take some of the blame, but so did her officers. It would play hard on Sanderson's conscience whatever the outcome, but it was ultimately *her* fault – the team was Helen's responsibility and, in failing to identify the growing hostility between her DSs, she had committed an unforgiveable oversight. If he died, they would all have to answer for it.

Helen had reached the gates now and paused to look down over Southampton. It was a dark, brooding night, relentless bands of rain sweeping over the city, and the lights twinkled mischievously below, as if revelling in the dark deeds that go undetected at night. Helen instinctively felt that their latest thinking was right – that someone within the BDSM community was responsible for Jake's murder. Samantha was potentially a good fit but, if so, why had she suddenly snapped? What had Jake done to provoke such savage treatment? And where was she now? As ever, there were more questions than answers.

The rain continued to sweep the hillside, but Helen didn't move. She remained stock still, a lone figure lost in her thoughts, surrounded on all sides by death.

61

'It's so nice to meet you. I just wish it could have been in happier circumstances.'

Emilia gave David Simons her best happy-but-sad smile. Jake Elder's former boyfriend had arrived on the first train from London and Emilia had been waiting for him. It was highly unlikely that another journalist would have got wind of his arrival in Southampton, but she'd decided not to take any chances, whisking him from the station back to base. They were now tucked away in her small office, breakfasting on strong coffee and the best doughnuts Southampton had to offer. In Emilia's experience, sugar was the best medicine for grief.

Simons was jetlagged following his flight from Los Angeles, which only exacerbated his disorientation and distress. Emilia had the sense that tears weren't far away and she was keen to keep him on track, gently coaxing his story from him.

'So you and Jake were together for . . .'

'Six, seven months.'

'And you saw each other regularly during that period?'

'Pretty much every day.'

'And how would you characterize your relationship?'

'Good. Very good at first. He was so generous and kind –'

'And then?'

Simons looked up at her, a flash of irritation crossing his face. Emilia sensed he was irked to have been dragged away from happy memories to the painful reality, but she didn't let her concern show.

'Most of the time it was great, but fairly early on it became clear that there were . . . limits to our relationship.'

Emilia leant forward.

'Meaning?'

'That I wanted more than he did.'

Emilia nodded, but said nothing.

'Contrary to the rumours, not all gay men are promiscuous,' he continued. 'I've only ever had long-term relationships – don't see the point in the other –'

'And you were hoping that Jake might be a keeper?'

'Isn't that what everyone's looking for?'

Emilia smiled, keeping her counsel. Was that what she was after? She'd had relationships of course, but they had been brief – her work schedule and family responsibilities always conspiring to kill off any potential romance. And now, after so long, she wondered if she was actually capable of commitment.

'So what was the problem?' she replied eventually, interested in his answer for more than just professional reasons.

'His heart wasn't in it.'

'Because?'

'Are you always this fucking blunt?'

Now his anger was clear. Emilia had misjudged how brittle he was and hurried to recover lost ground.

'I'm sorry if I sound rude. It's early mornings – I'm no good at them and I've a tendency to put my foot in my mouth. All I'm *trying* to do is get a sense of what you've been through. But please don't answer if you don't want to. I'm very happy to put you in touch with the police if you'd prefer, so you can get the answers you want from them.'

This had the desired effect. The police had clearly been in contact with Simons, but Emilia sensed that he'd been evasive about the precise date of his arrival in the UK. He seemed keen to avoid contact with them for as long as possible. In the meantime, Emilia was a useful source of information for him – it would pay him to keep her onside, despite his evident distress.

'I'm sorry, I'm just very tired . . .'

'Of course you are,' Emilia responded gently, offering him another doughnut. 'And there's no need to talk about anything you don—'

'He was in love with someone else, ok? He loved me in his own way but there was a part of him I couldn't reach.'

'I see. And do you have any idea who this other person was –'

'I glimpsed them talking once, but it was nobody I recognized.'

'Can you describe him for me?'

'Actually it was a she. Tall, shoulder-length hair, pretty.'

Intrigued, Emilia scribbled the description down before asking:

'So what happened?'

'I confronted him about it. He denied that he had feelings for her but he was lying, so I pushed it. He told me more and . . . well, I was bloody upset, so I called it a day. I've been in this situation before. And I didn't want the end of our relationship to be death by a thousand cuts.'

'You went your separate ways?'

'I took some work in the States. Tried to put as much distance between Jake and myself as possible. I'm not sure it worked though.'

Emilia kept her eyes glued to his as she scribbled – *female lover?* – on her pad. The tears that had threatened were coming now and she had the strong sense that this poor guy, who had loved Jake so much during his short life, now loved him even more in death.

62

He hammered on the door with his stick, but there was no response from inside. What was it with these people? Did they think that paying rent was optional?

Cursing, Gary Lushington looked down at the little book in his hand. There it was in black and white – rent arrears going back over three months. Paine had been a good tenant at first – if you ignored what he got up to for a living – but he'd been evasive and moody of late, which made Gary nervous. That type of behaviour usually meant only one thing – him ending up out of pocket. And that wasn't something he was prepared to allow.

Muttering, he leant against the door and, pulling the key chain from his pocket, began to search for his duplicate set. As he did so, he became aware of a very strange sensation. His back felt warm against the door – no, more than that, it felt *hot*. Gary pulled away quickly, turning to face the doorway.

And now he became aware that this corridor *was* markedly hotter than the couple he'd already visited on his rounds. He'd assumed his clamminess was the result of all those stairs – they were harder for him now he had to use a stick to get about – but now he realized that the heat he felt was emanating from within the flat. What the bloody hell was Paine thinking? It was a nice autumnal morning, for God's sake – there was no need to have the heating on full blast.

Suddenly Gary was seized by a nasty thought. Perhaps Paine had gone away, leaving the heating on. He might even have done a bunk, leaving his landlord with a hefty heating bill as a final fuck you.

Pushing the key firmly into the lock, Gary turned it hard and pushed the door open. Calling Paine's name angrily, he stepped forward, but almost immediately found himself stumbling backwards again. Crashing into the wall opposite, he remained rooted to the spot, momentarily stunned into silence. The temperature within the flat was *overwhelming* and a wave of choking heat now flooded out, crawling over the shocked landlord and escaping down the corridor beyond. But it wasn't this that rendered Gary Lushington speechless, nor even the sight of a figure hanging from the ceiling. No, what really stopped him in his tracks this morning was the smell.

63

All eyes were on her. The team had gathered in the briefing room for the morning update, looking to Helen for guidance and inspiration. But she felt empty this morning – despite a few hours' sleep she was still running on fumes – and had nothing new to give them. She had never been this deep into an investigation with so little to go on, and the morning papers – with their graphic accounts of Paul Jackson's suicide bid – had done little to improve her mood. Everyone at Southampton Central, from her DCs right up to the Chief Super himself, had been rattled by this unexpected development.

'The good news is that Paul Jackson is stable,' Helen said, as she continued her briefing. 'He's still in ICU, but he's conscious and the early signs are that there won't be any permanent damage to his brain or lungs. He's in a bad way, but the doctors are reassured that there's no immediate danger to his life, which is in no small part thanks to the decisive intervention of DS Brooks.'

Charlie acknowledged the compliment with a brief nod, but kept her eyes fixed to the floor. Was this to avoid meeting Helen's gaze or Sanderson's? Helen hoped it was the latter – evidence perhaps that her DSs had decided against antagonizing each other further.

'I know you were all shocked by last night's events,' Helen said, addressing the team once more. 'But right now we have to keep our focus on the case. How are we doing on the Snapchatters?'

'We've ruled out seventeen of the twenty now,' Edwards informed them. 'Nothing that links any of them to the club. Once we've run down the last three, we'll widen our field – look at Elder's emails, texts –'

'We've also just heard that David Simons is in the country,' DC Lucas interrupted gently. 'The Border Agency confirmed he landed at Heathrow last night. We'll get him in as soon as we can, but he's not in any hurry to contact us.'

'Keep on it. In the meantime, let's focus our attentions on possible suspects within the BDSM community, specifically "Samantha", formerly known as Michael Parker. The Edge of the Road has provided a mobile phone number, but it's not currently in use. I want us to investigate when and where that phone last made calls. Also, we have three former addresses for her, all of which she's spent time at within the last two years. We need to be knocking on doors, seeing if any neighbours or friends know where she might be now. Also, let's talk again to people who were at the club, the taxi drivers who were working that night – let's see if we can place her at the Torture Rooms. Any relevant info – good or bad – I want to hear about it straight away.'

Helen was about to move on to allocating individual tasks, when she saw the custody sergeant approaching. Nodding to Sanderson to take over, Helen drew him aside. The look on his face suggested he had something important to tell her.

'Uniform were called to an unusual death this morning,' he said quietly. 'We don't have all the facts, but it appears the victim was suspended from the ceiling in some sort of all-in-one body suit.'

Helen's heart sank, even as he said it. Gathering herself, she replied:

'Any marks on him, any signs of violence?'

'Not that I'm aware of. The boys are saying the place is in mint condition and that the whole thing looks kind of staged.'

Helen nodded, but her heart was beating fast.

'Do you have the address?'

The custody sergeant handed Helen a piece of paper, then withdrew. Helen was glad he'd done so, because as she looked at the address in her hand she got a nasty shock. She had only visited the address on two occasions but she knew exactly whom it belonged to. A man she loathed and hoped she'd never see again.

Max Paine.

64

What was wrong with her? She should be feeling relieved, elated, excited, but she felt none of these things. Her body ached, her brain throbbed – she was a mess.

Samantha lay on the bathroom floor, resting her forehead on the cold tiles. Returning to the flat last night, she had downed an entire bottle of vodka. Perhaps it was the adrenaline of the evening, perhaps the vodka was just low grade – either way she'd brought it all back up again an hour later. She normally never vomited but last night she couldn't stop, gagging on the bitter bile that was all she had left at the end.

If she'd had the energy, she'd gladly have killed herself. Her life was an endless merry-go-round of high hopes and crushing disappointments – each one harder to stomach than the last. She knew she was a work in progress, but still . . . Why were the highs so high and lows so low? Perhaps all those shrinks had been right after all. Perhaps she *was* a bad person.

Putting an unsteady hand on the sink, Samantha hauled herself upright. Turning on the tap, she cupped her hands together to collect the cold water and drank greedily from them. Then she threw the soothing water on to her face – she was burning up – and ran her wet fingers through her hair. A deep, sulphurous burp ensued and suddenly she was vomiting again, the water she'd just consumed disappearing down the plughole with obscene haste. It was as if the water couldn't stomach her, rather than the other way around.

Samantha dropped back down to the floor, exhausted and defeated. There was no point fighting it now and she finally gave way to despair. It was cruel but there was no point denying it. She had tried to embrace this world, but it always rejected her, raising the level of punishment each time. She was gone – dead behind the eyes now – and felt hollow, empty and utterly alone.

65

The SOCOs had already lowered the body to the ground and removed his clothing for further analysis. The victim now lay on the floor, naked save for a sterile sheet. It wasn't much dignity, but it was the best that they could do in the circumstances.

Crouching down, Helen used the tip of her pen to lift a corner of the sheet. She knew what to expect, but still it was horrific to behold. In life, Paine had been a handsome man, but now his face was waxy and mottled – numerous burst blood vessels giving his expression an unpleasant patchwork quality. He looked like he had exploded from within.

Helen shuddered silently. She had disliked – no, she had despised – Max Paine. He was a violent misogynist who took pleasure in bullying and degrading women. She had used his services a couple of times and had had cause to regret her decision, only escaping a dangerous situation by fighting her way out of his clutches. But still she wouldn't have wished *this* on him. This didn't seem like a similar situation, this wasn't a question of Paine overstepping the mark. This was a well-organized and premeditated attack on his life. This was an execution.

What connected Jake Elder and Max Paine? They

were two very different characters who'd chosen the same profession. Helen knew both of them – one intimately, one in passing. Was that important? If so, it was hard to see why. Max Paine was hardly a friend of hers and as far as she was aware the rest of the world wouldn't miss him either. So what was the point of his death? Were he and Jake chosen specifically or had they just hooked up with the wrong client? It seemed increasingly likely that their attacker *was* from the BDSM community, but the motive was still unclear.

Dropping the sheet, Helen stood up. She would not mourn Paine, but his death was still distressing and alarming. If the two victims were connected, then Helen was the obvious link. But if they weren't, the outlook was even worse. Helen and her team had put so much work in trying to link their killer directly to Jake Elder, but maybe they had been barking up the wrong tree? Perhaps it was the act of murder, not the identity of the victim, which was driving the killer here.

If so, then there was no telling when he might stop. Killing was like a drug – the appetite becoming sharper and more urgent with each successive act. If their killer was getting off on his total control over his victims – and his seeming ability to strike without attracting attention – then what would possibly induce him to stop? Helen had a nasty feeling that he was just hitting his stride.

Having exchanged a few words with Meredith, Helen

headed through the front door. Introspection and fear would get her nowhere. Their perpetrator had just raised the stakes significantly and she *had* to respond. It was time to summon what resolve she could if she was to stop him from killing again.

66

'If anyone asks, you say it's a police incident and move them on. No exceptions.'

The constable guarding the entrance to the flat nodded solemnly. They seldom said anything when Helen spoke to them. Was that out of respect? Or fear? Helen couldn't tell.

'You're not to move from here until you're relieved. Somebody gained unauthorized access to the crime scene on Wednesday morning. If it happens again, I'll be asking you for an explanation. This is off limits.'

'What a pity. I skipped breakfast to get over here before the others.'

Helen knew that voice. Turning, she saw Emilia Garanita walking towards her.

'I was just talking about you,' Helen replied.

'All good, I hope?'

Helen didn't dignify that with a response, instead turning and walking fast away from the flats towards her bike.

'I will find out, you know.'

'Find out what?' Emilia replied, as she hurried to keep up.

'Who your mole is. And when I do, I'll have their badge and you up on a charge of bribing a public official.'

Emilia tut-tutted gently.

'Why do you always see the worst in people? I'm just a jobbing journalist, playing by the rules –'

'You're a ghoul who trades in people's misery,' Helen retorted.

'Come off it, Helen. I only report the facts, I can't help what people read into that.'

Helen stopped in her tracks and turned to face Emilia.

'I saw the hatchet job you did on Paul Jackson. What was the headline? "The double life of the boardroom spanker"?'

'I don't write the headlines –'

'Bullshit. It had your fingerprints all over it. You have no regard for the consequences of your irresponsible journalism.'

'Back up a little, I have a duty to the public –'

'You have a duty to be a human being.'

For a moment, Emilia looked stung, as if Helen's accusations had finally landed. Then she seemed to relax again, a thin smile crawling over her face.

'Is there a reason why you're getting so wound up about this particular case?'

Helen stared at Emilia scornfully, but said nothing.

'You haven't been at any of the press conferences, so I haven't been able to ask you about your personal reaction to Jake's death.'

'I've got nothing to say about that.'

'But you were acquaintances. Friends even . . .'

Helen stared at Emilia, but said nothing. She'd known this moment was coming – Emilia was not the type to forget a tasty bit of gossip or past arguments – but now it was here, Helen still felt rattled. There was no point denying her connection with Jake, but this was not an avenue she wanted to go down. There was no telling where it might lead – blackmail? Exposure? – and this time she had no weapon with which to squash the wily journalist.

'We were friends, but I hadn't seen him for a couple of years and I'm treating this case as I would any other.'

'Please don't lie to me, Helen,' Emilia replied. 'You were very close to him, you must be in turmoil. I'm surprised they let you lead on this.'

'You're way off the mark,' Helen lied.

'Am I? I spared you last time because you persuaded me that that was the right thing to do. But I'm seriously starting to question the wisdom of my decis—'

'You *spared* me?' Helen replied, incredulous. 'You spared yourself. If you'd printed that stuff I would have had you up on a charge of illegal surveillance. Don't kid yourself that you're a decent person, Emilia, because you're not.'

'Fighting talk,' Emilia replied tersely, irked by this character assassination. 'Let's see where it gets you, shall we?'

Happy that she'd had the last word, Emilia turned and walked back in the direction of the flats. She had won the first battle. The question now was whether she would win the war.

67

Helen barely registered the other road users as she biked back to Southampton Central. She was riding slowly for once – she needed to buy herself time to think. This case was becoming ever more complicated, with no immediate or obvious solution in sight. What had started as a terrible personal tragedy had grown into something darker and Helen now faced a fight on two fronts – bringing in a devious and elusive serial killer, while fending off the very real threat of exposure.

Strange to say, the latter terrified Helen as much as the former. Privacy and discretion had always been her watchwords – it was the only way she knew – but now she was backed into an impossible corner. It would not be easy to spike Emilia's guns, nor tell what she might do with the information she now held close. Emilia would know that any attempt at extortion would be rebuffed – Helen would rather sacrifice her career than be turned – so what other option did she have but to publish? A detailed and lengthy exposé, highlighting the terrible conflict of interest that Helen had swallowed in the interests of gaining justice? Helen could well imagine how that story would play with the top brass.

Helen knew that there was only one possible solution, but still she recoiled from it. She had never wanted anyone to know her properly, never wanted anyone to get close to her. Her life was like it was for a reason. But the cat was out of the bag now and the only remedy was to confess, before Emilia beat her to the punch. The thought made her feel sick – how could she even find the words to begin? – and there was no question of her opening herself up for general entertainment. No, if she did this it would have to be targeted, controlled and brief. And it would have to be now – there was no telling what Emilia would do and Helen refused to be driven off this case by public outrage.

Leaving her bike in the Southampton Central car park, Helen stopped to look up at the windows above. There was no point putting it off.

It was time to talk to Gardam.

68

Charlie stared at the unshaven lump opposite her, trying to hide her distaste as he crammed a dripping fried egg sandwich into his mouth. Chewing noisily, the middle-aged cabbie eventually looked up, catching her gaze.

'You having something?' he asked.

'I've already eaten,' Charlie replied, lying. She was trying to lose a bit of weight and the fare at the transport café didn't fit the bill.

'Suit yourself,' the cabbie replied, taking a noisy slurp of his coffee, before popping a chipolata in his mouth. Charlie was paying for his breakfast this morning and he was clearly going to get the most out of her generosity.

'You spoke to one of my colleagues yesterday?'

The cabbie nodded.

'You told her you were working on Tuesday night?'

'I work every night, love. Don't have a choice.'

Charlie smiled sympathetically.

'And you had an unusual pick-up between the hours of midnight and one a.m.'

The cabbie shrugged. 'You get all sorts doing a night shift. But this one was a bit odd.'

'Odd how?'

'Well, it was a bloke for a start. I thought she . . . he was a bird at first. Long legs, long hair, nice clothes and that. But the voice was too low and he had an Adam's apple, so . . .'

'So what specifically was odd?'

'You mean apart from that?' the cabbie replied, laughing.

'Come on, there are lots of gay pubs and cabaret bars in that area. You must see stuff like that all the time.'

'It was more the state of him,' he conceded.

'Go on.'

'I could hardly understand where he wanted to go at first. He was white as a sheet and he'd been crying. He was trying to suck it in, but his make-up was a horrible mess,' he laughed again. 'I wasn't going to let him in, but he gave me a twenty up front, so . . .'

'Where did you take him?'

'To an address in St Denys – Newton Street. Only cost a tenner, but he didn't care. Got straight out of the cab when we got there and didn't look back. You ask me, he was about to puke. I don't know what they take in these places but –'

'Can you describe him to me?'

The cabbie paused, then said:

'Tall, like I said. Thin, very thin. He was dressed in a kind of cat suit, so you could see there wasn't an ounce of fat on him. Hairless too – no stubble or anything.'

'Can you describe his face to me?'

'Dark eyes, no eyebrows except what was drawn on –'

'Anything on the sides of his face?'

'Yeah, now you mention it, he had a little scar on the right side of his face. Make-up couldn't hide that.'

Charlie nodded, then pulled a photo from the file on her lap.

'Was this the person you picked up on Tuesday night?' she asked, offering the cabbie the photo. He took it between his greasy fingers, then after a moment's consideration handed it back.

'Yeah, that's him.'

Charlie took the photo and, having confirmed the address of the drop-off, thanked the cabbie and hurried on her way. Finally they had something to work with.

Her cabbie had just placed Samantha near the scene of the first murder.

69

'Thank you for seeing me straight away,' Helen said, her confident tone failing to conceal her anxiety.

'My door is always open,' Gardam assured her calmly. 'How bad is it?'

'Bad. He's definitely our second victim.'

'How can you be sure?'

'The MO is slightly different, but the victim was made to suffer as much as is humanly possible and it was a highly "professional" execution. This was a statement killing, just like Elder's.'

Gardam took this in – he looked as sick as Helen felt. Then he said:

'So the flat is owned by this Max Paine? How sure are we that he's our victim?'

'One hundred per cent.'

'Right,' Gardam replied. 'I thought we were still trying to contact his next of kin –'

'We are, but I know him. That's what I wanted to talk to you about.'

'I see. Have you come across him in a case before, or . . . ?'

The 'or' was left hanging and Helen knew she had to fill the gap. If she didn't say it now she would lose the confidence to do so.

'This is very difficult for me to say . . . but it would be unprofessional of me not to do so,' Helen said, just about getting the words out.

Gardam said nothing. He was watching her intently, which only made it worse.

'I know Max Paine, in fact I know both victims, because I've used their services.'

Gardam's face didn't move at all, but Helen could tell he was shocked by what she'd just told him.

'I used Paine's services twice, about a year ago. Before that I used to visit Jake Elder on and off, but I haven't seen him in over two years.'

This wasn't the whole truth. Helen had decided to omit the beating she'd given Paine – this was difficult enough without admitting to a criminal act.

'Right. I see,' Gardam finally responded, not quite finding the words.

'I don't really want to go into the details,' Helen continued. 'But I thought you ought to know.'

'And you didn't think this was worth telling me after Elder's death?'

'No, I didn't,' Helen replied firmly. 'I hadn't seen him in ages and couldn't add anything useful to the investigation by doing so. But now that a second man known to me . . . well, I wanted to be upfront with you and offer to remove myself from the case – if that's what you'd like.'

Helen had debated long and hard whether to offer this up, but she knew she was duty-bound to. It was the only thing she could do, given the circumstances.

There was a long silence. As Gardam processed his response, Helen examined his face for signs of an instinctive reaction. What was he thinking? Had she irreparably damaged herself in his eyes?

'Thank you for sharing this, Helen,' Gardam finally replied. 'This can't have been an easy thing to bring up.'

'It wasn't, believe me.'

'Can I ask if anybody else knows of your connection to the victims?'

Helen paused, then, closing her eyes, bit the bullet.

'Emilia Garanita knows about my connection to Jake Elder.'

'Bloody hell.'

'But she obtained this knowledge illegally and if she's smart she'll keep quiet. She knows nothing of my connection to Paine.'

Helen could have said more but didn't. In reality it was highly unlikely she'd be able to stop Emilia with the threat of prosecution – the original offence having been so long ago – but she had to play any card she could with Gardam in order to try and stay on the case.

Gardam pondered his response. Impatient, Helen now blurted out:

'Look, if this is awkward, I can obviously take sick leave. I don't want to, but if you feel it would be for the best, then obviously it's something we should consid—'

'Well, let's review what we've got,' Gardam interrupted. 'You knew both victims and have a personal connection to the case. Were you in a relationship with either of them?'

'No. Of course not. I liked Jake as a human being, but that's it. Paine meant nothing to me.'

'Right.'

What was that in his tone? Was it pity?

'And do you think you'll be able to discharge your duties in this investigation as normal?' Gardam continued.

'Definitely.'

'You're not *too* invested in it?'

'I don't think so. I'd tell you if I was.'

'And how sure are we that Garanita will keep shtum?'

'Fairly, though there's no guarantee of course,' Helen lied quickly.

Gardam looked at her, his mind turning. Helen was suddenly aware she was holding her breath and exhaled gently, trying to calm herself.

'Well, it's not an easy decision. But . . . I'm minded to keep things as they are for now,' Gardam said decisively. 'These deaths are alarming and I need my best people on it.'

Helen nodded, more relieved than she could say. She was embarrassed to feel tears pricking her eyes.

'And don't worry, Helen,' Gardam reassured her. 'This will remain between us.'

Helen thanked him and went on her way, keeping her eyes to the floor. Outside in the corridor, she leant against the wall and brushed the offending tears away. Odd though it was, she almost felt happy. It had been a tough conversation to have to have, but she was pleased she'd grasped the nettle. It had cost her something to take Gardam into her confidence – to reveal her weakness to him – but she now felt free to drive the investigation forward. Marching towards the incident room, Helen pulled her mobile out and dialled Meredith's number. There could be no more delays, no more setbacks now. Jake Elder and Max Paine deserved justice and Helen was determined to see that they got it.

70

Charlie drained the dregs of her coffee and tossed the paper cup in the bin. Would it be bad to have another one straight away? She was tired, but more than that she was cold, despite the autumnal sunshine. She had been pacing Newton Street for over an hour now and had little to show for it, except a mild headache and blocks of ice for feet.

Her cabbie was certain that he'd dropped his ride off near the top of the road. There were several blocks of flats there, but a little basic detective work in the shops and cafés had established that Samantha had been seen coming out of Ellesmere Heights on occasion. It was a fairly sorry-looking set-up and no one was answering the buzzers, despite Charlie having pressed them all several times. There had been nothing to do but watch and wait, so she'd parked herself on a bench outside the launderette with a coffee and a free sheet, arming herself with a puffed-out but empty laundry bag by way of cover. She seemed to spend most of her life on surveillance these days and she hungered for something a bit more challenging. The numerous lattes she was consuming were doing nothing for her waistline.

As the minutes, then hours, ticked by, Charlie's decision to keep this lead to herself began to trouble her. It was quite probable she was wasting her time and, besides, Helen had reiterated the importance of everyone sharing information from now on. But still . . . every lead Charlie had pursued so far had proved fruitless. Paul Jackson was a disaster and they were still trying to locate David Simons, though in truth no one genuinely thought he was a suspect. Which just left Michael Parker, aka Samantha. Charlie knew why she was keeping this lead to herself, and she knew it didn't reflect well on her, but still she sat here, ignoring the occasional buzz of her phone, intent on seeing it through.

How much longer could she stay? She would have to account for her time eventually and the longer she left it, the harder it would be to explain away. She was already in Helen's bad books, so why risk their friendship further by escalating her war with Sanderson? When all she might end up with for her pains was a stinking cold?

She rose to head back to the coffee shop and almost walked straight into Samantha. It took a moment for her to compute who it was – Charlie was busy apologizing for getting in her way when her gaze was drawn to the bloodshot eyes and the faint scarring on her right cheek. Samantha hurried on, and Charlie, realizing her mistake, flung her newspaper into her laundry bag and walked swiftly in the same direction.

Normally she would have waited longer, but Samantha seemed so determined to make it home that she was fearful of losing her. Samantha hurried up to Ellesmere Heights and pushed roughly inside, her gait unsteady and stumbling. The heavy door swung back on its hinges, then began its inexorable progress back to a closed position. Charlie jettisoned her fake laundry bag and ran. If she didn't apprehend Samantha now she would have to hand over her lead and take the consequences – and she was damned if she was going to do that. The gap was only inches wide, but Charlie shoved her foot into it, wincing slightly as the door pinched hard. But her intervention had been subtle and silent – she could hear Samantha stumbling up the stairs above, seemingly oblivious to her intrusion, so easing the door open again, Charlie slipped inside.

71

'I have a name for you.'

Helen was now standing in front of the team. A new case file in hand, she was determined not to waste any time.

'His landlord has identified the victim as Maxwell Carter, more commonly known by his professional name of Max Paine. He was a dominator who worked from his flat, so obviously one of our first lines of enquiry is whether he was meeting a client last night. There were no papers or diaries at the scene, so DC Reid, could you liaise with uniform on the house-to-house enquiries – see if we have any witnesses to activity at the flats last night. We'll also need to interrogate his digital footprint – did he run websites, was he on Twitter, Tinder? There were no devices in his flat, but we did find chargers for an iPhone 5 and a tablet, so check if he backed up at all and if so where to. Fast-track any warrants – we need to know who he was communicating with in the last few days of his life. McAndrew, can you take the lead on this?'

'On it,' McAndrew replied, rising and hurrying off.

'Max Paine is a local boy,' Helen continued, 'with one marriage behind him and a son, Thomas, aged six. He divorced three years ago – his wife Dinah now lives in

Portswood with their little boy. I will talk to them once we're done here. For now, let's focus on the facts. As with the Jake Elder murder, the killer has been very cautious, very precise. We won't have Jim Grieves's findings for a few hours, but so far Meredith has found no DNA evidence of our perpetrator within the flat.'

The way Helen said the word 'within' made a few of the team look up. Clearly she was building up to something.

'However, she has just confirmed to me that her team have found a partial footprint in the corridor leading away from the flat. The lino on the floor had been cleaned recently and we've got the faint outline of a size 6 boot. It was raining last night, the ground outside the flats was soft and dirty, so –'

'Does that suggest his visitor was a woman?' DC Edwards asked.

'Or a man with small feet. We've got an impression of the tread – which is ridged and in waved grip lines – DC Lucas, can you keep on forensics until we have a match?'

'Will do.'

Helen handed out the rest of the duties to the team – witness statements, Munch follow-ups, financial investigation, family histories – before calling time on the meeting. It felt good to be leading again, but even now something nagged away at her. She had asked for the whole team to attend the briefing – to push forward together on the new leads – but one officer was notably absent. Which left her wondering:

Where the hell was Charlie?

72

Charlie hammered on the door, but still there was no response. She had followed Samantha up to the fourth floor, calling out her name. But she appeared not to hear and in any event she was too slow to stop her entering flat 15, slamming the door behind. By the time she made it there, the music had already started up. Deafening techno shook the walls of the building and no amount of knocking could raise its inhabitant. What was she doing there?

Charlie walked across to the landing window and looked down on to the street below. Having spent a good five minutes wearing the skin off her knuckles, she'd given up knocking and descended to the entrance once more. Just inside the main door, next to the fire regulations, was a number for the caretaker. He was clearly more used to dealing with leaking roofs and blocked toilets, but once Charlie impressed upon him the urgency of the situation, he had been happy to comply. So why was he taking so long to get here?

This was a calculated risk and Charlie knew it. Technically she should have waited for a warrant, but as long as her entry was not illegal, she would probably be fine. Samantha was only a tenant and the caretaker had the authority to open her door. Furthermore, she had failed to stop when requested to do so by a police officer . . . Charlie knew she was scrabbling a bit, but she would need to have her story off pat, should the need arise. Helen would see through it, but might let her off if the arrest proved decisive and something told Charlie she needed to get into that flat as fast as possible. Samantha could be doing anything in there. Destroying evidence, preparing to flee, perhaps even making an attempt on her life? What was the reason for the deafening music? What was she trying to hide?

The squeal of brakes snapped Charlie out of her thoughts. Moments later, she heard the front door open. Shaking hands with the agitated caretaker, she ushered him upstairs until they were once more outside flat 15. The caretaker seemed to hesitate – as if tacitly asking Charlie if she was sure she wanted to do this – but Charlie wasn't in a mood to be put off.

'Open it, please.'

He turned the key in the lock and the door slid open.

'Do you want me to stay?' he asked half hopefully.

'You can wait outside. I'll call you if I need you.'

Grumbling, he complied. As he traipsed down the steps, Charlie didn't hesitate. Pulling her mobile from her pocket, she called base to request backup, then stepped confidently into the gloomy flat.

73

'This is him at Thomas's birthday party.'

Helen was sitting with Dinah Carter in her dingy living room, turning the pages of the family photo album. To Helen's surprise, Paine seemed to have had a strong relationship with his son – but this had been cut short. Thomas's dad was now on a metal slab across town, in the tender care of Jim Grieves.

'When did you last see Max?'

'Maxwell,' Dinah corrected her, 'he was always Maxwell to us.'

'Of course,' Helen replied, noting the hostility to Max's professional name. 'When did you last see him, Dinah?'

'Two weeks ago. He came round to take Thomas to football practice.'

There were no tears yet, just blank shock. Dinah was still trying to grapple with what she'd been told. The grief would come later.

'How did he seem?'

'Fine.'

'And did you speak to him at all after this?'

'We exchanged texts. Making arrangements and so on, but that was it.'

'When was the last time you received a text from him?'

Dinah was already scrolling through her phone.

'Sunday night.'

Helen read the message, which was everyday, anodyne, then said:

'And you've been separated for how long?'

'Separated for seven years, divorced for five.'

'And can you tell me why your marriage broke up?'

'Different lifestyles.'

'Can I ask what you mean by that?'

'Really? You have to ask?' she replied tersely.

'His choice of work.'

Dinah nodded.

'He wasn't working as a dominator when you met him?'

'No, he wasn't. He was a labourer, for God's sake. I'm not saying he was an angel. Neither of us were. I was open to stuff, we had a good sex life, but then he started watching a lot of porn, more and more BDSM stuff. He wanted me to go along to meets and stuff and I went to a couple out of loyalty, but I've never been comfortable . . . doing that sort of stuff in public. And once I was pregnant that was it. I called time on it and asked him to do likewise.'

'But he didn't?'

'He said he tried, but he didn't really. He was hooked. Said it was part of who he was. I don't think it was at all. In fact it changed him, I always said.'

'In what way?'

'He was always very generous, very kind and he loved being a dad. But he started staying out all hours, lying about where he'd been. I loved him, but I didn't love that side of him and in the end it all became too much.'

'Was it you who ended the relationship?'

'Yes. He got a flat and not long after that changed his name and . . .'

Helen nodded. It was clear that Dinah hated her ex-husband's alter ego, feeling perhaps that the name change was a rejection of her, of his past.

'Did you ever see his flat?'

'No, I wouldn't go round there and I wouldn't let Thomas either.'

'Did you ever come into contact with any of his clients? Anyone he worked with?'

'No,' Dinah replied impatiently. 'I wanted nothing to do with it. Because that wasn't him. Our Maxwell bought me flowers every Friday, took Thomas to the Saints, saved up to take us away on holiday. Whatever else came after, that was the *real* Maxwell. The man we both loved.'

Helen nodded, her gaze falling on the photo album that lay open in front of her. Looking at the photos of a smiling Maxwell, laughing and joking with his son, Helen reflected on how often people surprise you. She had been guilty of writing Paine off as a violent misogynist, but he was clearly capable of love, tenderness and devotion. Maybe it was impossible to know somebody else in this life. Perhaps it was only in death that one's true self was revealed.

74

'Samantha?'

The music was deafening, drowning out Charlie's voice. Outside the flat, it had been unpleasant and jarring, within the flat it was horrendous – the insistent, high-pitched computer beat and thumping bass arrowing straight through her. Charlie's first instinct on entering had been to turn back – her head throbbed and she felt unsteady on her feet, the vibrations crawling up through her bones, but she was here for a reason and was determined to see it through.

'SAMANTHA?'

Her cry was once again lost in the audio barrage swirling round her. This was the third or fourth time she'd called her name now without response, so summoning her courage she pressed on. It was dark in the flat and the carpet was old and ruffled up in places, making it fertile ground for trips and slips. Charlie found a light switch on the wall to her right, but the low-energy light bulb emitted only a weak, yellowing light that barely helped.

Ploughing on, Charlie came to a doorway. Cautiously, she poked her head inside to find a deserted kitchen. The fridge door hung open and a pile of dirty pots clogged the sink. It didn't look as if the room had been used for some time. Directly opposite was another door, this time leading to a tiny, faded bathroom. Again it was deserted and the small room smelt so overpoweringly of vomit that Charlie beat a hasty retreat.

Once more, Charlie hesitated. The source of the noise seemed to be further down the corridor, which arced round to the left ahead, disappearing from view. This was the bowels of the flat – hidden from public view – and Charlie was suddenly nervous of what she might find there.

Pulling her baton from its holster, she moved forward. There was not enough room in this place to extend it properly, you'd never get a proper swing, so she kept it short. Experience had taught her that this often worked best when it came to hand-to-hand combat in confined spaces.

She made her way carefully down the corridor. The further you got from the front door, the darker it became and she had to feel her way round the corner. The floorboards creaked loudly beneath her feet, threatening to give way, so Charlie upped her pace, eventually coming to a door that hung ajar. A sliver of light crept from within, illuminating a faded poster of a topless model that hung on the exterior of the door. Any beauty or glamour the image might have once possessed was lost now under the welter of depraved graffiti which covered it.

Taking a breath, Charlie grasped the handle and pushed the door open. This time the wave of sound knocked her back on her heels. It felt like she'd been struck, but gritting her teeth she stepped forward. The sight that met her eyes took her breath away.

The small room was in a terrible state of repair – bare boards, peeling plaster and exposed wiring hanging from the walls. There was no bed, no furniture – instead the room was piled high from floor to ceiling with dolls. Barely an inch of space was visible beneath the avalanche of painted faces, frills and stuffed limbs. Charlie stood still – she felt as if dozens of lifeless eyes were now fixed on her, chiding her for her intrusion.

Now the dolls were moving. Charlie took a step back, raising her baton in defence, flicking it out to its full length. The mound of dolls parted suddenly and from beneath them a figure emerged. It was Samantha but not as Charlie had seen her before. She was naked now, her pale form decorated only by the livid bruises on her ribs and the smeared mascara that had dried in streams on her face. Her expression was lifeless, her eyes cold and when she opened her mouth, Charlie could see that her teeth were yellow and brown. She looked the intruder up and down, then said:

'I've been expecting you.'

75

We think we're anonymous, but we never are. However we might try to protect ourselves, however smart we think we've been, it is impossible not to leave a footprint of some kind. Max Paine's killer had left his or her mark in the corridor outside the flat and perhaps he or she had left a digital mark too.

The latter was increasingly the case in police work and DC McAndrew was no stranger to content warrants and cyberspace. Rolling her neck with a loud click, she returned her attention to the screens in front of her, making a mental note to go to her pilates class later. Too much data sifting played havoc with your posture and she could feel her back beginning to protest at her lack of activity.

Click, click, click. McAndrew and the team were working on the supposition that Paine's attacker had deliberately cleared the flat of electronic devices – anything that could send or receive messages. Such a tactic might work in the short term but it was nothing more than a temporary fix. Paine hadn't been very assiduous about backing up, but the apps, downloads and messages from his tablet and smartphone were synced to the Cloud. McAndrew sifted through them now, searching for the important clue that seemed to have eluded them so far.

She flicked quickly through the dating apps, before finding what she was really after. His e-diary. Scrolling straight to yesterday's date, she took in his diary entries – a doctor's appointment at 11 a.m., coffee with a friend at 12 p.m., a Tesco's delivery at 3 p.m. After that came his work commitments – Paine was a nocturnal worker. A 'Mike' at 6.30 p.m., 'Jeff' at 8 p.m. and then the final appointment of the night at 9 p.m. None of the names gave them much to go on – no surnames and the first names probably false – but the last meeting of the day was even more oblique. Just a time and next to it a single initial:

'S'.

76

'If you want me, you're going to have to come and get me.'

Samantha remained stock still, despite Charlie's repeated demands for her to move. She lingered within the sanctuary of her strange doll cocoon and as neither of her hands was visible, Charlie had no intention of approaching her. Charlie had been stabbed, assaulted, even strangled in the line of duty and had no intention of risking another such attack.

'That's not going to happen and backup's on its way,' Charlie barked, crossing the room quickly to switch off the deafening music.

'Isn't that what they always say, just before something bad happens?'

'Threatening a police officer is a criminal offence,' Charlie growled back, irritated and angry.

'I think I can wear it, sweetheart.'

Charlie stared at her. She was treating this like a game. Was she just enjoying the moment or was there something else going on here?

'Well, that's all you're wearing, Samantha, so why don't you find yourself a robe? You've no idea what the sight of a naked woman will do to some of my uniformed colleagues.'

'Especially one like me,' Parker responded, suddenly

getting to her feet. The dolls fell away to reveal her full nakedness. She was utterly hairless and stick thin. With her toned body and full eye make-up, she could pass very convincingly for a woman, except for the bulky male genitalia between her legs. Charlie raised her eyes to hers and kept them there.

'Could you grab something for me, honey?' Samantha nodded towards a large wardrobe in the corner of the room. 'There's a jumpsuit two hangers from the left that should fit the bill.'

She ran her tongue over the last two words, amused by her little joke. The faint sound of sirens could be heard in the distance now, but this seemed to have no effect on Samantha. Her eyes were fixed on Charlie.

Charlie edged towards the cupboard, not once breaking eye contact. Samantha seemed calm, relaxed even – it was hard to see where the danger might come from. Was it possible there was somebody actually in the cupboard? The thought was crazy, but taking two quick steps towards it, Charlie threw the wardrobe doors open.

Nothing but a ragged collection of dresses and suits. Keeping one eye on Samantha, she reached for the second hanger from the left. A crimson jumpsuit hung on it and Charlie lifted it out. As she did so, the hook of the hanger snagged on the top of the hanging pole and Charlie had to turn briefly to free it. As she did so, she saw her go. Samantha sprang from her position in the middle of the room and sprinted through the open doorway. She had waited patiently, playing for time, but now she was making her bid for freedom.

Charlie dropped the hanger and ran after her. Samantha made it through the door and tore off down the dark corridor, hurdling the detritus in her path. Charlie was only seconds behind her, busting a gut to keep up.

Samantha raced to the bend in the corridor and took it hard, bouncing off the wall but keeping her balance. Charlie lunged at her, but in the darkness failed to see a discarded vodka bottle on the floor. Her left foot went from under her, the bottle skidding away and she hit the ground hard. Her momentum carried her forward and then she was scrabbling to her feet, ignoring the throbbing pain in her shoulder as she burst round the corner.

Now it was a straight race. The long, creaking corridor ran all the way to the front door – to freedom. Samantha had a head start and looked odds on to get there first, but Charlie knew she had to stop her. Redoubling her efforts she surged forward. Samantha was only twenty feet from freedom now.

Charlie had shut the front door behind her on entering and she was glad of it now. As Samantha approached the door, she was forced to slow down. And as she yanked the door open, Charlie saw her chance. Launching herself through the air, she cannoned into Samantha, slamming her naked body against the back of the door, before the pair of them fell to the floor in a heap. Dazed, Samantha tried to struggle to her feet, but the wind had been knocked out of her and within seconds, Charlie had her knee in the small of her back. Pulling her arms roughly behind her, she slapped on the cuffs and yanked Samantha to her feet.

They stared at each other for a moment, breathless and bruised, before Charlie eventually said:

'I think we've had enough fun and games for now. Let's make you decent, shall we?'

Samantha stared at her, shivering even as the sweat ran down her cheek, then suddenly spat hard in Charlie's face.

77

'What in God's name were you thinking?'

Helen had sped to Ellesmere Heights as soon as she had got Sanderson's call. Charlie had disobeyed a direct order by apprehending the suspect alone, so in spite of the presence of Sanderson, Lucas and numerous SOCOs, Helen didn't hesitate in taking her to task.

'You could have been killed or injured . . . You call, then you wait for backup, you *always* wait for backup.'

'Like you do, you mean,' Charlie retaliated, wiping the last remnants of Parker's saliva from her face.

'Excuse me?' Helen countered, stunned by Charlie's aggressive tone.

'You've broken protocol on numerous occasions. And have you *ever* been pulled up on it?'

Charlie would not normally have answered back, but she had just brought in the prime suspect and was not in the mood to be lectured.

'Only in life-or-death situations and besides it's different for me. You have a family –'

'So it's one rule for you, one rule for everybody else.'

'Why the hell are you doing this, Charlie?' Helen replied, beyond exasperated. 'You've got nothing to prove to me, nothing to prove to yourself. There's no need to keep putting yourself in danger like this.'

'I didn't know what she was doing in there,' Charlie countered. 'I could have waited another five minutes, but what if she'd done something to herself? You can see what state she's in – drunk, emotional, unpredictable –'

'Come off it, Charlie. You've always been impulsive, but that's not what this is. This is about you getting one over on Sanderson. This was *her* lead.'

'So why didn't she bring him in?' Charlie retorted, casting a quick glance at her rival, who loitered by the flat entrance nearby.

'I told every member of the team to report back to me straight away with any developments, but you deliberately kept this to yourself. You missed an important briefing, went off on your own. To prove what? That you're willing to risk your life for your career? You've got to get a handle on this – it's affecting your judgement, your ability to do the job –'

'Well, that's rich coming from you.'

Helen looked ready to explode, but Charlie continued:

'Ever since we found Jake Elder you've been acting oddly.'

'Don't think our friendship gives you the right to talk to me like that. I am your superior officer,' Helen snapped back, anger flaring in her.

'Then try acting like one,' Charlie interrupted. 'You were in pieces after we found Elder and you've been aggressive, over-emotional and unpredictable ever since. Take a look in the mirror, Helen, it's not me that's acting weirdly. It's you.'

Charlie turned and walked away towards her car.

Helen's first instinct was to go after her but even as she took a step in her direction, she became aware of the large audience watching on. There was no question of continuing the argument now. Helen had already let herself down by rowing with another officer – the same crime she'd pulled Charlie and Sanderson up on only a day ago – and she risked losing all authority if she made their confrontation look personal.

But in truth it *was* personal. Charlie had always been Helen's closest friend and ally at Southampton Central, but now it looked very much like her old comrade had cut her off for good.

78

Are some wounds too deep to heal? Is damaged love ever beyond repair?

Sally Jackson sat by her husband's bedside, clinging doggedly to his hand. She'd kept a vigil here since he'd been released from ICU, hoping that her support and encouragement might speed his recovery. Hoping that the Paul she knew would come back to her.

He was out of danger now, but he still found it hard to talk and was asleep for much of the time. Sally didn't mind – she'd hated being excluded from the intensive care unit, powerless to influence events and ignorant of what was happening within. Here at least she could try to help. In Paul's waking hours, she kept up a constant chatter, talking to him about mundane family matters as well as looking forward to things they might do with the boys once he was better.

Sally had no idea if it was true or just wishful thinking. It was hard to imagine they could ever go back to the way things were given the trauma of the last forty-eight hours. He had been in such a dark place, so despairing and rejected, that he had tried to leave them. Perhaps in her position some people might have felt rejected, but she didn't. She just felt guilt. Paul had asked for her help, for her understanding, and she had been too weak to give it to him. Paul had betrayed her – of course he had – but she had repaid him in kind and it made her feel dreadful.

Her conversation had petered out a while ago now. Much as she tried to remain upbeat, it was hard not to be consumed by dark thoughts. She'd overheard the nurses gossiping about a second victim and she suspected they were wondering if her husband would be the third. None of it made any sense and it filled her with trepidation for the future. Yes, she was here, doing all the things she should do, but really what hope was there for the future when the fissure in their lives was so great?

Wiping a tear away, Sally chided herself for being so morbid. There was no point looking too far ahead, she had to keep her mind anchored on the here and now. The rest – the future – was another world for them. She would remain here and do what was needed for Paul, for the twins. She would stay because she still cared deeply for her husband. She just didn't know him any more.

79

'This is your opportunity to tell us what happened. If I were you I'd take it.'

Samantha said nothing in response. She had seen the station doctor and was calmer now, though it was clear that she wasn't comfortable in these surroundings. She fidgeted endlessly, shifting in her seat, tugging at her clothes, obsessing about the broken nails she'd suffered when being escorted to the station. On more than one occasion, she had asked for replacements, as well as foundation, lipstick, mascara, but Helen had refused her requests. They would be good bargaining chips in the hours to come.

'What would you like to know, Helen? May I call you Helen?'

'If you like.'

Helen tried to keep the edge from her voice, but didn't wholly succeed. She was still stewing on her argument with Charlie and was not in the mood to be teased or mocked. Charlie had never spoken to her that brutally before – such an open act of defiance not only threatened their relationship but also morale within the team. It was tempting to blame Charlie's sudden and unexpected promotion for this problem but actually Charlie was right. Helen *had* been behaving oddly – this case was messing with her head, making her act in ways that were both unprofessional and unkind.

'And what should I call you?' she asked, trying to put these troubling thoughts from her mind.

'My name is Samantha.'

'Samantha Parker?'

'Just Samantha.'

Helen noted her aversion to her given surname – a small but telling sign. Opening her file, Helen digested the contents, taking a moment to compose herself. Her anger and discomfort still burnt, but the details of the case, and the rhythm of questioning, were comforting and familiar. Helen hoped that slowly she would regain her equilibrium in the hushed confessional of the interview suite. She was leading it alone, which was unusual, but in the circumstances what choice did she have? To include either Charlie or Sanderson would seem like favouritism. Another rod for her own back, Helen thought to herself.

'Samantha it is, then. But you've been known by other names, haven't you?'

'We all have many different personalities within us.'

'And, of course, there's your professional work as a drag act which requires an alter ego?'

'We're called performance artistes and, yes, a little creativity is required.'

'Would you say you're well-known on the club scene?'

'Pretty well.'

'And in the wider BDSM community?'

'It's a larger world than you'd think and, yes, I play my part.'

Helen nodded but said nothing, noting that Samantha was happy to be led towards an obvious trap.

'So you've visited the Torture Rooms then?'

'On occasion.'

'And you've run into Jake Elder during your time. If you need to refresh your memory here's a phot—'

'I believe I've seen his face around,' Samantha said, without looking down at the photo. 'At Munches, events and so forth.'

'And what about Max Paine? Have you ever met him? Ever used his services?'

'Once or twice. He's got a bit of a reputation, but then again every girl likes to be slapped sometimes, doesn't she?'

Helen ignored the assertion. 'Last night he had an appointment. His diary said he was meeting "S". Was that you?'

'Don't tell me something's happened to him?' Samantha came back calmly.

'Please answer the question. Was that you?'

Samantha sat back in her chair.

'Yes.'

'So you kept your appointment?'

Samantha nodded.

'Did he beat you?'

'Not particularly.'

'So how did you get your bruises?'

For the first time, Samantha hesitated, her cockiness temporarily deserting her.

'I forget.'

'Not good enough.'

'I honestly can't remember. I was in a bit of a state last night.'

'Why?'

'None of your fucking business.'

It was aimed directly at Helen. She sidestepped it and continued:

'Where were you between the hours of ten thirty p.m. and six thirty a.m. last night?'

'At my flat.'

'Can anyone verify that?'

'No.'

'How about Tuesday night? Cast your mind back three days – where were you then?'

'Out.'

Helen said nothing. The silence sat heavy in the room.

'I was at the ball, ok? It's a very popular event.'

'To be clear, you were at the Annual Ball at the Torture Rooms nightclub.'

'The Torture Rooms *nightclub* – Jesus Christ, you sound like my grandmother.'

'Yes or no?'

'Yes.'

Helen scribbled a note to herself to call Meredith. If Samantha's presence at the club that night could be confirmed, it would make a massive difference to their case. Otherwise they would always be open to the defence of false confession – a thorny problem in high-profile cases.

'Did you encounter Jake Elder on Tuesday night?'

'I saw him mooching about like a bear with a sore head. Poor boy looked like he needed cheering up.'

'Did you talk to him? Interact with him?'

'Did I . . . interact with him?' Samantha replied, wrapping her mouth round the words. 'Not that I recall, but then the night is a bit of a blur. As your colleague has probably told you, I have an issue with alcohol. I'd pay for the good stuff, but as it is . . .'

'So nothing out of the ordinary happened that night?'

'No. Same old, same old . . .'

'Have you ever used wet sheets?' Helen asked, changing tack sharply.

'Of course.'

'Other forms of restraints? Leather straps, hog ties –'

'Who hasn't?'

'A witness – a cabbie – picked you up that night after the Annual Ball. Said you were in a terrible state. Angry, distressed, unpredictable. If it was such a mundane evening, why were you so affected by it?'

Samantha said nothing, but Helen could see her eyes narrowing.

'What happened that night, Samantha?'

There was a long pause, as Samantha toyed with a broken nail. Then she leant forward, rewarding Helen with an ample view of her cleavage as she did so, before whispering:

'That's for me to know. And you to find out.'

80

Gardam leant against the two-way mirror, his eyes glued to the contest in front of him. In his younger days, he had loved the tussle of suspect and interviewer, revelling in the feints and parries, the carefully laid traps and elegant evasions, but he seldom got the chance to enjoy it now. His was a desk job, important but managerial, far from the front line, far from the fun. So he had to amuse himself vicariously, watching others do the job he once loved.

The experience was always sweeter when the interview took place under high pressure. The discovery of a second body and the ensuing media excitement had left no one in Southampton Central in any doubt about the need for a quick resolution to the case. Two men had been sadistically murdered, but worse still their initial suspect now languished in hospital, following a botched suicide attempt. Southampton was being made to look like a den of vice and its police force far from competent – Gardam had already had the police commissioner, the local MP *and* the Mayor on the phone, bending his ear about it.

His get-out-of-jail card in these situations was always Helen. She was an officer of such standing that nobody – least of all the local politicians, who liked to appear strong on law and order – could take serious issue with the way investigations were run. Yes, there were false starts and accidents, and you could never predict how people caught up in cases like these would react, but Helen's track record at getting results in the big investigations was second to none.

Gardam had used her name many times to smooth ruffled feathers, assuring his critics that justice would prevail, and in his heart he *did* believe that this case would be no exception. But another part of him knew that it was already very different. He and Helen had worked together on complicated investigations before, but never as closely as this. Something profound had changed in their relationship.

Was he genuinely falling in love with her? He'd had office crushes before, but he'd never been tempted to act on them. This was something else. She had opened herself up to *him*. He had replayed their recent conversation over and over in his mind. Did she know how he felt about her? Was it even possible she knew that he watched her? He hoped not because that made her confession even more unprompted. She had bared her soul to him, revealing things she hadn't confided to anyone else. He had the strong sense that she did this not just to unburden herself, but also to test him, to see how he would react. If he'd been obviously shocked or judgemental she might have backed off, but he had been accepting and encouraging, so she had elaborated, drawing him into her world. He hoped in time she would go further.

But that was for another day. Now there was work to

be done. Still, it didn't stop Gardam drinking in his subordinate now, noting the way she spoke, the way she held herself, the manner in which she teased and coaxed her suspect towards her traps. It was magical to watch and Gardam knew that his other duties would be neglected until she was done. While she was here, performing for him, the rest of the world could go hang.

81

'So why do you do it?'

Samantha arched an eyebrow, but said nothing, examining her nails.

'Is it about you? The victims? What is it about them that gets you riled?'

'Why should I hate *them*? They are nobodies.'

'So maybe it's about you, Michael.'

'Don't call me that.'

'It's your name, isn't it? Michael James Parker.' Helen pulled a couple more sheets of paper from her file. 'Born just outside Portsmouth, second child of Anna and Nicholas Parker, brother to Leoni. Are your parents still alive?'

'No, thank fuck.'

'But Leoni is. She's had to post bail for you on a number of occasions, hasn't she?'

'If you say so.'

'I see you've got form for credit card fraud. Tell me about that.'

'I was working at a café. Management took all the tips and I needed some money to survive –'

'So you lifted customers' credit cards and then what?'

'I feathered my nest.'

'Until you got caught.'

'Precisely.'

'Also charges of affray, assault . . . and false imprisonment.'

'That was bullshit.'

'Your victim didn't think so.'

'It was a game that went wrong.'

'Went wrong how?'

'I thought the guy had balls. Turned out he hadn't.'

'It's never your fault, is it? Everything we've talked about so far –'

'Why *should* it be my fault?'

Samantha snarled as she said it. Her female carapace was slipping now, her voice low and breathy, revealing a masculine side that was usually hidden from view.

'Tell me, when did you realize that you wanted to be Samantha, rather than Michael?' Helen said, changing tack once more.

'I didn't realize, I knew.'

'So it was from birth.'

'Of course. I was just born wrong.'

'And this desire to be a woman, how did it express itself when you were a kid?'

'How do you think? I had a mother and a sister.'

'You borrowed their clothes?'

'Sure. My mother said she never knew, but she did.'

'And your father?'

Samantha suddenly threw her head back and laughed.

'He definitely didn't know. Not initially at least . . .'

'And when he did?'

'What do you think?'

'He beat you?'

'Have a look at my past medical records. You'll see a lot of accidents there.'

'How long did this go on for?'

'Until he sent me away. He decided my mum and sister were the problem, so he packed me off to boarding school.'

Helen watched Samantha closely. The pain of this separation was still evident.

'It was all boys and I hated it. Nowhere to dress, no one to talk to and then puberty, God help me.'

'Your voice broke?'

'And the body hair, and walking round with a giant pair of balls between my legs like a fucking ape.'

'What did you do?'

'I cut myself, played the fool, I messed up in pretty much every subject I took. Still I was bullied to shit. Turns out the boys there didn't like sissies any more than my dad did.'

'So you've always been a victim of violence?'

'Pretty much, though they saved the best till last. I took their abuse for five years then one day I thought "fuck it". I turned up at the sixth-form disco dressed as Samantha. Immaculate, I was, far better-looking than the rest of the sad sacks there. And you know what? Nobody said a bad word to me. No, they waited until I was on my way back to the dorm. Doctors said I was lucky not to lose my sight.'

Samantha was looking directly at Helen, her eyes boring into hers.

'And the scar . . . on your face?'

'A present from my dad when I was eventually expelled.'

Helen nodded. She instinctively disliked Samantha, but her story was not so dissimilar to hers. The wounds inflicted by family are the deepest of all.

'Do you still self-harm?'

Samantha gave Helen a withering look that answered strongly in the affirmative.

'Do you think that's why you're drawn to recreational violence? To BDSM?'

'I'm not a shrink, sweetheart. Are you?'

Helen smiled and shook her head. She didn't like her attitude, but she was talking, which was good.

'Tell me what you like to do when you're having a session? What's your taste?'

'The usual.'

'Meaning?'

'Restraint, role play, punishment, isolation techniques, sensory deprivation –'

'Edge Play?'

'It's been known.'

'Give me some examples.'

Samantha looked at Helen. She had been warming to her, becoming almost garrulous and sociable, but now Helen saw her hesitate.

'In one of Max Paine's previous entries against your name – or your initial at least – he's written Phoenix. Can you explain that to me?'

Samantha looked dead straight at Helen. Was she looking for an excuse not to answer the question? A way out?

'We're not due to break for another thirty minutes, so please answer the question.'

'I'd like a lawyer now.'

'Your brief is on her way and should be here soon. In the meantime, what does Paine mean by "Phoenix"?'

'It's a scenario.'

'A scenario you act out?'

'Of course.'

'Describe it to me. Samantha, you can look away all you want, but I prom—'

'It's a scenario in which the bottom comes out on top, ok?'

'So the victim – you – are in control.'

'Right. Sometimes you act out a little bit first, where the top verbally abuses you, beats you up, but then the tables are turned.'

'Meaning that eventually *you* are the one handing out the punishment.'

'The Phoenix rising.'

As she said it, a smile crept over Samantha's face. Did she feel she was finally getting the upper hand with Helen too?

'Did you act out the Phoenix with Max Paine?'

'Sometimes.'

'I don't mean in the past,' Helen butted in, 'I mean on Thursday night. Is that what you wanted? Is that what he offered you?'

Samantha took a long time to think about her answer, before she finally said:

'Yes.'

82

The silence in the room was deafening. Normally the Incident Room was the epicentre of noise on the seventh floor – mobiles ringing, printers whirring and officers arguing, laughing, speculating. But not today. It was tense and hushed, the spectacle of both Sanderson and Charlie avoiding each other putting everybody else on edge.

Sanderson finished her tea and contemplated heading to the canteen for another. She'd been chivvying the computer operatives into carrying out their data checks on Paine's devices for over an hour, but with little success. This was especially galling, given Charlie's arrest of Parker. Despite her argument with Helen, Charlie would still get all the plaudits, if they managed to secure a confession from their prime suspect. Sanderson *had* started the day in conciliatory mood, thinking she should perhaps apologize to Charlie and try to make things right. But Charlie had gone her own way, stitched the rest of them up and now she had the upper hand. So her apology had been swallowed.

'Ok, let's park the smartphone for now, focus on the tablet instead,' she said, her patience finally wearing thin.

Her abruptness earnt her a reproachful look from

the data analyst, but Sanderson ignored it. She knew she was behaving petulantly, but she couldn't help herself. As her aggrieved subordinate punched the keyboard, Sanderson's eyes strayed across the room. She could see Charlie out of the corner of her eye, leafing through files. It made Sanderson smile. Hard though she was trying to look busy, she knew that all Charlie's thoughts were bent on the interview downstairs – an interview she was excluded from. This would be a big feather in her cap, if things played out as she hoped.

'Here you go,' her neighbour said, failing to conceal the hint of triumph in her voice. Sanderson turned to her, irritated with herself for being so distracted.

'What have you got?'

'Someone's using Paine's tablet.'

'Where?' Sanderson said, suddenly engaged.

'Not sure yet. They're hooked into a server in the city centre. Give me another five minutes and I'll give you a more precise location.'

Sanderson was already heading to the door.

'Buzz me in the car. I'm heading down there now.'

Sanderson pushed through the door and down the corridor, half walking, half running. She didn't want to overdo it, but she couldn't look this gift horse in the mouth. There *was* a chance that she could still redeem herself. More than that, there was a chance that DS Charlene Brooks had pulled in the wrong guy.

83

'So what do you think?'

Gardam had been waiting for Helen outside the interview suite. She'd been keen to get back to the team, but he'd pressed her for an update. So they now found themselves in the smokers' yard once again.

'I think she's a good suspect. She's admitted engaging in extreme BDSM practices with Paine on the night he died, she knew Elder and I'm pretty sure we'll be able to place her at both scenes. She's definitely damaged enough – she's been a victim of violence all her life and I suspect it's the only language she knows. Plus it's clear that she has an unhealthy interest in subjugating other people.'

'She told you all this?'

'She doesn't seem to mind, in fact she seems to enjoy it.'

'So why hasn't she confessed? If she's so willing to talk?'

'It could be that she's innocent – though she's never said as much. It may be that she's cornered and wants to enjoy the game for as long as possible. Or it may be that actually admitting what she's done is too hard for her. Don't forget she's a victim too.'

'So what's the next play?'

'We keep digging – see if we can link her to BDSM

purchases made with stolen credit cards. Anything we can turn up will increase our leverage.'

Gardam nodded and drew hard on his cigarette. A brief silence followed as Helen did likewise. They were alone today and the smokers' yard had a curiously intimate feel.

'I really should give these things up,' he said, exhaling.

'Me too. But somehow every time I make the decision to quit –'

'Something comes up.'

Helen nodded.

'Occupational hazard, I guess,' Gardam continued, flicking his ash on to the ground. 'How long have you been a smoker . . . ?'

'Since I was a kid,' Helen replied. 'There wasn't much else to do round our way when we were bunking off school. It was my sister who really got me into it.'

'I was the same. I wanted to be like my older brothers. Of course, they both quit years ago and now the bastards do triathlons just to rub my nose in it.'

Gardam finished his cigarette and rubbed it out on the wall behind him.

'Maybe we should both quit together?' he said. 'Keep an eye on each other.'

'Let's not run before we can walk, eh?' Helen replied, extinguishing her cigarette. 'We've still got a long way to go on this one.'

'I guess you're right,' Gardam answered, pocketing his packet of cigarettes.

Helen waited to be dismissed, but Gardam made no move to do so.

'Was there anything else, sir?'

'No. And don't feel you need to call me that. Jonathan is fine, as long as it's not in front of the troops.'

'Of course, thank you.'

'Good night, Helen.'

Helen took her leave and headed back to the seventh floor. Perhaps she had been wrong about Gardam. Against all the odds, they were starting to get along.

84

'It's so nice to have someone to talk to. Someone who *understands.* It must have been hard losing your dad so young, but you turned out ok, didn't you?'

Emilia Garanita nodded and gave Dinah Carter's arm a squeeze. The latter was clearly terrified that her son would be left traumatized by his father's sudden death and she desperately needed some female reassurance. Emilia was happy to oblige – she was good at making people feel better and what she'd told her so far was *mostly* true. The fact that her dad was not dead, but serving a sentence for drug smuggling, was a minor detail. It *had* been tough for her becoming a surrogate parent to her many siblings at such a young age, but the experience had been beneficial for her in the long run and now she didn't regret it. It was certainly useful in situations such as these.

Dinah Carter had been reluctant to open the door. She'd already had journalists round offering her money, but she'd run scared of them. Emilia sensed that they had been too aggressive, too obviously grasping for a piece of Dinah. Emilia by contrast had tried the softly, softly approach, mainlining on her sympathy for the bereaved ex-wife. And it had worked – Carter hadn't shut the door on her. Emilia suspected it was more than just her empathetic manner that had made Dinah hesitate – the extensive scarring on her face helped too. Emilia wasn't proud of the way she looked, but it certainly had its uses. People could see she had suffered – there was no need to explain – and more often than not that got her through the door.

They had already spoken at length about Dinah's son, Thomas, but there was a finite amount of copy in this, so Emilia moved the conversation on. The moral majority out there had limited sympathy for a man of Max Paine's alternative lifestyle, however loving a dad he might have been at the weekends. What they – and Emilia – were interested in was who might have killed him.

'Did DI Grace tell you what lines of enquiry they're pursuing, in relation to Maxwell's death?'

Dinah shook her head, fiddling nervously with the buttons on her cardigan.

'Do they have a suspect in mind?' Emilia enquired. She was aware that another suspect – Michael Parker – had been arrested in connection with the enquiry, but she wasn't sure how serious this new line of enquiry was yet.

'Not that they told me. They just wanted to know what kind of man Maxwell was. I told them about how he used to be, the good side of him, but beyond that . . .'

'And do you have any suspicions yourself? Do you know of anyone who might have wanted to harm Maxwell?'

For the first time, Dinah hesitated. She looked nervous, even a little tense.

'Has anyone harmed him before?' Emilia sensed a breakthrough.

Still Dinah paused, then:

'I don't know if I should be telling you this.'

'I won't print anything you don't want me to.'

It was an easy lie to tell and Emilia had done so many times before. Did Dinah smell her duplicity? She still seemed uncertain whether to trust her new friend, whether she should unburden herself. Then, making a decision, she said:

'He was attacked once before.'

Emilia nodded and looked concerned, giving this piece of info the weight Dinah obviously felt it merited.

'When was this?'

'About nine months ago. He had to cancel a day out with Thomas. I was livid, shouted at him down the phone, so he sent me a photo. Poor sod had been beaten black and blue.'

'Have you still got this photo?'

'Probably. On my old phone.'

'It would be great to have a quick look before I go,' Emilia said quickly. 'What did the police say about this?'

'I . . . I didn't tell them.'

'May I ask why?'

Dinah said nothing, but Emilia could tell there was more.

'Surely you must want to catch Maxwell's killer? For Thomas's sake, if not your own. Why *wouldn't* you tell them?'

'Because it was a police officer that did it.'

'How do you know?' Emilia asked.

'Because he told me. He wanted to do something about it, but how can you, when it's one of their own?'

'Did he say why he was attacked?'

'No, just that it was unprovoked. He didn't like talking about it much – he was embarrassed, I think, because it was a woman that did it.'

'It was a female officer?' Emilia responded, failing to contain her surprise. 'Did he give you a name?'

'No.'

'A description?'

'No, but he said she was well-known round here. He knew who she was, but he wouldn't tell me. Wanted to protect me, I guess.'

'Or protect himself,' Emilia thought, but said nothing. She was prepared to play along with Dinah's fantasy of Maxwell as the innocent victim for now. Thanking her for her time, Emilia began to wrap things up. She had come here with relatively low expectations, but was leaving with a major new lead. Could it be true? If it was, it presented some very interesting possibilities.

A narrative was taking shape in Emilia's mind that would trump all of the stories she'd penned so far in her brief, colourful career. She would need to be sure of her facts of course. And there was one person who would be able to help confirm her growing suspicions.

This was Emilia's next stop – one she hoped would finally blow this story wide open.

85

'Nobody moves unless I say so.'

Sanderson signed off and waited for the other members of the team to confirm that they would hold their positions. She had been keen not to repeat Charlie's mistake and had summoned backup as soon as she had pinned down where Paine's device was being used. It was routing via a server that was registered to an estate agent's on Banner Street in Portswood. It was pushing 11 p.m. so the agency was closed, but a light was burning in a third-floor window. The buzzers by the door adjacent to the agency suggested that the second and third floors of the building were flats. Perhaps they had an agreement to share the router or perhaps whoever was upstairs had gained access to it by some other means. Either way, they were about to find out.

Sanderson had tried and failed to contact the estate agency via its out-of-hours number, leaving her with no choice but to apply for a warrant. This had taken a couple of hours to source, but now she had the authority she needed to act. She rang the buzzer for the third-floor flat. No response. She rang it again, but still nothing. Losing patience she gestured to the nearby WPC to barrel charge the door. The weak lock yielded easily, the door swinging wide open, and Sanderson was inside and bounding up the stairs.

She moved past the second-floor flat, which appeared to be unoccupied and quiet. Another burst of speed and she crested the top landing. Marching straight to the flat door, she hammered on it.

'Police. Open up.'

She beat the door again, then moved aside quickly, allowing her uniformed colleague a proper run-up. Giving her the nod, she pulled her radio from her pocket.

'On the count of three. One, two . . .'

The door to the flat suddenly opened, prompting the uniformed officer to abort her swing at the last second. Sanderson hurried forward – to be confronted by a sheepish-looking student.

'What gives?' he said, trying and failing to be insouciant.

Sanderson pushed past him. She scanned left and right, darting in and out of the cramped rooms, but she already knew that this was not their killer's lair. It was a down-at-heel student flat – nothing more. You could tell by the smell of weed, the laddish posters, the unwashed pots and pans and, most tellingly of all, by the sight of an unshaven young man in his pyjamas playing Minion Rush on a battered tablet.

86

Samantha lay on her bed, staring at a spider crawling across the ceiling. It was a while since she'd been in a proper police cell. Normally they just put her in the custody cage with the drunk and the violent. This time they'd moved her to a solo cell. Had they done this to give her more time to reflect? To try and isolate her? Either way, it showed that they had plans for her.

She watched the spider scuttle its way to the corner of the room, settling itself back into its web to lie in wait for its prey. Was this Helen Grace's tactic too, lying in wait in the darkness, hoping that Samantha would offer herself as a sacrifice? If it was, she'd be a long time waiting. Grace had built up a considerable reputation over the years and Samantha had been surprised and disquieted at having to face her. She had thought she might get to talk to Brooks. But instead she had found herself opposite the boss, dancing on a wire.

Grace was determined, resourceful and well-prepared. Oddly, she was also adept at putting you at your ease, which made her more dangerous still. You could never be entirely sure what her next move would be, which was unnerving at first, but as she'd grown into the interview Samantha had begun to enjoy the sudden changes of direction and the attempts to wrong-foot her. It reminded her a little of the ghastly fencing displays she'd had to sit through during her brief period in private education. Lunge, retreat, parry, riposte. Lunge, retreat, parry . . . Grace hadn't landed a telling hit yet, though Samantha could tell she thought she was close. Was she out there right now, drawing all the strands together until she was ready to pull the net tight?

What she wouldn't give to be a fly on the wall, watching Grace sifting the evidence with her team and debating her next move. She had seemed so confident, so business-like when they started the interview, as if it were only a matter of time before she got her 'man'. But, by the end, her frustration was coming through loud and clear as she pressed Samantha for a confession. She had enjoyed refusing to play ball – that bitch was clearly full of herself and needed taking down a peg or two.

Grace was used to getting her way, to being on the winning side. But not this time. Perhaps she would be patient, waiting for her prey to come to her. Or perhaps her next move would be a full-frontal assault. Either way, one thing was clear to Samantha. DI Grace was clutching at straws.

87

'It would have been a lot easier if you'd contacted us earlier, Mr Simons.'

David Simons said nothing in response – he looked about as pleased to be in the interview suite as Charlie did. She'd been on the cusp of calling it a day when he had finally presented himself at the custody desk. Sanderson had just returned to the station and was locked in a private briefing with Helen, leaving Charlie no choice but to field the interview, as the only senior officer available.

'I might say the same thing to you,' Simons replied. 'I'm the only person on this planet who gave a shit about Jake Elder and yet I've no clue what's happening. Are you going to charge this guy Parker or not?'

'I'm afraid I can't comment on an ongoing operation –'

'Yada yada yad—'

'But I can assure you we are making good progress,' Charlie interrupted, resisting the temptation to punch Simons in the face.

The truth was of course a little different. Samantha was in custody but had not been charged, which made Charlie very nervous indeed. There was a lot riding on this for her, especially after her bitter argument with Helen.

'In the meantime, I'd like to go over a few details with you. Starting with where and how you first met Jake Elder?'

Begrudgingly, David Simons began to talk, giving brief details of his relationship with their first victim. Charlie listened, nodding and taking notes when necessary, but in truth her mind remained elsewhere. She didn't expect any revelations from Simons and her thoughts were full of the day's traumatic events. Her shoulder still ached from her fight with Samantha, but she would have happily worn that if she had helped bring this troubling case to a conclusion. As it was, she had all but destroyed her relationship with Helen, and Samantha remained a suspect, but no more.

Had the price been worth paying? She was determined not to come second best to Sanderson – but had it really been necessary to confront her mentor and friend so harshly? She and Helen had always got on and though it was true that Helen was in a very troubled place at the moment, she owed her more than bitterness and aggression. She had been right to call Helen out on her behaviour, but a lot of what Helen had said about *her* had also been on the money. Charlie did need to get a grip on herself. The fact that she wasn't planning on telling her partner Steve about her fight with Samantha told Charlie all she needed to know about the wisdom of entering that flat alone.

Would an apology cut it? Was it even advisable? Charlie had brought Samantha in and while there was still a good chance that she would be charged, it was probably best to say nothing. Once she had put Sanderson in her place, then she could try to repair her relationship with Helen. For now, there was nothing for it but to hunker down and see things through to the bitter end.

88

The kettle shrieked as it reached boiling point, jolting Helen from her thoughts. She had been briefed by Sanderson before leaving the station, her DS confirming that Paine's tablet was a dead end. The device had been found by two students in a park bin miles from his flat, its memory erased and the exterior wiped clean.

Frustrated and drained, Helen had spent some time in her office leafing through Meredith's latest reports, which worryingly did *not* include a positive DNA source for Parker at the Torture Rooms, before deciding to call it a day. It was late and she craved the sanctuary of her flat.

Once safely home, she'd tried to read, but when that failed to distract her, she'd opted for herbal tea and a hot bath instead. But, as ever, she couldn't stop her mind from turning. She didn't really remember filling the kettle, which was testament enough to her inability to drive Samantha from her thoughts. She was such a good fit for these crimes, but if she was guilty, why was she so cocky? She seemed to be enjoying the dance, as if she alone knew the punch line that was about to be delivered. Helen had the unnerving feeling that they were missing something significant.

Helen poured the boiling water into the cup and

watched the colour leach out of the tea bag. She had been looking forward to a soothing drink, but now she couldn't face it. What was the point of going through this ritual? She could have a cup of tea, lie in a warm bath, but she would still be thinking the same thoughts, teasing away at the same knotty problems. She'd smoked too many cigarettes and she didn't have the energy for a run – it was a bitter irony that she no longer had Jake to turn to, to rid her of her dark energy.

Throwing her tea into the sink, Helen turned to face the window. It was late now and the pubs would be emptying soon – perhaps some late-night voyeurism would help Helen unwind. The lights were off in her kitchen, shrouding her in darkness, but the moon was full and bright and as Helen looked out of her window she saw him. It was only for an instant, but there was no mistaking it. A man was standing in the derelict building opposite, watching her.

Helen's instinctive reaction was to pull away, but she managed to control herself, turning and walking slowly towards the back of the flat, as if nothing had happened. Then, as soon as she was out of view, she dashed to the front door and wrenched it open. She had no idea who was watching her, but he wasn't going to escape her tonight.

89

Helen burst out of the fire exit and into the communal gardens at the back of her flats. Whipping her key fob from her pocket, she buzzed herself out and sprinted round the corner. She now doubled back to her road but instead of turning left into it, she carried on past, coming to a halt by the lolling chain link fence which surrounded the derelict building – its only form of defence against the squatters and junkies who occasionally used it.

Finding a low point in the fence, Helen slipped over and padded towards the back of the flats. The building cast a tall shadow and Helen had to choose her path carefully – the ground was littered with broken glass and discarded needles. As she worked her way towards the empty shell, her mind was turning on what she'd seen. Was this the same figure she'd glimpsed a few months back? She'd thought nothing of it at the time, assuming it was just another drug user seeking temporary sanctuary. Now she chided herself for her complacency.

She had reached the back entrance and bending down picked up an empty beer bottle. It wasn't much, but it would have to do – in her haste she had left her baton and holster in the flat. Stepping into the building, she reached out a hand to steady herself. There was no light in the cavernous space – just moonlight creeping through the holes in the roof. It was an oddly magical sight, the moonbeams descending from above, but perilous too. Helen could barely see where she was going and knew that a wrong step might send her plunging into the basement below. More than that, she sensed that the person she was hunting was still inside somewhere. He might strike at any minute – if that was his intention – and Helen would be virtually defenceless.

She hesitated. Through the gloom she could make out a staircase in the far corner. Creeping forward, testing each floorboard as she went, she kept her head upright and alert, searching for danger. She remembered her words to Charlie earlier, but it was too late to call for the cavalry now. By the time they arrived, Helen felt sure her quarry would be gone.

Reaching the staircase, Helen looked up, suddenly feeling very small in the deserted building. There were fifteen floors above her, but she felt certain the figure she'd seen had been on the penultimate floor. She had fourteen floors to climb. What was her best strategy – slow and steady or swift and decisive? The stairs were made of concrete and seemed the one element of the building that hadn't rotted away, so summoning her courage, Helen raced up the stairs.

Fourth floor, fifth floor, sixth floor. Helen drove herself on, keeping her pace steady. She was bouncing lightly from step to step, moving as silently as she could, but it was hard to move this fast without creating a little noise. Would this prove costly? Was she walking into an ambush? Fear once more seeped into her consciousness. She was not by nature fearful, but something about this place was messing with her head. She didn't want to end her days here.

She had reached the thirteenth floor now. Gripping the beer bottle firmly, she dropped her pace, taking the stairs two at a time in giant, silent strides. If he was going to come for her, it would be now. But she wasn't going to walk into his trap tamely.

There was nowhere for him to hide now, so Helen burst into the room, her arm raised to protect herself. The floorboards protested and a cloud of dust flew up, but no attack came, so Helen moved on to the next room, expecting to be thrown backwards with a savage blow at any minute.

Still nothing. Then suddenly there was a noise. At the other side of the building – what was it? A crash? Someone putting their weight in the wrong place? Helen bounded forward. She was sprinting as if her life depended upon it, eating up the yards to the far wall and suddenly she burst out into a large open space. A penthouse apartment that was never built, it was now a vast receptacle for dead birds and drugs detritus. Other than that, it was empty – save for the door to the fire escape that lolled open.

Helen raced over to it. Pushing out into the fresh air, she came to an abrupt halt. The fire escape on which she now stood was old and rusty and could potentially give way at any moment – suddenly her impulsive bravery seemed foolhardy in the extreme.

Taking a step back, she looked through the grille to the steps below. The metal staircase zigzagged down the building and Helen scrutinized it for signs of movement. But all was still, apart from a few startled pigeons and the fire escape door moving back and forth in the wind.

Suddenly a thought occurred to Helen and mounting the fire escape she climbed to the top floor. This was the only remaining place her voyeur could be hiding. But it was as deserted as the rest of the shell.

Crouching down, Helen breathed out, trying to slow her heartbeat. Despite her endeavours she had been left empty-handed. There was *no one* here. She had been so sure – had seen the figure so clearly. She couldn't have imagined it all.

Could she?

90

'I don't think we have a choice. We have to charge her.'

Charlie's tone was flinty and unyielding. Despite the failure of Samantha to confess, she seemed determined to nail her for the brutal double murder.

'If we don't we've got at best another twenty-four hours and I don't think that's enough. She's too confident of herself, we need more time to wear her down.'

'You really want to dive in again, after what happened last time?' Sanderson replied, as coolly as she could. 'We have got to be sure.'

'She was the last person to visit Paine on the night he died.'

'That we know of.'

'And she's never once protested her innocence, despite numerous opportunities to do so.'

'Nor has she confessed. So what have we actually got?'

Helen watched her two deputies debate the evidence. It was still early and she was exhausted and irritable after her night-time excursions. She hadn't slept a wink last night, replaying what she'd seen over and over to see if she could have been mistaken. Her defences were up and every tiny noise had seemed so ominous that in the end she'd given up trying altogether and headed into the office. She knew that today would be crucial for the investigation, so when Sanderson and Charlie arrived, she called them both into her office.

She had thought about apologizing to *both* of them for her recent behaviour, but the events of last night still hung heavy on her mind and with the clock ticking on Samantha's custody there was no time to waste. So they'd pressed on with the case, just about managing to ignore the tensions bubbling beneath the surface. Helen would have to force the pair of them to work together if necessary, as they were both good officers whose recent misdemeanours were mostly a product of her own fractured focus.

'What have we got on the credit cards?' Helen asked suddenly, interrupting the debate.

'The Zentai suit and hog ties that killed Paine were bought with a different credit card to the one used to buy Elder's wet sheets,' Sanderson replied.

'Have we cross-referenced the stores and websites that the two different cloned cards were used in? To see who might have stolen the details?'

'Yes, but it's already a massively long list. The supermarkets, Boots, W. H. Smith, Amazon, PayPal, iTunes . . .'

'Can we link either of the cloned cards to Samantha? We know that as Michael Parker she had form for this kind of thing.'

'Nothing on her home computer, phones or devices. And we didn't find any cards at her flat.'

'Does she work anywhere other than the bar?'

'Not that we know of.'

'What about the deliveries of the bondage items themselves?' Helen said, turning to Charlie.

'As with Elder, the BDSM stuff was delivered by courier to a vacant address. A domestic property awaiting new tenants.'

'Get on to the estate agents that rent them out. See if there's any connection between the different properties and a particular agency.'

'Sure thing.'

'What about the boot print?' Helen continued. 'Meredith said the print she found at Paine's was a size six. Parker is a size seven, but that doesn't necessarily rule her out.'

'There was loads of stuff in the flat geared towards sizing down, corsets, heels –' Charlie responded.

'Trying to make herself as petite as possible.'

'Exactly. But no sign of any boot or shoe that fits.'

Helen nodded, but her frustration was clear.

'We've got the tread pattern,' Sanderson interjected. 'It's quite unusual, so we'll chase down which outlets sell it.'

'Good. We're not letting Samantha believe she's anything other than our number one suspect and we exhaust *every* avenue, up to the last minute to link her to these murders. Understood?'

Sanderson and Charlie nodded and left. Helen picked up the phone to dial Meredith Walker, but as she did so DC Reid knocked on the door. Replacing the cradle, Helen beckoned him in. Reid approached clutching a DVD. He handed it to Helen without a word, clearly worried about being the bearer of bad news.

Helen slipped the DVD into her laptop and the screen filled with a CCTV feed.

'What is this?'

'CCTV taken from a street near the Eastern Docks. One of the night watchmen down there saw someone matching Parker's description, so we checked it out.'

Reid reached over and fast-forwarded the footage, before eventually pressing play. Helen leant in, looking closely at the date and timeline.

'This is the night Max Paine was killed?'

'Correct.'

The camera gave a decent view of the dockside and Helen now saw a woman walk into view. She paused the image – slicked down hair, a large, light-coloured coat over a skin-tight suit – it was Samantha all right. Helen resumed playing the footage and watched as the woman struck up a conversation with a man idling near a stationary van. Parker appeared to take the man's hand and put it between her legs. Moments later, the two figures climbed into the back of the van.

'The van doesn't move for the next three hours. Then Parker exits. She doesn't look in a very good state and gets out of there as quickly as she can.'

Helen nodded, but her eye was already straying to the timeline at the bottom of the screen, rewinding the footage to the moment Parker got into the van with her bit of rough. The clock read 22.02.

'How accurate is the time on this feed?'

'To the second.'

Helen breathed out, then suddenly stepped forward,

kicking her office chair with all her might. It careered across the room, slamming into the wall before toppling over. Without bothering to offer an explanation, Helen walked out of the door and away across the incident room, dozens of pairs of eyes following her as she went.

91

'Not up to my usual standard. But pretty damn good in the circumstances, wouldn't you say?'

Samantha offered her nails to Helen, clearly pleased with the few cosmetics items she'd managed to source.

'Very nice,' Helen told her, keeping her temper in check. It had taken the best part of twenty minutes to pull Samantha up from the cells, but the interval had done little to calm Helen. Jim Grieves had put Paine's time of death as somewhere between 10.30 p.m. and 6.30 a.m. the following morning. Notwithstanding the fact that Paine died slowly, Parker's presence at the docks at 10 p.m. meant it was more than likely that someone had visited Paine's flat after her.

'I want to keep myself looking my best. You never know what's around the corner, do you?'

Her tone was teasing and playful.

'Absolutely. But I don't want to string this out any more than we have to. I expect you're anxious to get home.'

Samantha shrugged, disappointed with Helen's response. Was she expecting – hoping – for more aggression from Helen?

'You're right. It doesn't do to leave my babies alone for too long.'

'Quite.'

Samantha's dolls were in fact all in evidence bags at Meredith's lab. Surely Samantha would have guessed that, so was this yet another game? Helen looked down at her file, leafing casually through the pages, saying nothing. She could see in her peripheral vision that Samantha was twitchy and ill at ease, as if this exchange was not going as she'd hoped.

'I'd like to clarify a few details about your night with Max Paine.'

'Of course.'

'We talked a little about "The Phoenix" last time.'

'Got your juices flowing, did it?'

'I want a little more detail about what you got up to specifically,' Helen demanded, ignoring Parker's jibes.

'A lady never tells.'

'Was it straight S&M or something more exotic?'

'The latter.'

'Details, please.'

'Restraint and suffocation. I want total control.'

'And how do you achieve that?'

'Force of personality.'

'What about the restraints? Do you ever use hog ties, for example?'

'Of course.'

'Have you ever used them front ways on? Securing the hands to the ankles so the back is bent forwards?'

'Yes, it's more painful that way.'

'Did you do that to Paine?' Helen said, looking Parker directly in the eye.

'Yes,' she replied, refusing to be intimidated.

'Did you use any other restraints?'

'Tape, leather – I was very thorough. I wanted every inch of that boy to be covered.'

'And can I ask what time you left Paine's flat?'

'I honestly can't remember.'

'Roughly.'

'Around eleven, I suppose.'

'And then you went home.'

'As I've said before, yes.'

Helen sat back in her chair. She had won this battle but lost the war and suddenly felt drained of energy. Her sincere vows to bring Jake's killer to justice seemed a mockery now.

'Why are you lying to me, Samantha?'

'I'm not.'

'You didn't leave Paine's flat at eleven, you left much earlier and headed straight down to the docks for some rough trade.'

'That's bullshit.'

'We've got you on CCTV so there's no point lying. Is that how you got those bruises? Things get nasty in that van, did they?'

'I was *with* Paine,' Samantha insisted.

'Yes, but he was fine when you left him.'

'I've told you what happened, how he died –'

'You've recycled the details of Jake Elder's death. Max Paine died in a Zentai suit, with his arms tied *backwards* in hog ties. You tried hard, but you were wrong on pretty much every detail.'

'You're lying.'

'Did something similar happen at the Torture Rooms? Why *were* you leaving in such a state? Did someone reject you, push you away?'

Samantha hesitated too long, giving Helen her answer.

'I thought so.'

'This is bullshit.'

'You know, this is a first for me. I've never had a suspect who's so keen to be charged with a double murder. You've been wasting my time, haven't you, Samantha?'

'You've got it wrong,' Samantha said, now visibly flustered.

'No, you've got it wrong,' Helen said, rising. 'We're done here.'

Helen stabbed off the tape and walked to the door, pausing as she opened it.

'Good luck, Samantha.'

Then, without waiting for a reply, she left.

92

It was mid-morning and the Pound Shop was heaving. Beleaguered mums juggled maxi packs of Monster Munch, while old age pensioners scoured the shelves for bargains, keen to eke out their weekly budget a little further. It was an odd place to be plotting a murder.

The tall, slender figure sailed through the crowds, amused by the sights on display. All these people were so bound up in their own lives, scrabbling in the bargain bins, ladling pick-and-mix into crumpled bags, that they couldn't see what was right in front of them. What would they say if they knew? Would they be horrified? Or excited?

The police were no better. Grace's team had pulled in a messed-up shemale who might interest them for a while. But they were wide of the mark and, though Grace would presumably cotton on soon, she wouldn't be in time to prevent the next death. It was only hours away and already those same feelings were rising. Excitement. Tension. Control. Release.

This one would be a little bit different though. It wouldn't do to become predictable and now was the time to really give the police something to think about. Whereas the others had been works of art, this would be more down to earth, more homespun. This one would make them sit up and take note.

The cashier was ringing through the basket, chatting amiably. In her own mindless way she was becoming an accessory to murder. This was probably the most exciting thing that would ever happen to her and yet she was totally unaware of it, believing that this was just another routine sale of mundane domestic items.

But it was more than that. Much more than that. This was the beginning of the end.

93

'I need everything you've got.'

Meredith Walker had been about to tuck into a well-earnt sandwich when Helen Grace burst through the doors. Her colleague seemed angry and frustrated and, as Meredith was brought up to speed with developments, it wasn't hard to see why. The pair of them were now shut away in Meredith's office, reams of paper spread out on the desk in front of them.

'Every last detail. The answer *has* to be here somewhere.'

'You'd think, wouldn't you?'

'This guy's not a ghost, he's flesh and blood. He can't just visit these scenes and leave no trace.'

'I'll admit it's odd, but he has clearly been *very* careful. He wears a body suit, perhaps a mask, and never takes his gloves off. There are no prints on Paine's thermostat, nothing on the door handles or on the Zentai suit, the hog ties –'

'What about more circumstantial stuff? From the corridors, outside Paine's flat, in the bins.'

'We're still sweeping, but any defence would have a field day with the possibilities of cross-contamination –'

'I need *something* here.'

'I understand that, but we can't magic up the evidence.'

'What about the Torture Rooms? What have we got there?'

'Twenty-three different sources of DNA at the crime scene. I think your lot have been over these already.'

'What else?'

'We've got a number of DNA sources in close proximity to the corridor which we haven't been able to match.'

'What do you mean by "a number"?'

Meredith lifted a file on her desk to reveal another, from which she now pulled a sheet of paper.

'We have . . . a few beer bottles, a cigarette butt, a used condom, a glove. All of them containing DNA which we can't match to anyone on file.'

'He's unlikely to have had sex – the MO doesn't suggest it's that sort of crime – but perhaps one of the others?'

Meredith half nodded, half shrugged – she looked as unconvinced as Helen sounded. Helen rubbed her face with her hands and stared at the sheets of paper on the desk. So much data, such little progress.

'Do you think we'll catch him?' Helen said suddenly.

'It's early days, Helen.'

'There's always going to be one that gets away though, isn't there?'

'He'll make a mistake. They always do. And when he does, you'll be waiting for him. I have every confidence in you.'

Helen thanked Meredith, then headed off. She was

grateful for her support, but the truth was that this case was so unusual and so puzzling that she was genuinely concerned about the outcome.

For the first time in years, Helen was beginning to doubt herself.

94

'They haven't got a bloody clue.'

David Simons's tone was withering.

'They arrest someone, let him go. Arrest someone else, let *her* go . . .'

Emilia nodded and let Simons rant. Like many in the BDSM community, he had had his hopes raised by the arrest of Michael Parker. News of Parker's sudden release was therefore a kick in the teeth that had been met with a wave of anger. Many were confused, others were scared, but none had the personal connection that Simons had. Which is why he was blowing a gasket now.

'It's incredibly frustrating,' Emilia said, when Simons eventually drew breath. 'We all want to get justice for Jake and the investigation seems . . . unfocused at best. Which is why I wanted to talk to you.'

Simons suddenly looked up, intrigued and surprised.

'Forgive me for revisiting painful memories, but you said when we talked before that there was someone *else* in Jake's life? A woman he had feelings for?'

Simons stared at her, clearly unhappy to be reminded of this.

'I know this is difficult for you,' Emilia continued, 'but it's really important. What did Jake tell you about the nature of their relationship?'

'Not a lot – I had to prise it out of him.'

'And?'

'And it was complicated. At first, he denied he had feelings for this woman. Then he said he was over her, but I'm not sure that was true either. He used to follow her around at one time, after she'd dropped him –'

'He *stalked* her?'

'I didn't say that. But he had issues . . . letting go.'

'So what happened?'

'She walloped him,' Simons said, smiling grimly.

'She attacked him?'

'He gave her a fright and got what was coming to him. She lamped him with her motorcycle helmet, I think, and he left her alone after that. He didn't like telling me of course, but I needed to know everything. For all the good it did me . . .'

Emilia hesitated – scribbling down 'motorcycle helmet' – then asked:

'You mentioned that you saw them together once – Jake and this woman. Did you see her face?'

'Only for a moment, but I was intrigued so . . .'

'Would you recognize her now?'

'Why? Why are you asking me these questions?'

'Look, David, I know this probably seems odd but I'm trying to put together the fullest picture of Jake's life that I can. For reasons that you'll understand in time, I'm not convinced we can have full confidence in the police investigation and somebody needs to carry on the fight on Jake's behalf.'

Simons looked at her and then said:

'Yes, I think I would.'

Emilia delved into her bag. Pulling a photo from inside, she laid it on the table.

'Is this her?'

Simons leant forward. Emilia watched him closely. She was trying to remain calm, but her heart was in her mouth. Finally, Simons looked up at her and said:

'Yes, it is.'

95

Angelique lay on the bed, her eyes glued to the television. The news was on, leading with the latest developments in the Jake Elder case and the early-evening audience were being treated to grabbed images of Michael Parker – 'Samantha' – scurrying back to his flat while being harried by local journalists.

Despite her height, Samantha looked so diminished, so pathetic, that it was a wonder the police ever had her in the frame. She was clearly a nasty piece of work, but did they really believe she had the organizational skills to pull off such an intricate double murder? Details of Paine's death had seeped out online, triggering a wave of reaction on social media. Some commentators were sickened, others strangely impressed by the elaborate nature of the crime. But nobody had publicly pointed the finger at Samantha, despite the common practice these days of trial by innuendo. That should have told the police something – sometimes it pays to listen to the word on the street.

As it was, they had accused two innocent people with predictable results. What would Samantha do now? She had always been wound tight – how would she react now to the shit storm that was coming her way? Huddling up inside her stale little flat with nobody to comfort her but her dollies? It wouldn't be at all surprising if she went the same way as Paul Jackson, though something told Angelique that Samantha might be rather more effective at finishing the job.

What were Grace and her team doing now? Now that they were back to square one? Did they still have faith in their leader? Would they trust her to get a result? Not knowing was tantalizing, but there was nothing to be done about it. The next few days would reveal everything and in the meantime there was nothing for Angelique to do but watch and wait.

96

'I want us to look again at the credit cards.'

Helen had made Charlie jump when she appeared by her desk. However long you worked with her you never got used to her stealth.

'We've run them several times,' Charlie replied quickly. 'Both credit card owners used many of the same stores and internet sites, so the point of fraud is going to be hard to pin down. Look at the list – Amazon, Ticketmaster, Trainline, Sainsbury's, Gumtree, iTunes, Pets at Home –'

'Let's come at it from another angle then. If it's internet fraud, then it's going to be virtually impossible to trace, so let's focus on the retail outlets. We've been assuming that our killer has specifically cloned cards to facilitate these murders. But it's more likely he was involved in petty crime first, only later graduating up to more serious offences.'

'So we want to look for seasoned credit card fraudsters –'

'Exactly. Get on to the local outlets that the fraud victims used regularly. It would be easy enough for an employee to lift their details when ringing through a transaction, so let's see if any employees – past or present – had form for credit card fraud. Don't limit yourself to recent offences – this kind of crime is a long time in the making.'

'But if they're on file, wouldn't we have got a match to a DNA source at one of the crime sites?'

'Not necessarily. It may be they were questioned but never charged. Or it may be that our killer is just too cautious. He didn't even touch Paine, yet managed to kill him. The same may be true of Jake Elder.'

Charlie nodded, but it was a depressing thought. Were they chasing shadows?

'I originally thought forensics would be crucial, given the lack of credible witnesses,' Helen continued. 'But now I don't think we even have that luxury. So we're looking for tiny mistakes, small pieces of the puzzle that put together –'

'Lead us to our man. You should know, though, that even with just the retail outlets highlighted it's a seriously long list –'

'I know it's a needle in a haystack –'

'Look, I'm happy to do it, of course I am.'

'Good. Thank you.'

Helen turned to go, but Charlie had more to say.

'Look, Helen, I know I said too much yesterday.'

'It's not your fault, Charlie, it's mine.'

'Whatever, I just wanted to let you know that I'm really sorry and that I'll do whatever is necessary to help you break this case.'

'Thank you.'

Helen should've gone further, apologizing for *her* erratic behaviour, but she didn't really trust herself and something in Charlie's demeanour meant it wasn't necessary. The mark of a true friend.

'Call me if you find anything,' Helen said, turning to leave.

'Sure. Where are you going?'

Helen paused in the doorway of the incident room and turned back to Charlie.

'To climb inside the mind of a killer.'

97

Control. Sadism. Restraint. Victim. Dominator. Knowledge. Power. Anger. Disgust. Self-hatred. Pain.

Helen scribbled fast, covering the white board with her scrawl. She had commandeered one of the more remote interview suites, covering the table with files and dropping the blinds. She wanted to be alone with the perpetrator, testing their rudimentary profile of him again to see if she'd missed anything obvious. She read through their behavioural indicators, probable motives, evidence analysis, trying to picture what went through their killer's mind at the point of death.

'Can I join you?'

Surprised, Helen looked up to find Jonathan Gardam standing in the doorway.

'Sorry, I was miles away. Come in.'

Gardam pushed the door to and walked towards the board. He stood for a minute, taking in the words written on it.

'How's the profile coming on?'

'Slowly. We haven't got much to go on.'

'Tell me.'

'Really, it's pretty basic . . .'

'I'd like to help if I can. I was a decent DI once upon a time.'

Helen hesitated. She preferred to do her soul searching alone, but Gardam's tone brooked no argument and perhaps she could make an exception. She wasn't getting very far by herself.

'I think the key element is control. Control of himself, control of his victim, control of us. He's a high-functioning individual with an inflated sense of his own importance, someone who feels the world doesn't understand him. He wants to engage but will only do so on his terms, leaving statement killings for us to interpret.'

'So he enjoys the game?'

'Absolutely. I think he likes to tantalize, to tease, to play God.'

'Is he likely to live alone, then? To have a home environment that he can control?'

'Possibly but he may have a partner, even a family. Maybe he controls them like he controls his victims or it may be that they dominate *him*.'

Gardam nodded, taking this in.

'Do we think his victims were targeted specifically?'

'If they were I would expect to see more signs of overt violence against them.'

'So does he have something against people in the BDSM world?'

'Possibly.'

'Does he have a moral issue with S&M? Was he on the wrong end of a bad experience? Could some incident within the community have triggered this?'

Helen considered this.

'I don't mean to pry,' Gardam ventured, 'but you

must have come across these kinds of people – what sort of world is it?'

'It's not as weird as you'd think,' Helen replied quickly. 'People go into it for all sorts of reasons, but generally it's professional, discreet and consensual.'

'But there must be people who want to push it to the extreme . . .'

'In private encounters perhaps. Professional sessions have strict safety rules, which are religiously observed.'

'So this guy has graduated beyond the entry level? He's experienced?'

'Judging by his knowledge and activities, I'd say he knows this world well. He doesn't seem to want to be punished or exposed or abused, he wants to be the one with the upper hand. It is possible he comes from a place where he has no control, no sense of hope. He could be an abuse victim, someone trapped in an unhealthy relationship, someone saddled with emotional baggage that he can't expiate any other way.'

'Do any of those apply to you?'

Helen stopped, surprised by the question.

'Look, tell me to fuck off if you want to, but you're our best asset in trying to understand this guy. I appreciate you don't want to broadcast this side of your life to the team, but between us . . .'

Helen stared at Gardam, then said:

'I do it because it works.'

'Because you feel . . . guilt?'

'Guilt, regret, anger.'

'And it works for you? It gives you reassurance, comfort . . .'

'For a while.'

'But then those feelings come back again?'

Helen shrugged, but didn't deny it.

'Do you think those feelings will *ever* go away?' Gardam persisted.

'I'm not sure. It sounds stupid . . . but sometimes I feel . . . that I'm stained. That I'm marked by what's happened in the past . . .'

'It's a mark no one else can see.'

'*I* can see it.'

Gardam looked at her for a moment. He seemed to be struggling for the right words. Finally he said:

'Do you really think you're . . . cursed?'

'That's exactly how I feel.'

'It doesn't have to be that way, you know . . .'

'Believe me, if I could find a path through this I would.'

'Then let me help you. You've taken the first steps by confiding in me. Don't let this opportunity go to waste. Let me . . . help you.'

He took a step forwards, holding out his hand to her. The smile on his face was kindly but firm.

'I know you're lonely, Helen, I know you feel lost . . .'

Helen took a step back, but still Gardam advanced.

'And I hate to think of you alone in that flat, with all this going on.' He gestured at the board.

'I'll be fine. Look, I think it's best that –'

'You opened yourself up to me for a reason. So don't be scared now.'

He put his hand on Helen's cheek.

'This will be good for both of us.'

Helen lifted her hand to remove his, but suddenly Gardam pulled her towards him. Now she felt his mouth on hers. She raised her hand to his chest to push him off, but he kept coming, his teeth biting down on her lower lip.

Helen pulled away sharply. But his arms were still around her and as she tried to wriggle out of his grip, she collided with the table.

'Don't run from this, Helen,' Gardam chided, running his hand down her back and on to her buttocks.

He moved towards her again, but this time Helen struck first, dragging her nails down the side of his face. Gardam recoiled in shock, giving Helen the opportunity she needed. She drove her knee hard into his groin – once, twice, three times.

Gardam crumpled to the floor.

Helen stepped over him, moving fast across the room. Reaching the doorway, she burst through it, leaving her boss lying on the floor, gagging quietly into the carpet. Helen didn't look back once. Now she just wanted to be away.

98

The eyes of the world were on her now.

Samantha hated mockery, she hated attention, she hated judgement. But she was getting all three in spades now. She'd pulled the curtains to, turned off her mobile, but still the intercom buzzed, buzzed, buzzed. She knew bugger all about electrics, so in the end she'd ripped it off the wall, hurling it at the door with a stream of invective. Shortly after, the handful of journalists who'd harried and jostled her on her way home had gained entry to the block. She could hardly call the police and her useless landlord wasn't answering his calls, so they were still at the door, calling, hammering, joking. To them this was all in a day's work.

She had stuck it for a while, ignoring their pleas for an interview, sitting in silence in the living room. But in the end it had got to her and she'd retreated to the back of the house. Cranking up the stereo, she'd treated them to a bit of Dark Metal. They would love it of course – it would add 'colour' to their articles – but she didn't care. She just wanted to block out the world for a while.

The police had stolen most of her possessions, her clothes, even her babies. But they had missed a couple. A pair of dolls she'd picked up at a flea market and had called Duke and Duchess on account of their finery.

They now resided in the corner of a bedside drawer, temporarily exiled there due to lack of space in the room. Samantha pulled them from their hiding place and laid them on the floor in front of her. They were all she had for company now, yet even they seemed to be looking at her oddly today, their dead, black eyes giving back nothing but suspicion and disappointment. She had seen that look a lot when she had been a kid.

God, how she craved a drink, but there was no way she could head out to get one. She had gambled and lost, revelling in the attention the police gave her as she led them a merry, pointless dance, only to be tossed aside once they realized she was lying through her teeth. All she'd wanted was a moment in the spotlight, but what a bitter harvest she'd reaped.

She wanted company but there was none to be had. She wanted sanctuary from the world, but even that seemed to have been taken away from her now. This dingy, rotting flat had been her haven for so long. But that was all over. Now it was just a home without a heart.

99

Sanderson finished her drink and considered the wisdom of having another. It was only a pint of weak lager – not exactly Oliver Reed standards – but still she hesitated. She'd known many a copper ruin a perfectly good career by slipping into bad habits. The Mermaid pub had been the location for several falls from grace over the years, hidden away in a back street close to Southampton Central.

She should have been at a spinning class, but somehow she couldn't face all that shouting and positive energy tonight. The alternative was going back to her badly heated flat and empty fridge, so she'd retreated to the warmth of the pub instead, ignoring the occasional glances of the hopeful males at the bar, to enjoy an overpriced pint of continental beer.

'Can I get you another?'

Sanderson looked up to find Emilia Garanita standing over her.

'I'm meeting someone here shortly, but I've got half an hour to kill. Judging by the looks you're getting, you could use a chaperone.'

Sanderson assumed she was lying, but didn't immediately tell her to sling her hook. Garanita had been useful in the past and maybe some company was better than none. She would need to be on her guard, but what the heck?

Minutes later, Emilia returned with two pints.

'I would have thought you'd be burning the midnight oil.'

'Taking a break. We've done as much as we can for tonight.'

'I dare say.'

Sanderson detected the note of sarcasm, but didn't begrudge Emilia her scepticism. Sanderson had set several lines of enquiry in train, but she had little confidence that any of them would pay dividends in the short term. Furthermore, Helen seemed to have gone AWOL, underlining Sanderson's sense that things were drifting. The investigation appeared to be stymied, morale fractured and her own career going nowhere. Her conflict with Charlie risked dividing the team and she still feared that her popular rival would be the natural winner.

'So how *are* things going?' Emilia said brightly.

'Do you mind if we don't talk shop?'

'By all means, but if there's anything you want to tell me, off the record . . .'

'I'm good.'

'Well, let me help *you* then. I know things aren't going your way.'

Sanderson looked up from her drink.

'It must be tough now there are *two* DSs, especially as Brooks and Grace are so close. I'm not a betting woman, but when Grace eventually moves on, I'd say Brooks was favourite to take her place, wouldn't you?'

Sanderson stared at Emilia, but said nothing.

'Must be galling being pushed out, which is why I wanted to talk to you.'

'Look, things haven't been easy – I'm sure you've heard the gossip – but I don't do quid pro quos, Emilia. If you want to know more about the case, there's a press conference starting in ten minutes at Southampton Central –'

'I'm not interested in that. The kind of questions I've got for you can't be asked at a press conference.'

Sanderson looked at Emilia, intrigued now in spite of herself.

'What I'm about to tell you is in confidence. I have important information regarding these murders.'

Emilia let her words settle, then continued:

'If we act on this information, the implications for Hampshire Police will be profound, so I need to know I can trust you. Can I trust you, Joanne?'

'Of course.'

'Good.'

Emilia smiled and leant in close, dropping her voice to a whisper.

'Because I'm about to make you an offer you won't be able to refuse.'

And now Sanderson knew Emilia had been lying about meeting a friend. She had come here for *her*.

100

'You're going to have to handle it on your own.'

'I can't go out there without an SIO. I'm a bloody Media Liaison Officer.'

'Then do your job – liaise with the media,' Gardam replied curtly.

'Not having DI Grace is one thing – I'm used to that – but I can't go out there without you. They'll smell a rat and call me on it.'

'Then find Brooks or Sanderson.'

'Believe me, I've tried. And next time – fyi – I would appreciate a call rather than an email. Bailing at the last minute is not on –'

'But it's happening, so get over it. This is not a fucking debate.'

DS Maddy Wicket looked sufficiently put out for Gardam now to soften his tone.

'Look at me. I can't face them like this.'

Maddy stared at the scratches on his right cheek.

'What happened?'

'Thought I'd go for a run to make a change from the police gym. Ran straight into a bloody branch and now I look like I've been mugged. Hardly the best advert for local policing.'

Maddy wanted to disagree but even she saw that Gardam was right.

'We could cancel, if you want,' Gardam suggested. 'Unless you want to knock it back a couple of hours and try and raise Brooks in the meantime?'

Predictably Maddy now latched on to this. She loved nothing more than riding to the rescue and started to run through their options. Gardam nodded, but he was no longer listening. He was back in the interview suite with Helen.

She had come to him. She had worked him hard, appearing frosty and defensive at first, but that had all been part of her game. Slowly she had unpeeled herself and in the last few weeks she had come on to him directly. You don't tell a man that kind of thing without expecting a reaction. It was an explicit invitation and when he acted on it, she'd attacked him.

Was she running scared? Was it because he was married? No, her reaction was far too aggressive to be explained like that. In other circumstances, he would have had her up on an assault charge, but he couldn't do that here. Had she done this kind of thing before? He rather suspected she had. Her previous boss had been a woman but the one before that had been a man. He had left suddenly having crossed swords with her – had she tricked him in the same fashion?

She needed saving from herself – she *wanted* to be saved – and she'd led him to believe that he was the man to do so. He loved her pain, but wanted to purge her of it, to protect her from the darkness out there. He had always thought of her as an injured bird requiring warmth, comfort and love. But now he knew that Helen Grace was nothing more than a heartless prick tease.

101

Helen shut her front door, locking it behind her. Leaning against it, she closed her eyes and tried not to cry. She had left the station and headed straight home, driving too fast, barely registering the other drivers. Her head was pounding and she now pulled her cigarettes from her pocket, but they tumbled from her grasp. Her hands were shaking – she was still in shock.

She kept replaying the last couple of hours in her head, barely believing they were real. It was over twenty years since anyone had been sexually aggressive towards her and she would never have expected it to happen at Southampton Central. The station had been her sanctuary for so long, the place where she could be a normal, functioning human being – but Gardam had destroyed all that.

What the fuck was he thinking? She'd told him about herself in confidence and as a friend. She'd been worried about the impact of her past on the case, but that was it. She had never encouraged his interest in her. Quite the opposite: she had put his close attention down to him being a good manager, a front-line officer who knew what it was like to lead a major investigation. What signs had he picked up on to make him think that he could behave like that?

It was scarcely believable and she wanted to wish it all away, but she still had his skin under her nails and the scent of his aftershave on her face. She hurried to the bathroom and, pulling off her jacket and blouse, scooped handfuls of hot water over her face, neck and hands. Before long her hair was dripping, her make-up smeared, but she was clean.

Towelling dry her hair, she looked at herself in the mirror. What should she do now? Should she report him? What he'd done was totally unacceptable but he hadn't harmed her and if he contested her account of what happened, how on earth could she *prove* that she was telling the truth? It would be his word against hers.

She should report him. She *had* to report him. But the thought made her sick to the stomach and besides she might very well come off worse – Gardam had friends in high places. There'd be no question of carrying on with the investigation, of getting justice for Jake. But could she really go back to work as if nothing had happened and report to Gardam in the usual way? She now knew what he thought of her and it was impossible to stop thinking about it.

Buzz.

The noise had been somewhere on the periphery of her consciousness, but now she heard it clearly.

Buzz.

There it was again. It was coming from somewhere within the flat. Scenting danger, Helen drew her baton and extended it, creeping forward towards the source of the noise.

Buzz.

It was coming from the kitchen. What the hell was it?

Buzz.

Losing patience, Helen now stepped quickly inside. There was no one in the kitchen, but the sight that greeted her still stopped her in her tracks. Her private phone was sitting in the middle of the kitchen table. The mobile that she had dropped down a drain three days ago. It was powered up and now buzzing in receipt of a text message.

Helen inspected the room. Who had put it there? Were they still in the flat? The kitchen window was secured, but what about the living room? The bedroom? Baton raised, Helen charged from the kitchen, checking the windows, the cupboards, under the bed. Her heart was beating fast, but there was no sign of an intruder. She was alone.

Who had seen her drop the phone? Who had returned it to her? *Why* had they brought it back?

Helen walked quickly into the kitchen. Pulling a tea towel from the hooks, she covered her hand and carefully picked the phone up. Through the cotton fabric, she pressed READ. The message sprang up – it was from Angelique and it was short and sweet:

We need to meet.

102

Helen parked her bike three blocks away, then began to walk hurriedly towards Angelique's flat. The sun had set now and Helen stuck close to the wall, avoiding the sodium glow of the streetlights. She had no idea what she was walking into, but she didn't want to announce her arrival.

Had Angelique followed her that night? Seen her drop the phone down the drain? If so, why had she fished it out and how had she gained access to her flat? Helen's cleaner had been in today, it was possible she'd forgotten to lock the door properly, but she was usually very scrupulous about security. Had Angelique got a key somehow?

It made little sense but the shadow of a memory now rose in her mind. Helen remembered looking through the list of names drawn up by Sanderson, detailing people who'd attended her Munch or who were regular visitors there. There was an Angelique on that list somewhere – Helen was sure of that – but she'd thought little of it at the time. Sanderson hadn't met her, they had nothing specific on her and there was no guarantee it was even the same person. But she had been on the list – she was part of the community. It was very possible she was a size 6 shoe and from memory she did like to wear boots. Did she know Paine? Had she frequented the Torture Rooms? And if she was responsible for these crimes, what was driving her?

The chief question in Helen's mind was why she had gone to such lengths to summon her. If she wanted to be anonymous or discreet there would have been easier, less sinister ways to do so. So what was this then? Some kind of power game? A signal that she was in control?

Helen paused at the top of Angelique's street. It was near the docks and largely made up of converted warehouses and a few specialist shops – most of which never seemed to be open. There didn't appear to be any CCTV on the street, so Helen moved quickly forward, walking down the opposite side of the road to get a better look at Angelique's building.

It was plum in the middle of the quiet street, backing on to another large set of flats. There appeared to be no back entrance, nor any fire escape either. Her only means of entry was through the front door. This made Helen nervous, but it had one advantage. There were two other sex workers operating from the flats, which meant that the front door was often in use, especially after dark. Helen crossed the road, taking up a position a few yards away from the front door, shielded by a couple of large municipal bins.

Helen breathed out, trying to calm her racing heart. Was she foolish to come here? She had no choice really – she had to find out why Angelique was playing games with her – but it didn't make her any less apprehensive. This was not her turf, nor was she arriving under circumstances of her own choosing. She was dancing on the end of somebody else's line.

A noise made her look up – a man with an overcoat and briefcase was hurrying away from the flats. Helen gave him a couple of seconds start, then emerged from her hiding place – to see the heavy front door swinging to a close. Darting forward, she grabbed at the handle, arresting its progress just in time.

Moving inside, she eased the door shut, then looked up the stairwell. There was no one in sight and all was quiet, so Helen walked quickly but quietly up the stairs. Soon she was on the third floor, outside Angelique's flat. Now she didn't hesitate, pulling a credit card from her jacket pocket. If the dead lock was on, she would get nowhere. But if it wasn't . . .

She eased the card through the gap between the door and the frame and, moving it upwards, felt for the latch. The card hit metal and, having gained traction, Helen kneaded it back and forth, manoeuvring the metal tongue out of its mooring. She increased the pressure of her body on the door and moments later it opened with a gentle sigh.

Helen stepped inside and listened. A distant beat drifted down from above – someone upstairs had the music ramped up – but there was little sound in this flat. Nor was there any light – the whole place stood in utter darkness. Silently slipping her baton from her pocket, she extended it and took a step forward.

The floorboard creaked under her weight, so Helen took a step back. Changing her route, she now clung to the wall, moving faster and with less clamour. The flat was a small one-bed affair and wouldn't take long to scout. Helen was suddenly keen to have this over with – it occurred to her that perhaps the place was so quiet because there was no one here. Wouldn't that be rich if she was creeping around an empty flat, braced for an attack that was never going to come?

She had reached the kitchen and darted her head in. But it was deserted. She moved forward now into the living room, ducking low to avoid any possible attack. Whatever misgivings, there was no point taking unnecessary chances. But this room too was deserted. She could see through the open door opposite that the bathroom was empty as well, which just left the bedroom.

Helen padded towards the door, which hung ajar. Perhaps the place was unoccupied? Perhaps Angelique was waiting until Helen was inside before following her in? She shot a look over her shoulder, but all was still, so using the point of her baton, she pushed the door open.

Still nothing. So cautiously Helen took a step forward. The curtains were closed and it was dimly lit, but something made Helen hesitate on the threshold. Something – or someone – was in here. They had the advantage, but Helen suddenly flicked the light on to level the playing field.

And there was Angelique, lying on the bed. She wasn't moving, so checking the corners of the room, Helen moved forward. As she got closer, it became clear that Helen had come too late. Angelique lay there in her catsuit, her limbs tethered to the four corners of the bed with Japanese bondage cords. Her face was blue and as Helen now leant over she saw that the unfortunate dominatrix had a ball gag secured in her mouth. Worse still her entire head, from chin to crown, was covered in clingfilm.

Helen had been right all along. She had just walked into a trap.

103

'Now tell me, what happened to your colleague? DC McAndrew, was it? I rather liked her.'

Sanderson smiled tightly, as Maurice Finnan presented her with a cup of tea and ushered her towards the living room.

'On operational duties, I'm afraid.'

'And now they've sent a sergeant along. I *am* going up in the world.'

It was said lightly, but Sanderson sensed the question behind Maurice's joke. Clearly he was sharp as a tack beneath his cultivated eccentricity.

'Nothing too exciting, I'm afraid. Just some follow-up work.'

Maurice sipped his tea and said nothing.

'You very helpfully provided us with a list of vehicle registrations that you've seen near Jake Elder's flat.'

'I did.'

'Would you mind if we went through a few of them with you now . . . ?'

Maurice was only too happy to help, so Sanderson crossed the room and sat down next to him. Maurice pulled his reading glasses from his top pocket and cast an eye over the list of registrations.

'This one, DE59 VFB. A blue Transit. Can you remember the driver at all?'

Maurice thought for a second, then replied:

'No, I'm afraid I can't. Normally I've got a pretty good memory for these things, but . . .'

'What about this one? BD05 TRD – a Corsa.'

'Little fellow. Raincoat, with one of the little rucksack things for computers –'

'Laptop bag.'

'That's it.'

'And VF08 BHU. An Astra estate –'

'Big guy, unshaven, a labourer or something like that.'

'Very good and what about this one – LB52 WTC?'

'Well, that was an unusual one – a motorbike.'

'Right. And the driver?'

'A woman. That's what made her stand out. I didn't think they were into that kind of thing.'

'Could you describe her for me?'

Sanderson took down the particulars, barely believing what she was hearing. She hadn't wanted to believe Emilia at first, telling her to take a running jump. But as the journalist had laid out the evidence in front of her, troubling questions had been raised in her mind. Garanita had photographic evidence going back several years that suggested Helen had used Jake Elder's services and it appeared she knew Max Paine too. Why had she withheld this from her team? What did she have to hide? Sanderson's head had been spinning by the end of their conversation and she had hurried here, hoping against hope that Maurice would contradict Emilia's story, but he hadn't. Quite the opposite. He had in fact just given her a perfect description of Helen Grace.

104

She'd called in sick, but actually had never felt better – her lie was simply designed to let her work at home in peace. In the past, when she was still learning the ropes, she'd come a cropper by being too open about her stories. Leads had been 'borrowed', witnesses snaffled, and suddenly her exclusives had become yesterday's news. There was no way Emilia was making the same mistake again. Not with the story that was going to define her career.

It was clear from her chat with Sanderson that no suspicion had yet alighted on Helen Grace. The loyal DS was disbelieving at first, but over the course of their chat she could see a step change in her perception of her boss, but also in her view of Emilia. She sensed that Sanderson was dissatisfied professionally and she'd played on that – highlighting the opportunities Grace's exposure might throw up, while also appealing to her sense of duty. One bad apple can make the whole force look bad, she'd said, somehow managing to keep a straight face as she did so.

Sanderson had bitten on it and run off to do her bidding, leaving Emilia free to write her copy. She had already drafted the leader page – a masterpiece of pithy exposé – and had the building blocks in place for pages two and three. What she needed now was some context.

People thought they knew Helen Grace, but she'd had such a rich and difficult life that it was a story that was always worth retelling. It was Emilia's profile piece at the centre of the paper that would be the true heart of this story – after all, nobody had better access to or a deeper history with Grace than she did.

In the interests of fairness, Emilia had listed Grace's many triumphs – the unmasking of Ella Matthews, her heroics in rescuing Ruby Sprackling, not to mention her apprehension of a pair of serial arsonists. Set against this was Grace's propensity for violence – the fatal shooting of her own sister most notably – and her dark obsession with sado-masochism.

Like Emilia, Helen Grace was a woman with two faces. Looked at from one side, she was Southampton's finest serving police officer. Looked at from another, she was a deeply troubled woman who seemed to curse everything and everyone she touched. Some, like her loyal comrade Charlie Brooks, survived the ordeal, but others were not so lucky. Mark Fuller had killed himself while in captivity, her nephew, Robert Stonehill, had had to flee after Helen exposed him, and at least three serving police officers – two of them at Detective Superintendent level – had had to resign after crossing swords with her. Disaster, death and violence seemed to stalk Helen wherever she went.

Her whole life seemed to have been a prelude to the events of the last few days. Jake Elder had been obsessed with her – he had stalked her and been assaulted as a result. Max Paine had also pushed his luck with her and, by the looks of the photo his widow had given Emilia, had been viciously attacked. Emilia had asked around and discovered Paine had a predilection for unwanted advances. Emilia could see the scene clearly – Paine trying it on and receiving a nasty beating for his pains. In their differing ways – one emotionally, one sexually – they had both tried to force themselves upon Helen Grace and paid a heavy price for their boldness.

How had this all come about? Had their paths crossed together by chance or was it by design? Had they threatened to expose Helen, as Emilia had previously, unless she played ball? Or had Helen's anger been simmering for years, just awaiting a spark to ignite it?

Emilia had historic photos of Grace visiting Elder, plus a positive ID and testimony from David Simons confirming that they had a troubled relationship. She also had robust evidence from Dinah Carter and a decent ID – how many well-known female officers with a penchant for sado-masochism were there? Emilia had most of the answers now, but still this final piece of the puzzle eluded her.

Why had Helen Grace finally crossed the line? What had finally pushed her into becoming a murderer?

105

He didn't have to wait long. The front door opened slowly and moments later she emerged, hurrying off down the street in the direction she'd come from. From his elevated position, she seemed so small, so vulnerable, that for a moment he almost felt sorry for her. But it was only a fleeting emotion – the rage that had sustained him for so long devouring this brief spasm of pity.

What was she thinking now? She had been at the scene for a short time, but had reaped a bitter harvest. By contrast, he had enjoyed himself enormously. This murder had been the most meaningful. And the most satisfying. Angelique had begged for mercy once she realized what was happening – as much as you can beg when you've got a plastic ball clamped into your mouth. But he had barely heard her as he went about his business – it was so much noise in the background. She was just an offering – an offering to lay at the feet of Helen Grace.

Helen had almost reached the end of the road now. Had she left her bike out of sight to avoid drawing attention to herself? If so, she was wasting her time. This was about her – this had always been about her.

Suddenly she slipped from view, disappearing around the corner and away from him. But their meeting was not far away now.

You can run, Helen. But you can't hide.

106

The Incident Room was deserted. Sanderson had left it until late to return to base, hoping that the rest of the team would have called it a day, given that there were no breaking leads. As she teased the handle of the main door, she was pleased to find it locked – she didn't want to have to explain her presence here. Letting herself in quickly, she secured the door behind her. She couldn't risk being disturbed, given what she was about to do.

Picking her way through the desks, she made her way to Helen's office. Her boss always operated an open-door policy and never bothered locking her office. Helen liked to be one of the foot soldiers and was at pains not to erect false barriers between her and the team. This was useful now, as Sanderson walked into her office unimpeded, but it made her betrayal all the worse. Whatever she thought of Helen now, she had always been an inspirational figure in Sanderson's life.

Crossing to the desk, she opened one drawer, then another. But it was as she opened the bottom drawer that she found what she was after. Helen had long straight hair and always kept a hairbrush in her office, in case she suddenly found herself facing top brass or, worse, the press. Slipping on latex gloves, Sanderson picked up the brush and carefully extracted three hairs from the bristles. Dropping the hairs into a small evidence bag, she sealed her haul and placing the brush back in the drawer, pushed it firmly to.

Twenty minutes later, she was buzzing herself into the Police Scientific Services building. It was a short hop up to the lab on the third floor, where she found Meredith Walker waiting for her.

'This had better be good,' Meredith said on seeing her. 'I'm missing *First Dates* to be here.'

'New lead in the Elder case. DNA source. We need it done –'

'Asap, I know.'

The forensics officer turned to begin her work.

'Oh and Meredith . . .'

She turned to look at Sanderson once more, intrigued by her serious tone.

'It's for my eyes only.'

107

They ate in silence. Jane was well tuned to his moods and could tell when Jonathan had had a bad day at work. Her default tactic in those situations was not to probe or hassle him; instead she would hand him a glass of cold white wine and get on with the business of cooking their dinner.

She had cooked one of his favourites – linguini alle vongole – but he could barely taste it tonight. He was on auto-pilot, twirling the pasta slowly round his fork then lifting it to his mouth, barely conscious of what he was eating. He didn't care a jot for the consequences of his actions today – he felt confident he could ride out any formal complaint Helen might make. It was the betrayal that burnt. He had wanted her like he hadn't wanted any woman for years and she had pushed him away. Why had she toyed with him if she wasn't interested?

Gardam finished eating and pushed his bowl away. Looking up, he caught Jane staring at him. She'd obviously been concerned when he returned home with two deep scratches on his cheek, but seemed to accept his story of a jogging accident. Now, though, Gardam wondered if she was having her doubts. The scratches were long, straight and clean. Would you expect that type of injury from a low-hanging branch? The question was whether she would respond to these doubts, asking him outright. He wanted her to ask. He would tell her that he hadn't slept with another woman, but he wanted to. He would tell Jane that he found her predictable, bourgeois and anodyne – both in the bedroom and out. He would tell her that their marriage was comfortable and routine, characterized by his career ambition and her appetite for a nice, middle-class lifestyle, but that when you boiled things down, when you got down to primal needs and desires, she meant little to him. Helen was the woman who occupied his thoughts now. Despite her savage rejection, she remained there still – in his brain, in his gut, but worst of all in his heart.

108

It was nearly midnight and the air was biting cold. Helen walked briskly through the trees, working her way to the deepest part of the wood. She had come this route many times during her runs and knew it like the back of her hand. She was following a path that few knew of, which gave her some comfort, some respite from the paranoia now gripping her. Here at least she would be safe.

Angelique had been left for her to discover. This was a new phase in a game that was clearly directed at her. All three victims were known to Helen – she had used their services and allowed them to see a part of her that no one else did. Was jealousy driving someone to destroy these people? Or something else? And what did the text message sent by Angelique's killer summoning Helen imply? That she was being set up? Or just that she was meant to know? Perhaps the killer had just lost patience with the real target and had decided to bring her into the game.

Time would tell, but if Helen wanted to survive, she would belatedly have to get smart. Pulling her private mobile phone from her jacket, she flipped open the back and removed the SIM card. She looked around for any signs that she was being watched, but seeing nothing, removed her lighter from her jeans and ignited the flame.

It was an oddly beautiful sight – the plastic melting slowly as the metal chip of the SIM card blackened and distorted. Holding it in her gloved hand until it was destroyed, Helen dropped it to the ground, into a small hole she'd dug with the heel of her boot. Kicking earth over the hole, she then moved away quickly, clutching the phone in her hand.

On the edge of the woods, she hesitated. A couple were wandering home across the Common, arm in arm. Helen waited until they had disappeared, before venturing on to open ground. She had always felt at home here, but now she felt exposed and vulnerable. Upping her pace, she soon found herself sprinting, keen to get this over with.

Within minutes, she was by the cemetery lake. Checking the coast was clear, Helen pulled the body of her phone from her pocket and threw it as hard as she could, watching it arc through the sky before landing in the water with a splash. The noise echoed briefly then died away.

Helen had already turned on her heel and was marching towards the southern exit. She had to regroup now, which meant heading back to her flat. She would have to search every inch of it and secure every lock before she would feel safe, but she would do whatever was necessary. It was her home after all – her only safe space now – and she was damned if she was going to be driven from it.

109

Charlie held her hand to her mouth, sickened by the sight in front of her. It shouldn't have made a difference to her that their third victim was a woman, but it did. Charlie could see the naked terror frozen on her pretty face, she could feel her desperation to breathe, to live, even as the oxygen in her lungs ran out. Her nostrils were dilated, her mouth wide open – one almost felt she might lurch back into life suddenly with one big breath. But her lifeless eyes, staring monotonously at the low ceiling, gave the lie to that.

She went by the professional name of Angelique, but her real name was Amy Fawcett. The flat was registered in her name and the imprint of her real life could be seen in framed photos hung up in her private space at the back of the flat. She was a musician and performance artist, who paid the bills by her extracurricular work at night. She didn't appear to be a prostitute – there were no condoms in the flat, no history of arrest – in fact this work appeared to be a sideline, which made her death all the more tragic. There was a photo next to her bed of a young Amy gripping a viola awkwardly under her chin. It had brought tears to Charlie's eyes when she first saw it, such was the guileless innocence and optimism of the image, and she'd had to absent herself from the team for a few moments. She needed a break – she realized that now – but quite when and how she would get one was another matter.

They were still in the midst of a major investigation with no clear suspect in mind. Charlie had crunched the credit card details and sent them to Helen, but progress was incremental rather than revelatory and Charlie had the uneasy feeling that things were starting to go south. Normally, Helen would have been all over this, stalking the crime scene, bullying the forensics team and coordinating the uniformed officers on the street. But she was notable by her absence this morning. Charlie hadn't been able to raise her on her landline or mobile. Was she sick? Surely not, Helen was *never* sick.

She had tried Sanderson, thinking it might be wise to defer to her greater experience, but she couldn't get hold of her either and was told by one of the girls at the station that the DS was 'unavailable' and 'on operational duties'. What those were Charlie couldn't fathom – what could be more important than a triple murder?

It fell to Charlie then to marshall the troops. This should have felt exciting – calling the shots at a murder scene was the natural culmination of her career thus far. But the gnawing uncertainty that something bigger was going on, from which she was excluded, was sapping her energy and optimism. Equally debilitating was the sight in front of her – a beautiful and talented spirit whose life had been brutally cut short.

110

Helen hadn't wanted to leave Angelique like that, but she'd had no choice. She could hardly call it in, so instead she had deliberately left the front door open. She had no doubt that one of Angelique's neighbours would notice and investigate further. It wasn't ideal and might delay her discovery for a few hours, but there was no other way. Helen couldn't risk incriminating herself and, besides, she had work to do.

She had lowered the blind and turned off her phone. The whole of the kitchen table was covered in papers and files – the sum total of their work on these murders so far. She had the strong sense that they had been looking the wrong way the whole time, guided to do so by a killer who was organized, diligent and determined. Helen blamed herself – she had been wilfully blind to the growing evidence in front of her, burying her personal connection to the victims because it was inconvenient and unsettling. By retrieving her private phone, by summoning her to the third murder, the killer had let it be known that he would not let her involvement with Jake, Max and the unfortunate Angelique remain hidden.

Helen had a growing sense of who might be responsible, but she refused to let paranoia guide her thinking.

She had to follow the evidence, focusing on the choice of victims, the manner of their deaths and the way their killer had gone about organizing these murders. The devil was in the detail in these cases and Helen returned once more now to Charlie's credit card searches.

This was their killer's only weak point, the one area where he might show his hand. They now had a third victim to work with and two new instruments of torture – Japanese soft cord bondage ties and a ball gag – which had presumably been purchased for the occasion.

Helen knew that their perpetrator favoured online bondage retailers so, plugging into the police network via remote access, she started to run the searches. She eschewed the chain sex shops in favour of the more boutique operations. And before long she found what she was looking for – the necessary items paid for by a Geoffrey Plough, an 87-year-old former teacher, now living in Shirley. He was an unlikely recipient for S&M products, but more telling still was the fact that the delivery address did not match Plough's. The items had instead been delivered to a vacant retail outlet in Woolston.

Helen didn't hesitate now, emailing Plough's bank and using her name and reputation in the subsequent phone call to persuade the manager to release the necessary information to her. Moments later, her home printer was spewing out Plough's debit card activity for the last three months.

Helen was excited to see that the list of transactions was

fairly short. Whereas the other two credit card victims were keen shoppers, spending frequently at a large number of stores and sites, Plough was parsimonious. He presumably didn't have much in the way of income, given his meagre spending, and he didn't seem to shop online, preferring face-to-face transactions. He was also a man who didn't like to go too far afield. Most of his purchases were made locally in Shirley and he was clearly a repeat customer. One location particularly stood out – one he seemed to visit daily. Wilkinson's on Park Street.

Helen knew that Wilkinson's had figured on the other fraud victims' transaction lists and she pulled them from the files now. Her finger ran down one, then the next and sure enough both had been regular shoppers at the same store.

Which is where Helen was heading now. If she was right, the answer to this deadly game of riddles was waiting for her there.

III

Sanderson paced up and down, fervently wishing she were a smoker or a nail biter. But she was neither – never had been – so there was nothing to do but wait.

The divers had been in the lake for nearly twenty minutes and Sanderson had by now got used to the strange, repetitive rhythm of their work. Dive, resurface, discuss, dive, resurface, discuss . . . Each time they came back up, she was convinced that this would be the breakthrough she needed. And each time she saw that they were empty-handed another little part of her died.

This was a massive gamble on her part. She had gone over Gardam's head straight to the Chief Constable. It had been hard enough to get him to agree to surveillance, it was harder still to get them to agree to the expense of a dive. But in the end the Chief Constable had agreed that there were grounds for concern and Sanderson's decisiveness initially appeared to have paid dividends. Helen Grace had had a five-person team on her as she made her way across Southampton Common. They had lost her initially as she disappeared in the depths of the woods, but a pair of young officers posing as lovers had picked her up again a little later on, as she emerged back on to open ground.

Sanderson had been beyond relieved at this news – she'd feared Helen was on to them and had deliberately lost her tail – and had radioed another member of the team to watch her from a safe distance. This officer had clearly seen Helen throw something in the lake and from then on Sanderson hadn't stood still, petitioning the Chief Constable for a dive, detailing more people to the surveillance effort and drawing DS McAndrew into her confidence to run some further checks.

Standing by the side of the lake, a brisk autumnal wind whipping around her, she wondered whether she had made a mistake. What if the item that Helen had discarded was something else entirely, something personal and unrelated to the case or, worse than that, merely a piece of rubbish. She shuddered at the thought of how she would explain that to her paymasters.

A shout made her look up. One of the divers was signalling that he'd found something and was returning to the shore. Sanderson set off towards him and moments later she was in possession of a mobile phone, neatly encased in an evidence bag. She didn't recognize it but it could be Helen's – there was a lot they didn't know about her boss, it appeared. Slipping on gloves, she opened the back of the phone, but there was no SIM card inside. Sealing the bag, Sanderson now pulled her phone from her pocket and called McAndrew – even without the SIM card there was lots they could do with the phone's memory, the serial number and so on. Concluding her call, she handed it to a colleague to ferry back to Southampton Central and resumed her position on the edge of the lake, hopeful that there might yet be more discoveries.

They were inching forward, but painfully slowly and Sanderson wondered how long it would be before Helen smelt a rat. Time was ticking and Sanderson knew her case against Helen would have to be bulletproof before she made her move. If she fudged the execution or, worse still, was just plain wrong, it wouldn't be Helen's neck on the block – it would be hers.

112

'Check again.'

Helen virtually barked her order at the startled manager. Peter Banyard, the new manager of the Park Street Wilkinson's, was not used to dealing with police officers, but he knew bad manners when he saw them and bridled at the request.

'I'm more than happy to check again, Inspector, but I can assure you that this is the complete list of all our employees.'

Helen ran her eye down them again. Jeff Armstrong, Terry Slater, Joanne Hinton, Anne Duggan, Ian McGregor . . . There was nobody here she recognized, no one who might be relevant.

'Could these names be fake?'

'Of course not,' the aggrieved manager responded. 'We check their ID, get National Insurance numbers, their bank details –'

'How far does this list go back?' Helen interrupted.

'Eighteen months.'

'Ok, I'll need a list going back five years, everything you've got.'

'Then I'll need a warrant. I think we've already gone way beyond the call of duty –'

'You'll have one before the end of the day. Thank you for your time.'

Helen was already halfway out of the door, heading fast for the store exit. The fraud victims had all shopped here for several years, so it was possible their credit and debit card details had been garnered some time back. And yet . . . she had only known Paine for eighteen months and Angelique considerably less than that. This felt recent and Helen knew that she was missing something significant. Their killer was still out there, thinking, plotting, waiting for his moment to strike.

113

'Amy Fawcett's body is currently at the mortuary – Jim Grieves is working on a more accurate time of death –'

'But . . .' Sanderson interrupted, wishing McAndrew would get to the point.

'But I've run the Automatic Number Plate Recognition and DI Grace's bike was in the vicinity of Fawcett's flat last night.'

'What do you mean, "in the vicinity"?'

'Three blocks away.'

'What time is this?'

'She heads into the docks area around nine p.m. And leaves via the same route shortly before ten.'

'Ok, call Grieves on the hour every hour until he gives you a time of death. He won't like it, but he'll have to wear it.'

'Sure thing.'

They were standing in Helen's office. It was the least suspicious place for a private conference, but even so it felt profoundly odd to be talking about her while standing in her space.

'Look, Ellie, if you feel uncomfortable doing this,' Sanderson said quickly, 'you just have to say –'

'It's ok. I'm fine. And you can rely on me to be dis—'

'I know I can. Why do you think I asked you?'

This earnt a crooked smile from McAndrew, so Sanderson continued:

'Have we got anything from the phone yet?'

'Not much but we're still doing most of the checks. The serial number shows that the phone was stolen five years ago. I'd imagine it's been used with a bastardized SIM card since. The phone's history has been deleted, I'm afraid, and the boys aren't convinced that we'll be able to retrieve it.'

'What about prints?'

'Only partials, unfortunately. It's been rubbed down pretty well.'

'Shit.'

'That said,' McAndrew added, 'Amy Fawcett's phone was still in her bag and the boys have had more luck there. She sent a text message last night to an unregistered mobile number – 07768 038687 – asking someone to meet her at her flat. We've looked at the phone contacts of Jake Elder and Max Paine – this is the only number that links all three. We've got Elder and Paine's phone content going back years. The same unregistered user used this number to make appointments with them – just as he or she did with Fawcett.'

Now Sanderson smiled – the first time she'd done so in a while.

'Ok, let's run with that. Go back to the phone company – who is it?'

'Lebara – a pay-as-you-go service.'

'Go back to them and do a location search. Find out which mobile masts that phone has been pinging over the last few weeks, months. I want to find out where that person has been.'

McAndrew nodded and headed off, leaving Sanderson to contemplate her next move. She had already received several phone calls from Emilia asking for progress, but she would have to wait. They didn't yet have the smoking gun, but the case was steadily building and, if they were going to bring Helen in, there was something she needed to do first.

114

'I'm sorry, I just don't believe it.'

Charlie tried to keep her voice steady, but there was no hiding the emotion she felt.

'What you *believe* isn't really relevant. We have to be led by the evidence,' Sanderson countered.

'DI Grace is a highly decorated officer – she has more commendations to her name than the rest of us put together. Her integrity and professionalism have never been questioned –'

'That's not true. She was nearly kicked out of the force for shooting her own sister.'

'She saved my life that day.'

'And you've been peas in a pod ever since, haven't you?'

Charlie was about to take Sanderson's head off, but Gardam intervened, holding up his hand to silence her. He had called Charlie to his office as soon as Sanderson had brought these latest developments to him – Charlie was of equal rank and needed to be included. She was very grateful he had – Sanderson clearly wasn't going to fight Helen's corner.

'This is difficult enough as it is,' he said calmly. 'Let's try to keep personal issues out of it. So what have we got?'

'We have a personal relationship with all of the victims –' Sanderson began.

'According to a journalist,' Charlie countered.

'Garanita has a number of photos showing DI Grace visiting Elder's flat, plus I now have the testimony of a neighbour who saw her there on numerous occasions. Max Paine was brutally attacked nine months ago by a female police officer – a client who'd turned on him. Interestingly, Paine left a voicemail for Emilia Garanita hours before he was killed, saying he had important information relating to Jake Elder's murder.'

This time Charlie said nothing.

'We can place Grace's bike near the scene of the latest murder at exactly the right time. *And* we believe we can link DI Grace to all the victims via an unregistered mobile phone she attempted to discard on Southampton Common last night.'

'Come on, Sanderson, that's speculation and you know it.'

'We'll see,' Sanderson said confidently. 'We also found a partial boot print near the crime scene at Paine's flat. It's a size six – DI Grace is a size six – and the pattern on the bottom is deep, wavy tread, reminiscent of soles you often find on biker boots. As you know, DI Grace –'

'I get the picture. Can we place Grace at the scene of the first murder?'

'Not yet.'

'What about Paine and Fawcett's flats?'

'Still processing the evidence, sir,' Sanderson replied, sounding slightly hesitant for the first time. 'But the fact remains that DI Grace has been evasive and secretive from the off. She has been behaving erratically and emotionally, making decisions and calls that the evidence just didn't justify. The use of clingfilm on the third victim can't be a coincidence, given her history. Perhaps she got bored of waiting for us to work it out.'

'But why? Why would she do something like this?' Charlie virtually shouted.

'Maybe they blackmailed her and she killed them. Now she's trying to cover her tracks, make it look like a serial killer, when actually she's just covering her arse. Or maybe she's just snapped, she's been doing this stuff for so long and nobody has a closer affinity to this type of killer than her. After all, it runs in the famil—'

At this point, Sanderson's phone rang out, loud and shrill. Apologizing to Gardam, she answered it and retreated. Charlie saw this as her opportunity and leapt in.

'With the greatest of respect to my colleague, I really don't think arresting DI Grace is the right thing to do. We need to evaluate these leads, for sure, but I don't think an arrest – with all the attendant publicity – is a smart move.'

Gardam looked at her, but said nothing.

'Look, I know hunches and personal relationships don't count for much,' Charlie acknowledged, 'but I've known Helen Grace longer than anyone here and she just isn't capable of these crimes. Her first and *only* priority is to save lives, to serve the ends of justice. Whatever may have happened in her personal life, she wouldn't do this. She would never murder someone in cold blood, so for everyone's sake, let's not rush into something we'll regret. She is *innocent*, please believe me.'

Charlie finished her impassioned speech and now became aware of Sanderson standing by her side.

'That was Meredith Walker at the lab,' Sanderson said, failing to keep the note of triumph from her voice. 'We've got a match, sir. A cigarette butt found in the corridor by the crime scene at the Torture Rooms has DI Grace's DNA on it. She was there that night.'

Charlie felt physically winded, stunned by this development. And her discomfort increased still further as Gardam now turned to them both and said:

'Ok. Let's bring her in.'

115

Helen checked her mirrors, but the car was still there. She'd first noticed she was being tailed when heading north up Kingsway. She had sped fast round the Charlotte Place roundabout, then forked left up The Avenue. The grey saloon kept pace without ever seeming to speed up or slow down. The tactics she recognized, the car she didn't – which made her very nervous indeed.

It had to be police, but who and why? Helen suddenly had the nasty feeling that she hadn't walked away from Angelique's flat unseen after all. Were they watching her then? If so they would have photos of her entering and leaving the flat – photos that would look pretty damning if given the right twist. If they were following her from the flat, then had they followed her on to the Common too?

She could see the large expanse of green to her left now, as she flashed past on her bike, though trees shielded the lake from view. Were the police there right now? Searching for evidence? There was an alternative scenario – that they had just picked up her tail this morning, following her to Wilkinson's and beyond. But that scarcely made her feel any better. They clearly still had their suspicions about her. In normal circumstances she would have gone straight to her boss to get the lowdown, but how could she do that now? Failing that she would have gone to the team, to her DSs, but perhaps even they were working against her? Someone must have raised concerns with top brass.

Helen tugged at the throttle, speeding north. The tailing car kept pace. Helen *could* call Charlie to try and get the lie of the land, but it was an inherently risky play. Her communications might be monitored, and even if Charlie *was* onside – as Helen fervently hoped she was – it would put her in a terribly difficult position. Nobody had called her this morning, which was unheard of. They were deliberately giving her a wide berth, which meant that something was up.

There was no one she could turn to, so she would have to handle things herself. Someone was intent on setting her up and it was up to her to resolve the situation. But first she would need to lose her tail.

Highfield Lane was fast approaching. Helen lowered her speed, then suddenly cut hard right, yanking the throttle once more. Her back wheel skidded, screeching loudly, then suddenly she was shooting forward. Moments earlier she'd been heading due north, now she was tearing west, testing the speed limit as she did so. She was expecting the blues and twos to come on, but the grey car remained as unobtrusive – but persistent – as ever. She raised her speed now – 40 then 50 mph. She could get pulled over for speeding, but that was the last thing on anyone's mind at the moment. The fact that they hadn't pulled her in meant either that this was just a surveillance gig or that they wanted to do so discreetly.

They would obviously be radioing her progress in and there was every chance she might be riding into a trap. Cobden Bridge was coming up – this was a good place to trap a fleeing suspect, as they generally didn't fancy a swim. It looked clear, but . . . Helen pumped her speed up to 70 mph, overtaking three cars before zooming back into lane. At any moment she expected unmarked cars to appear, blocking the other end of the bridge. But as she ate up the yards to the end of the bridge, the way remained clear. As she reached the end, she dropped down on to her right knee, biting hard into the tarmac as she spun down Bullar Road. She roared down it, then braked hard, not daring to cross Bitterne Way without looking. It was busy today, vans and lorries speeding along, and as Helen awaited her opportunity, she flashed a look in the rearview mirror.

The grey car was still with her, moving fast down Bullar Road towards her. It was fifty yards away, now forty, now thirty . . . Throwing caution to the wind, Helen tore across the four-lane carriageway, narrowly avoiding another bike, before speeding on. The pursuing car bided its time and Helen now became aware of a red estate car up ahead that seemed to be taking its time to reach Freemantle Common, almost as if it were waiting for someone.

The road was pretty quiet today. It would be a great place to strike and sure enough the Astra now pulled across the road, blocking her route. The blue light was out now, the doors opening in readiness for an arrest. The grey car was not far behind, so Helen didn't hesitate, lowering her speed, then ramming back the throttle to mount the pavement. The officers were already getting back into their car, so Helen raced down the empty pavement before joining the road and speeding off.

There was no need for stealth – now it was all about speed. She sped through Merry Oak and Itchen, paying heed only to the space in front of her, ignoring the traffic signals that attempted to arrest her progress. And as she reached Weston, Abbey Hill cemetery came into view in the distance.

This had been her destination all along. If she could get there she had a chance of escape. The pursuing cars were not far behind, their high-powered engines helping them to keep pace with her Kawasaki. Now Helen was leaving the main road, mounting the single-track road to the cemetery. There was no way down now – she was boxed in – so she cut loose, ripping her speed up to the max. Within moments, the cemetery gates appeared in front of her. Jamming the brakes, Helen skidded to a halt in front of them and was off and away before her bike had stopped moving.

As she vaulted the gates, she heard the cars pull up but Helen didn't hesitate, darting off down the main path towards the far end of the cemetery. This was her terrain and she planned to use her knowledge of it to her advantage, cutting diagonally across the minor paths, making maximum use of the cover the tombs and statues provided. She could hear shouts behind her, but they seemed a way away – she had a few minutes' grace now but she would have to use them wisely.

She found herself in the most secluded part of the cemetery. She had bent her path this way partly out of an instinct to stay hidden but also out of habit. This was the location of her sister Marianne's final resting place and as Helen approached her grave she suddenly slowed her pace dramatically. Not because she thought she was safe, but because of what she now saw in front of her.

Leaning against Marianne's grave was a simple bouquet of flowers. Suddenly Helen knew exactly who wanted to destroy her. And, more importantly, she knew why.

116

Her heel dug sharply into the turf and the ground seemed to give way beneath her. Hearing her pursuers approaching, Helen had vaulted the railings at the far end of the cemetery and thrown herself down the hill, hoping to disappear from view and confuse her pursuers. But the ground was wet and slippery and she lost her footing almost immediately, careering down the hill on her back, picking up speed as she did so.

For a moment, Helen didn't know which way was up. Then suddenly she came to an abrupt halt, somebody punching her hard in the side. Recovering herself, Helen now realized she was in a thorn bush and the sharp pain in her side was a thick branch that had rammed into her ribs. She was winded and muddy, but as she was still wearing her leathers and helmet, was largely unscathed.

Picking herself up, she looked up at the cemetery, now a good seventy or eighty feet above her. She could still hear voices, but no one was peering over the railings in her direction. If she moved swiftly, she had a chance of evading her pursuers completely, so breaking cover she ran down the side of the hill. She moved from bush to thicket to bush, occasionally casting a wary look behind her.

Before long she'd made it to the bottom of the hill

and, cutting her way along a footpath, made it back to civilization. Hurrying down a side street, she spotted Chamberlayne College, then heading left, hurried towards Weston. Spotting a bin, she pulled off her helmet and jacket and dumped them. The call would have gone out to uniform as well as other surveillance officers now, so she would have to be careful.

Her side was hurting her now, but she pressed on. She couldn't head home and needed somewhere – a sanctuary – to gather her thoughts. Somewhere public but not too public. Suddenly a Ladbroke's came into view and Helen ducked inside. There were a smattering of punters about, but they were far more interested in the dog racing and fruit machines than her. Buying a coffee, Helen sat down at the betting bar, a copy of the *Racing Post* open in front of her. She barely took in the text on the page, her brain pulsing with urgent, disquieting thoughts. Why had she been so complacent? Why had she ignored the evidence that was staring her in the face? She had seen someone in the derelict flats opposite her months ago but had dismissed the apparition as a junkie. But the person within had been watching her all the while, waiting for the moment to strike. How long had he been there? How many times had he seen her sitting at her window? How many months had he been inveigling his way into her life?

Since Max Paine's death, she'd feared the murders might be connected to her, but she'd suppressed these thoughts. Her chat with Gardam had reassured her, but how naïve and foolish that looked now. The fact that she was summoned to the third murder confirmed to her that she was being set up and the use of clingfilm confirmed for her the identity of the perpetrator. Her sister, Marianne, had killed their parents in the same way, securing their limbs then wrapping their heads in clingfilm. She too was now dead but her son, Robert, was alive. Helen had ruined his life by accidentally outing him as the son of a serial killer. He had remained hidden for several years since that devastating moment, but had finally resurfaced. Helen had wanted to be his guardian angel but her cursed touch had brought him only misery, rejection and pain.

Now he was back for revenge.

117

'Do you have any eyes on her?' Sanderson barked, her stress levels hitting the roof.

'Negative.'

'Any idea where she might have gone?'

'She probably hopped the fence and made her way down the hill – but I couldn't tell you in which direction.'

Sanderson cursed. Another member of the team looked up, intrigued, so pushing the door to Helen's office shut, Sanderson lowered her voice.

'Where is the nearest road? If she wanted to head back into town, where would she head to?'

There was silence on the other end, as the surveillance officer conferred with his colleague, then he eventually replied:

'Probably Weston or Newton.'

'Ok, leave one man at the cemetery in case she doubles back for her bike, but the rest of you get to Weston and Newton and fan out from there. We'll circulate her description to uniform, but keep your eyes peeled. You lost her, you can bloody well find her.'

Sanderson clicked off, realizing too late that she had raised her voice once again, to the evident interest of her colleagues. It was not surprising – in spite of everything she'd experienced with this team she had never felt so stressed as she did right now. Getting Gardam to agree to the arrest had been hard enough, but then to lose her . . . They had got too close, blown their cover and Helen now knew that she was being pursued. Having been so upbeat earlier, Sanderson suddenly felt deeply anxious. She had no idea where Helen was right now and, more importantly, no idea of what she might do next.

Her phone rang suddenly and Sanderson glanced down eagerly at the screen. But it was just Emilia Garanita – again. Rejecting it, she marched from Helen's office, slamming the door behind her.

118

What the hell was she playing at?

As her call went to voicemail, Emilia clicked off and threw her phone angrily on to her desk. She and Sanderson had made a pact to keep in touch, but she had the distinct feeling she was being kept at arm's length. Sanderson wouldn't have a case at all if Emilia hadn't given her the story. That whole team – Sanderson included – had been so infatuated with Grace that they'd never stopped to ask any questions of her. She'd had to lead them to Helen's wrongdoing and she was damned if she was going to be shut out at the moment of triumph.

She wanted to wait until they had made an arrest before publishing the story. With a suitable tipoff from Sanderson, Emilia could be in position to get a photo of Grace being marched to the cop car in cuffs or driven through the back door in custody. She'd had a four-word text this afternoon, suggesting an arrest warrant was imminent, but since then nothing from Sanderson.

Suddenly Emilia wondered if she'd backed the right horse. She couldn't have approached DS Brooks of course – it was clear where her loyalties lay – and everybody else was too inferior in rank. She'd felt certain that Sanderson was the one – she was suggestible, frustrated and lacking in confidence – but, then again, you never know how people will respond when it comes to the crunch. Perhaps Sanderson was just inexperienced at playing the game or maybe she was a little less innocent than she let on. Could she have taken Emilia for a ride?

She sincerely hoped not. Because Emilia was in a position to do serious damage not only to Sanderson's career but also to the Hampshire Police in general. She needed them and vice versa, yet they had always treated her badly – at best like an irritant, but more often as a necessary evil. Grace had been a particularly bad offender in this regard – her hostility to Emilia very clear. Often Emilia had been on the back foot in their relationship, but now finally she was poised to attack.

And her weapon of choice would be tomorrow's edition with its screaming banner headline:

COP TURNED KILLER.

119

Helen walked quickly towards the back of the store, keeping her head down. She was an odd sight for a cold autumn evening – boots and leathers on her bottom half, but only a thin black vest top above. More curious still were the scratches on her face and arms. She looked a little like she had been dragged through a hedge backwards, which of course she had.

It was cold in the refrigerated section of the supermarket and Helen didn't linger, marching to the manager's office at the rear and pushing inside. Peter Banyard was still unnerved from their first meeting and looked positively shocked now by her second appearance of the day.

'Are you ok? Can I get you anything?' he eventually said, clocking her strange appearance.

'I'm fine, but I need to ask you another question.'

'I haven't got your paperwork ready yet if that's –'

'That's not why I'm here. I want you to look at this picture, tell me if you recognize this man.'

Her hand was shaking slightly as she held up her phone for him. On the screen was one of the photos the press had used when they'd 'outed' Robert Stonehill several years earlier.

The manager stared at the photo.

'Do you know him?' Helen repeated more loudly.

'Well, yes. That's Aaron West.'

'He works for you?' Helen continued, insistent.

'He's one of our temporary workers. We take them on around Halloween, Bonfire Night and so on.'

'Does he work the tills?'

'Tills, shelves, wherever we need him. He does a few shifts a week – has been for a few months now.'

Just enough time for him to plan Helen's downfall. He had lifted customers' credit card details while working the tills, then used their details to purchase his specialist S&M gear – gear that would eventually lead the police back to her.

'Did you check his credentials? His ID?'

'Yes,' Banyard replied, looking unnerved, 'although the checks for temporary workers aren't perhaps as rigorous as for our permanent staff.'

'I bet they're not,' Helen snarled back, just about containing her anger. 'Do you have an address for him?'

'We should do,' the manager replied, 'but I'm not sure that will be necessary.'

'What do you mean?'

'I just saw him out the back. In the locker area. I can take you th—'

But he didn't get to finish. Helen was already gone.

120

She sprinted across the store, scattering shoppers in her wake. The Staff Only door was fifty feet away and Helen charged towards it, glancing around for someone to help her open it. But there was no one to hand and she couldn't delay, so she launched herself at it. Her shoulder hit the cheap door hard, wrenching the lock from its socket.

Two alarmed faces stared at her as she hurried inside – two employees who were about to return to work, dumbfounded by Helen's dramatic entrance.

'Where are the lockers?'

For a moment they were speechless.

'The lockers,' Helen barked.

One of the workers now pointed to a door on her left. Helen was off again, eating up the yards to the door and pushing through it. To her dismay, the dingy locker room was empty, but Helen sensed movement and now saw the fire exit at the far end of the room swinging gently to a close. Had he heard her coming and taken flight? If so, he was only a few seconds ahead of her.

Helen burst out into the night, scanning desperately left and right for signs of her quarry. And there he was. Not forty yards away from her down a narrow alley, sprinting as if his life depended on it. Helen took off in pursuit, pounding the concrete as she pushed herself to narrow the gap between them.

It looked as though the alleyway would lead them back into the main shopping precinct where most of the big stores were to be found. Was that Robert's plan? To lose himself in the crowds? Helen couldn't allow that so, even though her lungs were burning, she upped her speed again. The bitter irony of her pursuit wasn't lost on her – she'd been searching for her nephew for so long and now here he was, intent on escaping her.

He had now reached the end of the alleyway and darted round to the left. Helen couldn't afford to let him out of her sight, but she was only fifteen feet behind now. Reaching the end of the alley, she tore around the corner in the same direction as Robert – running smack into a middle-aged man laden with shopping bags. She cannoned off him, falling to the ground, jarring her frame nastily on the concrete floor as she did so. Pain seared through her, but she was already clambering to her feet. Holding her hand up in apology, she side-stepped the concerned shoppers hurrying to help her.

She ran her eye over the sea of shoppers but couldn't see Robert. Had he taken advantage of her accident to disappear into one of the main shops? No, there he was. Helen glimpsed his deep-red hoodie, bobbing as he hurried north towards the precinct exit. Shaking herself down, Helen tore off in the same direction.

The chase was on.

121

'We've just had a call from Wilkinson's in Shirley. Apparently, DI Grace just left there in a hurry.'

McAndrew's tone was hushed. She clearly felt awkward working against their boss, but orders were orders, so she'd brought her news straight to Sanderson and Charlie.

'This is the address of the store –'

'I know where it is,' Sanderson interrupted. 'Alert uniform in the area to be on their guard – I want any sightings radioed in immediately.'

'I'll advise officers in outlying areas to head towards the precinct – they can form a wider net in case she slips through.'

'Was she on foot?'

'I believe so.'

'Good, then we've got a good chance of taking her. I'll take the car down there now.'

Charlie watched Sanderson head off, her emotions in riot. Since the arrest warrant had been finalized, she had been torn in two. One part of her wanted to do her duty like McAndrew, but the greater part of her wanted to warn Helen of the danger she was now in. She couldn't call or text her as that would be too easily traced back to her, but perhaps there was a payphone in one of the local pubs? Charlie had the sense that the net was closing on Helen now and, unless she did something to help her, she was doomed.

'DS Brooks is coming with me. You can take point here.'

It was said to McAndrew, but was aimed at Charlie. Sanderson was looking at her as if she could read her mind, sensing her disloyalty. The eyes of the room were on her now so with a heavy heart, Charlie said:

'Sure. Let's go.'

There would be no escape for Helen today.

122

Helen grasped the chain link fence and vaulted it in one easy motion, landing gently on the other side. Her nephew had veered away from the city centre as fast as he could, seeking out the footpaths and back alleys that would be deserted as night closed in. Before long he'd reached an allotment and was now cutting across it, heading towards the south of the city. Helen was close behind, running as fast as she could over the hard, rutted ground.

Had Robert always planned this as an escape route? He seemed to know his way without thinking, avoiding public places and possible obstructions. Normally Helen would have called in her pursuit in an attempt to cut him off, but that wasn't an option now.

When they'd first met, Helen would have been confident of winning this contest. Robert was just a young man then – he didn't have her physical training, nor her experience. Now there seemed to be something different about him. He was leaner, fitter, and she could see that his head was shaved. He had a smooth, militaristic look, almost as if he were the one who had now been in training, preparing to avenge himself on the woman who had killed his mother and ruined his life.

Robert was only twenty feet ahead but vaulted the

boundary fence without hesitation before sprinting on. His levels of fitness really were impressive and Helen suddenly had the nasty thought that it would be she who'd tire first. Clearing the fence, she touched down hard, narrowly avoiding a tree root, then burst forward once more. If she lost him, who was to say when she would get another chance to confront him. It was now or never.

They had been running for over ten minutes, but Helen knew that Robert's escape options were narrowing. They were nearing the outskirts of the docks. There were many warehouses, in use and derelict, for him to hide in, but the whole of the Western Docks was fenced off and unless Robert had a craft of some kind waiting for him, he couldn't keep heading south.

Up ahead of her, Robert slammed into the dock's perimeter fence, scaling it as he did so. Helen could see he was wearing gloves, but as he reached the top, he yelped in pain, the razor wire clearly doing its work. But he pushed on through, falling to the ground on the other side, obliging Helen to follow him. She scampered up the links, pausing only at the top to manoeuvre herself through the coiled wires. It would lose her valuable seconds, but it would be disastrous to get caught up in it and a false move would cut her to ribbons.

The metal teeth of the wire caressed her cheek as she eased her head through, but didn't draw blood. Twisting again, she wiggled her torso through the gap, feeling the back of her vest tear slightly as it snagged on its way through. Now she could grip the fence on the other side and, pulling her legs through, quickly swung down on to the ground – just in time to see Robert disappearing into Quay 42.

Helen stumbled as she moved forward – her legs were growing weary of the pursuit – but she drove herself on. Quay 42 was a derelict outpost of the Western Docks and was a fitting place for this endgame to play out. The last time Helen had visited the mothballed warehouses that littered it was to recover one of Marianne's victims. Perhaps the historic associations were too much to resist – Helen couldn't believe he'd made his way here by chance.

She was entering the dock area now – great, empty warehouses looming up on all sides. Helen hurried towards the old dockside, peering into the shadows on either side, searching for her prey. Was he hiding in the shadows, waiting to attack her from behind, or had he come here to make his escape? Peering over into the water, Helen could see no craft, no signs of movement. Turning she cast a look further down the quayside, but it too was deserted. She had been too close behind for Robert to have made it out of the quay completely, so he was here somewhere. Was he watching her right now?

There were four main warehouses on this part of the quay, all in equal states of disrepair, shattered windows giving a fractured view of the darkness within them. If Helen picked wrong, then he would escape. There was no margin for error now. He was unlikely to be hiding in the first as he had veered round to the left past it when entering the quay. Presuming he hadn't doubled back, this left three more. The next-nearest one was little more than a shell, the roof having collapsed some time ago. There was plenty of detritus within to provide cover, but the moon that now hung overhead was full, lighting up the interior clearly. It would be a gamble to conceal yourself there in plain sight, so Helen moved on to the last two. Both of these were in good repair and would be smart places to hide, the fire escapes that snaked down the sides providing a possible means of escape if need be. If Helen was being pursued, she would have picked one of these two.

Helen wrenched open the door to the nearest one and peered inside. It was one vast hangar, littered with abandoned crates and dead pigeons. Again there was plenty of cover but there were no internal walls to hide behind, so now Helen's gaze strayed to the last warehouse, which bordered the quayside. This was a two-tier building – a series of offices and small units on top of the main hangar. This seemed much more promising, so, making her choice, Helen hurried towards it.

The main hangar doors lay in front of her, but the fire escape that led up to the second floor intrigued her more, as it would have been out of view when Helen entered the quay complex. She walked forward confidently, then came to an abrupt halt. A dark spot lay on the ground by the steps and bending down Helen dipped her finger in it. Holding it up to the light, she could see that it was blood, glistening in the moonlight, fresh and wet.

Now Helen moved quickly up the steps. Reaching the

top, she paused. There was every chance that Robert was inside. She was about to face him unarmed, with nothing but her experience and training to protect her. If he meant to do her harm, even kill her, then who would ever know that she'd been down here? That she had solved the case? For the first time since this desperate chase had begun, Helen paused to catch her breath, pulling her mobile from her pocket. She sent a quick text, then switching the phone to silent, stepped into the darkness within.

Immediately, something came at her. She flung her arm up to protect herself, then watched in alarm as the startled pigeon flew away, the sound of his flapping wings echoing around the empty rooms. Any element of surprise was gone now, so Helen pressed on, walking swiftly down the corridor that stretched out in front of her the full length of the building. There were small offices off it and Helen checked them over as she walked past. She wasn't keen to get caught in one of these – she wanted him to make the first move, rather than walk into a trap herself.

Her eyes scanned the space ahead of her, looking for signs of movement, and then, in the distance, she saw it. At the very end of the corridor there was a room which was probably the biggest in the building. It overlooked the water, was the width of the warehouse and all roads led to it. And unlike every other room in this decaying edifice, it was emitting a pale-blue light.

Intrigued, Helen crept forward. As she did so, she spotted a few abandoned bits of scaffolding. Bending down, she picked up a short length of pipe and carried on, getting closer and closer to the office ahead. She was fifteen feet from it, now ten, now five. Helen stood on the threshold, then pushed into the room, braced to defend herself.

But no attack came. Was Robert even here? It was hard to make out the outer edges of the room – her eye was drawn to the computer whose weak light she had noticed from the corridor. Next to it on a rickety table was a camping lantern and Helen grabbed it, turning it up. Now the room came into focus – empty coffee cups, an ashtray full of cigarettes, discarded sandwich wrappers, a hoodie hanging over a chair, but also a white iPhone 5 nearby. Helen guessed it was Max Paine's – but time would tell. And flanking all this, pinned up on the walls were maps of Southampton, picking out Banister Park, Bitterne and the docks.

This then was Robert's bolthole – a perfect hiding place from which to plot his killing spree. And as Helen took another step forward, turning the lantern to get a better view of the room, she saw him, framed by the large windows behind him. He was silhouetted against the moonlight, but as Helen stepped closer she took in his face. He looked pale, impassive and oddly effeminate – there didn't seem to be a single trace of hair on his face, head or neck. She hadn't seen him in years, and now as he took *her* in, his blue eyes sparkled malevolently.

'Nice to see you again, Helen. It's been a long time.'

123

The unmarked car hurtled down the road, sirens blaring and light flashing. Even though she was safely strapped in, Charlie held tight to the armrest. Sanderson was wound tight tonight and driving way too aggressively. She didn't dare say anything, but she didn't want to become a casualty of her colleague's desperation to nail their boss either.

They were heading fast towards Shirley, but as they reached the outskirts, Charlie's phone pinged loudly. Sanderson gave her an accusing look, as if Charlie had deliberately done this to distract her, before returning her attention to the road. Irked, Charlie pulled out her phone. But as she did so, her finger froze, hovering over the Read button. The message was from Helen.

Charlie glanced sideways at Sanderson, then pressed the button. The message was short and sweet.

'Western Docks. Quay 42.'

It was timed as having been sent three minutes ago. Was Helen in trouble? Did she need help? Was this her covert way of asking for it, by texting instead of calling? Charlie stared at the message, unsure what to do. Should she text back? Probably – that's what a good friend and colleague would do – but if it was later discovered that she had been communicating with a suspect on the run, then that would be her career over. She owed Helen so much – her livelihood, her position, her life even – but there was too much at stake now and, if she was honest, there were too many unanswered questions.

Which is why, with a heavy heart, Charlie turned her phone towards Sanderson and said:

'I think you'd better see this.'

124

They stood stock still, sizing each other up. Robert showed no signs of wanting to attack her, but neither was he preparing to flee. He was boxed in, Helen blocking his route from the room, yet he seemed oddly unconcerned.

'When did you know?' he said suddenly.

His voice was as she remembered it – young and raw – but the warmth he used to possess had vanished. He seemed older, but not happier.

'After Paine maybe. But I hoped I was wrong.'

'Isn't that just like you? Always in denial.'

'About what?'

'The harm you do. The pain you cause.'

'I've only ever wanted to help people. I spent months looking for you, trying to make amends –'

'But you didn't find me, did you?'

'Not for the want of trying. I know I turned your life upside down –'

'Is that how you'd put it?'

'You were happy, you had nice parents, a good home, but you were my only blood relative. I wanted to look after you, help you make the right choices –'

'Then I guess I'll be another thing on your conscience, won't I?'

This time his tone was gleeful and taunting.

'You did all this because you wanted to,' Helen said, gesturing to the maps, the phone. 'It's nothing to do with me.'

'In some ways I did them a favour. Jake was hopelessly obsessed with you, Paine was eating himself up with bitterness –'

'And Angelique? What the hell had she done?'

'Nothing yet. But you would have harmed her, just as you did the others. Everything you touch dies, don't you know that yet, Helen?'

Helen stared at him. He knew her better than anyone else and was determined to make that count.

'Including yourself?' she said quietly. 'Isn't that what all this is about?'

'Well, the last time you faced off with a blood relative, you shot her. So it would be kind of poetic, wouldn't it?'

'I never wanted to kill your mother. She forced me to.'

'Isn't it a coincidence that you always end up in a position where you are *forced* to hurt people? Do you never ask yourself if you *like* inflicting pain?'

'That's not true.'

'Isn't it? What did you feel when you were beating Paine? Wasn't there a part of you that didn't want to stop?'

Helen wanted to deny it, but couldn't find the words.

'You see, Helen, you're no better than the criminals you chase. Think of me as your subconscious, acting out the fantasies and desires that lie within you.'

'Tell that to the judge.'

'There's not going to be a trial, Helen. This starts and ends here.'

Helen said nothing. She had sent her text over ten minutes ago. She would have expected to hear distant sirens by now, but there was nothing. Robert stood in front of her, framed by the dark sea, looking relaxed and happy. Helen had no idea what he was planning, but his mood made her decidedly nervous.

'How did you know?' she said suddenly, breaking the silence.

'That wasn't hard, Helen. I've been your quiet shadow for nearly a year now. Little boy blue following you around day after day after day. I saw you meet Jake Elder in that city centre bar. I heard him arguing with his boyfriend afterwards. Did you feel lonely after that exchange, Helen? I saw you sitting in your window looking beautiful and sad –'

'And a day later I visited Max Paine,' Helen replied, suddenly realizing how careless she'd been.

'I watched you visit him then and the time after. I saw how agitated you were after you'd come to blows. And the next morning, I saw him. He had a cap on and was covered in make-up, but boy was he a mess. You must have really gone to town on him.'

Helen looked at Robert. The boy who had once cried on her shoulder now stared at her, hateful in his triumph.

'Am I really worth all this?' Helen said finally.

'You have no idea.'

'You've been stalking me for months, giving up your own life –'

'I *had* no life thanks to you.'

'Bullshit. You don't have to play the cards you're dealt. You can choose a different path, make good choices –'

'You killed my mother. Nobody told me about that – for years I was given half-truths and evasions. Then you came along and told the whole fucking world.'

'That was never my intention.'

'"Son of a Monster" – that's what they called me. "The Spawn of a She-Devil". I was a nobody – don't you get that? – and suddenly I was famous.'

Helen stared at him. The memory of the press pack descending on his quiet family home in Aldershot still haunted her.

'After that I couldn't go anywhere. People knew who I was, what she'd done, they wanted nothing to do with me. As if her sins were mine. And yet what had she done? She'd killed to protect you. To save her little sister.'

'I know that's what she thought she was doing –'

'I was going to kill myself,' Robert interrupted. 'I was going to call you up, tell you where I was and then do it, before you could get to me. I'd saved up my pills, found a hotel room, but when it came to it, I couldn't do it.'

Helen looked at him as he took a step forward.

'Not because I was scared, but because I was angry. It's my rage that has sustained me all these months. My rage and my hatred of *you*.'

Helen stayed where she was, refusing to be intimidated. And in the far distance, she now heard the sound of sirens. Robert seemed oblivious, continuing his rant against her.

'After you shot her, you danced on her grave.'

'I loved your mother, I still do. But she was a murderer –'

'You tried to justify your own actions by denigrating her.'

'What she did was wrong.'

'No, what she did was right,' Robert barked back at her. 'Which is why it felt right.'

Helen suppressed a shudder. Marianne had been utterly unrepentant at her trial, even confessing to enjoying murdering their parents.

'What did she say at her trial? "I enjoyed watching their faces, knowing they couldn't hurt me any more." I read the transcripts, I read everything about her. Her testimony was all I had left of her.'

Helen felt the emotion rising in her – Robert had been the innocent in all this, yet he too had been swallowed by the darkness.

'You were never like her.'

'But I am now. Thanks to you.'

'And does it make you happy?'

Robert looked at her oddly, as if trying to read the trick in the question.

'Yes. I think it does. You see I could have killed you at any point during the last twelve months, but I wanted you to suffer. To feel the pain that I've endured since you ransacked my life. All your dirty little secrets put on view for the world to enjoy. Jake, Max and poor Angelique . . .'

The sound of the sirens was now unmistakable. Help could be only minutes away. There could be no triumph for Helen, but at least she could bring this thing to an end.

'I contacted my colleagues before I came in here, Robert,' she said softly.

'I assumed you would, but I'm glad we've had this time together.'

'So what happens now? If you want to hurt me, you've got a couple of minutes to do it.'

Robert stared at her, his hands hanging by his side.

'I'm not going to hurt you, Helen. That was never the plan.'

Still Helen braced herself, ready to roll with his attack. But Robert simply turned and opened the windows behind him, flinging them back so they crashed loudly on the wall outside, sending glass tumbling downwards. A blast of cold air roared in, whipping Helen's hair around her shoulders. Suddenly everything outside seemed amplified – the sound of car doors slamming echoing around the deserted quay.

'Don't be stupid, Robert. You'll break your legs and where are you going to run to? We've boxed ourselves into a corner here.'

Robert turned back to her. Illuminated by the full moon behind him, he seemed even more ghostly than before.

'Speak for yourself.'

Helen took a step forward, her anxiety spiking. Why was he so calm? What was she missing here? Did he want to be caught? She could hear footsteps climbing the metal fire escape now, hurrying towards them.

'Like I said, this is about you, not about me.'

The footsteps were getting closer. It could only be a matter of moments before Robert was apprehended.

'That's why everything in this room is yours, Helen. The coffee cups, old cigarettes, food wrappers. Even an old hoodie you thought you'd lost. Your DNA, your prints. There's nothing of *me* here, I'm afraid.'

Now Helen knew exactly what he intended to do and lunged forward, but she was too late. Hopping up on to the lip of the window ledge, Robert leapt out into the night. Helen launched herself at him but was a second too slow. She slammed into the wall – just in time to see Robert land with a splash in the inky water below. Her adversary had chosen his spot well – an old loading bay overhanging the dock.

Now the full extent of her stupidity came crashing home. But she had no time to react as suddenly she felt rough hands upon her, dragging her back from the window. She tried to speak but her face was pushed hard into the dirt, even as her hands were wrenched backwards and cuffed. Now she was being read her rights by breathless officers too drunk on their own success to listen to her pleas.

Robert's victory was complete.

125

Emilia rubbed her hands together in a vain attempt to keep warm. She had lain in wait behind Southampton Central on numerous occasions, but had never found an effective way to keep warm. She was a naturally cold person – however many layers she wore, she could never stop her teeth chattering.

Tonight though, she didn't mind one bit. Any personal discomfort she felt was forgotten – this night was her night, the crowning achievement of her professional life thus far. She had endured much over the years – parents who maltreated her, an acid attack that had permanently scarred her, endless mockery and abuse – but tonight she would show them all. She was about to break the story of the year – one that would make her career and finish another in the process.

She had made it down to Southampton's main police station in record time. Sanderson's text was to the point – 'in custody. back entrance. 20 mins.' – and Emilia had wasted no time, grabbing her camera and heading out of the door. There was a darkened doorway out the back which made perfect cover and she was poised there now, waiting for the tell-tale saloon. This was supposed to be a discreet, unpublicized entry to the station, but thanks to Sanderson it would be anything but. Perhaps Emilia had misjudged her – maybe she could be trusted to honour their deal.

Emilia checked her camera again. Battery level high, night exposure set, rapid fire mode on – then a sound made her look up. It was low but persistent, the sound of a car moving swiftly but quietly along the deserted street. Emilia readied herself.

Now the car swung into the alleyway behind the station and as if by magic the heavy rear doors started to creak open. The car swung round towards them, slowing slightly to allow a sufficient gap to open up. Emilia now stepped forward shooting quickly, grabbing as many photos as she could. She had timed it right, for seconds later the car disappeared inside, the doors clanging shut behind it.

Emilia stepped back into the shadows. Her article was ready to print, barring one small addition. Flicking the camera on to viewing mode, Emilia broke out into a smile. She had what she needed, her coup de grâce.

A shot of Helen Grace's ashen face, staring out into the night.

126

'Look at the camera, please.'

Helen stared straight ahead as the flash fired – once, twice, three times. It was blinding, disorienting, the pain piercing her brain. But Helen knew it was just the beginning of her torture.

'Now to the left, please.'

Flash, flash, flash.

'Now to the right.'

Helen knew the drill – had watched this process countless times – but she had to be led through it now by the custody sergeant. She nodded when prompted, but none of it felt real. She was still in shock, her mind turning on the ingenuity of Robert's scheme. He had trailed her patiently, picking up the detritus of her life, carefully assembling the narrative of her destruction. He had selected his victims well – choosing people who were not necessarily close to Helen, but who were nevertheless part of her secret life. Their exposure through death posed the question of who might want to silence them, leading the police straight back to Helen. She had no doubt now that Robert would have planted further DNA evidence at the Torture Rooms and possibly at Paine's too. She had a connection to all the victims, so her only escape route was to establish a bona fide alibi.

With a shudder, Helen realized that this too would be denied her. She had been out running on the night of the first murder – had someone seen her running north, as if heading home from the Torture Rooms? On the night of Paine's murder, she had visited Marianne's grave – her route from Southampton Central would have taken her right past Paine's flat. She was a creature of habit and Robert had taken full advantage of that, knowing all the while that there was no one waiting at home to confirm her version of events.

'Right. Now we're going to strip-search you.'

Helen felt hands upon her and looking up she saw a female custody officer removing her clothes. Her vest, trousers and boots were removed and bagged. She would be allowed to keep her underwear on, but only after they had been searched. Helen submitted to this indignity, all the while feeling the sergeant's eyes on her. Helen's torso was riddled with scars – evidence of her historic addiction to sado-masochism, which would no doubt strengthen the case against her. Very few people had seen her like this – naked and exposed – and Helen could feel the sergeant's silent judgement.

This was nothing compared to what was to come, however. Helen knew that her life would be pored over now, her every misdemeanour and insecurity exposed as she was hung out to dry. She was at the bottom of the well, with no means or hope of escape.

Standing there half naked in the weak light of a flickering bulb, Helen was utterly alone.

127

It felt like she was in the middle of a nightmare. Charlie stood still in the middle of the room, making little effort to help the SOCOs who manoeuvred around her. Helen was innocent – she *had* to be innocent – and yet she had led them here. The phone looked like it was Paine's, the hoodie was hers and the cigarettes that lay half smoked in the ashtray were unquestionably Helen's brand. The coffee cups were Costa not Starbucks, the sandwich wrappers were from the local deli by the station . . . The place even smelt of Helen – her signature Obsession perfume seeming to hang in the room. This was her space, her brain, but still it made no sense.

Sanderson walked swiftly past towards Meredith, brushing against Charlie as she did so. It was a subtle reminder that they were here to do a job, to gather and process the evidence. Charlie had played her part in Helen's capture, but it had been Sanderson's persistence and instincts that had brought them to this place and she clearly felt that she was in charge. Had her colleague been driven by conviction or ambition? It probably didn't matter – either way she was well placed to step into Helen's shoes if – when – she was charged with triple murder.

Charlie would suffer as a result. Her life would be

made as difficult as possible and she had no doubt that, before the end of the year, she would find herself in Gardam's office, asking for a transfer. Perhaps this was no bad thing. How could she carry on now that her mentor had been disgraced? How could she look anyone in the eye when it appeared her faith had been badly misplaced? Tonight was Helen's nadir, but Charlie felt her life unravelling too. They had been so close – Helen was godmother to her only child. Could she really have got it so wrong? Was it possible that Helen's barren life had finally led her to . . . this?

'I'll check the perimeter, see if we have any witnesses.'

Sanderson grunted, but didn't look up. They both knew there wouldn't be any witnesses on the deserted quay and that this was just an excuse for Charlie to leave the room. Perhaps she *was* a bad copper, perhaps she was blindly loyal, but she was still a human being. She walked quickly from the room to hide the tears that were threatening. Guilty she might be, but Helen had always been Charlie's friend and confidante and she was damned if she was going to watch Sanderson dance on her grave.

128

Jonathan Gardam watched through the two-way mirror as the questions rained down on Helen. As soon as her arrest had been confirmed, he'd called in officers from Sussex Police to lead the interviews. There was no question of Sanderson or Brooks questioning Helen, given their relationship with her. Gardam could have fielded the interview himself of course, but he had decided to take a back seat. He would get a much better view of the action that way.

Helen looked pale and weary, but she was not quite beaten yet. She was patiently taking the officers through the events of the evening, trying to convince them that *she* was the victim. But even from here, Gardam could feel their scepticism. Helen's story was coherent and measured, but detectives of this ilk were not prone to flights of fancy – they followed the evidence.

'Listen, we'd like to take you at your word, but there was nobody there. We checked the surrounding buildings, the dockside –'

'He was there.'

'Then why can't we find any trace of him?'

'Do you think I made him up? Why would I have

called my colleagues to the docks if I was responsible? Why would I do that?'

'You tell us.'

Helen was getting angry now, insisting that she had acted properly throughout the investigation. She was telling them that she hadn't kept her connection to the first two victims to herself – she had discussed it with her commanding officer and been asked to continue on the case. They promised to follow this up, before launching into a series of new questions about her relationship to the deceased. Helen brushed these off, urging them to verify what she was saying, before asking her anything else. Again they batted her back and Gardam was surprised to see Helen now turn towards the two-way.

'I'm not saying another word until you get him in here,' Helen was saying. 'Ask him under caution if I raised the issue.'

'With all due respect, you're the only one under caution here and I'd like *you* to answer my questions . . .'

Helen ignored her interrogator, staring straight at Gardam. It was a bold gesture but a pointless one. She would only see her own face staring back, whereas he could see everything. He had the advantage now, which is how he wanted it.

They would come to him, of course, asking if what she claimed was true. He had the opportunity to extend a helping hand to her now . . . but why should he, when she had already sunk her teeth into it? He would dismiss her claims. He would be surprised, bemused, even saddened that she should try to draw a fellow officer into her depravity.

He had been fascinated by her – maybe he was still – but she had poured scorn on him. And for that she was going to pay.

129

The door closed behind her and Helen heard the key turn in the lock. It was strange how different it sounded on the inside. Out there, among colleagues and friends, the turn of the key had always sounded like a job well done. In here, it was like a death knell.

Helen sat down on the bed and stared at the walls. Her mind was turning on a thousand points, searching for the weak points in Robert's scheme, but she could find none. She knew already that there would be no help coming from Gardam. If he'd wanted to save her, he would have done so by now. No, this was the perfect get-out for him – if she reported his assault now, who would believe her? Still, Helen wondered if he was enjoying her destruction. Or did it hurt him, knowing that he would never see her again?

She heard footsteps and looked up. The door remained closed, but a newspaper slid under the gap at the bottom. The footsteps moved away and Helen could hear the custody officers laughing. It wasn't hard to see why. Their gift to her was a copy of the *Evening News*. Picking it up, she flicked past the sensational headline to the inner pages. Much of the paper was devoted to the story, but the crowning glory was Emilia Garanita's profile piece of her. It was entitled: *Fall from Grace*.

Helen binned the paper and lay down on the bed. The fight had finally gone out of her. There was nothing to do now but lick her wounds.

Robert had waited for his moment, then struck with devastating effect. He was a man possessed – his loneliness, bitterness and rage altering him beyond all recognition. He had stayed alive purely to gain vengeance for his mother and Helen had paid dearly for her sins. Robert had taken from her everything she held dear. Her reputation, her job, her friends.

And, worst of all, her freedom.

DI HELEN GRACE WILL RETURN IN ...

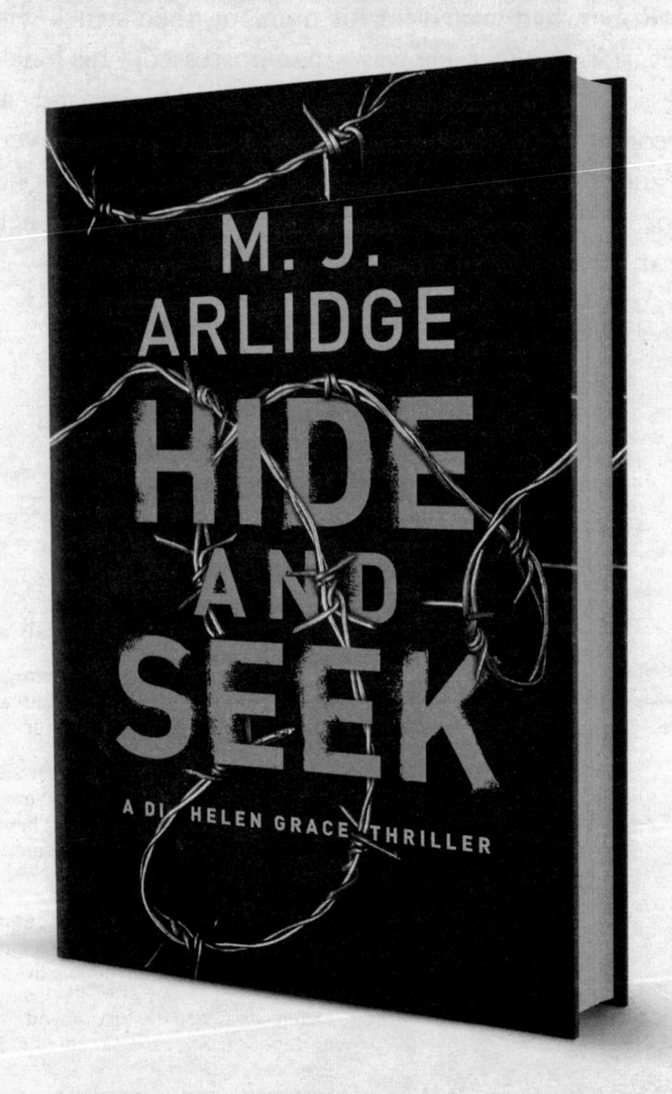

SEPTEMBER 2016

THE FIRST DI HELEN GRACE THRILLER

The girl emerged from the woods, barely alive. Her story was beyond belief. But it was true. Every dreadful word of it.

Days later, another desperate escapee is found – and a pattern is emerging. Pairs of victims are being abducted, imprisoned then faced with a terrible choice: kill or be killed.

Would you rather lose your life or lose your mind?

)etective Inspector Helen Grace has faced down her own demons on her rise to the op. As she leads the investigation to hunt own this unseen monster, she learns that may be the survivors – living calling cards – who hold the key to the case.

And unless she succeeds, more innocents will die . . .

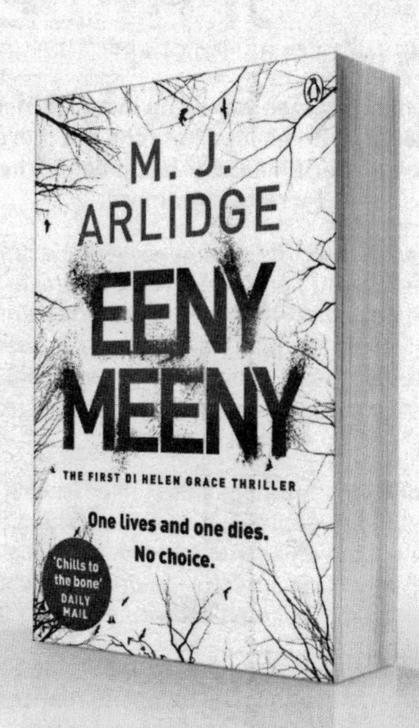

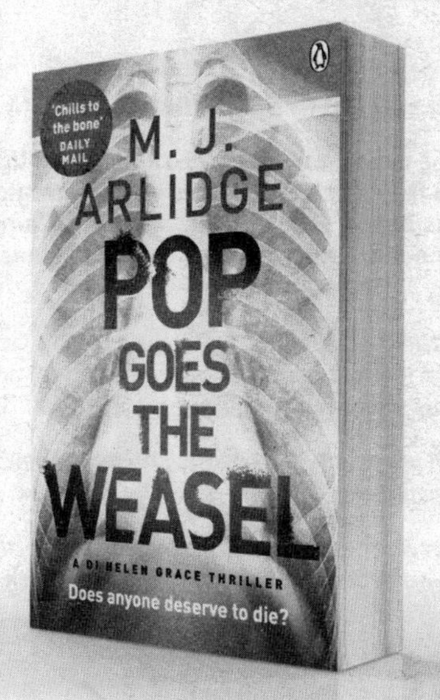

THE SECOND DI HELEN GRACE THRILLER

A man's body is found in an empty house. His heart has been cut out and delivered to his wife and children.

He is the first victim, and Detective Inspector Helen Grace knows he will not be the last. But why would a happily married man be this far from home in the dead of night?

The media call it Jack the Ripper in reverse: a serial killer preying on family men who lead hidden double lives.

Helen can sense the fury behind the murders. But what she cannot possibly predict is how volatile this killer is – or what is waiting for her at the end of the chase . . .

THE THIRD DI HELEN GRACE THRILLER

A young woman wakes up in a cold, dark cellar, with no idea how she got there or who her kidnapper is. So begins her terrible nightmare.

Nearby, the body of another young woman is discovered buried on a remote beach. But the dead girl was never reported missing – her estranged family having received regular texts from her over the years. Someone has been keeping her alive from beyond the grave.

For Detective Inspector Helen Grace it's chilling evidence that she's searching for a monster who is not just twisted but also clever and resourceful – a predator who's killed before.

And as Helen struggles to understand the killer's motivation, she begins to realize that she's in a desperate race against time . . .

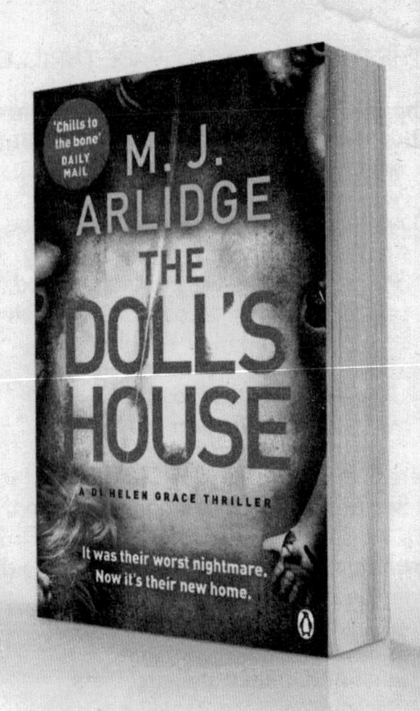

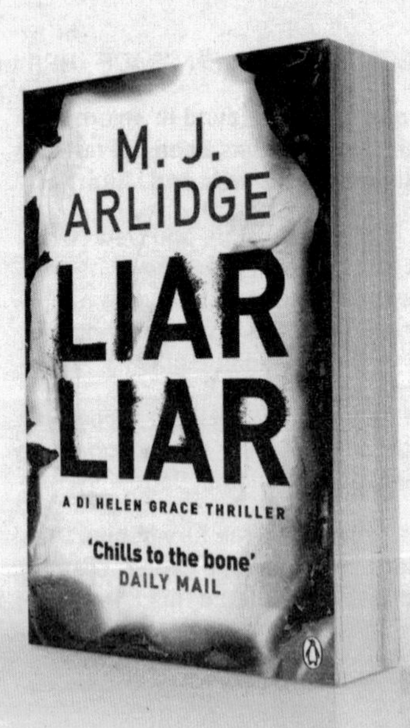

THE FOURTH DI HELEN GRACE THRILLE

In the dead of night, three raging fires lig up the city skies. It's more than a tragic coincidence. For DI Helen Grace the flam announce the arrival of an evil she has never encountered before.

Because this is no firestarter seeking sic thrills, but something more chilling: a series of careful, calculating acts of murd

But why were the victims chosen? What' driving the killer? And who will be next?

A powder keg of fear, suspicion and drea has been laid. Now all it needs is a spark set it off . . .